SPY DUST

Laureline Ducros

Spy Dust by Laureline Ducros

Book One of the Russian Gambit Series

ISBN: 9798863919560.

First published in 2020 under the title Russian Gambit

Copyright © 2020, 2025 by Laureline Marie Ducros.

All rights reserved.

DEDICATION

For those who find strength in their scars, and who see beauty in the broken—this is for you.

PROLOGUE

Opéra Garnier — Paris, France
Thursday, 27th June, 21:49

The rain had stopped as suddenly as it had begun, leaving the pavement of the *Boulevard des Capucines* glistening like a black mirror under the muted glow of the streetlamps. Everything was exactly as he remembered, unchanged since that night when he had kissed her here, in the shadows of the opera house, her wet hair clinging to her cheek as the summer rain soaked them both to the bone.

They had been reckless in their happiness, intoxicated by love and the belief that they could outrun fate. But that memory belonged to another life—another man.

He hadn't been a killer then—at least, not in the way he was now.

He stepped over the body.

The counter-sniper had fallen at an awkward angle, slack-jawed and wide-eyed in death. His expression held a hint of surprise, as though he hadn't expected to die here tonight—on a balcony high above the opera square. But sometimes fate had a peculiar way of catching up with one's sins. And the man at Mercury's feet had surely been no stranger to sin. Quite the opposite.

Sliding the garrotte back into his pocket, Mercury crouched beside the body.

The sniper had died as men like him always did: quickly, quietly, and for the simple reason that he'd been protecting the wrong man. The one Mercury had come here to kill.

Reaching out, Mercury prised the sniper rifle from the dead man's hand. Even through his gloves, he felt that the weapon's grip was still warm. Once, the reminder of how recently a life had ended might have given him pause, but he'd learned to shut his mind to it.

Checking the weapon's scope and load, he moved to the edge of the balcony. Satisfied, he knelt, braced the stock against his shoulder and eased the rifle barrel between the stone balusters. Then, with a gentle twist of the scope, the world below came into focus: the red carpet looked darker than it should have, wet from the rain, its surface catching uneven streaks of light. Operagoers in well-tailored tuxedos and flamboyant evening gowns paraded across the soggy stretch of fabric, separated from the host of spectators, protesters, and journalists by barriers and security guards.

"Mercury, this is Moscow Ops Control. CCTV is down. Target on schedule," a voice rasped in his earpiece.

Without a word, Mercury removed the earbud and shoved it into his jacket pocket. He didn't want to hear the Kremlin's voice—not here, not tonight.

Returning his attention to the scene below, Mercury watched through his scope as three black limousines moved in slow procession across the square and then eased to a halt at the red carpet. The moment the cars stopped, the doors swung open and men in trim suits spilled out—their movements so tightly synchronised it was hard to tell where one man ended and another began.

Mercury's gaze settled on the middle car.

A moment later, one of the bodyguards—larger, more seasoned—stepped forward and opened the door. First, Mercury saw only the polished tip of a patent leather evening shoe, then the rest of the man emerged from the car.

Victor Orsin.

The man Mercury had come here to kill.

Cameras flashed, capturing Orsin's image as he strolled towards the entrance under the furious shouts of protesters and a barrage of questions fired at him by the press.

Orsin ignored them.

Walking down the red carpet, he seemed untouchable—a man beyond justice and above fear. Yet the bodyguards trailing him told a different story. This was a man on edge, and he had every reason to be: after all, few made enemies of the Kremlin and lived to tell the tale.

Kneeling behind the balustrade, Mercury adjusted his scope—compensating for distance, wind, and lighting. Then he became still, his finger caressing the trigger guard, as he waited for that perfect moment when Orsin was in full view—when he could take one life without risking another.

Then Orsin stepped into his crosshairs.

And for the briefest of moment, time seemed to fold in on itself, carrying him back into the past—to that day, that moment, when he had picked up that crisp, pristine copy of *The New York Times* and realised what *she* had done.

Despite all warnings, she had laid bare the full scale of Orsin's evil: money laundering, election fraud, arms trafficking, and worse. Much worse. Torture. Summary executions of civilians. War crimes.

It had been her final gift to the world.

The truth she had died for.

Oh, Natalia.

For a moment, the pain of her absence became almost overwhelming—the quiet, unending ache too much to bear. Mercury shut his eyes, forcing her image from his mind, knowing that if he didn't, he would see her there, in the crosshairs. When he opened his eyes again, the world was stripped to its rawest form:

him, Orsin, and the bullet that would bridge the space between them.

Carefully, he let his finger slip past the guard and settle lightly on the trigger. And then—very gently—he began to squeeze. No rush. No force. Just a slow, steady increase of pressure until he reached that point of slight resistance that was the final, mechanical barrier between life and death.

For justice.

He pulled the trigger.

The shot was clean—a quiet, muffled pop, barely louder than the ambient noise of the square. But the impact was instant. Lethal.

Orsin's head snapped back, a mist of red blooming in the air, bright against the night, dull against the sodden carpet. For a moment, Orsin swayed, still upright, frozen in death's grip, then his body gave in, tipping backwards, stiff and final, dead before he hit the ground.

For a split second, there was silence. Then the chaos began to ripple out from the centre—fast, frenzied, panicked. People scattered in every direction, bodyguards rushing in the opposite direction from the crowd, converging on Orsin's body, eyes frantically searching for the threat they knew was out there but couldn't see.

Mercury didn't move. He couldn't. Not yet.

He had to be sure.

And then he saw what he had been waiting for: the solitary figure of a man—squat and square-shouldered—moving calmly through the chaos, unhindered by police. When he reached Orsin, the bodyguards formed a tight circle around the man, as though he were extension of their fallen master.

And in some sense, he was.

Mercury tracked the man's movements through the scope, watching as he knelt beside the Orsin's body and slipped his hand beneath the dead man's collar—not to check for a pulse, but to retrieve what had been there all along: a small, steel pendant.

For an instant, it dangled in the half-light—utilitarian and unremarkable. Then it was gone, tucked into the man's pocket. But Mercury didn't need to see more. He knew what it was. And what it could do—the utter, unspeakable destruction it could unleash.

It was the proverbial key to Pandora's box—the ultimate tool of geopolitical dominance.

He'd seen enough. It was time to move.

Mercury slung the rifle over his shoulder and withdrew into the shadows of the façade.

Below, the opera square was a maelstrom—bodyguards scrambling to secure the exits, police rushing to corral the crowd. They would focus on the ground level first and work their way up. Standard procedure. Routine. Predictable.

Mercury looked up at the rooftop. It would be his route out. Up and over. Away from the chaos below.

A quick leap, and his fingers caught the stone ledge. Quickly, he pulled himself up, the tips of his patent leather evening shoes finding footing on the narrow ledge still wet from the rain.

In the distance, he could already hear the faint wail of sirens. They would be here in four minutes. Helicopters would follow in five. At that point, everything would be locked down—searchlights sweeping across the rooftops, while police officers sealed off the streets.

But their effort would be futile.

By then, he would be gone.

Mercury scaled the side of the building—quick and silent—then pulled himself over the edge of the roof. Crouching low, he scanned the adjacent rooftops for any sign of unexpected threats:

the flash of a scope, the movement of a body, anything that might complicate matters.

Nothing. Only the lone silhouette of a man on a distant balcony, lighting a cigarette while he calmly watched the chaos in the square far below. But he was supposed to be there. He was his ripcord in case things went south.

Staying low, Mercury moved across the uneven rooftop, keeping close to the stone ledges and scanning the crowd below for his second target. And then he found him: Orsin's man—squat, square-shouldered—moving through the crowd with the unhurried poise of a seasoned spy put out to pasture long ago.

The Kremlin didn't care whether Orsin's underling lived or died; all that mattered was the pendant. Or rather, what it could control.

Mercury kept pace, moving in perfect sync, tracking Orsin's man from above.

His target was heading left now, towards the *Rue des Mathurins*—away from the panicked crowd and towards a waiting limousine.

A moment later, Mercury reached the edge of the rooftop. He had the perfect view now: Orsin's man, the limousine, and a clear path between them.

Mercury knelt, bringing the rifle up in one smooth motion, his body automatically adjusting to the weight. The stock settled firmly against his shoulder. He looked through the scope, zeroing in on Orsin's man.

One shot. That was all it would take.

Back in Moscow, men in grey suits were eagerly awaiting the news that the pendant was on its way back to them. And he could give it to them. Right now. Right here. A twitch of a finger was all that was needed.

Mercury aligned the crosshairs over the man's forehead.

His finger tightened on the trigger until he reached that point of barely-there resistance, where all that separated life from death was a hair's breadth of tension.

This was it. The point of no return.

Mercury paused, then—carefully, deliberately—he tilted the rifle to the left by a fraction of an inch. Just enough.

He squeezed the trigger gently.

The suppressed shot was lost in the clamour, but the result was as intended: The bullet missed its mark by the slimmest margin, grazing the man's cheek, drawing blood but sparing life.

The perfect miss.

Just as planned.

Mercury lowered the rifle. He couldn't afford to waste even a second.

Leaving the weapon behind, he stepped to the edge of the rooftop and looked down. It was chaos—people fled mindlessly in all directions while a handful of police officers pushed against the flow. No one looked up. And even if they did, the shadows would conceal him.

He pulled a lightweight rappel line from his evening jacket, secured one end to the stone ledge, and clipped the other to a hidden hook inside his cummerbund. Then he slid over the edge, descending the façade quickly, quietly, and entirely unnoticed. Moments later, his feet touched the ground. And now, back on the street, he was nothing more than yet another frightened operagoer: unarmed and dressed to the nines.

Across from him, on the other side of the street, the limousine pulled away, tyres screeching against the wet pavement. Mercury watched its taillights disappear around a corner, knowing exactly where the pendant was headed—and who would be waiting for it there.

He could have stopped it. He had been ordered to stop it. And no doubt, both the Kremlin and the man in the limousine had expected him to succeed. But what none of them had anticipated—what none of them could possibly have imagined—was that Mercury had never intended to stop the pendant from reaching its destination.

To the contrary.

He had meticulously planned for it to arrive there.

PART ONE
Sophie Madelaine Akehurst

CHAPTER I

The Atlas Bar at the Valmont Palace Hotel
London, United Kingdom
Friday, 28th June, 19:00

Sophie Akehurst first saw him on a balmy summer evening in June, at precisely seven o'clock, just as she stepped behind the counter of the Atlas Bar to begin her shift.

It was one of those lazy, early summer evenings when the warmth of the day seemed to linger forever. The French doors to the grand terrace stood open, inviting the gentle breeze and fading sunlight to filter into the room. Inside, guests in smart evening attire sipped champagne cocktails under the muted glow of crystal chandeliers, while waiters in cream-coloured dinner jackets scurried between them, pouring drinks, and carrying trays.

For some strange reason, her eyes were drawn to him almost instantly, spotting him through a gap in the crowd.

He sat alone at a table by the window, in the shadow of a marble pillar that dimmed the fading sunlight just enough to render him part of the background, yet not entirely invisible. His drink sat forgotten at his elbow, while his eyes rested on the open doorway to the lobby, watching the arriving guests with detached curiosity.

It wasn't his looks that had drawn her attention—though the strong, chiselled jawline and the scar above his cheekbone were hard to ignore. No, it was something subtler, a stillness, as if the room around him existed in motion, yet he remained unaffected, separate.

Stepping out from behind the bar, Sophie grabbed a tray and headed over to the scar-faced man.

As if sensing her approach halfway across the room, the man looked up. For an instant, a trace of recognition seemed to pass over his hawkish features—but it was gone so quickly that she might have imagined it.

Shaking off the sudden sense of unease, Sophie forced a polite smile. "Good evening, sir. Is everything to your satisfaction?"

He didn't smile back. "Everything's fine."

The way he spoke—curt, clipped—hinted at something foreign. Eastern European, perhaps Russian, but she couldn't be sure.

"I see you haven't had a chance to finish your drink. May I offer a replacement on the house?" Sophie motioned towards his watered-down whisky. "Or a different drink, perhaps?"

"No." He flicked a finger towards the neatly folded copy of *The New York Times*, which—judging by its pristine condition—had never been opened. "But I'd appreciate if you'd get rid of this for me."

"Certainly, sir. I'll take care of that for you."

Sophie took the paper, absentmindedly noticing the price tag in its top right corner proclaiming in bold letters that it had been bought at the *Gare du Nord* in Paris.

Something about that struck her as odd, though she couldn't say why. It wasn't important, just one of those tiny, inconsequential details. Like a stranger's mismatched socks or a door left slightly ajar—it made you pause for a second, but then you moved on.

"Is there anything else I can assist you with?" Sophie asked, her tone smooth and professional.

A brief shake of his head, that faint accent grating at the edges of his English. "No. Thank you."

"Very well, sir. Enjoy your evening."

Sliding the newspaper under her arm, Sophie stepped away from the table. As she turned, his eyes shifted towards the open doorway again, half-absorbed in his own watchfulness. Though his gaze didn't follow her, Sophie had the uncanny sense that, somehow, she had been noted—her face, her words, her presence. Filed away. And something about it made her strangely uneasy.

A gentle brush at her elbow pulled her from her thoughts. "Sophie," the floor manager—tall, grizzled, French—murmured, "Gabriel's asking for you. He's in the lobby."

She gave a brief nod. "On my way."

Paper still in hand, Sophie weaved through the crowded bar towards the Valmont's lavish entrance hall. The noise dimmed as she stepped into the foyer, the rich sound of a piano drifting through the room, the calm a serene contrast to the chaos she had just left.

"Light reading?" a voice said from behind her.

Sophie turned to see Gabriel Dunbar step around the counter of the reception desk.

In his early thirties, tall, and dark-haired, the Valmont's newly minted head concierge was handsome in a disarming, almost dangerous way. Dressed in a tailored navy suit and white shirt, he was the very picture of an English gentleman, but there was an edge to him, a sense of someone always watching, always aware. Nothing ever slipped the attention of those ink-black eyes, which, right now, were watching her with good-humoured amusement.

"Just the usual front-row seat to Armageddon," Sophie replied, angling the paper towards Gabriel so he could see the title page—the headline about a Russian oligarch gunned down in the middle of Paris framed by the depressing string of articles about conflicts and bloodshed that had long become a fixture of the daily news.

"Well, the world really *is* going to hell." Gabriel laughed softly, his gaze flicking across the article, then back up to meet hers. "And speaking of which, how did your exams go? Comparative politics, wasn't it?"

Of course, Gabriel hadn't forgotten. He never forgot anything.

"Not too bad, I think," she replied.

"Glad to hear it." Gabriel's smile widened a fraction. "So, what's the plan? Heading out to celebrate after work?"

"Not sure yet. There's some party everyone's going to, but I'm working the weekend—and I've still got a ton of thesis research waiting for me."

Gabriel arched an eyebrow, watching her with an expression of mild amusement. "So that's a no, then."

"Sometimes you're just a little too perceptive, Gabriel."

He laughed very softly. "Part of the job, which—by the way—is also why I'm accosting you," he admitted, his voice tinged with an apologetic note. "Are you staying late today?"

"Yes, I'm doing the till. Why?"

"Because I might have a late-night guest for you. Want to get rid of the paper, so we can have a look at the file?" Gabriel nodded towards the polished table on their left, where complimentary copies of the world's major dailies were laid out for the Valmont's guests to peruse.

"Can't leave it here." Sophie held up the newspaper so Gabriel could see the sticker. "It's not one of ours."

Casually, Gabriel took the paper from her hand and slipped it to the bottom of a newspaper pile. "Now it is," he said with a wink.

"Management would fry you alive if they saw that," Sophie remarked, mildly amused by Gabriel's casual rule-breaking.

"I'd love to see them try," Gabriel replied drily, motioning for her to follow him to the reception desk.

"So, who's your mysterious late-night guest?" Sophie asked, following Gabriel behind the counter.

He turned serious, taking on the quietly efficient manner that spelled work.

"One Alexei Alexandrovich Zorin." Gabriel tilted one of the computer screens towards Sophie and pulled up a reservation, his platinum cufflink briefly catching the light as he typed. "He's booked into the Royal Suite."

Sophie stepped closer, her eyes flitting across the file.

Alexei Zorin, despite his Russian-sounding name, was travelling on a Dominican passport. Diplomatic. According to his file, he was flying-in private. And as customary for the world's moneyed aristocracy, Mr Zorin was accompanied by a king-sized entourage of pilots, bodyguards, and private assistants.

"Anything I need to know?" Sophie asked, her gaze fixed on the screen.

"We extend him a half-million credit line, so whatever he wants, you just bill it. No questions asked."

"Half a million pounds? Are you serious?"

"He's got a taste for the finer things..."

"I'm sure. Anything else?"

"He's the no-nonsense type: no chitchat unless he starts it. That's pretty much it."

"Sounds charming," Sophie said dryly.

The corner of Gabriel's mouth twitched upward in a faint smile. "Oh, he is."

At that moment, the sound of footsteps echoed in the lobby.

Sophie looked up.

Three men in trim suits had just stepped through the revolving glass doors into the Valmont's entrance hall. Walking shoulder to shoulder, they moved with a kind of unsettling precision towards the reception desk, and for a brief moment, one of them glanced at Sophie, the slight turn of his head revealing a hard-cut profile and an earpiece with a wire that vanished discreetly into his collar.

Bodyguards.

Sophie glanced at Gabriel. "The vanguard of your important arrival?"

Gabriel's mouth tightened, but amusement lingered in his eyes. "It's the Valmont, Sophie, every arrival is an important one."

With a conspiratorial smile, Gabriel slipped out from behind the reception desk and strode towards the grand entrance, smoothing the front of his immaculate suit as he walked. Instantly, a small army of white-gloved porters, butlers, and bellboys began to assemble in his wake to receive their orders.

Sophie stayed behind, her eyes fixed on the window front stretching along the length of the hotel. She wanted to see Zorin for herself.

A moment passed, then another, and finally, a convoy of identical black SUVs pulled into the forecourt, the fading sunlight flashing off the tinted windscreens.

The motorcade circled the *Lalique* fountain and then rolled to a stop in front of the hotel entrance. There was a moment of motionless suspense, then the passenger doors—manned by liveried porters—swung open: Bodyguards—tall, well-built men sporting trim suits and stern faces—issued like a small army from the waiting cars. For a second, they stood on the curb, their eyes sweeping the forecourt for any sign of danger, then one broke rank and turned to open the rear door of the only car that hadn't yet disgorged its passengers. From it emerged the solitary figure of a man—tall, lean, dressed in a light summer suit and wearing sunglasses.

Undoubtedly Zorin.

Shielded from view and danger by half a dozen bodyguards, Gabriel and Alexei Zorin exchanged a brief greeting.

At that moment, Sophie noticed a flicker of movement in the corner of her eye.

She turned.

Her reclusive, scar-faced guest had stepped out of the bar and now stood in the shadows at its entrance, speaking quietly into his phone while his eyes tracked the men crossing the atrium.

As if sensing her attention on him, his gaze flicked to Sophie.

It was a fleeting glance, one that might have been mistaken for a casual sweep of the room, yet there was nothing haphazard about it. His gaze swept over her, meticulous and probing, taking in every detail before moving on and leaving Sophie with a prickling sense of unease—like ice spreading under her skin.

CHAPTER II

The Atlas Bar at the Valmont Palace Hotel
London, United Kingdom
Saturday, 29th June, 01:00

The ormolu clock in the hotel foyer struck one o'clock, and with its chime, the Atlas Bar began to slip into its nighttime lull—the light of the crystal chandeliers dimming to a twilight glow, the staff numbers dwindling to the bare essentials, while the stragglers finished their drinks and gradually trickled out into the night.

But the departing figures barely registered in Sophie's mind. Her attention was focused on the receipts sprawled across the counter before her, mentally checking the numbers to make sure nothing was off. The task wasn't exactly thrilling, but work after hours paid double, and—as a perpetually cash-strapped fellowship student surviving on grants and waiting tables—that made all the difference.

She paused when she reached the last receipt, tapping her pen against the counter for a moment before checking it off. With a small sigh of relief, she leaned back slightly, letting her gaze drift around the room. It was empty now, the marble floors and polished wood gleaming under the chandeliers. She liked this hour. The dim light, the silence and for a second, she let herself enjoy the quiet, the stillness of it all.

But then, out of the corner of her eye, she noticed a flicker of movement.

It was him.

Her reclusive, scar-faced guest.

Why are you still here? she thought, with a hint of irritation.

As if to answer her unspoken question, the distant din of footsteps echoed in the lobby, and at their sound, something changed in her unsettling guest. It wasn't a grand, conspicuous movement, but rather a faint, almost unnoticeable change in his posture—an ever so slight tensing of the shoulders, a barely perceptible lifting of the head—as if every fibre of his being were tuning into the rhythm of the approaching steps.

Feeling a hint of unease, Sophie followed his gaze.

Gabriel was leading the way, Alexei Zorin beside him, and a protection detail—five men with earpieces, stern expressions, and necks like bulls—trailing two steps behind.

"This way please, Mr Zorin," Gabriel said, holding the door and motioning ahead.

There was no reply, no thank you, not even a casual nod of the head, just a dismissive silence accompanied by the sound of a dozen footsteps as Zorin and his entourage swept into the room. For a brief moment, Alexei Zorin paused at the entrance, staying in the shadows as if to take stock of the room then—with a deliberate stride—he stepped into the soft glow of the crystal chandeliers.

He looked younger than she had expected.

He was in his thirties, tall and lean, with light brown hair and a face that seemed carved from stone—all sharp angles and precise lines. He was handsome, devastatingly so, but it was a kind of beauty that came with an edge, something dark and dangerous lurking just beneath the surface.

But what truly captured her attention were his eyes. They were of an impossibly deep blue colour, like the sea, but there was no warmth in them. Only depth.

He didn't look at her immediately. Instead, he surveyed the room, his sharp blue eyes taking in every detail before his gaze settled on her.

She felt it like a jolt, as if he'd reached out and touched her across the room. His eyes lingered for just a fraction too long, and there was something in his gaze, something that seemed to see right through her.

And then the moment was shattered when Gabriel stepped forward and into her line of sight.

"I'll leave you in the capable hands of our staff," Gabriel announced with the well-practised smile of the consummate host. "Should you require anything at all, my team and I are at your disposal."

Zorin didn't bother with a response. He waved Gabriel off with a lazy flick of the wrist and stalked off to a table at the far end of the room—his stone-faced bodyguards following at his heels like a pack of well-trained and very silent terriers.

Gabriel, unfazed by the lack of response, watched them go for a moment before stepping over to Sophie.

"The bodyguards are not particularly squeamish," Gabriel whispered, leaning in close, his hand brushing briefly against hers—the touch like a spark, almost electric, a tingling of nerves. "Try to keep your distance and make sure they can see what you're doing." He paused, measuring her, as if concerned about leaving her alone with Zorin. "Think you can handle it?"

"Don't worry," Sophie replied, her voice sounding more confident than she actually felt. "I'll manage." She glanced over at the scar-faced man, still sitting there with the same unsettling calm. "What about him? Should I ask him to leave?"

Gabriel's gaze followed hers, his eyes razor-sharp in their attention as he studied the man, then shook his head. "It's fine. If Zorin's security has concerns, they'll let you know." He paused. "I'll stay in the lobby if you need me."

Gabriel gave her a quick, reassuring nod and then disappeared, leaving Sophie alone with Zorin and his stone-faced minders.

For a moment, she stood there, preparing herself with a slow breath—the kind one took before jumping into cold water—then she headed over to Zorin's table.

With an apologetic nod, Sophie stepped past the bodyguards and greeted their overlord with a tactful smile—polite, restrained yet sufficiently obliging to placate even the most demanding scion of the moneyed aristocracy.

"Good evening, Mr Zorin. It's a pleasure to have you with us tonight. May I guide you through our exclusive selections, or do you have a particular preference?"

Zorin took his time looking at her, his gaze slow, almost bored. When his eyes finally met hers, they reflected a quiet hint of irritation, as if she had already failed some unspoken test just by addressing him.

"A Macallan 72, neat, and a glass of water," he said finally.

Zorin's voice, now that he had finally deigned to speak, took Sophie by surprise. It was the kind of voice that never needed to be raised to reach the listener's ear—a rich, deep timbre, soft and melodious, yet, like the man himself, of a cold, restrained yet powerful intensity.

"Certainly, sir. Just to make you aware, the Macallan 72 is one of our rare vintages, so we only offer it by the bottle."

"I'm aware," Zorin replied with a hint of impatience, casually placing one elegant, perfectly groomed hand on the armrest, and tapping his finger against the leather, as if counting down the seconds before his patience ran out.

The sight made Sophie pause momentarily.

It wasn't the testy gesture or the glint of his intricate white gold watch that caught her attention—it was the tattoos.

Extending across the back of Zorin's hand was an Orthodox cross with three horizontal beams, the lowest one slanted. At its base, inked in the same dark, almost black colour, was a star-shaped symbol, its points extending outward like the cardinal points of a compass. But even more disturbing than the markings on the back of Zorin's hand were the Cyrillic letters adorning his long, graceful fingers—one below each knuckle.

O M Y T

For the fraction of a second, Sophie's gaze was transfixed by the tattoos, at once repulsed and fascinated by their sinister overtone, and then her eyes snapped back to his.

"Anything else, sir?" she managed.

Her indiscretion, however fleeting, hadn't gone unnoticed. Zorin measured her with a hint of contempt—just a pinch—as if he couldn't muster any greater emotion for a mere servant, then he said: *"The New York Times.* And some privacy."

Sophie felt her polite smile waver momentarily, but she checked herself, countering his scorn with a courteous nod. "Of course, sir. Right away."

Mentally kicking herself for her indiscretion, Sophie hurried back to the counter. Making sure Zorin's goons could see everything she did, she unlocked the solid steel vault and retrieved the one-hundred-and-fifty-thousand-pound bottle with a careful hand.

For a brief moment, Sophie stared at the flask, painfully aware that it was worth enough to repay her student loan twice over. She pushed the thought from her mind. She would deal with that once she completed her exchange programme here in London and returned home to the States.

She twisted the Macallan's cork carefully and it came loose with a gentle pop. With the greatest of care, Sophie poured a generous measure of the sinfully dark whisky, while Zorin's bodyguards watched with unrelenting scrutiny, as if afraid she was about to poison their overlord with a shot of overpriced single malt.

He'd probably deserve it, she thought sardonically.

Sophie added Zorin's order to his tab, then slipped out to the lobby to grab a newspaper for him.

The vast hall was empty and quiet, but to her relief, housekeeping hadn't cleared the newsstand yet, and the papers were still laid out on the polished mahogany sideboard.

There was only a single copy of *The New York Times* left.

The one with the sticker.

Cursing inwardly, Sophie picked up the paper and studied it with a critical eye, then began to carefully peel off the price tag. It came off satisfyingly clean, its adhesive residue sticking to her fingers.

Behind the reception desk, Gabriel lifted his head—his handsome features obscured by the shadows. "Do you need a fresh copy?"

"No, it's fine. Thanks, Gabriel!" Sophie replied, rolling the price tag into a curl between her fingertips, then stashing it into the pocket of her black cocktail dress, to throw it away later.

When she returned to the bar, the scar-faced man shifted. His eyes were on her now, watching her movements in a way that made her skin prickle. Pretending not to notice, Sophie placed the newspaper between the whisky tumbler and the water glass.

The short walk to Zorin's table felt longer than it should have. When she finally reached him, she set the glass and newspaper down with a steady hand. "Your whisky, sir, and *The New York Times*."

As she placed the newspaper on the table, Sophie noticed that it was a little damp. And so were her fingers. She silently cursed herself for having placed the paper between the glasses, letting it soak up the faint trace of condensation that the ice had created on the water glass.

But Zorin said nothing; he simply dismissed her with a barely perceptible nod, unfolded the paper, bowed his patrician head, and began his silent study of the day's headlines.

Retreating to a shadowy corner behind the counter, Sophie took up her observation post, where she could maintain a watch over her guests. For a moment, her eyes lingered on Zorin, watching him from across the room, then her gaze instinctively shifted to the scar-faced man.

Her unsettling guest sat motionless, his hand resting casually on the armrest, while his gaze—ostensibly fixed on the ornate Art Deco clock mounted on the whisky tower—watched Zorin in the reflection of the mirrored wall behind the bar counter. For a moment, the scar-faced man seemed almost pleased at the sight, but the impression was so fleeting that she might as well have imagined it.

But whether imagined or not, Zorin seemed to have noticed the man's interest too, and unlike his goons, he didn't seem to take kindly to it.

Zorin's cold blue eyes lifted from his newspaper and fixed on the figure by the window. There was a stillness to him, a calculated pause like one predator observing another and assessing whether he was a threat or merely a nuisance. Then Zorin folded the newspaper, pulled a wad of cash from his pocket, and dropped it disdainfully beside his untouched whisky—as if both the money and the drink were beneath his standards. Without a word, Zorin got up and strode to the exit—his stone-faced bodyguards falling into step behind him like Praetorian guards.

I wish you a very pleasant evening, too, Sophie thought wryly, watching them disappear into the lobby.

As soon as they were gone, Sophie grabbed a tray to clear the table. But before she could even step around the counter, the scar-faced man stood. He headed straight for the exit and as he passed the table Zorin had just vacated, he casually grabbed the discarded newspaper, tucking it under his arm. Without a glance back, he slipped through the glass doors into the foyer and out of sight.

The whole thing was so casual and quick that if Sophie hadn't been watching closely, she might have missed it. And it was the ease, the nonchalance, that somehow made her uneasy—making her feel as if she had seen more than she was supposed to.

CHAPTER III

The Valmont Palace Hotel
London, United Kingdom
Saturday, 29th June, 01:49

Sophie stood in the fluorescent light of the hotel staff rooms, her fingers fumbling with the buttons of her black cocktail dress as she stared at her own reflection under the unkind glow of the strip lights—their unforgiving brightness highlighting every shadow under her eyes.

Something about the evening felt off. She couldn't pinpoint it exactly, but the whole thing had a weird undercurrent to it.

She closed her eyes and pressed her forehead against the cool glass of the mirror.

Don't be ridiculous, she thought, pushing the thought from her mind.

It was nothing. Of course it was nothing. Between work and studies, she'd been running on fumes and now her mind was running wild because she hadn't given it a break in weeks. Everything was fine. She was just tired. Ridiculously tired, and nothing more.

Go to bed, she urged herself silently.

Her phone buzzed, shattering the fragile moment of blissful solitude. Sophie didn't even need to look at the screen to know it was Gina. She was nothing if not consistent.

With an entirely silent sigh of resignation, Sophie reached for her phone, swiped her thumb across the cracked screen and opened the text.

'Free tables at Viper's Den tonight! You in?'

Sophie closed her eyes for a second, wishing she could ignore it. She wanted to, really. But her social life—already a perpetual casualty of her studies and her work—was unlikely to survive another quiet ducking out.

Sophie sighed, her fingers tapping out a reply with a resigned acceptance. *'I'll be there in 30.'*

'Get here ASAP! I've got someone for you to meet!'

Resisting the urge to roll her eyes, Sophie slipped her phone into her clutch. It seemed she would have to endure another one of Gina's ill-fated matchmaking schemes tonight.

Pushing the thought of impending drama from her mind, Sophie rifled through her bag in search of her *pièce de résistance*—a daringly short black sequin dress. She had found the barely worn, five-hundred-pound designer frock at a thrift store in Soho and acquired the treasure for the paltry sum of twenty pounds.

The fabric clung to her as she slipped it on, the black sequins catching the light and shimmering with every movement.

Standing in the wash of the cold light, Sophie reapplied her eyeliner, whose dark colour brought out the darkness of her brown eyes in a way she always found quite pleasing.

Through the door, she could hear the soft chime of the lobby clock. It was time. Quickly, Sophie shoved the rest of her clothes into the locker and gave herself one last look in the mirror before stepping out into the hotel foyer.

It was almost empty.

The lights had been dimmed, and the polished floors reflected the soft glow of the chandeliers overhead. The night manager stood at the reception desk, handing a dark-haired man a room key, while a butler carried his luggage after him with loving care.

As Sophie passed the newsstand, she noticed the missing copies of *The New York Times* had been returned, a neat stack of crisp, unread papers now arranged at the centre of the table. She paused, her gaze drifting over the pile. Out of idle curiosity, she reached for one and flicked it open, her eyes lazily skimming the opening lines of the lead story, more out of habit than interest.

The New York Times

THE FALL OF A TITAN

Written by K. Hirst, R.T. Bell and T. Birch

In memory of Natalia Vetrova, who gave her life in service to the truth.

Last night, in a scene seemingly straight from The Godfather's playbook, Victor Orsin, a billionaire Russian defense tycoon, was fatally shot outside the *Palais Garnier* in Paris.

Orsin, officially a successful defence contractor and generous patron of the arts, was less coy in off-record settings. Alleged of being a figurehead of the Twelve—a multi-billion criminal empire—Orsin represented the murky nexus between Russian statecraft and the criminal underworld.

He owed his meteoric rise to the Kremlin's relentless pursuit of "plausible deniability": As the Russian president consolidated his grip on power in the early 2000s, the Twelve became the Kremlin's go-to address for murky, deniable operations. However, they soon expanded their client base beyond the Russian state. Over the past two decades, the Twelve deployed their mercenary troops to support beleaguered dictators, funded disinformation campaigns, laundered billions in illicit funds, sold arms to sanctioned regimes and militias, and corroded electoral processes the world over.

However, despite his critical role in advancing Russia's geopolitical interests, Orsin's relationship with the Kremlin was complex—a blend of loyalty, fear, mutual exploitation, and, in the end, confrontation.

His death on the steps of the Paris Opera House was the final act in a life that was always flirting with danger. His legacy will endure in the annals of history—a testament to the perils of power in a land where the line between the state and criminal underworld is blurred beyond recognition.

For a brief moment, Sophie's eyes lingered on the words before her gaze shifted to the image on the title page. The caption identified the man as Victor Orsin. It showed the oligarch slumped on the stone steps of the opera house, his suit bloodstained. The photographer had captured the scene just as a man—squat and square-shouldered—was kneeling beside the body, one hand reaching beneath Orsin's shirt collar to retrieve a small pendant. But this wasn't what held her attention. It was Orsin's hand. Lifeless. Limp. Resting on a stone step. And on the back of that perfectly manicured hand was a tattoo: a star-shaped symbol, its points extending outward like the cardinal directions of a compass.

It was the same tattoo she had seen on Alexei Zorin's hand.

The connection between the two men felt suddenly too strange, too coincidental, too horrifying in what it implied.

She stood there for a moment longer than she meant to, letting the thought form, but only halfway. Then, almost instinctively, she pushed it aside.

It was just *one* tattoo. One among many, in Zorin's case. Tattoos like that weren't exactly rare. And just because something seemed connected didn't mean it was a clue to some grand conspiracy.

"So you *are* going out!" came a voice, unexpected and close, from behind her.

Sophie turned, startled. Gabriel leaned casually against the doorframe, his face shadowed. He wore a leather jacket over his tailored suit, looking ready to leave as well.

"You doubted me," she said, hastily placing the newspaper back on the table, feeling caught out, as if her thoughts about Zorin's tattoos had been not only entirely inappropriate but also somehow visible to anyone who might have glanced her way.

Gabriel smiled and inclined his head in an apologetic nod. "I did." He paused, then added, "Where are you going?"

"My friends somehow managed to get free tables at the Viper's Den."

"That's right around the corner from my place. Should I give you a lift?"

The offer caught her off guard—not unwelcome, but unexpected from this otherwise intensely private man.

"Sure, that'd be great, Gabriel."

The chime of the elevator echoed through the entrance hall, drawing their attention. Both turned towards the sound.

The doors slid open, revealing a pair of bodyguards stepping out first, forming a menacing vanguard. Behind them, Alexei Zorin materialised, an eight-man-strong coterie of guards and aides trailing at his heels.

The men crossed the lobby in a well-rehearsed formation; Zorin at the centre, his acolytes behind him, and his bodyguards around them all.

Halfway across the foyer, Zorin slipped his phone from his jacket pocket and answered a call. With his attention momentarily diverted, he veered slightly to the left, out of the immediate orbit of his sworn protectors. And just as they walked past the reception desk, the dark-haired guest—oblivious to the choreographed flow of the procession—pocketed his room key and, smiling at the night manager, took a step back, his shoulder grazing Zorin's. The contact was light, a whisper of fabric against fabric, almost tender in its brevity. But the collision, though slight, seemed to break some unspoken rule of proximity around Zorin. Still on his phone, Zorin raised his left hand by just a fraction of an inch. In response, his bodyguards seamlessly spread out around him, creating an invisible barrier between Zorin and the rest of the world.

Focused solely on the sanctity of his master's space, one of the bodyguards, walking at the back, took a step aside, and before Sophie could move out of his way, the man's shoulder collided with hers. The clash was minor, but the bodyguard's reaction wasn't. He reached out to push Sophie out of his path, but Gabriel was quicker. He stepped forward, moving with surprising speed and catching the man's wrist.

"Is there a problem, sir?" Gabriel's voice, though calm, carried a quiet authority that made the bodyguard pause.

Zorin, momentarily distracted from his call, turned to observe the scene. Phone still in hand he took in the exchange with the predator's interest, his focus zeroing in on Gabriel. For a moment, Zorin stood motionless, simply watching, then he ended the call, slipped his phone back into his jacket pocket and signalled his lapdog to back off with a small flick of his wrist.

And like a well-trained terrier, the bodyguard took a step away from Gabriel. "No problem," he said with a thick Russian accent and an apologetic nod. "Just... misunderstanding."

For a fleeting instant, Zorin's goon wavered, as if uncomfortable with the idea of turning his back on Gabriel, then he stepped back into formation.

Zorin, however, seemed to have no intention of moving on. Slipping his phone into his jacket pocket, he measured Gabriel with intense, focused interest and then said something in Russian—his words directed not at his guards or his underlings but at Gabriel. And to Sophie's surprise, Gabriel acknowledged Zorin's words with a polite nod and a quiet response, not in English, but in Russian.

An ever-so-faint smile formed on Zorin's lips. "Your Russian is excellent, Mr Dunbar. Like a true Muscovite." And with that, Zorin turned on his heel, his bodyguards closing ranks around him—transforming into a solid wall of muscle and menace as they slipped through the revolving doors out into the night.

"What a prick," Gabriel remarked under his breath, his eyes following Zorin before turning to her. "Are you okay?"

Sophie hesitated for the fraction of a second, still slightly taken aback by what just happened, then she gave a nod. "Yeah, I'm fine."

"Good. Let's get out of here."

Gabriel courteously held the door open for Sophie and then followed her out into the balmy summer night. It was still surprisingly warm, and the air was heavy with the latent promise of rain. And somehow, the fresh air seemed to lift her oddly sombre mood.

"I didn't know you spoke Russian," Sophie said after a moment.

"My mother was Russian," Gabriel replied distractedly. "But I didn't practise a lot, so I can barely string two words together."

"Well, it seemed good enough for Zorin."

"I doubt it. Nothing ever is."

Sophie laughed softly. "You sound like you had to deal with him way too many times."

"Far too many. He was a regular at the *Palazzo Volterra* in Florence."

"I didn't know you worked in Florence."

"It was a rather short stint. Pretty much like here. A few months filling in for an absentee front desk manager who cracked his skull in a climbing accident."

"So you always work like that, as a temp, I mean?"

"I'm an itinerant odd-job man. I do whatever needs doing, wherever it needs doing."

"You sound like a buccaneering adventurer."

Gabriel laughed softly. "Oh, I am."

She followed Gabriel across the street, her eyes lingering briefly on the dark band of the River Thames, its banks linked by ancient bridges and flanked by the illuminated wheel of the London Eye on one side and the steeple of Big Ben on the other.

"My bike is over there," Gabriel said, pointing across the road towards a sleek black motorcycle that stood under the no-parking sign of a deserted loading bay.

"You didn't strike me as a rule breaker until today."

"I only ever break the rules I know I can get away with," Gabriel replied in a playful tone, handing her his helmet, then he slipped his phone from his pocket. "One sec, I'll be right with you."

Taking a step away, he typed a quick text, then turned back to her. "Ready?"

"Yes."

Gabriel swung his leg over the bike, settling into the seat and looking back at her.

Sophie hesitated, suddenly unsure whether it was a wise thing to do, then dismissing the thought, she slipped on the helmet and positioned herself behind Gabriel. Tentatively, her hands found a place on his torso that—even through the twin layers of his suit and leather jacket—somehow felt far too toned for a man who spent his life in the plush, velvety world of luxury hospitality.

As if sensing her thoughts, or perhaps her hesitation, Gabriel bent his head a little to the side. "Don't worry, I'll get you there safely."

CHAPTER IV

London, United Kingdom
Saturday, 29th June, 02:02

Sophie clung to Gabriel as he manoeuvred his motorbike through the streets. The warm air rushed past them, carrying with it the scents of summer and the faint yet persistent stench of the city. Gradually, the streets began to narrow, the buildings crowding closer together, their facades a tapestry of old brick and modern graffiti.

After a few more turns—some legal, some not—Gabriel finally brought the bike to a gentle stop in front of what had once been a nineteenth-century factory building. Across the street, Sophie could already see the queue of revellers stretching under the neon sign of the Viper's Den, the pulsating beat of music echoing faintly from its direction.

"Let me help you," Gabriel offered, holding out his hand to help her off the bike.

Sophie grasped his hand, feeling the rough calluses against her skin as she fought for balance on the uneven cobblestones with her heels. Gabriel steadied her, and they stood facing each other, both frozen in the moment, neither moving nor speaking as they held each other's gaze.

And before either of them could make a move—away or towards the other—the sky cracked open, unleashing the torrential downpour that had been looming over them all evening.

Caught off guard, they dashed under the awning of a nearby pub. The rain hammered down with relentless fury, turning the pavement into a canvas of shimmering reflections and the gutters into raging torrents.

Sophie leaned against the cool brick wall, water dripping from her hair.

"Should be over in a minute," Gabriel said, casting a glance at the sky as he slid a cigarette pack from his inside pocket, the words *Fumer tue* written in bold black letters on the pack.

He offered her one, but she shook her head. "I don't smoke."

"Wise choice. It's a nasty habit."

He lit a cigarette, his cufflink—an intricate platinum knot wrapped around a centrepiece of burnished steel—glistening ever so slightly as he moved, the light running over it in a playful cascade.

They stood in silence for a moment, the smoke from his cigarette curling up into the rain, disappearing before it could form properly. He leaned back, his shoulder just brushing the wall, watching her for a second before asking, "So what's the plan once you finish your master's? Are you going back to New York? Or are you staying here?"

"I hope to get an internship back home in New York, at the UN or maybe a think tank."

Gabriel leaned against the wall beside her, giving her a pensive nod as if digesting that information. "So there's nothing to keep you in London? No family? No boyfriend?"

Gabriel's question was thrown casually into the conversation, but Sophie was aware of the weight it carried—the subtext she wasn't sure she wanted to decipher.

"No," she said, keeping her tone light. "There's no one."

"That sounds lonely," he said, quietly.

Sophie hesitated for a moment, aware the conversation was veering into treacherous waters. "Alone isn't necessarily lonely, Gabriel."

"Agreed," he conceded.

Sophie hesitated again, watching the smoke of Gabriel's cigarette swirl and disappear, then asked, "And how about you?"

Gabriel tilted his head, his expression contemplative. "Alone? Yes. Lonely? I think that's more introspection than I can bear."

"That *does* sound lonely."

He smiled, and it was that rare, genuine smile that started as a spark of warmth in his dark eyes and then spread across his face, making the fine lines around his eyes more visible before finally reaching his mouth, making his lips curl upward, almost hesitantly, as if he were unsure of himself—or her.

"Do you want to come over to my place for a drink?" he asked, his question hanging between them, heavy with implication. Then, as if realising how the invitation sounded, he quickly added, "It's a gentleman's offer."

Sophie looked up at him. The dim streetlight cast shadows across his hard-cut features, and his dark, slightly tousled hair gave him a carelessly handsome look that was hard to ignore. He was so likeable, so relatable, and yet, beneath the veneer of the everyday man, she saw a man who was anything but ordinary.

Part of her wanted to reach out, to peel back the layers and discover what lay hidden beneath them. But it was too early. She wasn't ready. Not yet. She needed control, distance, time to understand where this was headed.

"Not tonight, Gabriel," she said softly. "But I'd like to, someday."

He held her gaze for a beat longer, as if weighing her words, and then, with a slight incline of his head, he acknowledged her decision. There was no disappointment, no change in his expression, just a quiet confidence, as if he knew she'd come around eventually.

"Come, I'll walk you over to the club," he said, flicking his cigarette into the street, where it hissed and died in a puddle.

"No, I'm fine. It's just across the street."

"It's late, Sophie, and I just want to make sure you get there safely."

"I'm fine, Gabriel, really."

Gabriel measured her for a moment, the idea of letting her walk alone stirring visible discomfort within him. Then he gave a reluctant nod, bent, and kissed her, ever so gently, on the cheek. "Take care, Sophie."

He smelled of cologne and just the faintest tinge of cigarette smoke, and for a fleeting second, she was tempted to slip her hand up his chest and kiss him. But she checked herself, knowing that if she gave in now, she might lose more than she was ready to risk. She took a step back, creating a necessary distance between them.

"Good night, Gabriel."

Unsure whether she regretted her decision, Sophie turned away slowly.

Keeping herself from looking back, she stepped out onto the rain-soaked street, her shoes splashing in the shallow puddles.

Her mind was still so preoccupied with Gabriel that she almost didn't notice the car idling in the shadows of a dilapidated brick building. It registered only fleetingly, a small detail in the periphery of her mind.

Still, something about it struck her as odd and she glanced back.

The outline of a figure was visible in the back seat, his features obscured by the darkness. As she watched him, a bus lumbered past, its headlights sweeping through the car windows. The man, as if recoiling from the light, turned his face away from the window, shrouding his features in shadow. A heartbeat later, the car pulled out onto the road and drove away, its taillights disappearing into the night.

CHAPTER V

London, United Kingdom
Saturday, 29th June, 02:26

Trying to keep her mind off Gabriel, Sophie idly scrolled through the messages on her phone as she waited outside the Viper's Den. Above her, the neon sign flashed red and green, its light reflecting on the rain-soaked streets.

The bouncer, a brawny giant, glared at the queue, his meaty fingers clutching a list. When his gaze finally settled on Sophie, he nodded at her and asked, "Oi, you alone?"

"My friends are already inside," Sophie replied.

"Name?"

"Sophie Akehurst."

"All right, you're on the list. Go ahead."

"Thanks."

As Sophie stepped inside, a woman about her age approached her.

"Wrist, please."

Sophie held out her arm. The woman's fingers closed around her forearm as she pressed a stamp onto the inside of her wrist—leaving a mark invisible to the naked eye.

"Thanks," Sophie mouthed over the beat of the music, and the woman graced her with a tense, professional smile, mouthing something back that Sophie couldn't understand.

Slipping past bored security guards and drunk revellers, Sophie moved deeper into the club, the bassline resonating within her chest as she walked through the entryway. A moment later, she slipped through another set of doors into the club's pulsating heart, where she was instantly swallowed by a seething throng of human bodies.

The half-acre dance floor—surrounded by roped-off booths and illuminated bar counters—was packed to the brim. Drunken dancers swayed to the beat, while those too intoxicated to stand congregated around the tables. The music blared at full volume, and occasionally, the DJ's voice echoed above it to spur on the crowd. And over it all hung the nauseating stench of spilt drinks, stage smoke, and sweat.

Cursing her life choices, Sophie navigated between clusters of gyrating bodies. Even though it was almost impossible, she did her best to evade the fleeting touches of strangers while her eyes scanned the faces on the dance floor in search of the one she wanted to find. Finally, in a clearing amidst the sea of bodies, she saw Gina—lounging in the VIP section, surrounded by a fawning court of admirers.

Carving her path through the crowd, Sophie finally reached her friend.

They hugged briefly, then Gina pulled back, her face lit with a conspiratorial gleam. "Come, you've got to meet Erik," she shouted over the music. "He's your type: smart enough to be dangerous, handsome enough to be distracting, and tall enough that you won't be able to look down on him." Briefly, Gina's gaze flicked over Sophie's shoulder, most likely to the mysterious Erik who was waiting somewhere in the throng. "Fair warning though—he's already a bit drunk. But don't worry, he's decent when he's not."

"Oh, come on, Gi."

"You've got to relax, Soph. Don't let one bad relationship derail your life. Plus, he's loaded, so you can stop working yourself to death at Valmont, pretending to care about people who drop your monthly rent on a bottle of champagne."

"Thanks, Gina. That's exactly what I'm looking for in a relationship—total dependence. Who needs a degree when you can just get laid, right?"

Gina smirked. "You know what I mean. You're grinding non-stop just to stay afloat. You deserve more than that. And hey, if *more* happens to be rich and nice to look at, I'm not seeing the downside."

Sophie stifled a groan. There was no point in arguing with Gina in her state of inebriated exuberance. She could say hi, talk to the guy for two minutes, and then abscond.

Letting Gina drag her along, Sophie crossed the dance floor and then walked up to the bar to meet her mysterious would-be suitor.

"He did an exchange term in Paris too, *Sciences Po* like you, so you have something in common. His French is horrible though," Gina said, pulling her along, then she raised her hand and pointed to a man at the far end of the bar. "That's him."

He looked about her age. Twenty-four, maybe a bit older. He was definitely handsome, unquestionably drunk, and—judging by the way he imperiously snapped his fingers at the bartender—quite full of himself.

As they approached, Erik swung around on his barstool, looking at Gina and then at Sophie—eyeing her with less-than-subtle appreciation. For a second, she regretted not taking Gabriel up on his offer. At least she wouldn't be here right now.

"You must be Sophie," Erik slurred. "You really *are* pretty." He laughed, a sound more in line with a snort. "Wanna get out of here? My flat's in Russell Square. It's way nicer than this place, and the drinks are better too."

Sophie forced a smile. "Maybe another time. How about I call you an Uber?"

Before she could move, Erik reached out, grabbing her wrist—not forcefully, just enough to pull her slightly closer. It wasn't the strength of his grip—it was the fact that he touched her at all, without asking. The suddenness of it, the familiarity of feeling trapped.

Sophie felt the walls close in around her. Her heart pounded against her chest, and the room suddenly felt too warm.

She yanked her wrist back.

She couldn't do this. She wasn't ready—not even when temptation came in the form of the dashing Gabriel Dunbar and most certainly not if it tottered at her with beery breath and the promise of a warm bed close to campus.

"I'll be right back," she said, voice tight, stepping back.

Desperate to escape this stomach-turning compost of sickening odours and uninvited advances, Sophie wandered through the crowd, looking for a place to which she could escape. On the other side of the stage, she spotted a few people she knew from her fiscal policy course, but the booth was already overcrowded and not one person seemed even remotely sober. And then she spotted the toilet sign to her left.

Better than nothing.

Quickly, she slipped into the room, closed the door behind her and leaned against it.

What the hell am I doing here?

As a narrow survivor of a shipwrecked relationship and now convinced repudiator of romantic entanglements of any kind, she kept her admirers at a distance with steadfast conviction. And yet, here she was, exiled in the toilets of a seedy club, hiding from a drunk admirer.

Taking a deep breath, Sophie stepped over a pile of soaking-wet paper towels to get to the sink. She slipped her phone from her clutch and checked the time. It was half past two.

One drink. Then I'll be off.

Sophie placed her phone on the edge of the wash basin, turned the tap and let the cold water run over her wrist. At that moment, her phone buzzed. Without turning off the water, Sophie leaned to catch a glimpse of the screen. It was a voicemail notification.

'You have three missed calls from Gabriel Dunbar,' read the automated message. 'The caller left no message.'

One reception bar at the top of the screen briefly flashed and then vanished again, leaving the bars greyed out completely. Sophie sighed. She would have to go outside to call Gabriel back.

She turned off the tap. The sound of the water abruptly ceased, leaving only the muted thumping of the bass from the other side of the door.

Stepping closer to the mirror, Sophie pulled her lipstick out of her clutch and applied it carefully, the soft, rose-coloured tone still dark enough to stand out against her pale skin. She pressed her lips together, blending the colour, then she slipped the lipstick back into her purse, brushed her long chestnut hair over her shoulder, and took a last glance at her reflection. In the wash of black light—used to prevent the odd drug addict from shooting up in the club's toilets—she suddenly noticed the luminous stains on her fingertips.

"Dammit," she muttered, holding her wrist under the black light to inspect the admission stamp.

The stamp was intact—smudged slightly at the edges but still clear enough to pass muster. The symbol and date were perfectly legible. It was something else that caught her attention.

The stains were a different colour than the stamp—cooler, bluish rather than white.

Sophie frowned, turning her hand this way and that, as if a different angle might explain it.

What was it? A smeared stamp from brushing past someone in the crowd? Something left on the bar, or the door handles?

Water hadn't worked earlier, and there was no soap here—just the broken dispenser hanging from the corner of the sink. She rubbed her fingers against the hem of her dress but achieved nothing beyond a faint shiver of static. Whatever it was, it would have to stay.

The stamp, at least, was fine. And as long as that passed the bouncer's scrutiny, she could step outside for a breath of fresh air.

With a sigh, Sophie let her hand drop, reached for her phone, then slipped outside into the dimly lit hallway.

The music boomed at full volume and the air was stifling. To her right was a fire escape, flanked by a bull-necked security guard and topped by a sign labelled unmistakably with the words 'No Exit'.

Let's see about that.

Drawing herself up to her full height, Sophie stepped over to the guard and graced him with that coy, endearing smile that always got her what she wanted. "If I pop out there for just one minute, will you let me back in?"

He flashed her an eager grin that, even before he replied, told Sophie that she had won.

"Of course," he shouted over the music and opened the door for her.

Rewarding his generosity with a wink, Sophie slipped out into the night and drew a deep breath.

The air outside was cool, far cooler than the sticky heat of the Viper's Den. Breathing it felt like a lifeline. Right then, her phone buzzed again, and a text appeared on her screen. It was from Gabriel.

'Sophie, please call me. It's urgent.'

For a second, Sophie stared at the message, then she hit the call button. There was an odd click on the line, a long silence, and then, finally, the call connected. It rang once, twice, and then once more.

"Come on, pick up," Sophie whispered, walking past a rusty dumpster—its pungent odour mingling with the smell of urine.

Out of nowhere, hands—gloved and impossibly strong—grabbed Sophie from behind.

Her scream was smothered by the hand that closed over her mouth. In mindless fear, Sophie bit down until she tasted blood. There was a dull grunt of pain and then her assailant dealt her a resounding slap, so powerful that it sent her reeling to the ground. The sheer force of the impact pressed the air from her lungs, and then a booted foot settled on her neck, keeping her down on the pavement.

For a moment, her attacker stood motionless above her, as if to assert his control over the situation, then he bent and roughly pulled her arm out from under her body. Something clicked faintly. A bluish-purple beam of light cut through the darkness. It moved in an erratic arc and came to rest on her hand, making the luminescent stains on her fingertips glow.

"That the *metka* stuff you're looking for?" the man asked, studying the glowing stains on Sophie's fingertips, then glancing over his shoulder at a second figure standing in the shadows.

"Yes, it is," a man's voice—deep and vaguely familiar—confirmed.

"Then we have your bird, so let's pack her up."

Sophie felt terror run through her. Gathering all her strength, she tried to free herself. But her attacker moved with lightning speed, drawing a gun, and placing it against her forehead.

"You make a scene, I put a bullet in your head. Got it?"

Petrified, Sophie gave a nod, hoping that her compliance would keep her alive.

The man's smile broadened a little. "Good. Now listen; when I say so, you get up nice and easy, and you walk to that car on your left. No noise. No fuss. Clear?"

Sophie nodded again, keeping her eyes on the gun as if, by staring at the weapon, she could somehow control it. Her attacker waited for a moment, looking over his shoulder to make sure that they were alone, then he glanced at the man in the shadows as if to get his permission for whatever was about to follow and finally, he lifted his foot off her neck. "Up."

Mechanically, Sophie pushed herself up from the pavement and staggered towards the car. When she reached out to open the door, her captor slammed her against it. The sheer force of the impact pressed the air out of her lungs and turned her scream into a pathetic, gurgling wheeze. And then something pricked her thigh. The sharp pain was over before her mind could fully register it. From the corner of her eye, Sophie saw her attacker step back and slip a plastic cap over the needle of a syringe. Almost instantly, a creeping numbness began to spread through her arms and legs. She felt drowsy and, strangely, less afraid.

"I trust you'll complete the job as agreed," the second man said from the shadows. "I can't have another body in the streets."

"I know what Morozov wants. Don't need you breathing down my neck."

Sophie's phone rang, the sound far away, then stopping abruptly as her attacker crushed the phone under the heel of his boot.

A moment later, his hand closed roughly around her arm. Sophie tried to resist, but her limbs were heavy, unresponsive, betraying her with their sudden uselessness. The ground seemed to tilt and sway under her feet and then he hauled her into the car.

She fought to keep her eyes open, to maintain a grip on the slipping threads of consciousness, but her eyelids felt heavy, weighted down by an invisible force.

The last thing Sophie saw before she drifted out of consciousness was the tall figure of a man stepping out of the shadows and turning his face towards her.

It was a face she knew.

A face she had seen only hours ago when she had stepped behind the counter of the Atlas Bar to begin her shift.

It was him.

Her strange, reclusive, scar-faced guest.

CHAPTER VI

London, England
Monday, 1st July, 18:22

Sophie awoke slowly, her mind fighting through the haze of sedation and strange disjointed memories. A sharp, metallic tang filled her mouth and the air she breathed was stale—carrying the faint scent of mould and something acrid.

For a moment, she lay with her eyes closed, feeling the cold seeping into her bones from the hard surface beneath her. Then, slowly, agonisingly, she pried her eyes open—blinking against a wavering light that glowed overhead.

With a soft groan, Sophie rolled onto her side, the rough concrete scraping against her hip, and then a sharp pain shot through her wrists—stopping her movement instantly.

Her eyes found her wrists—bound tightly together in front of her. For a moment, all she could do was stare at her hands, and then her eyes traced down to her legs—naked, like the rest of her body.

A slow wash of alarm met the sight. Some distant part of her mind knew she ought to scream or rage, but her body—rendered sluggish by sedation—wouldn't answer.

Gingerly, she arched her back from the cold concrete floor, only to drop again when dizziness struck. For an instant, the ceiling seemed to crouch closer, pressing in on her with its ugly grey corners. A single bulb dangled from an unprotected wire, offering no warmth, only a sputtering half-light. The rest of the room stretched away—concrete walls beaded with damp. A rusted pipe overhead released periodic drips, each one spattering into a puddle with a hollow *plop* that set her nerves on edge.

Bit by bit, other sounds peeled away from the drip of water—distant footsteps, muffled voices, and the soft hum from a ventilation shaft—all running together in a horrifying tune.

Then, abruptly, a sound pulled her back to reality with a jolt. It was faint at first, a distant echo of footsteps that grew steadily louder as they approached, coming closer than any others had before. Then came the sound of a door and the din of male voices.

"Eight girls, just like we said. All the usual specs— eighteen, nineteen, pretty, clean, and of course, pure. Plus, snagged you a bonus. American. Picked her up a couple of days ago while I was doin' a job for Morozov. Figured she'd catch your fancy," said a voice that Sophie recognised as her kidnapper's.

A man's voice replied, speaking English with the clipped, precise accent of the British upper class. "Nikolai Morozov? Since when does he dabble in the trade?"

"Nah, he don't. But this one's a liability, see? Morozov's boy wants her gone—fast and quiet. Doesn't want another body in the streets for the Met to find."

"I do not deal in locally sourced products, Liam, especially if they might attract undue attention from the Metropolitan Police. That is not my risk profile."

"Don't worry, she ain't gonna cause any trouble. The Colonel's taking care of it."

The steps halted. Silence. Then the rustle of paper. And finally, the Brit's voice broke the hush again. "Liam, she is twenty-four years old. Spoiled goods. Essentially worthless. Dispose of her and show me the others."

"Trust me, she's a real knockout. Not the kinda merch you toss out before a proper look."

"Very well, then let us have a look."

The hollow clang of a key turning in a lock filled the cell, followed by the soft sound of metal grating over metal. Then the door swung open, the garish glow of artificial light streaming into the cell. A moment later, booted feet moved into Sophie's line of vision, walking towards her over the wet floor. She recoiled but lacked the strength to fend off the hands that dragged her upright.

Someone touched her chin, quite gently, tipping her face up. Sophie looked up. In front of her stood an elegantly dressed man in his late fifties, with greying temples, wire-rimmed spectacles and the air of a venerable art connoisseur. But the face she looked at wasn't just any face. It was one she knew. Its pale, contemptuous features had stared back at her every so often from the society pages of the shoddy free dailies she used to read on the tube.

Lord Harper.

"Quite a beauty indeed," Harper said, sounding pleasantly surprised.

Adjusting the signet ring on his pinkie finger, he took a step back and circled her, his footsteps echoing in the cell.

"I must apologise, Liam, she is indeed exquisite. Quite marvellous in fact."

Reaching out, Harper let his fingertips brush over the tip of her breast. His touch was gentle, not salacious, but cold and professional, so utterly devoid of sexual interest as if he were appraising some rare piece of art. Apparently satisfied, he gave a nod and turned to Liam.

"Does she have a clean bill of health?"

"Yeah, she's clean—tests all came back clear, no nasty surprises."

"Very well, we have a deal," Harper said, slipping a marker from his pocket. Then he looked at her and held out his left. "Give me your hands."

Sophie didn't move.

Without another word, Harper reached for the zip ties and pushed them up towards her elbows until the plastic cut into her skin. Holding her still with one hand, Harper wrote something on the inside of her wrist with the other. The ink was invisible, just like the stamp at the club, but Sophie still felt what he had scrawled on her skin: the Roman numeral nine.

Harper pocketed the pen, then took off his spectacles and stepped aside. "Bring her upstairs. We must not keep the bidders waiting."

Liam pushed her out of the cell. Barely able to hold herself upright, Sophie staggered along as he dragged her through a gloomy passageway, past a long row of steel doors and cross-barred cages in which women languished like cattle—naked, bound, more dead than alive.

"Please," Sophie whispered, her speech slurred.

"Shut up," Liam hissed, pushing her along the dank passage and through a steel gate into a darkened room where a man in a dark suit stood waiting.

"She's the last," Liam announced.

The man turned, grabbed Sophie's wrist, and turned it upwards, then he shone the purplish beam of a penlight on it, so that the Roman numeral on her skin flashed briefly. Apparently satisfied, he shoved her through another door into a darkened room so vast that her steps echoed in it. Then he pushed her down to her knees.

The instant Sophie hit the floor, a single spotlight flickered to life, its garish beam trained firmly on her. For a beat, the light blinded her completely, but then her eyes adjusted and a vast, semi-circular space—like a Roman amphitheatre—came into focus.

Like the floor beneath her, the curved structure was built entirely from red and white marble. Lined up along its single rank sat around two dozen spectators: Men, all dressed in formal dark suits as if they had just left a dinner party. A handful of the attendees regarded her with the same detached curiosity that museumgoers might afford a moderately interesting exhibit, while the others ignored her completely, continuing their hushed conversations as if nothing had happened.

Suddenly, a disembodied female voice filled the silence. "Lot number nine. American. Twenty-four years old. We will start at two hundred thousand British pounds."

Briefly, the fog lifted, and in that fleeting, terrifying moment of clarity, Sophie finally understood the gravity of her situation: The bids were for her.

With almost inhuman strength, Sophie staggered to her feet, but her weakened limbs couldn't support her body. She swayed and stumbled into the spectators. Strong hands caught her shoulders, breaking her fall and holding her in a half-kneeling position, with her head hovering over her saviour's knees. Sophie looked up.

It was Alexei Zorin.

CHAPTER VII

London, England
Monday, 1ˢᵗ July, 19:22

For a fleeting moment, Sophie felt hope at the sight of a familiar face, her addled mind convinced that Zorin would intervene—that their acquaintance, however vague, would somehow save her.

"Help me," she whispered, her voice tremulous.

Zorin held her gaze. His expression was unreadable, but in his eyes, Sophie saw a flash of recognition and something far more terrible: indifference.

Hands grabbed her from behind and hauled her up. And Zorin allowed it to happen, his gaze lingering on Sophie for a moment longer before he turned back to the man beside him, continuing the conversation that had been so rudely interrupted.

As Sophie was dragged back into the spotlight, the woman's voice chimed once again through the speaker. "Two hundred and fifty thousand."

Frantically, Sophie's eyes darted over the ranks, searching for whoever had placed the bid. Just then, one of the men raised his hand.

The voice—female, sterile—spoke again. "Three hundred thousand."

Sophie's vision blurred, obscuring the bidder's face. In a desperate attempt to steady herself, she reached for the guard's arm, one hand gripping his wrist, the other clutching the hand holding the flashlight. For a fraction of a second, the penlight flared up, its blue light revealing the invisible stains on her fingertips. Her vision cleared again, her eyes settling on the blond man to Zorin's left. He was leaning forward now, so that the overhead light illuminated his hard-cut features. He regarded her for a long moment, idly blowing cigarette smoke through his lips, then he raised his hand.

"Three hundred and fifty thousand. We have three hundred and fifty thousand from the gentleman on the left," the disembodied voice announced.

Zorin—so far indifferent to the drama that unfolded on the stage—looked up. First his eyes shifted to the bidder, then swept over the audience and finally his frosty gaze settled on Sophie. For a beat, Zorin seemed to assess her, weighing her worth and deciding whether it was enough to warrant the effort, then he lifted one finger by just a fraction of an inch.

"We have four hundred thousand from the gentleman at the centre. Four hundred thousand."

Zorin's seatmate placed another bid.

"Four hundred and fifty thousand."

Zorin raised his bid.

"We have five hundred thousand," the woman's voice announced.

The man to Zorin's left lifted his hand again, this time holding up two fingers.

"The bid has been doubled to one million pounds," the woman's voice announced.

Zorin raised his hand again, in the same lazy manner as before, mirroring the blond man's gesture.

"Two million," the disembodied voice proclaimed.

The blond man matched him.

"Four million."

Zorin outbid his opponent once more, with a languorous twitch of the hand.

"Eight million," the faceless voice chimed from above her. "We have eight million pounds."

There was a moment of hushed silence, the men sitting motionless, their faces sharp and pale in the glow of the spotlight. Then the blond man's lips curled into a disdainful, mirthless smile, and he shook his head.

The disembodied voice spoke again. "Eight million pounds. Going once. Going twice. Sold for eight million to the gentleman at the centre."

The spotlight went out.

She couldn't think.

She couldn't feel.

And then hands—callous and careless—seized her and hauled her out of the room.

Sophie didn't fight as she was dragged back into the dank hallway—she was like a figure in a dream, an impotent observer of her own tragedy, watching herself being marched through the passageway past rows of metal doors and steel cages, into a small room.

The space was dank and disgusting. The walls, if they had once known colour, had long since surrendered to a uniform shade of neglect, and the air reeked with the scent of stale smoke and sweat. Sophie didn't know how long they waited there, but finally, someone came and mumbled instructions to her minder in a language she didn't understand, then she was ushered out into the corridor again and frogmarched into a cramped cell with white-tiled walls and strip lights for illumination.

"Get yourself cleaned up," barked the guard, tossing a bar of soap at her feet.

Sophie stared at it, unable to move.

"The buyer doesn't want you all filthy, so pick up the damn soap and scrub, or I'll do it myself."

Trembling, Sophie bent to pick up the bar of soap. The moment her hand closed around it, a torrent of frigid water washed over her, making her retreat against the white-tiled wall, but there was no escaping the freezing cold. Shivering violently, Sophie rubbed the soap between her bound hands and then did as she had been told, washing herself down from head to foot.

"Enough!" shouted the guard, and the torrent of water stopped as suddenly as it had started.

Exhausted, Sophie dropped the soap and sank to the ground. But the respite lasted only seconds, and then her minder grabbed her hair and hauled her upright.

"Dry off and get the fuck on with it," he sneered, shoving a towel into her trembling hands. "I ain't got all night."

Trembling from cold and fear, Sophie feebly towelled herself down. Once dry, the guard cut the zip ties around her wrists and handed her a short black dress—barely long enough to cover the apex of her thighs. Struggling to stand, Sophie slipped the skin-tight garment on. When she was finally done, the guard put a new pair of zip ties around her wrists, pulling them tight, and then tossed a pair of impossibly high heels at her feet.

"Put 'em on."

For a fraction of a second, Sophie felt the insane urge to refuse but mastered herself. *Pull yourself together*, she urged herself in her mind. *You have to be smart now.*

She bent and did as she was told.

As she looked up, she saw the guard reach for a small metal box. It was scratched and dented, much like the rest of this place, used too many times to count.

He unlatched it with a soft click and opened the lid. Inside: syringes, small glass vials, rows of sharp, gleaming needles. The guard pulled a vial from the box, holding it up to the light. He flicked the top with one thick, calloused finger and then reached for a syringe. The needle glinted in the guard's hand as he plunged it into the vial.

"No, please," Sophie whispered, backing away.

"That's for the next one, darling, not for you," the guard said with a sick grin, his eyes still on the syringe. "Your buyer wants you clean, not all fucked up on junk."

At that moment, the sound of familiar voices echoed through the hallway.

"I am delighted to finally count you among my clients, Alexei," Harper said, sounding as if he were genuinely overjoyed. "Trust me, it is money well spent."

"I'm certain it is," Zorin replied, the soft, low timbre of his voice resonating eerily in the hallway.

"And should she fail to meet your expectations, you will undoubtedly find a willing buyer in Stiva. He flew in from Paris today solely for the auction, and I hear he was quite miffed to be outbid on his home turf—especially by the man who, if rumours are true, has become something of his arch-nemesis."

"You talk too much, Harper," Zorin remarked coldly.

An instant later, the door swung open, and Alexei Zorin stepped into the cell, Lord Harper and a stern-faced bodyguard following in his wake.

The guard stepped to Sophie's side and hauled her up by her arms, while Zorin and Harper stood waiting by the door.

For a moment, Zorin looked her over, taking in her damp hair and skin-tight dress, then he shrugged off his suit jacket, stepped to her side and slipped it around her shoulders.

"Let's go."

CHAPTER VIII

London, England
Monday, 1st July, 20:51

The bodyguard shoved Sophie forward, his fingers digging into her flesh as he marched her through an endless series of narrow, claustrophobic hallways.

She didn't fight, merely stumble along, the drugs dulling everything—the ache in her wrists, the sounds, even the fear.

Zorin and Harper walked ahead, their voices calm and steady, as if this were nothing more than routine. Zorin never looked back, never even glanced at her—as if she were nothing but cargo being ferried from one point to another.

Suddenly the air changed—becoming cooler, sharper. And then they stepped outside into a courtyard.

It was vast, enclosed by high walls and surrounded by surveillance cameras. At its centre, four black SUVs stood waiting, their engines running, their headlights dimmed.

The scene felt unreal, like a stage where nothing moved, yet everything was waiting.

Somewhere beyond the walls of the courtyard, she heard voices and laughter. Sophie understood, dimly, that this was the moment. If she was going to call for help, it had to be now. But the thought floated, untethered, never quite reaching her limbs. She couldn't summon the will, couldn't make herself feel the sharpness of the fear that should have been there. The urgency, the panic—it was all smothered, buried beneath the thick, drug-induced fog.

And then, before she realised it, she was in the back of a car, with Zorin beside her, and a driver and bodyguard sitting in the front.

With a click, the doors locked and then Sophie felt the subtle jolt as the car began to move, its headlights sweeping across the forecourt one last time before they passed through the archway and onto a dark, tree-lined road.

She pressed her bound hands against the back of the driver's seat, trying to steady herself.

"Please, you don't have to do this," she whispered—her voice low, pleading, but distant, as if it belonged to someone else.

Zorin didn't look at her.

"Indeed, I don't," he said, his tone impossibly calm, almost matter-of-fact, as though they were discussing something mundane. Something small.

"Then let me go," she said, quieter now. "Please, I beg you, I won't tell anyone what happened."

Zorin's lips curved, just slightly, the faintest shadow of a smile. He didn't laugh, but the suggestion was there, as if she'd said something so obviously naive it barely deserved acknowledgement.

"I think we both know that's impossible."

Evidently considering the conversation over—and uninterested in anything else she might have to say—Zorin pulled a phone from his pocket, dialled a number, and pressed it to his ear. The conversation that followed was short and in Russian. The words washed over her, their meaning lost, but the sound of them familiar now, the cadence of his voice steady, almost lulling her.

And then, through the fog, a name broke through.

Nikolai Morozov.

The name drifted to the surface, cutting through the fog, and for a moment, her mind latched onto it, as if it was a key to something. Something bigger. Something darker.

But the effort to hold on to it was too much. Her eyelids felt heavy, her thoughts scattered. The name slipped away again, sinking back into the confusion that surrounded her.

She wasn't sure how long it had been—minutes, seconds—but the next thing she noticed was the rush of cool air against her face. It snapped her back, if only for a moment. She blinked, trying to focus. The window was open, the River Thames stretching along the left side of the car.

The night air whipped into the car, tugging at her hair, chilling her skin. She reached up to brush the hair from her face and at that moment, she saw Zorin's hand, the phone in his palm.

He tossed it out the window, a casual flick of his wrist, as if it meant nothing. The phone disappeared into the dark, swallowed by the river below.

At that moment, she felt the stark reality of her situation closing in around her—about who Alexei Zorin really was and what he was planning to do to her.

"Are you going to kill me?" Sophie whispered.

Zorin turned his head fractionally, allowing a slice of light to catch the planes of his face. He was handsome—devastatingly so—but it was a handsomeness that seemed out of place now, nothing but a mask hiding his evil.

He arched an eyebrow. "It would be quite a waste to kill you after I took the trouble of buying you, wouldn't you agree?"

"Then what do you want with me?"

Zorin finally turned to look at her. "If I remember correctly, you begged me to save you."

"Not like this..."

Zorin laughed softly, so quietly she almost didn't hear it. He tilted his head back against the seat, as if savouring the memory. "Like this...," he repeated, tasting the words. "I'm not sure where you've gleaned your assessment of my moral constitution, but let's not pretend tonight was a chivalrous errand."

"Please," she tried again, voice hoarse. "You have money, influence. You don't need me. I won't tell anyone what happened here."

"It's too late for that," he said finally. "Far too late. So consider this your second chance. Not everyone gets one. I suggest you make the most of it."

The words settled between them, heavy and inevitable. Sophie knew exactly what it meant—there was no mistaking it, no room for false hope or misunderstanding.

The reality of it all settled into her like a weight on her chest. Her options had shrunk to nothing. She was an object to him, a commodity—beneath his concern, beneath his pity.

Closing her eyes, she pressed her body harder against the seat, trying to keep her distance from the man beside her. She felt suddenly violently sick, as if the drugs were winning over the adrenaline again—and for a moment everything went black.

A while, her mind seemed to float in and out of consciousness, and when she finally came to again, the world outside had changed. The car was still moving, but somehow, without her noticing, they had left the city and the lights along the road had begun to thin out, leaving stretches of darkness between the streetlamps.

The car slowed slightly, taking a turn, and Sophie's eyes drifted up, catching sight of a street sign. In her drugged state, Sophie couldn't read the words written there, but the plane-shaped icon was all she needed to see.

They weren't just traversing the city; they were leaving it.

"Where are you taking me?" Sophie whispered, her eyes shifting to Zorin.

"To a friend's house," he replied with a pinch of scorn. "You'll like it—the view is marvellous."

His blatant mockery made Sophie shiver. He was enjoying this.

Before she could say anything else, they took another turn and drove towards the airport. And there, at the end of the tree-lined road, Sophie saw the blue flashing lights of police cars. Around a dozen officers stood on the street, waving drivers to the side, checking their papers and cars—inside and out.

Sophie's heart leapt with a flicker of hope. *They'll stop us.*

The motorcade slowed as it approached the checkpoint. The bodyguard tensed, his hand moving instinctively towards his gun. Zorin remained calm, his eyes never leaving the police ahead.

Zorin's motorcade didn't stop with the other cars that were heading for what looked like the road to the main terminal of the airport. Instead, they shifted to an empty lane on the very left, bypassing the waiting cars and finally coming to a stop in front of a ten-foot steel gate, topped by barbed wire and flanked by a dozen uniformed police officers.

Someone panned a floodlight in their direction, then one of the officers—carrying a submachine gun and a walkie-talkie—strode to the vehicle in the front. He spoke a few words with the driver, subjected the car to a cursory inspection, stepped back, and raised his hand to signal that everything was in order. The gate groaned and began sliding sideways, opening the path to the airstrip beyond—vast and empty, save for a single black jet that sat bathed in the glow of the runway lights.

And just like that—quietly, without spectacle—they drove unchecked past the police barriers onto the tarmac.

"That's impossible," Sophie whispered.

Zorin laughed again—that terrible, soft, melodic laugh, nearly inaudible, and almost pleasant. "You'd be surprised how cheap a man's loyalty is."

The steel gate closed behind them, and as the police lights faded behind it, that fleeting moment of hope dissipated with them, replaced by a chilling certainty: No one would come for her.

Sophie turned to Zorin, ready to beg, to plead for mercy, anything that would spare her from whatever horror lay ahead. But just at that moment, a shaft of yellow light fell in through the window, splitting Zorin's face in half, shadow and light, and falling onto the black grip of a handgun in his shoulder holster.

And finally, the terrible lethargy seemed to fall from her, her body moving before her mind had consciously made the decision. She lunged at Zorin, her hands grasping at the gun.

But Zorin moved faster.

His hand shot out, his fingers hooking into the zip ties binding her wrists. With effortless strength, he twisted her arms and forced her down. She was on her knees in an instant, her body shoved into the confines of the footwell. He maintained his grip on her wrists, holding her in place with unyielding force.

And in that moment, a wave of fear finally broke through the narcotic haze, primal and raw. It was a fear unlike any she had felt before. In an instant, her world narrowed to isolated sensations and minute details—the silk lining of Zorin's jacket brushing against her arms, the woody scent of his cologne hanging in the air, and the timepiece on his wrist, its seconds hand ticking away with unerring precision, like an inexorable countdown of her mortality.

"Please don't hurt me."

"I'll let it go, just this once," he said, his tone very calm, almost soothing. "But fear won't buy you leniency forever, so don't make me regret my choices."

For a moment, he held her gaze, as if to make sure she had truly understood him, then he released her. "Now, it's time to board, so you better get up."

Sophie did as she was told. Trembling, she slowly rose from the footwell, settling back into her seat. A moment later, the car rolled to a stop. Zorin's bodyguards opened the doors, and Sophie was pulled from the car into the night air.

She stumbled slightly, her legs heavy and uncooperative. The effects of the drug hadn't worn off yet, and the ground seemed to tilt beneath her feet, a slow, nauseating spin that made her want to vomit. She caught herself, willing her body to stay upright, to not give Zorin and his goons the satisfaction of seeing her break down completely.

The jet loomed ahead, its engines humming. With swift strides, they marched her over to the plane, their hold on her unyielding and for a brief moment, panic overcame Sophie again. She struggled against the guards. "No, let go of me."

The men didn't even budge, simply ushering her forward.

In a desperate attempt to leave behind some kind of evidence, Sophie glanced over her shoulder, looking at the terminal, and then back at the entrance gate, hoping that somewhere, a security camera would catch her image.

And then she was already halfway up the steps to the jet, ascending them as she would a scaffold—with trembling knees and flanked by henchmen.

CHAPTER IX

Venice, Italy
Monday, 1st July, 23:16

Sophie's eyes fluttered open as the jet began its descent. The flight had lasted just over two hours. Two hours in which she found herself the solitary passenger in a plush private sanctuary at the rear of the plane, all polished wood and cream-coloured leather. No one, not even Zorin, had entered her space. The isolation was unnerving; it gave her too much time to think, too much time to fear what lay ahead.

When the plane touched down, the landing was so smooth it was almost imperceptible, but it jolted her heart into a frenzied rhythm. She could hear the shuffle in the cabin outside—footsteps, voices, the clatter of luggage hastily unloaded. Finally, they came for her—two sharp-eyed, tight-lipped bodyguards who dared neither touch nor look at her. One of them motioned for her to stand, and she complied—stumbling slightly as she got to her feet, still unsteady from the drugs.

Accompanied by Zorin's goons, Sophie exited the plane, stepping down onto the tarmac and breathing in air dense with the briny scent of the sea.

"Where are we?" Sophie asked, glancing at the bodyguards who walked a step behind her.

Her minders didn't respond, either not understanding or simply not caring to. Without a word, they led her across the tarmac towards a massive black helicopter—dark and angular, as if made for combat. The door was opened for her, and Sophie was ushered into the plush interior. She hesitated for a moment, the hum of the slow-moving rotors filling her ears, then climbed in, her fingers brushing against the cool, smooth surface of the leather seat. She sat, and the door closed behind her, trapping her inside.

Twisting her wrists in her bonds, Sophie reached for the safety belt, awkwardly fumbling with the buckle as the zip ties cut into her wrists.

Moments later, Zorin slid into the seat next to her—his presence sudden and unwelcome.

For a fraction of a second, he watched her struggle with the safety belt—her movements made clumsy and ineffective by the restraints—then he reached over, his fingers brushing hers as he took the strap from her. His hands moved quickly, fastening the seatbelt with practised efficiency. Then, unexpectedly, his fingers were on her wrists, adjusting the zip ties and loosening them just enough to relieve the pressure on her chafed skin.

Sophie flinched at his touch—unnerved by the strange intimacy of the moment.

The corners of Zorin's mouth curled into a faint, disdainful smile, but he said nothing, turning his attention to the window.

And then the rotors began to pick up speed, the ground falling away beneath them to reveal a fantastical mosaic of meandering canals and clustered terracotta roofs. At that moment, as they took to the sky, Sophie finally realised where he had taken her.

Venice.

The helicopter flew in a wide arc over the ancient city, then banked to the left, veering out over the Adriatic Sea and heading towards a secluded island half a mile away from the lagoon. The small archipelago was dominated by a sprawling complex—a colossal Byzantine edifice with two sweeping wings and an illuminated glass cupola that sat like a capsized half-moon atop the building.

It looked like a fortress.

One from which there would be no escape.

In an impotent attempt to shut out the fear, Sophie closed her eyes—feeling rather than seeing the helicopter's descent. And then they touched down. For a moment, the clatter of the rotor blades filled the night, drowning out every other sound, then the engine hum faded, replaced by the sound of waves and a distant gull's cry.

A dozen armed guards—clad all in black—emerged from the shadows of the building, seamlessly forming a protective ring around the helicopter. The doors swung open, and before Sophie could even move, callous hands grabbed her bound wrists and dragged her out onto a neatly cut lawn.

Sudden panic gripped her—a primal instinct to fight flaring up. She twisted against the iron grip of the guard, trying desperately to yank her hands free.

And then Zorin's voice cut like a whip through the nocturnal hush. Just a single word in Russian. Clipped. Hard. Clearly a command. Instantly, the painful grip on her wrists eased. Then Zorin beckoned her to his side with a lazy flick of his hand.

She hesitated briefly, but deep down, she knew that—at least for now—Alexei Zorin was her safest bet.

Just be smart, don't provoke him, you'll find a way out, she thought and summoning every ounce of her dwindling courage, fell in step behind him.

Accompanied by a retinue of bodyguards, they crossed the forecourt, walking past terraces lined with fragrant orange trees, and then up a wide Romanesque staircase to the brilliantly illuminated entrance gates.

As she walked, she tried to get a sense of the place, of the exits and the windows, but her mind still didn't fully engage, a fog clinging to her thoughts, slowing everything down. And then she was already inside, standing in the entrance hall.

The space was enormous, like something out of a different time.

Fashioned from red and white marble, the foyer was an extravagant space—adorned with intricate *Pietra Dura* floors, carved alabaster columns, and a soaring lead glass cupola that shone with the refracted light of a dozen crystal chandeliers. From the colonnaded ground floor rose an ornate staircase, its two symmetrical flights stretching in half-curves up to a balustraded gallery that encircled the entirety of the room. Just like the ground floor, the gallery itself was lined with outsized Baroque paintings that hung at precise intervals between the windows. And beside each window stood a bodyguard, their weapons visible under their jackets.

Even though Zorin's suit jacket covered her body to mid-thigh, Sophie felt exposed—as if every man in the room could somehow see how little she wore.

Her captor, perhaps sensing her discomfort, beckoned her to his side with a flick of his wrist. She moved closer, and as she did so, Sophie realised that it wasn't concern for her well-being that had sparked Zorin's unexplained affection—but the arrival of another group of men.

Through the ten-foot windows, Sophie saw half a dozen bodyguards ascend the Romanesque staircase outside. Between them walked a tall figure, his blond hair slightly tousled. For a brief moment, the man paused to light a cigarette and cast a casual glance up at the illuminated edifice. Then he exhaled a great puff of blue smoke, discarded the cigarette and stepped through the door into the illuminated entrance hall.

At that moment, as the blond man stepped inside, Sophie recognised him. He was the second bidder from the auction, her almost-buyer and—if Harper was right—Zorin's declared nemesis.

Stiva.

Dressed casually—dark slacks, white shirt, sleeves rolled up to the elbows—Stiva strode across the foyer amidst a phalanx of bodyguards. Like the black-clad guards who surrounded him, Stiva moved with an easy grace, but compared to their raw heft, he was lean and elegant—a jungle predator rather than a wolf.

As the procession approached, Stiva's gaze shifted to Sophie, the slight turn of the head revealing not only hard-cut features but surprising youth. He looked even younger than Zorin. No more than thirty.

Briefly, Stiva's gaze lingered on her, then it moved on to her captor. For a fraction of a second, Sophie saw a flash of hate in Stiva's eyes. It lasted only a beat, and then Stiva regained control of himself. He said something in Russian, and Zorin replied in the same language and with a dismissive tone.

Stiva smiled, his eyes returning to her.

"Good evening, my dear. I trust you had a pleasant journey, despite the dismal company." Stiva's voice was soft, and just like Zorin's, without so much as a trace of an accent.

Zorin laughed very softly. "Dreaming of things you can't have, Stiva?"

"Not at all, Alexei. I don't waste my time on dreams. I tend to make them reality. This is why I'm here. Just like you."

Zorin laughed softly. Mirthlessly. "There's a fine line between confidence and delusion."

"Is that so? And you think you're the man to replace Victor Orsin? Take his seat in the pantheon as one of the Twelve?"

Victor Orsin.

For a fraction of a second, the name hung in Sophie's mind, *The New York Times* headline flashing before her eyes, then her gaze dropped to Zorin's hand—to the tattoos that graced his skin.

So it hadn't been a coincidence after all.

This was real.

Alexei Zorin wasn't some kind of cartel satrap, or mafia drug baron, or corrupt Russian oligarch; he was a member of the

Twelve, a criminal organisation so far beyond the reach of justice, that its leaders had gotten away with waging proxy wars for the Kremlin and committing war crimes all over the globe. And apparently the man at her side was powerful enough to vie with Stiva for a leadership position within this shadow empire.

No law enforcement agency in the world would pursue Alexei Zorin for what he had done—she would be left to rot at his mercy.

Briefly, the sensation of despair became almost overwhelming, but Zorin's voice pulled her from the haze.

He had switched back to Russian, as though uncomfortable to have her as a witness to a conversation that had been started out of spite in English and had transformed into something clearly not meant for her ears. But the damage control came a little too late. With one careless remark, Stiva had given them away.

But the two men, oblivious to her newfound knowledge, continued the conversation for a few tense moments, then a butler caught up with them, his posture as rigid as his expression.

"Good evening, gentlemen," the butler began, his voice smooth and measured. "May I extend a warm welcome to you on behalf of Mr Volkov? He has been eagerly anticipating your arrival."

He paused, allowing his words to settle before continuing with a polite inclination of his head.

"Mr Volkov is presently in his office and would be delighted if you joined him, Lord Cavendish, and Admiral Kirov at your earliest convenience," the butler announced, his voice echoing slightly in the vast space, as if to underscore the importance of the summons.

"So Arthur and Leonid have beaten us to the punch. How long have they been here?" Stiva asked.

The butler's eyes narrowed a little, as if Stiva's question surprised him. "As far as I'm aware, sir, Lord Cavendish joined us two hours ago, straight from London. And Admiral Kirov arrived only thirty minutes ago from Istanbul, though I believe he flew out of Moscow."

"Damn sanctions," Stiva said, motioning ahead. "Well then, let's not keep them waiting—after all, we wouldn't want to upset three sitting members of the Twelve by being late, would we, Alexei?"

The butler gave Stiva a tense smile, then turned to Zorin. "Sir, would you like me to show the lady upstairs to your quarters?"

Zorin's gaze slid towards her, as though she were an afterthought. For a moment—just a moment—there was something in his eyes, something distant, as if he'd have preferred she simply disappear. But it passed quickly, almost imperceptibly, as Zorin's expression shifted back to its usual guarded calm.

"She'll stay with me," Zorin announced calmly. "Now, let's go. We wouldn't want to keep Ivan waiting—after all, the Tsar isn't known for his patience. Nor am I."

CHAPTER X

Isola di San Clemente, Venice, Italy
Monday, 1st July, 23:31

Stiva raised his eyebrows at Zorin's decision to bring her along, but the butler gave an obliging, albeit tense bow. "Of course, sir. If you would be so kind as to follow me, I shall take you to Mr Volkov straightaway."

Zorin motioned for her to follow. Sophie hesitated, suddenly afraid of where he would take her and what would happen there. Clearly in no mood to play games, Zorin placed a firm hand on her arm, his grip gentle but insistent.

Sophie felt her body move, more out of instinct than decision, as though some unseen force had shifted her forward. Zorin fell into step beside her, releasing her arm but keeping his hand at her back—not touching, but close enough to remind her of his presence.

They followed the butler across the lobby to an arched doorway manned at either side by armed guards. They passed through it into a reception room where two dozen suited men and a handful of beautiful, long-legged women mingled.

Neither Zorin nor Stiva acknowledged the attendees, but the wide berth everyone present afforded the two men left little doubt as to the rank and status her companions enjoyed in this shady world.

"This way," the butler said, guiding them to the other side of the reception room to a tall double door that a portly valet in a dark tailcoat opened for them.

"Mr Volkov, your guests are here for you," the butler announced, then stood aside to let them pass.

Sophie hesitated, and Zorin, apparently sensing her fear, placed his hand on the small of her back and steered her gently but firmly over the threshold.

The office that awaited them on the other side was lavish, with buff marble floors, elegant designer furniture, and a wall of French windows that stretched the length of the cavernous space. At the far end of the room, behind an opulent desk made of polished brass and exotic wood, a man sat waiting. His face was regal and stern, with ashen hair and keen grey eyes that seemed to take the measure of them all in one fell swoop. Dressed in a sleek dark suit and white shirt, there was a grim majesty about him—the sinister splendour of a man accustomed to absolute power.

When Zorin stepped over the threshold, a faint smile spread over his even features. He rose and came towards them with swift steps.

"*Alexei Alexandrovich,*" he said, grasping Zorin's hand.

"*Dobryy vecher, Ivan Sergeevich.*"

Ivan Volkov. So this was the tsar.

Releasing Zorin's hand, Ivan Volkov turned to greet Stiva, grasping his hand and patting his shoulder with the ease of long acquaintance, but none of its warmth. "*Stiva.*"

Stiva replied something in Russian and with an ever-so-slight bow of the head, as if addressing royalty.

For a moment, Ivan's eyes lingered on Stiva, almost probing, then—ignoring Sophie's presence so completely as if she didn't exist—his gaze shifted to the butler who still stood by the door.

"No disturbances," Ivan commanded, dismissing his servant with a casually contemptuous wave of his perfectly groomed hand. Then, turning around, Ivan moved the same hand across the room, including in its sweep an outsized marble fireplace, elegant Italian furniture, and two men who sat casually in wide-armed chairs. "Please, gentlemen, make yourselves comfortable."

Everyone turned to follow Ivan's invitation, but Sophie didn't move, letting herself fall back as her eyes shifted to the men at the back of the room, whose features were illuminated in the soft glow of the overhead chandeliers.

Their faces—just like their names—were vaguely familiar, tied to some long-forgotten news reports or articles.

The first—tall, lean, with grizzled hair and the distinct air of the soldier—had to be Admiral Leonid Kirov. The man beside him—gaunt, keen-eyed and elegant, with the bearing and gravitas of someone not only well-moneyed but well-born—was undoubtedly Lord Arthur Cavendish.

When Zorin and Stiva approached, both Kirov and Cavendish got up and exchanged silent greetings, then everyone settled around the table; Zorin and Stiva on one side, Lord Cavendish and Admiral Kirov on the other, and Ivan Volkov—presiding over them all like some sinister grand master of the underworld—at its head.

Sophie's brief hope of being forgotten vanished when, without so much as a glance in her direction, Zorin snapped his fingers in her direction—as if calling a dog to heel.

There was no chair for her, only the option of standing behind Zorin like a servant or kneeling at his feet like a slave.

The thought of doing what he demanded made her sick and yet—knowing that the consequences of refusal would be far more terrible than the temporary humiliation of obedience—she stepped to Zorin's side.

Zorin didn't look up as she stepped to his side, as if he simply expected compliance, and somehow, that expectation was enough to ensure her obedience.

But Stiva, perhaps to spite Zorin, perhaps out of genuine concern for her, placed the tip of his polished shoe on the frame of a footstool and turned it a little in her direction, then motioned for her to sit down.

Zorin laughed softly. "Always the gentleman, Stiva."

"We all have our flaws," Stiva replied, a hint of mirth lingering in his voice, then he extended his hand towards her. "Please, take a seat, my dear."

For a brief moment, fear of Zorin's reaction nearly made her refuse Stiva's offer. But her head was spinning, the drug still clouding her mind, and she knew she couldn't manage the simple act of sitting without collapsing.

Stiva's grip was steady, firm without being rough, as he helped her lower herself onto the stool, all the while his eyes never left her face, as if gauging just how far the drug's grip held her.

Sophie folded herself onto the stool, while the men shifted their collective attention to their overlord, who leisurely selected a Cuban cigar from the humidor on the table and then offered them to his guests. Only Cavendish and Kirov accepted.

Sitting back, Ivan trimmed the cigar, lit it, and took a slow, deliberate puff.

"I'm sure you are all wondering why I've brought you here at such short notice. So let me satisfy your curiosity."

He paused, taking another puff of the cigar, while he watched the men around the table through the smoke.

"As you know, the U.S. is quietly pushing yet another Security Council resolution to reinforce the ban on nuclear weapons in space. The reason for this move is an illicit, off-the-books Russian weapons system lovingly nicknamed Pandora."

Ivan paused and, without shifting his gaze from his guests, reached into the inside pocket of his jacket and retrieved a small, pendant attached to a simple, sturdy chain. Its metal surface had been burnished to a dull sheen and there was something unmistakably military about it—solid, utilitarian, practical.

Sophie froze.

She had seen it before.

The image flashed in her mind, unbidden, sharp and immediate—the front page of *The New York Times*, the photograph of Victor Orsin, slumped and lifeless on the steps of the Paris opera house, the pendant barely visible in the grasp of the man kneeling over him, pulling it from beneath his bloodied collar.

It was the same pendant.

The one Orsin had carried.

"This," Ivan said quietly, letting the chain dangle from his hand, "is one of two launch keys. Alone, it's nothing but a paperweight. But together with the second key, it controls Pandora."

CHAPTER XI

Isola di San Clemente, Venice, Italy
Monday, 1ˢᵗ July, 23:47

"What the hell is Pandora?" Kirov inquired.

Ivan smiled and blew a puff of smoke into the air: "An orbital ASAT platform equipped with high-yield nuclear warheads, capable of simultaneous EMP strikes across low Earth orbit."

Zorin, Stiva and the admiral exchanged astonished looks, while a frown gathered on Cavendish's brow. "Ivan, I'm the money man. I need this in layman's terms."

"The most destructive weapon ever developed, Arthur," Ivan paused and smiled quietly at Cavendish through his cigar smoke. "Imagine a nuke parked in space. At the push of a button, it unleashes a massive EMP burst that obliterates every satellite in orbit, crippling military and civilian infrastructure on a global scale. Missile defence, GPS, power grids, financial systems, even weather forecasting—all gone in an instant. In military terms, losing primacy in space means losing wars on Earth. In civilian terms, it's just as bad. Life as we know it will grind to a standstill. And there's absolutely nothing that can stop it."

"Jesus," Cavendish hissed.

"Oh, it's a masterpiece," Ivan said with a smile, pocketing the pendant again.

"And what precisely has this masterpiece to do with us?" Stiva asked, slipping an elegant platinum cigarette case from his jacket pocket and opening it with a flick of his thumb.

"It's up for sale."

"How the hell can anyone sell an orbital nuke?" Stiva demanded. "The technology, maybe—but an entire operational system? That's ludicrous."

"Ah, here's the sweet part." Ivan's replied, blowing a puff of smoke into the air. "The American's, always ahead of the game, came up with the glorious idea of paying off an entire roster of... *ideologically susceptible* engineers and programmers to install hidden 'back doors' into the weapon's software. Of course, Moscow found out, put the chaps up against the wall and patched over the flaws. But, as it so happened, they didn't catch everything."

"So the weapon can be controlled by the Americans?" Stiva asked.

"No. It can be controlled by anyone who has two launch keys and a working ground station. As of last week, that's neither the Americans nor the Russians."

"Are you saying the Kremlin lost control of it?"

Ivan exhaled slowly, smoke curling around his face.

"Six days ago, the primary launch keys were stolen from a secret military facility near Nizhny Novgorod—alongside specialised hardware modules that circumvent standard authorisation. At the same time, the main ground station and its fallback hubs in Murmansk and Khabarovsk were sabotaged: communications relays fried, power grids overloaded, entire racks of servers gutted. It was an inside job. Years in the panning. And highly effective. And now, with the base hardware and backups offline, the Kremlin can't get so much as a status ping from the weapon. They have no control over the weapon, and until now, every attempt to regain it has failed."

"So who's controlling this orbital strike marvel now?" Kirov asked.

Ivan paused, exhaling a cloud of smoke. "An insider. A former Russian general who was in charge of the program. And this gentleman—aware of how... dysfunctional our relationship with the Kremlin has become—entered into an exclusive agreement with Victor to sell us the weapon. On the night Victor was killed, he acquired the first launch key and access to a repurposed Cold War uplink station. The second launch key was supposed to follow after that."

"I assume, now that Victor is dead, the deal is off. Or are we still rolling?" Stiva asked, lighting his cigarette and blowing smoke through his teeth as he spoke.

"The transaction is going ahead," Ivan replied. "Tomorrow night, the second pendant will be handed over to us on board the *ITS Giuseppe Garibaldi*, a decommissioned Italian aircraft carrier currently mooring off the Faroe Islands."

"I hate to be a killjoy, Ivan, but what kind of price tag are we talking about?" Cavendish interjected.

"Fifty billion," Ivan replied. "I'm talking dollars not sterling," he added.

Cavendish's eyebrows shot up. "That kind of money will raise red flags the moment we start moving it. It will take days to funnel through our structures, weeks if it needs to be pristine."

"You have twenty-four hours. I need it gilt-edged, on-shore. Every penny traceable to a legitimate source."

Kirov shook his head. "I don't like this. Why risk exposure by rushing matters?"

"The Kremlin is moving heaven and earth to get its toy back. There's chatter in intelligence circles that they're closing in on the seller, so if we want Pandora, it's now or never."

Kirov gave a tentative nod. "Very well, I'm willing to take that chance, provided we have the operational capabilities to see this through." Kirov's eyes went to Stiva and then to Zorin. "Can we do this?"

Zorin gave a slow, pensive nod. "It will require some adjustments, but we can handle this." His eyes shifted to Ivan. "Where are the codes now?"

"They are already on the vessel." Ivan smiled condescendingly. "The seller is somewhat twitchy about his security, afraid that the Kremlin will put a bullet in his head before he can vanish into his hard-earned retirement."

"A decommissioned aircraft carrier in the Norwegian Sea is a risky choice of location," Zorin remarked. "Are the security measures laid out for that threat level?"

Ivan gave a slight smile. "Not at all. The *Giuseppe Garibaldi* was undergoing refurbishment at one of our dockyards before being transferred to its new owner. Everyone knows it's there, so no one's looking closer. It's just another ship, doing what's expected. And those few who are supposed to look closer, have been paid well to look the other way. And if we can use it as a platform to demonstrate a stolen experimental fighter jet, we can use it for anything."

"The Kremlin knows how we operate. They know what to look for," Zorin remarked. "And a decommissioned carrier with a heavily upgraded short launch ramp and partial catapult that the new owner didn't commission is sure to draw attention."

"It's my security disposition, Alexei," Stiva interjected, his voice cold. "It has been devised to protect the prospective buyer of the Chinese J-20S naval prototype. If it's good enough to hold up with a jet in action, then it's good enough to hold up in any scenario. Or do you doubt my ability to keep effective measures in place?"

Zorin turned to Stiva, measuring him briefly before he spoke. "Not in the least. You're the naval man, Stiva. The call to review the measures is entirely yours."

Stiva looked at Ivan. "The measures are good enough. No change is needed."

Ivan smiled, clapping his hands together. "Well then, gentlemen, it's time to get the process moving. The deal dossiers and system specs will be hand-delivered to you tonight. As for the rest, I believe everyone knows what to do."

Ivan reached out and pressed a discreetly recessed brass button on the side of the table. An instant later, the door opened, and Ivan's butler stepped into the room.

"How may I be of service, sir?"

"Show the gentlemen to their accommodations, and make sure they have everything they need."

As if on cue, the men around the table rose. Exchanging a few last words in Russian and English, they moved towards the door, where they finally parted. While the others left, Zorin and Admiral Kirov lingered behind, speaking quietly for another ten minutes under the patient gaze of waiting butlers. Then Zorin's hand rested once more on the small of her back, steering her out of the room like a petulant child.

CHAPTER XII

Isola di San Clemente, Venice, Italy
Tuesday, 2nd July, 00:16

A butler led them up an elegantly curved staircase, through a doorway framed by marble architraves, and finally into a vast gallery lined with neoclassical masterpieces that hung at precise intervals between the outsized windows.

Through the three-inch windowpanes, Sophie caught a glimpse of the vast gardens, the sea, and a private pier where Stiva—now dressed casually in all black—was slipping into a sleek speedboat moored at the jetty's farthest end. For a moment, the boat's solitary headlight cast a garish glow on the water before the vessel unberthed and sped into the night, its dark silhouette blurring with Zorin's reflection in the armoured glass. A second later, the light vanished amidst the dark waters of the Adriatic, and as the world outside plunged back into darkness, the window turned once again into a perfect mirror, showing her only Zorin's hard-cut features and his eyes— still fixed on the spot where the boat had vanished.

"We have prepared the Rialto suite for you, sir," the butler announced. "It offers an exquisite view of the lagoon and the city."

Zorin acknowledged the butler's words with an absentminded nod, either indifferent to this particular aspect of his stay or too preoccupied with the boat's departure to pay attention.

The butler, in turn, brushed off Zorin's terseness with a polite smile and conducted them to a tall double gate at the end of the gallery. "I believe there have been a few changes to the security disposition since your last visit—one of them is our new biometric access system." Taking a step back, the butler gestured to a small, square device on the wall beside the door. "If you would be so kind, sir."

Zorin, standing behind Sophie, reached out and pressed his right thumb to the glass. Instantly, the device lit up. For half a second, nothing seemed to happen, then a series of faint hissing noises echoed in the silence, followed by the unmistakable sound of disengaging deadbolts.

Stepping forward, the butler opened the door for Zorin. "Please, sir."

Zorin, standing an inch from Sophie's back, bent a little over her shoulder. "After you," he whispered, his mouth close to her ear.

Gathering her courage, Sophie stepped over the threshold into an elegant antechamber.

The room was large, almost cavernous, bathed in the soft glow of chandeliers whose crystals that hung like frozen teardrops in the muted light. Even in the gloom, Sophie could make out the room's fantastical architecture: the *Pietra Dura* floors, the massive arched windows, and the marble columns that stretched all the way up to a high ceiling adorned with intricate frescoes and gold leaf accents.

"Your luggage has already been brought up, sir, and everything has been prepared as usual," the butler announced, following Zorin into the room. "In addition, I have taken the liberty to arrange an assortment of suitable garments for your companion, as I have been informed that she is travelling lightly. Is there anything else I can do for you, sir?"

"Yes, you can. I've sent for a safety deposit box. Make sure it's delivered to me directly when it arrives."

"Of course, sir. Is there anything else I may assist you with?"

"No. You can leave. And make sure we're not disturbed," Zorin commanded in a tone that made it clear he expected obedience without question.

The butler retreated, countering Zorin's discourtesy with a restrained little bow before he slipped out of the door and closed it behind him.

The instant it fell into the lock, Zorin's hand closed around her upper arm, urging her forward. Well aware that she had no power to resist, Sophie followed her captor in a state of mute terror, walking through a series of rooms and a short hallway to a stately bedroom with white marble floors, French windows, and a carved fireplace.

Zorin let go of her, closing the door and turning the key in the lock.

For a moment, Sophie expected him to descend on her like a starving vulture, but he didn't. Instead, he stepped past her, leisurely slipped one hand into his trouser pocket, and strolled over to the fireplace. For a moment, he stared at the neatly stacked logs inside, then he reached out and pressed a small, recessed brass button just below the mantelpiece. Flames flared up from some hidden mechanism, crackling as they curled around the logs.

"Nights tend to be cool in Venice," he said, staring into the flames for a moment and then directing his attention back to the mantelpiece.

On it, beside an enormous Chinese vase painted in red and green hues, lay a slim leather briefcase and an ivory-coloured envelope. Zorin reached for the latter, opened the unsealed flap, and removed the contents: a single sheet of paper—folded twice widthwise—and an American passport with a distinctive red paperclip attached to its back cover.

It was hers.

Zorin opened it and read the data page containing her name and details, then leafed through the rest of the booklet, idly perusing the entry and exit stamps of the countries she had visited, and finally stopping when he found her UK student visa.

"What do you study?" he asked, not lifting his gaze from the document.

Sophie had to force the word from her mouth. "Politics."

He laughed softly. "Oh, the glamorous world of policymaking. Trust me, it's filthy business. No place for starry-eyed idealists." He snapped the passport shut, turned to the fireplace, and fed it into the flames. "You won't need it again."

The flames leapt, greedily consuming the paper, curling it into nothingness. Her name, her identity—all incinerated in a heartbeat.

Never in her life had she experienced such horror, such utter misery, as she did in that moment. "What are you going to do to me?"

He turned now, his gaze shifting lazily to her. There was no rush, no sense of urgency. He was savouring this, the way a cat might toy with its prey. "Scared?"

"Yes."

He gave her a cold smile. "Good."

Nimbly, like a magician conjuring a flower out of thin air, Zorin slipped a thin-bladed knife from his sleeve. Sophie recoiled in terror. But this time, her captor didn't relent. He closed the distance between them with swift strides.

Sophie acted on instinct, her hands going up over her face, her body cowering down to the ground. But the blow didn't fall. Instead, she felt the blade brush against the inside of her palm, cool and strangely smooth, then the zip ties came off, and the blood rushed painfully back into her hands.

For a moment, Zorin towered over her, as if to drive home the point of their respective roles in this twisted game, then he crouched down in front of her. Now they were almost at eye level.

His jacket had slipped from Sophie's shoulders, and so had one strap of her dress, offering him a careless glimpse of one bare breast. But his eyes didn't even waver—not bothering to steal a glance at what he had purchased at such a steep price. He wasn't interested in her body. He was interested in her fear—the raw, sharp edge of it.

This was the real game. The real intimacy.

For a brief moment, a memory flashed in Sophie's mind, the memory of another man who had made her feel just as helpless. She had escaped the horror then, though not unscathed, but here and now, she no longer had the ability to end the game by turning her back on it. The balance of power wasn't simply upset, it had shifted to the extremes—to the absolutes of power and powerlessness.

A single tear slid down her cheek. She hated that tear, hated the way it betrayed her.

It was Zorin's voice—its soft, seductive timbre—that pulled her from the void. "Shh," he said, his voice low and smooth, soothing in a way that made her skin prickle. "No tears, they won't help you. I want you to listen, not cry."

Sophie closed her eyes, pulling herself together before she looked at Zorin. "I am listening."

"Good," he said, his tone calm, his voice terribly soft, almost a whisper. "I'm sure you're quite keen on surviving our little adventure. Whether you do or not is entirely up to you." He let the knife in his hand tilt towards her, so that the tip of the blade came to rest on Sophie's lip. "The rules are simple, someone with a mind like yours shouldn't have any trouble following them." He watched her very keenly now, as if to make sure that she was really listening. "What I expect of you is obedience and silence. You will follow my every command without question or hesitation, and you will not speak—neither to me nor anyone else—unless I give you leave to do so. Do we understand each other?"

He was watching her, testing her, waiting to see if she understood. Waiting to see if she would submit.

And, though she despised herself for it, she nodded, her head dipping almost imperceptibly.

Zorin smiled very vaguely, though there was no pleasure in his smile. "Seems you're a fast learner. Good for you."

He rose and sheathed the knife, then stepped around her and began to unbutton his shirt—his movements calm, methodical, each button undone with the same care he had given to every gesture, every action.

"No, please."

Zorin laughed softly. "What are you afraid of? That I'll have my way with you right here on the floor and kill you when I'm done?"

Her silence hung between them, answering in its own way.

"I prefer my companions sober," he said, his tone almost light, as though discussing a matter of taste. "And at least reasonably clean. You, I'm afraid, are none of those things at the moment."

He slipped his gun from the shoulder holster and tucked it into the back of his waistband. Then, without ceremony, he shrugged off his shirt and holster and let them drop to the floor.

Sophie didn't mean to look, but her eyes remained locked on his body in the quiet horror of her own helplessness.

He was all hard lines and controlled power—a body honed for battle but just as capable of seduction. The tattoos came alive as he moved—the skull, the reaper's scythe, the stylised Byzantine eagle whose jagged wingtip arched over his heart. There was no vanity here, no decoration for decoration's sake—each piece seemed to stake a claim, to reinforce what was already obvious: this was a man who had lived with death and wielded it like a tool.

Had circumstances been different, perhaps she might have appreciated the disquieting allure of his dangerous, unsettling beauty. But here, in the claustrophobic intimacy of her captivity, all she could feel was the cold, creeping fear that came with knowing exactly what he could do. And knowing that he had no reason to hold back.

Zorin didn't acknowledge her stare. He didn't need to. He knew she was watching, just as he'd intended. The message was clear—as clear as the message of a poisonous snake: Stay away and I'll let you live.

Then, as if the revelation had fulfilled its purpose, he turned away and pushed open a set of narrow, double doors to his left. Behind them was a spacious dressing room. Stepping inside, he plucked a pristine white shirt from one of the many racks that lined the walls and picked a pair of cufflinks from the velvet-lined tray. Slipping on the shirt, he turned back to her.

"I have business to attend to." His eyes shifted to her hair, the pointed look making her feel unkempt. "I suggest you use the time to sleep off the drugs and clean yourself up. I expect you to be presentable when I return." Deftly fixing the links on the cuffs, he nodded to the holster at his feet. "Pick it up."

Sophie hesitated for a fraction of a second, then reached for the leather strap and handed it to Zorin. When he took it from her, their eyes met, and Sophie realised that this had been a test and that, by hesitating, she had failed it.

"I think we'll try that again later," Zorin remarked, slipping on the holster, and placing his weapon in it.

He measured her with a cold look.

"No antics while I'm gone. Trust me, it's not worth it," he said, his tone warning. Then, with a last stern glance at her, Zorin turned to the door, stepped out and closed it behind him. And then the key turned, locking her in.

CHAPTER XIII

Isola di San Clemente, Venice, Italy
Tuesday, 2nd July, 06:37

Sophie jolted awake, heart pounding, her legs tangled in the silk nightgown that some unseen servant had thoughtfully laid out for her last night.

The was still dim outside, the dim light of dawn lapping at the horizon. Sophie's eyes scanned the room, searching for whatever it was that had woken her. There was no movement, no sound, not even a shadow. But she felt instinctively that she wasn't alone.

Tremulously, she reached for the brass-plated switch panel on the nightstand and pressed a button at random. Muted light flooded the room, reflecting on crystal vases and three-inch windowpanes.

There was no one in the room now, but Zorin had been here. He had come and gone like a ghost. And the only trace of his passing was the door, unlocked and standing slightly ajar by just a fraction of an inch.

Then she heard voices, very faint, coming from somewhere beyond the door.

Silently, Sophie slipped out of bed, her bare feet soundless on the cold floor. For a moment, she considered walking out in the nightgown, but Zorin's words from the night before echoed in her mind. He expected her to be presentable and she didn't dare to defy him—she couldn't afford to fight pointless battles.

Shivering slightly, Sophie walked over to the closet. For a moment, she pondered the assortment of *suitable* garments Ivan's butler had so thoughtfully provided. It was a closet fit for a prized whore: dresses dreamt up by the great fashion houses of Paris and Milan, flimsy shreds of fabric that left nothing to the imagination apart from the price, which—according to the still-attached tags—

was available upon request only. Finally, with a vague sense of disgust, Sophie picked a black dress and a matching pair of heels.

She showered quickly and dressed while she brushed her teeth, then added some mascara as an afterthought. When she was done, she glanced at the mirror without really seeing herself. For a moment, she could feel her heart race, its frantic beat echoing in her ears as fear—thick and suffocating—threatened to pull her under.

Breathe, she urged herself. *Come on, breathe.*

She closed her eyes, inhaling slowly, deeply, willing herself to calm down. Slowly, she opened her eyes, staring at her reflection. A tear had slipped down her cheek without her realising. She brushed it away, annoyed at the weakness.

You can do this.

Trying to control the lingering sense of dread in the pit of her stomach, Sophie slipped out of the bathroom. Briefly, she was tempted to wait for Zorin to come to her, but she knew she would have to face him eventually, and she preferred to face him on her own terms rather than his.

Heart in mouth, she walked through the gallery to the large drawing room. At its opposite end, another door stood ajar—just wide enough for her to glimpse what lay beyond.

It was an elegant octagonal room, filled with half-lights like a sanctuary. Zorin sat in a wing chair beside the window, the light of the rising sun dancing on his handsome face. He was dressed in black, with only a peek of a white shirt visible under the black quarter-zip. His left hand rested casually on the armrest, while his right was raised to his shoulder, lightly massaging it, as if he had fallen asleep in an awkward position and woken to a stiff neck.

Opposite him, by the fireplace, sat another man. He was about sixty, very tall and with the trim build of an avid sportsman whom age had cost little of his vigour. His attire—bespoke suit, monogrammed cuffs, and platinum links—had something stiffly aristocratic, but his grizzled hair, lightly tanned skin and distinct yet pleasant lines around the blue eyes spoke of a life lived fully, if not always wisely.

"What about the girl?" Zorin asked.

Zorin's visitor pulled a buff manila envelope from his bag. "The charming Miss Akehurst stirred quite a bit of trouble back in London," he said, handing Zorin the envelope. "So much so that even Ivan got word of it."

The mention of her name made Sophie's blood run cold.

"Why is that?" Zorin asked, tossing the envelope onto the table beside him without bothering to open it.

"Someone was going to extraordinary lengths to save her. Someone with a lot of clout. Well-paid lawyers, shady enforcers, and big media houses all gearing up for a field day. Harper had to pull every conceivable lever to shut this one down."

"I trust Harper was thorough," Zorin remarked, evidently bored.

"Oh, Harper fabricated a marvellous story to tank the investigation: There's evidence of drug abuse, money troubles, a bit of casual escorting to pay for another line of coke. That kind of thing. Media bailed at once. The Yard is pushing paper and waiting for her body to turn up in a ditch."

Sophie felt a cold shiver run down her spine, and for a heartbeat, desperate, red-hot anger almost won over. But she mastered herself.

"Do we know who was looking for her?" Zorin asked, his voice cutting through the haze of her fury.

Zorin's visitor looked at her captor for a long moment, his eyes narrowing. "No," he said finally. "But whoever it was is gone. So I assume Harper's tale was good enough to fool Miss Akehurst's would-be saviour."

"I don't like to take unnecessary risks," Zorin said.

"Do you want me to do something about it?"

"I want you to check out Harper and his filthy associates," Zorin replied, his voice dripping with disdain as he mentioned Harper's name. "If he or any of his friends are a liability, see to it that we cut our losses. Discreetly. And make sure that there aren't any trails that Miss Akehurst's would-be saviour can follow."

Sophie closed her eyes. For one foolish, desperate moment, there had been hope. Real hope that somewhere, someone was looking for her. Searching. And she wanted to hold on to it, that fragile, foolish flicker of the possibility of rescue, even though there was nothing to hope for anymore.

Her knees went weak, and she reached out to steady herself against the doorframe, needing something—anything—solid to anchor her. It was such a small, insignificant movement, a minute rustle of fabric, but it was enough.

He didn't look up. He didn't speak. But Sophie felt Zorin's attention turn to her. The shift was subtle, almost imperceptible, but Sophie felt it like a physical thing. She was caught. She knew it. And he knew it, too.

A second passed, then another, and finally, he spoke. "Only children listen at doors."

A slight shudder passed over Sophie, but she straightened herself and stepped into the room. Zorin's head turned towards the door, his cold blue eyes resting on her as she entered.

"We were just talking about you," he said, holding her gaze for a moment, then gesturing lazily towards the older man sitting across from him. "May I introduce you to my guest? Doctor Thomas Frost, head of Interpol's European Response Team, and my... loyal friend." Zorin smiled his ever-mirthless smile. "Doctor Frost was kind enough to work his contacts in London to update me on the investigation into your disappearance."

Frost inclined his head in a polite and entirely silent greeting.

"You have made a lot of trouble. It's impressive, really, how much chaos one person can stir up without even trying." Zorin leaned back in his chair, his gaze never leaving hers. "I do hope you don't plan on causing more."

For a moment, Zorin continued his silent study of her, as if waiting for the slightest hint of rebellion, then he stood slowly.

Frost, evidently startled by the movement, shot to his feet, like an obsequious servant standing at attention for his master.

"I think we're done here, Doctor Frost," Zorin said, dismissing his guest with a disdainful flick of the wrist, as if he were a mildly annoying insect.

"Of course, thank you for your time." Frost's eyes briefly flitted downwards in a silent acknowledgement of his subservience, and then he turned on his heel, leaving the room with the kind of swift steps that told Sophie he was glad to have survived Zorin's hospitality.

The door clicked shut behind Frost and Zorin's eyes, which had followed his visitor, now shifted to her. Sophie felt a cold shiver run down her spine. She knew that she had treaded dangerously close to the red line by listening at the door. And perhaps now, she would suffer the consequences.

"You're trying my patience, Sophie," Zorin said, taking off his black cashmere quarter-zip to reveal the crisp white shirt underneath. "And that's not a wise thing to do."

He tossed the sweater over the back of his chair, then turned to her. She didn't dare to meet his eyes, so she focused her attention on his shirt. There was a tiny speck of blood on it, just above his collarbone and for a brief moment, Sophie wondered whose blood it was, and if hers would look quite the same on the white fabric if he spilled it.

"Look at me."

She did.

As she looked at him, Sophie noticed the subtle signs of tiredness beneath his otherwise youthful appearance: His light brown hair was just a touch dishevelled, as though he had run his hand through it during some moment of frustration, and his eyes bore a heaviness that spoke of long hours and thankless tasks.

"You are treading dangerously close to the line, Sophie, and I *will* punish you if you cross it. Do we understand each other?"

He was close, too close, and yet she couldn't bring herself to step back. She forced herself to stand straighter, despite the cold grip of fear tightening around her spine. "We do."

Zorin regarded her for a long moment, the faintest hint of a mirthless smile forming on his lips at her vague show of defiance. Then he stepped towards her, his eyes fixed on her. And suddenly, Sophie felt the fear rise in her stomach again. She didn't back away. She couldn't anymore. It was as if her body had stopped working.

Zorin shook his head ever so slightly, raising his hand to brush a stray strand of hair from her face, the gesture deceptively gentle.

"Never forget," he said, in that soft, silken tone, "how delicate this little arrangement of ours is. One misstep, and it all unravels."

He observed her almost thoughtfully, as his fingers brushed a strand of hair from her face. The touch was light, barely more than a whisper against her skin, but it made her shiver. And instantly, the fear returned to her full force.

Zorin smiled vaguely, but there was no pleasure in his smile.

"You should listen to what you feel now, Sophie," he said, his voice dropping to a near-whisper. "Fear is useful. It will keep you alive."

There was something almost tender in the way he spoke, as if he were offering her a gift, a twisted lesson in survival.

Sophie felt her pulse quicken. The room felt suddenly too small, too tight, the threat too real.

For a moment, he didn't move, simply allowing the threat of his presence to wash over her, and then he pulled back just enough to meet her eyes. "Do you understand what I am telling you, Sophie?"

As he spoke, he watched her very closely, his gaze unwavering, daring her to defy him once more and for a moment, it was as if the entire world had narrowed down to this—just the two of them, locked in a battle she couldn't win.

She nodded. "I understand."

"Good," he said, stepping back, his voice losing its intimacy but not its threat. "I hope you'll remember it this time."

He held her gaze for a brief moment, then turned.

"And now, get out of my sight," he said, walking towards his desk, his hand once again going to his shoulder, as if he were in pain. "I have work to do, and I don't want to be disturbed."

CHAPTER XIV

Isola di San Clemente, Venice, Italy
Tuesday, 2nd July, 09:59

Three interminable hours passed, but Zorin didn't leave his study. Outside, the cloying mist had given way to the rising sun.

Sitting in the wash of the golden rays, perched on the edge of an elegant wing chair, Sophie listened to the steady beat of the waves, occasionally disturbed by the distant throb of a landing helicopter or the melodious chime of the ormolu clock on the mantelpiece. Sporadically, a maid or a butler quietly intruded into her space to perform tasks too menial for Zorin or to serve Sophie breakfast. But none of it—the food, the people, the sounds—could penetrate the suffocating stillness of her despair.

No one would come to save her. Not the police. Not anyone else. If she wanted to survive, she had to become her own saviour. And time was running out.

So far, Zorin had made no attempt to touch her and, by his sordid standards, he might even have shown her compassion. But she harboured no illusions about the fragility of this forbearance. The moment would come, and she could either endure it or fight.

The low hum of a powerful engine cut through the steady beat of the waves, pulling her from her thoughts. A cigarette boat, its sleek wooden body glistening in the sun, approached the pier. Its engines hummed a low, urgent dirge, its hull barely disturbing the water's surface. The man at the helm cut the engines, allowing the vessel to drift the final few feet, guided by the gentle hand of the tide.

As the man emerged from the boat, he was at first no more than a silhouette framed against the morning sun. It was only when he stepped onto the pier, moving into the softer light, that Sophie recognised him.

Stiva.

He was wearing sunglasses, slacks and a crisp white shirt, its sleeves casually rolled up to his elbows. Just like last night, there were no bodyguards swarming around him and without them, he seemed almost normal.

As he walked along the short pier, he reached into his jacket pocket, pulling out a sleek silver cigarette case. He opened it with a flick of his wrist, selected a cigarette, and lit it with a gold lighter. For a moment, he stood there, contemplatively exhaling a cloud of smoke as he surveyed his surroundings with an air of ownership—as if looking out over his kingdom.

Then, suddenly, a man stepped to his side. From her vantage point, Sophie couldn't see his face clearly—only the sharp line of his jaw and his dark hair, both of which felt vaguely familiar.

Shoulder by shoulder, the two men walked towards the entrance together, their heads bent in deep and earnest conversation.

As she watched Stiva disappear into the building, her thoughts reeled back to last night. To the auction. To Stiva's face, illuminated in the darkness.

She wondered if any of this would be different if Stiva had bought her that night. Most likely it would be. Without doubt guilty of each and every crime the Twelve stood accused of, Stiva still stood out from the ranks of his abhorrent peers. He had shown her courtesy when no one else had. More, he had openly disapproved of Zorin's sadistic tastes.

And then a crazy thought flashed through her mind. *Maybe it's not too late.*

Stiva had wanted her enough to offer four million pounds for her. Perhaps, with some luck, she could convince him that she was worth more than that. More even than Zorin had paid.

Her hopes were far-fetched, but there was nothing else she could cling to. Fear had made her surrender twice and with each capitulation she had slipped further down the rabbit hole. The compliance she had hoped would save her had doomed her instead. Maybe it was too late to save herself, but whatever waited for her, she wouldn't endure it kneeling at Alexei Zorin's feet. And if getting away from her captor meant spreading her legs for his nemesis, so be it.

It was a desperate, reckless plan, but it was better than having no plan at all.

The sound of the door opening roused her from her thoughts. A maid, wearing a midnight-blue uniform with gold buttons, stepped into the room. She moved with the grace of one who had been trained to be neither heard nor seen, her steps barely whispering against the marble floor. In her arms, she carried a silver vase with an enormous bouquet of white roses.

"Good morning, ma'am," she said in a low voice. "Would you like me to come back later?"

Sophie shook her head. "No, it's fine."

The woman graced her with a discreet smile and set about her task, replacing the still perfectly beautiful flower arrangement on the table with the fresh one.

"Is there anything I can do for you, ma'am?" the maid asked once she had finished.

Sophie considered the question. There were a thousand things she wanted, a thousand plans swirling in her mind. But she knew the futility of voicing them. "No, thank you."

The maid nodded. "Very well, ma'am. If you need anything, please don't hesitate to call." She motioned to the discreetly recessed brass button on the side of the table.

"I will."

The maid gave her a small smile—kind, courteous, professionally detached. Then she turned to the door. Holding the heavy silver vase with both hands, the maid awkwardly extended a single finger and touched it to the biometric scanner embedded in the wall beside the door. The device emitted a soft beep, followed by a quiet click from within the door. The maid shifted, gracelessly opening the door handle with her elbow.

Sophie stood up to give her a helping hand.

"Thank you very much, ma'am." The maid gave Sophie another smile, a bit unsure of herself, as if the random act of kindness had somehow upended her routine, then she slipped out into the hallway.

The maid didn't turn back to check if the door had fallen into its lock, and so she missed that Sophie had stuck the tip of her shoe into the door, keeping it open by just a fraction of an inch.

A shiver ran down Sophie's spine. This was it, the ultimate prize, the gate to freedom—if she only dared to step through it.

She hesitated, Zorin's warning echoing in her mind like a prophecy of doom. If he caught her, she might not survive his wrath. But tonight, the Twelve would wrap up the Pandora deal and then Zorin and his peers would most likely part ways. If they did, there was no guarantee she would ever see Stiva again. And that meant if she didn't take her chance to bargain with Stiva, another might never materialise.

Taking a deep breath, Sophie placed her palm on the door's polished veneer. Beyond it lay the hallway that would lead her down to the entrance hall and from there, she could reach the palm court—the direction in which Stiva and his designated butler had set off last night after the meeting.

All that separated her from Stiva was the length of Ivan's palace—but it might as well have been a battlefield.

If she dared to venture out, she would likely encounter one or more of Ivan's uniformed guards. If she couldn't avoid a confrontation, she would have to convince them that there was nothing suspicious about her brief excursion from Zorin's quarters.

The thought made her hesitate.

She didn't want to press her luck, but if it came down to it, she would have to lie and do so convincingly.

But she was good at pretending. She had always been good at it. Every false smile given to a testy guest had prepared her for this moment.

You can do this.

With a gentle push, she opened the door. The hallway was deserted. Sophie hesitated one last time, then, with a shuddering breath, she stepped outside.

Everything was quiet. The only sounds came from outside—the occasional calls of pheasants which seemed to live all over the island, the distant sound of a passing *Vaporetto*, and the constant rush of the waves breaking on the shoreline.

Proceeding quietly, Sophie walked down the gallery—more museum than hallway—and slipped through the arched gate at its end. Once again, she found herself on the wide walkway that ran around the circumference of the entrance hall. Above her was the massive glass cupola, below her the foyer with its polished marble floors and priceless artworks. And descending in two graceful symmetrical arcs was the wide staircase—guarded at the foot by two of Ivan's henchmen.

As if he had somehow sensed her presence, one of the guards looked up, his eyes shifting along the balustraded walkway.

Sophie retreated back into the hallway, hoping he would relent. But he didn't. Instead, he turned and began to ascend the staircase.

Sophie hesitated. If she forced a confrontation and failed to maintain her act, she would have thrown away her only chance in mere recklessness. No, it was too early to stretch her luck to the limits of its capacity.

Quietly, she backtracked into the gallery, scanning it for a place to hide. There was none. Only the door that led back to Zorin's suite and a second one just to her left.

She made her decision in a split second. Quietly, she stepped to the door, pressed her ear to it and listened for a moment. Nothing. With a trembling hand, she tried the handle. It yielded without a sound. Swiftly, she opened the door and slipped inside.

The room on the other side was empty. The morning light filtered in through the stained-glass windows, casting kaleidoscopic patterns on the polished floor. To her right stretched bookshelves stacked with precious leather-bound tomes, to her left a windowfront overlooking the sea and straight ahead, flanked by two marble columns, was a mahogany door. It stood ajar. Just a little. But enough for her to see a man's hand tapping impatiently on the armrest of his chair.

Sophie froze. She was trapped on both ends now.

CHAPTER XV

Isola di San Clemente, Venice, Italy
Tuesday, 2nd July, 10:22

Sophie crouched behind the high-backed divan, making herself as small as she could. The silk upholstery felt soft against her cheek, and she concentrated on the sensation. Gradually, the blood-thrum in her ears eased and the muddled voices in the adjoining room began to resolve themselves into distinct words and sentences.

They were speaking English—one with a vague Scottish burr, the others with the faintest trace of a Russian accent. The voices sounded familiar and she forced herself to register each snippet of conversation. Then all at once, one of the voices—low, resonant, calmly authoritative—fell into place. Ivan Volkov.

A tremor coursed through her. She felt the vibration in her own bones.

"We've had an incident on the *Giuseppe Garibaldi* last night," Ivan was saying. "The vessel was breached in the early hours of the morning. The pendant is gone."

For a moment, no one spoke, as if the enormity of Ivan's announcement needed time to sink in—to be processed in the minds of the men gathered in that room. Finally, Kirov's voice broke through the hush. "Do we know who they are?"

"Not *they*, Leonid. Just *he*. A single, lone operative," Ivan replied, still in that unsettlingly contained tone.

"One man?" Kirov echoed. "How the hell is that possible? How the hell could a single operative breach our carrier and waltz away with a firing key to an orbital nuke?"

"That's what I'd like to find out too," Ivan replied.

"What do we know about the guy?" Kirov asked.

"At this point, we're still piecing together the evidence," Ivan said, then added in a tone that was more command than request. "Andrew will walk you through what we have so far."

From her narrow vantage point, Sophie glimpsed a man's frame shift in his seat—squat, square-shouldered, with a half-healed wound on his cheek. And as she looked at him, she remembered the image on the front page of *The New York Times*: Victor Orsin sprawled out on the staircase of the Paris opera house and a man, this man—the same squat, square-shouldered man—kneeling over him with the Pandora launch key handling between his fingers.

It was him.

The man cleared his throat and leaned back, disappearing again from her narrow field of view, but the voice that followed now seemed to be his. The Scottish accent pronounced.

Andrew.

"Our new friend killed six of our sailors to get to the pendant. Snapped their necks. Clean fracture of the C2 vertebrae. Each one of them," Andrew began, his voice was tight, clipped. "You don't learn to kill like that in back-alley fights or barroom brawls. That's training. Serious training. I'd say special ops. Naval *Spetsnaz*. But now, let's get to the interesting part: The ligature marks." There was the rustle of paper being pushed across a table and then lifted up. "He uses some kind of garrotte, not to strangle, but to break their necks. Classic hangman's fracture at the C2 vertebrae. Quick. Silent. Always fatal. Now, that's not just exceptional skill, that's a unique operational fingerprint. A personal calling card if you will."

There was a pause, then Andrew continued.

"Now, wind back to Paris. We have a dead counter-sniper on a balcony. A longstanding member of Victor's security detail—big chap, well-trained, not easy to kill. He died of a broken neck. clean fracture of the C2 vertebra. Classic hangman's fracture. And you know what he has around his neck?" Andrew paused, for effect. "Ligature marks."

"Are you saying that the thief from the Faroe Islands and the killer from Paris are one and the same man?"

"I'm certain of it," Andrew replied. "The guy that stole the Pandora launch key is the same one that killed Victor. And about Victor's killer we know quite a lot by now."

Sophie pressed her back harder against the divan, painfully aware that the details of this conversation were lethal knowledge—and if they discovered her, absolutely nothing would save her life.

Kirov's voice pulled her back to the present: "The last intel I received on Victor's death was that it was the Moscow. Most likely military intelligence, but that's not confirmed yet."

"Oh, it's worse than that," Andrew said, and Sophie heard the soft clink of ice on glass. "It's Ural 16. An off-the-books covert action unit, operating outside the official structures of Russian intelligence," Andrew replied. "Focus is on highly sophisticated deep-cover operations, wet work, influence operations, you name it. Massive budget. Accountable only to the very top."

"And who is our friend, do we know?" Kirov asked, his voice tense.

"The commanding officer of the Ural 16 black-ops team. Codename's Mercury."

"Mercury," Kirov repeated, letting the name linger. "Is there anything we know about him? Apart from the fact that he's the Kremlin's boy?"

"Well, we know almost nothing about him," Andrew replied. "In fact, we don't even know for sure if he's Kremlin's boy anymore," Andrew replied, each word clipped and careful now. "You see, according to my sources, Mercury hasn't returned the pendant to his masters. The Kremlin doesn't have it. At least not yet."

"So he's a double agent?"

"Maybe he's screwing the Kremlin up the ass, but we don't know. Not for sure. However, what we do know is that Moscow was worried enough to send a scalp hunter after him. They think Mercury might've slipped the leash and they want to determine if he's theirs, someone else's, or no one's."

"So we're dealing with a Russian agent, potentially with a rogue Russian agent or a double, who now has one of the two Pandora firing keys," Kirov said musingly. "Do we know what he's after?"

"No," Andrew replied. "Could be anything. Power. Money. Ideology. Even a girl. Who knows."

"Well, let's leave motives aside for now. I'm more interested in how he pulled this off," Kirov said.

Ivan let out a low, mirthless chuckle. "That's the question, isn't it? How could he worm his way onto that ship and escape with the pendant, all without raising the alarm?"

Sophie heard the sound of a glass being set down, the ice clinking like tiny chimes.

"I'll tell you how," Ivan continued, in the slow, deliberate tone of a man unwrapping a particularly nasty truth. "It was someone who knew exactly what they were doing. Someone who knew the location and layout of the vessel, the security protocols, the possible escape routes."

"Stiva handled the security," Kirov replied. "The operation was airtight. And the flow of information was restricted to the inner circle. The keys were well-secured, the ship's location known only to a select few. Our contacts at every stage were reliable, vetted over years of close and successful collaboration. Nothing could have gotten out. I don't see how this could have happened."

"It happens," Ivan said, his voice as cold as ice. "When someone on the inside *makes* it happen."

There was a pause, a silence heavy with implication.

"You think it's one of us? Someone from the inner circle?" Kirov asked.

Ivan's voice again, cool, imperious: "No, I don't think. I know," he said, as if forcing everyone to consider the unthinkable. "The operation was precise. Surgical. Clean. Mercury was well-informed. Too well-informed. This wasn't something an outsider could pull off—not within that timeframe, not with that level of detail."

"So Mercury had help..." Kirov said slowly.

"Yes. And that means we have a rotten apple in the basket. A traitor. Someone at the very top. He's responsible for last night. And if I'm right, he's responsible for Paris too."

There was a moment of stunned silence, then Kirov asked, "Do we know who it is?"

"No. But we'll find him. He'll slip. They always do. Eventually," Andrew replied.

"Do we have some kind of starting point to find him?"

Once again, Andrew's voice filled the room: "Our traitor? No. Mercury? Maybe. If we leave the bodies aside for now, it all boils down to a single piece of hard evidence—an abandoned safehouse in Paris, rented under the name of Monsieur Armand, a Frenchman. Official records are fake, so is Monsieur Armand himself. No one ever laid eyes on him. The elderly landlady claims she spoke to him once on the telephone. Swears he's Parisian—pitch-perfect accent, not a sliver of foreignness anywhere. The deposit was cash, untraceable. No prints, no notes, not so much as a smudge on a mirror. And that is it. That's the sum total of our leads. At least so far."

"What do you mean by so far?"

"I need to check this first before I come up with wild theories. But if I'm right, we'll have our traitor tonight."

"What if he's already gone by then?"

"I doubt it. Whoever it is, he's after Pandora. To get it, he needs both firing keys. He has one; and he's sticking around for the other."

For a moment, no one spoke, the three men apparently all lost in thought, then Ivan's voice broke the hush.

"Very well, Andrew," Ivan said. "I expect results tonight."

There was a brief moment of silence, followed by the scraping of chairs and the soft sound of leather-soled shoes on marble floors as Ivan and his henchmen left their private war council. A second later, the three men walked past her—first Ivan, then the towering figure of Leonid Kirov, and finally Andrew—squat, square-shouldered, with a visible, freshly healing wound on his cheek.

The men stopped at the door and shook hands, then vanished one by one into the sun-drenched hallway outside. A moment later, the door closed behind them.

Sophie waited for a second—heart thundering.

And in that moment, realisation finally sank in fully. Ivan suspected a traitor, but did not know who. Moscow feared a rogue agent, but lacked proof.

There were perhaps a handful of people who knew about this. And now she knew too. This was her chance. Her path to freedom. If she played her cards right, she could use her newly acquired knowledge to her advantage. If she found the traitor before Ivan did, she might be able to cut a deal with him. She had little to offer—but in this snake pit of treachery and deceit, the information she had just overheard was worth something, as was her silence. And she could exchange both for protection and a way out.

Slowly, she rose with trembling knees.

At that moment, the door opened quietly, and Sophie turned to see the tall figure of a man step into the room.

CHAPTER XVI

Isola di San Clemente, Venice, Italy
Tuesday, 2nd July, 11:47

It was Stiva.

Moving with the furtive, soft-footed tread of the uninvited guest, Stiva slipped into the library—casually trailing one hand along the edge of the sideboard as if he were simply brushing away dust. And then, with all the skill and dexterity of a pickpocket, Stiva plucked a tiny object from the underside of the table and slid it into a tiny, hidden compartment in his cufflink.

And right at that moment, he seemed to sense her presence in the room.

He turned around.

A hint of surprise flashed in Stiva's grey eyes as he caught sight of her, but it was gone in an instant, replaced by an impenetrable mask of cold reticence and absolute self-control.

"What a surprise: Alexei's lady friend," he said softly, nimbly shutting the door with one foot. "We haven't been properly introduced yet, I'm afraid. So let me rectify the omission." He gave a small, gallant bow of the head. "Stepan Ivanovich Volkov."

"Sophie Akehurst," she replied, her voice trembling.

"Sophie," Stiva echoed, letting her name roll off his tongue in an almost pleasant way.

For a moment, he regarded her—the sharpness of his hard-cut features almost inhuman in the garish glow of the morning sun—then he slipped his hand into his trouser pocket and began to stroll towards her at a slow, measured pace.

"So, Sophie, I see you're exploring your temporary accommodation. I can assure you, the amenities are quite terrific." He picked up a beautifully painted Chinese vase in passing and weighed it pensively in his hand. "Unfortunately, the use of the house facilities is the prerogative of my father's esteemed guests." His eyes narrowed just a little. "Which begs the question: What exactly are you doing here?"

The desperate entreaty that had hovered on the tip of her lips died at the revelation that the man she faced was Ivan Volkov's son. Somehow, that new and entirely unexpected piece of information made her whole fantastic plan seem suddenly ludicrous.

Instinctively, Sophie backed away from him, trying to distance herself from the danger. But Stiva moved with almost inhuman speed, hurling the vase across the room. It shattered on the wall, a mere inch from her head, making her freeze.

The miss had been deliberate, its precision hinting at the deadly skills that lurked under Stiva's polished veneer.

"Ah, let me warn you, my dear, running is never a good strategy. Someone is always quicker," Stiva said, his voice soft, its tone warning yet with a hint of benevolence. "Now back to my question." He stepped closer and placed one hand on the wall beside her head. "What are you doing here?"

Sophie felt a chill run down her spine. There was something dangerous about him, some heightened sensitivity, as if his senses were more keenly attuned to his surroundings than hers.

"Are you listening to me, Sophie?" Stiva asked, his eyes narrowing, his voice soft, almost soothing, as if he were speaking to a frightened child.

"Yes, I'm sorry."

"Then answer me: What are you doing here?"

"I—"

The sound of a frighteningly familiar voice cut her answer short. "I don't usually get to watch my women from that vantage point, but it surely has its appeal."

Sophie's eyes snapped to the door. There stood Zorin, one shoulder propped against the stuccoed frame, one leg crossed over the other at the ankle, one corner of the lip curled into that derisive sadist's smile.

Sophie expected Stiva to step away, but he didn't even turn to Zorin. Instead, he kept his eyes firmly on her—his expression warning.

"Oh, Alexei, you have a terrible penchant for interrupting my fun. But be that as it may. I caught your pretty companion here," he brushed a stray lock from Sophie's face, "roaming around in places where she doesn't belong. Seems she doesn't know the house rules yet. Should I fix that for you, my friend?"

Zorin chuckled, pushing himself away from the doorframe in a movement that looked oddly stiff. "No need, Stiva, I'll take care of it. I'm sure your attention is required elsewhere."

"And where would that be?" Stiva asked laconically, his grey eyes still on her.

"Mexico," Zorin replied, his tone suddenly harder, less mirthful. "It seems that your operation down there is missing three Kilo-class submarines that were destined for the cartels. And now the would-be narco-subs turned up thousands of miles away at the *Gremikha* Naval Base, safely back in the hands of their rightful owners. If I didn't know better, Stiva, I'd almost suspect you of working for the Kremlin." Zorin's eyes dropped to Stiva's hands, to his cuffs, and the platinum links holding them together. "Especially with those cufflinks. GRU standard issue, I believe. Is it just another product you deal in or was it a gift for services rendered?"

The slight was deliberate. So was the choice of language: English instead of Russian. Zorin didn't simply mean to insult Stiva, but to do so with an audience.

The hint of displeasure in Stiva's eyes turned to a cold, terrifying hatred. He rounded on Zorin, requiting his offhand slight in Russian. Zorin didn't respond, but his lip curled once again into that derisive, mirthless smile, and for a beat Sophie feared that Zorin's overt condescension would push them both past the breaking point. But neither man was willing to cross that line. Standing motionless, they stared at each other—two predators poised to strike—then they let up: Stiva stepping back while Zorin beckoned her to his side.

She complied instinctively, but Stiva held her back with a raised hand—the intricate platinum knot catching the sunlight. For a moment, her eyes hung it, held there by a memory she couldn't quite place.

"We're having a small party tonight, my dear, and I'd be honoured by your presence." He smiled, his eyes oddly probing as if he were trying to read her mind, then he turned his attention back to Zorin. "Don't disappoint me by keeping your little friend away, Alexei."

"I would hate to let you down, Stiva."

Stiva acknowledged Zorin's reply with a curt nod, then stepped past him and out of the door, leaving Sophie at her captor's mercy.

Zorin regarded her for a long moment, then he slipped one hand into his trouser pocket and began to walk around her at a leisurely pace. He didn't speak, apparently deep in thought—most likely contemplating her punishment. As he sauntered past the sideboard, Zorin ran his hand casually along its edge and plucked a tiny black device—no bigger than a grain of rice—from its underside. With a smile, he held it up and inspected it briefly, then he stopped, dropped it, and ground it under his heel.

"It's just you and me now, without any other ears listening to what we say."

Sophie heard Zorin's voice and yet his words didn't reach her mind. Others echoed there: *We have a rotten apple in the basket. A traitor. He's responsible for last night. And if I'm right, he's responsible for Paris too.*

And for the briefest of moments, the image of Ivan's son—dressed casually and all in black and slipping away under the cover of the night—flashed in her mind's eye. And then the image gave way to another, darker one—to a white tiled cell in London, and Lord Harper's voice, echoing through the hallway. *Stiva just flew in from Paris last night.*

Paris...

Zorin's voice pulled Sophie from her reeling thoughts.

"Do you know who that was?" Zorin asked, leaning casually against the sideboard and resting his palms on its edges while he observed her.

Sophie hesitated for a beat. Zorin couldn't know what she had overheard in London. To his knowledge, she had never been properly introduced to Stiva, and unless she had casually picked up Stiva's name during their meeting with Ivan, there was nothing at all for her to know. Zorin, perceptive as he was, might spot her lie, but she would be damned if she didn't at least try to give him the impression that she was nothing but an unwitting, frightened hostage. At least not until she had decided what to do with her newfound knowledge.

"No, I don't."

"Ivan's son. Stiva to his friends. Stepan Ivanovich to you." He paused. "You tangle with powerful men, Sophie. And you're picking fights that you can't win."

His words, so casually spoken, brought home the true meaning of fear: Zorin would make her pay for her transgression.

"Please, I'm sorry, I—"

"Shh." Zorin shook his head, stopping whatever apology was about to fall from her lips. "You don't speak unless I give you leave to do so."

She kept quiet, hoping that her silence would appease him. And it did, for Zorin smiled his lazy, ever-mirthless smile, then raised his hand to summon her to him with a deliberately disdainful crook of the forefinger. Sophie didn't dare to refuse, but the muscles of her thighs trembled as she stepped to him.

His casual stance—hips propped against the ledge, hands resting on either side of him—cost Zorin a little of his considerable height, but even so, he still towered over her.

Sophie didn't dare look into his eyes, so she focused them once more on his shoulder, noticing that the tiny speck of blood on his shirt was no longer there. So he'd changed, and in the process, he'd probably noticed that she had gone.

"Look at me," he commanded, in the quiet voice of someone accustomed to being heard and obeyed.

She looked up.

She had expected to see anger in his face. Even fury. But there was no trace of it in his handsome features. He was calm, so terribly calm that she felt her blood run cold under his gaze.

"I thought you understood the rules," Zorin said.

The question that lingered in his statement made it clear that this time, he expected her to answer.

"I do."

"Then you're a fool indeed." He hooked his finger under the fallen strap of her dress and slipped it up over her shoulder. "But don't worry, Stiva will enjoy your tears while you undress for him tonight. And so will most of my friends."

"No, please—"

"You chose to ignore my warning, Sophie, what's coming is… just deserts." Zorin's expression hardened, even the pretence of mirth disappearing from his handsome features. "Still, you should consider yourself lucky; after all, you could have ended up in a traitor's bed instead of mine. And trust me, in a world like this one, that means death by association."

Sophie felt her blood run cold. In one breath, Alexei Zorin had confirmed all her suspicions.

Stiva was the traitor.

Zorin held her gaze for a long time, as if to observe the effect of his words on her. Finally, he gave a slow nod, as if he were satisfied with whatever he had seen in her expression, then he reached out and rapped his knuckles against the lintel.

Instantly, the door swung open and two of Ivan's uniformed goons stepped into the room. "Sir?"

"Escort my friend back to my lodgings. And make sure she stays there."

CHAPTER XVII

Isola di San Clemente, Venice, Italy
Tuesday, 2nd July, 18:43

Sophie stood alone in the grim silence of Zorin's bedroom. The light of the evening sun banked in through the wall of armoured windows and bathed the pale marble floor in hues of red and gold.

Zorin had mercifully not returned to his quarters after their dreadful encounter that afternoon, and apart from a butler who had come by to deliver a safety deposit box and inform Sophie that 'Mr Zorin wishes for the lady to be ready at seven', she had been left to her own devices. For a while, she had cried, then paced around in her cage, and finally she had done what her captor undoubtedly expected: she had readied herself for tonight. And now she stood here—face painted, body primed, dressed in lace—like a whore waiting for her suitor.

The thought made her stomach churn.

Wrapping her arms around herself, Sophie walked to the window and pressed her forehead to the cool glass. A helicopter approached from the sea, its empennage gleaming in the sun, the black fuselage casting a shadow on the dark blue waters of the bay below. It flew a wide circle over the rugged coastline, then began its slow descent over the island, hovering in the air like a hummingbird before vanishing behind the treeline. Below her, men in tailored suits and bodyguards in black military fatigues walked across the forecourt. In their midst, Sophie spotted Cavendish and Kirov, and a step behind them walked the man whom fate had made her unlikely ally.

Stiva.

This morning, she had been ready to beg for his protection on her hands and knees. But things had changed. Stiva was a hunted man—one who was entirely oblivious to the fact that his secret had been uncovered by his greatest enemy. And this made him her ally—a reluctant one perhaps, but an ally nonetheless.

The ormolu clock on the mantelpiece chimed the quarter hour. She had fifteen minutes. A cold shiver ran down Sophie's spine, the sensation of fear so acute that it was almost enough to send her over the edge.

You can do this, she told herself in her mind. *Stay calm.*

Tremulously, Sophie stepped away from the window and turned to the spacious walk-in closet. On a Dalbergia sideboard—beside a Dupont lighter and an exquisite Patek Philippe wristwatch that had been carelessly discarded on a gilt-edged deck of cards—sat a metal case engraved with the telltale logo of a Swiss bank. Fleetingly, Sophie ran her hand over the cool steel, wondering what treasures Zorin hid inside, then her eyes fell on something rather unexpected: Beside the bank box lay a well-thumbed book, its cover once blue, but now faded and some of its pages folded at the edges as if its sinister owner secretly liked to mark his favourite passages as he read.

Hesitantly, Sophie reached for the volume and turned it over. The cover was topped by a gilt-edged title and the author's name in Cyrillic letters. The words didn't mean anything to her, but the stylised face on the cover did.

Pushkin.

The last thing she expected to find among Zorin's belongings was a dog-eared volume of poetry. But now wasn't the time to dally over Zorin's secrets.

Painfully aware that her hand was trembling, Sophie replaced the book exactly as she had found it—spine to the wall, cover down—then she turned around and picked up the dress she had selected hours before. Black. Short. Skin-tight. She slipped it over her head, the cool fabric caressing her body as she pulled it down, the neckline covering just enough to leave what little it covered to the imagination. She adjusted the dress, donned a pair of matching heels, then glanced at the mirror.

A whore indeed.

The thought made her shiver. Closing her eyes, she composed herself. She couldn't afford to lose focus—not if she wanted to survive.

All she had to focus on was getting to Stiva, to tell him that she knew of his secret and was willing to strike a deal—a devil's pact. One that would get her out of here.

You can pull this off. Just stay calm.

The sound of a door opening pulled Sophie from her thoughts. Footsteps echoed on the marble floor. Then she heard Zorin's voice—soft and clear—speaking flawless French to someone on the phone and pausing occasionally to listen to whatever the caller at the other end of the line had to say.

A few moments later, Zorin entered the master bedroom, ending his call with a terse command and no goodbye.

He was close enough to know where she was, close enough to walk in if he chose. But instead, in a rare gesture of what might have passed for mercy in his world, the sound of his footsteps retreated towards the balcony—granting her one last moment of privacy.

Staring at herself in the mirror, Sophie smoothed the dress over her hips, then stepped out of the closet.

The balcony doors were open, a breeze carrying in the scent of the sea.

Zorin stood on the balcony, his back to her, his eyes scanning the dark expanse of water. He was impeccably dressed, as always, in a formal dark suit. The cut was sharp, the fabric exquisite, and if not for the tattoos on his hands, he would have passed as a scion of the moneyed aristocracy.

Composing herself, Sophie stepped out onto the balcony. Zorin turned slightly as she approached, his eyes flickering over her for the briefest of moments before returning to the view. His expression was unreadable, a mask of composure that revealed nothing and concealed everything.

Sophie moved to his side, her hand lightly brushing the balustrade as she looked out at the sea.

The view was magnificent. The moon hung low over the sea, casting a silver path across the inky water that seemed to stretch endlessly into the night.

"The sea has a way of drawing you in, doesn't it?" Zorin's voice was low, almost a whisper. "It's easy to lose yourself in it, to forget everything else."

Sophie nodded, not trusting herself to speak.

"Do you know what fascinates me most about the sea?" He wasn't asking. It was the kind of question that needed no answer. "It's the way it can look so calm, so deceptively inviting. Safe. But beneath the surface, it's a different story. Currents that can pull you under before you even realise you're in danger."

Sophie tensed, her fingers tightening around the stone, but she kept her gaze fixed on the horizon, willing herself to remain calm. "That sounds terrifying rather than fascinating."

"Indeed, it does. But that makes it all the more important to remember that there are depths you don't want to explore. Waters that, once entered, offer no return."

"I've never been one for deep water."

"Good," Zorin replied, his voice so low that it was almost a whisper. "Because sometimes, those who venture too far find themselves lost at sea. And as much as I might wish to, I can't always save those who've strayed beyond the shore."

"I'll remember that."

Zorin looked at her, and there was something in his eyes that she couldn't quite place. A fleeting moment of concern perhaps, or something else she didn't quite understand. But it was gone in a heartbeat, replaced once again by Zorin's cold, frightening façade.

"Very well, then I think it's time to go," he said, offering her his arm.

Sophie hesitated for the fraction of a second, then she took it, slipping into the role that was expected of her.

CHAPTER XVIII

Isola di San Clemente, Venice, Italy
Tuesday, 2nd July, 19:04

Zorin hadn't forced her to walk at his side as they made their way through Ivan's palace, but now, as they were about to enter the reception room, Zorin caught her arm—lightly, but with that proprietary confidence that made her feel paraded and displayed—and steered her through the open doors.

The room that welcomed them was vast, too large for comfort—a hall of mirrors stretching out into infinity, fractured reflections catching the light of the chandeliers above. It was a room meant to impress, to dazzle. But as Sophie's eyes adjusted to the dim light, the glamour began to fray at the edges. The mirrors, the chandeliers, the endless reflections—they were meant to distract, but nothing could truly obscure the ugliness of what was happening here.

Dance poles stood between marble columns, and around them women moved—naked, adorned with nothing but diamonds. Their bodies swayed, slow and deliberate, as if they were underwater, as if the poles they clung to were the only things tethering them to this world. The men watched, impassive, their eyes sharp, perhaps vaguely amused, but untouched by anything resembling compassion. The women's eyes, however, were emptied out, vacant, not with sadness but with nothingness, as if they had been drained of life itself, left to exist only as ornaments for the men lounging casually among them. Bruised punctures marred their arms, small scars of forced injections, like marks of ownership and possession. They were there to fill space, to entertain, but most of all, they were there to be consumed—their suffering multiplied to infinity by the mirrors on the walls.

Suddenly, she felt Zorin's presence like a weight pressing down on her—his hand on her back the only solid thing in the room.

Zorin hadn't touched her, not like that, not the way these men touched these women. Not yet. But standing here, beneath the thick veneer of luxury and rot, she felt the reality of it creep into the corners of her mind.

She had been spared so far, untouched by the bruises, the needle punches, the degradation. She had been kept at the edge of the abyss, dangling just far enough to feel the weight of what could happen but not yet falling into the void.

Not yet.

But her time would come.

It was only a matter of when.

Zorin's hand returned to her waist, pulling her attention back to him. His eyes met hers, and there was something cold, calculating, in them.

"I think you'll find tonight... educational." Zorin's voice was soft, low, the kind that slipped into your bones. "But while I encourage curiosity, I'd advise you not to wander too far—unless you're ready to put into practice what you've learned."

Sophie's stomach turned at the casualness of his words and she only gave him a silent nod.

They moved deeper into the room. A few men glanced up at her, their eyes lingering a little too long. Sophie could feel their glances. The eyes of men moving over her like grease, lingering just long enough to strip her bare. She knew those glances. They were the glances of men who could and did buy anything they desired.

This was their world. They had purchased it—every inch of flesh, every soul—and they could do with it what they pleased.

Only hours ago, the sight of this place—the mirrored walls, the dead-eyed women, the endless parade of well-dressed predators—it all would have reduced her once again to a quivering, frightened shadow of herself. But now, for the first time since she had been brought here, the oppressive sense of terror that had become as much a part of her as the rhythm of her breath—was gone. She had a purpose now. A plan. She wasn't just drifting through the currents of Alexei Zorin's world anymore, tossed from one sickening moment to the next. She had her footing, and with it came the beginnings of something like hope, even if it was a hope born of desperation.

Trying to push the thought from her mind, Sophie kept by Zorin's side, while secretly searching for the man that she had chosen to be her salvation—or her doom.

And finally, she saw him.

Stiva sat at the far end of the room, watching her with a kind of bored impertinence—one hand draped over the armrest, one polished shoe perched disdainfully on the edge of a low brass table. A woman, raven-haired and glassy-eyed, knelt at his feet, her cheek resting against his knee. His fingers wound lazily through her hair—the gesture disturbingly tender—but the woman didn't seem to register his touch. She had checked out, her mind elsewhere. Sophie could see it in the way her eyelids fluttered, the way her body swayed ever so slightly, the way her lips parted, not in pleasure but in numbness.

And at that moment, as if sensing Sophie's eyes on him, Stiva looked up, returning her gaze with a kind of bored impertinence—one hand stoking the woman's head, one polished shoe perched disdainfully on the edge of a low brass table.

But it was only show. Stiva knew that she had observed him today, and he was desperate to talk. They both were. And that conversation would have to happen here. In this room. Under Zorin's eyes. Somehow.

It was risky, almost suicidally so, but it was also the only chance she'd have.

Somewhere out there, beyond Alexei Zorin's reach, was a life she had almost lost hope of ever reclaiming. She could taste it now, just within reach, if only she was willing to gamble everything on this one slim chance.

And she would. She had to. The alternative was unthinkable.

She turned to Zorin. "Please excuse me for a moment, I'd like to powder my nose."

"Don't stray too far," he said, his voice low, almost tender. "It's easy to get lost..."

For the fraction of a second, the ease with which he let her slip away made her chest tighten—but this was her only chance, and she couldn't let a vague notion of fear or suspicion get in the way.

"I'll be right back."

"Then go," he said, in a low voice.

Sophie turned away from her captor and crossed the room.

A man in an immaculate dinner jacket whirled by, pressed a drink into her hand, then vanished through a forest of potted palms.

At the far end of the room, a balcony door, half ajar, promised cooler air. Sophie drifted there, pushing through shoulders and half-heard conversations.

When she reached the doors that lead out to the terrace she paused, her hand resting on a Baalbek pillar as she looked back at the room. Zorin was watching her, his expression unreadable, his eyes locked on hers. She felt the weight of his gaze even from a distance, a reminder that no matter how far she went, she could never truly escape him.

With a shuddering breath, she turned away and walked out onto the terrace.

The night air was warm, the sky black, the stars distant.

Slowly, she stepped to the railing, letting her eyes trail over the torchlit sculpture garden below. Silhouettes of date palms fanned along its edges and beyond them lay the sea—dark and oddly calm.

"Thinking of jumping, my dear?" The voice, soft and rich, slid into her ear like a snake and then Stiva stepped to her side, setting a hand on the balustrade a mere inch from hers.

"Just enjoying the view," she replied, keeping her tone neutral, polite, though her heart raced against her neck.

Stiva leaned in closer, the scent of his aftershave overpowering as it invaded her space. "No one ever enjoys the view at a party like this one. People are either forced to be here, or they come for a... purpose." His gaze flickered over her body, lingering too long on the neckline of her dress, before he met her eyes again.

"Some are here for both reasons," she said, turning back to the sea.

Stiva laughed very softly. "Oh, a woman with a purpose, that's a rare thing indeed." He edged closer, his voice dropping to a conspiratorial whisper. "Tell me then, what's yours?"

She felt a shiver run down her spine. Suddenly, she was frightened to confront him. He wasn't just a spy. He was a killer. But she could not afford to let her only chance slip. "I know what you did today. And why. And others know it too, and they're closing in on you."

Stiva's face showed her nothing, yet she noticed his fingers tighten around the glass. "Is that so?"

"Yes."

"And without doubt you've come here with some kind of proposal, am I right?"

"Yes."

"And what do you suggest?"

"Help me, and I'll help you."

"Protection for information, is that the deal you're trying to cut?"

Sophie gave a vague nod. "Yes."

Stiva laughed softly, turning around and leaning against the railing, so that he could watch the crowd inside through the French windows. "I think you overestimate your value."

"Perhaps you underestimate mine."

Another voice cut through the conversation. "I think she's right, Stiva. Which means you're standing awfully close to something you can't afford."

Sophie turned to see Zorin step out onto the terrace, strolling towards them, one hand in his trouser pocket, the other holding a drink he clearly hadn't even tried.

Stiva laughed very softly, entirely unimpressed by Zorin's sudden appearance.

"Oh, come now, Alexei, we're like brothers, and brothers are supposed to share." Stiva ran his hand suggestively down her arm. "I'd really like to know if your pet is worth the price you've spent on her." He nodded towards the stripper pole, just beyond the French windows, then looked at Zorin. "Send her up on stage. Show us her charms. Or are you concerned that you can't control your pet?"

Stiva's tone was casual, almost playful, but there was something darker underneath. He was testing the waters, pushing at the boundaries, seeing how far Zorin's control could be stretched.

Zorin stepped closer, sliding a casual arm around her waist, drawing her to him. "She's not here for your entertainment, Stiva. She's here because I want her to be. And you'd do well to remember that."

For the briefest of moments, Sophie felt an absurd sense of gratitude for Zorin's unexpected protection, even though she knew it was more a subtle tensioning of the leash than a rescue.

Stiva chuckled, but it was a forced sound, his grin faltering slightly. He wasn't used to being put in his place. Not like this.

"Well then, keep your pet to yourself. The evening's entertainment is about to start, and we wouldn't want to miss it."

Zorin gave a vague nod and motioned ahead. "After you, Stiva."

They left the terrace and stepped inside. Just before the French doors closed behind them, Sophie glanced at Zorin. In that fleeting moment, Sophie caught the ghost of satisfaction in Zorin's eyes—and realised the unthinkable.

Alexei Zorin had orchestrated this.

Briefly, his words from this morning echoed in her mind: *You should consider yourself lucky; after all, you could have ended up in a traitor's bed instead of mine.*

Not knowing that she was already privy to Stiva's secret, Alexei Zorin had initiated her. Not to warn her, but to make her act. He had stage-managed the revelation, steering her towards Stiva so she'd deliver the warning. He had wanted for Stiva to absorb the rumour—sense the crackle of approaching thunder.

The question was why.

CHAPTER XIX

Isola di San Clemente, Venice, Italy
Tuesday, 2nd July, 20:12

Following Stiva, Zorin led Sophie back into the mirrored hall, its pale marble floors reflecting the crystal chandeliers strung overhead. Inside, the air was cooler, scented with Moroccan rose.

They circled to a corner where Stiva's raven-haired companion still sat waiting on low, upholstered chairs that flanked a sunken seating area. As Stiva approached, she lifted her eyes and offered him a smile that came and went, like a service light switched off too quickly.

Stiva sat heavily beside her. With a peremptory wave, he indicated Zorin and Sophie should join them on the wide leather couch. Sophie caught the woman's slow, sideways glance—the perfect image of compliance—then let herself slip onto the seat next to Zorin.

Drinks were replenished, half-introductions made, then the waitress placed a silver plate with white powder on the table.

"For the ladies," the waitress said, with a wink and left.

Stiva's companion reached out, dipped a finger into the powder and licked part of it off, then held her hand out to Sophie. There were needle punctures all over the crook of her arm—tiny bruises, some faded, some new. Their eyes met. Hers were very black, but now Sophie could see how dilated her pupils were, her gaze cloudy from all the drugs, yet not clouded enough to hide the fear.

Zorin's soft laugh pulled Sophie from her state of paralysed horror. "I wouldn't try it, if I were you. The same goes for the champagne." He took another sip of his whisky, then he brought the glass to her lips. "Try this."

The mere idea of sipping a drink from his hand like an obedient pet made her skin crawl and for a brief moment, she doubted that she could maintain this illusion much longer, but there was no choice.

You can do this.

She parted her lips, feeling the cool rim of the glass against her mouth. And then she took a small sip of the sinfully dark whisky, feeling its smoky, peaty flavour burn her throat.

For a moment, Zorin sat motionless, his gaze fixed on her face with unwavering intensity, and then he tilted the glass away, his thumb brushing over her lower lip, wiping the remnants of the whisky away.

Gently, he ran his fingertip over her lip, then let it linger there—a silent command.

Her stomach churned as she realised what he expected of her, and for a moment the room seemed to close in, the music and chatter fading to a dull roar. But then she mastered herself. Slowly, deliberately, she parted her lips and slowly, sensually licked the drop off his thumb, her tongue brushing against his skin.

It was a private moment, but like everything in this room, it was meant to be seen. The mirrors caught it and multiplied it, the simple act becoming something else entirely—an intimate performance for those who understood the subtle power dynamics at play.

Across the table, Stiva watched the exchange with lazy amusement and said something in Russian which made the corner of Zorin's lip lips slightly in a mirthless half-smile.

Zorin set down the glass and, ignoring her, continued the conversation.

Keeping up the pretence of petrified stillness, Sophie watched Zorin from under half-closed lids, trying to assess him—to gauge how far she could go before he would strike.

At first glance, Zorin appeared relaxed, a man engrossed in deep and earnest conversation, but to the keen observer—to one willing to see not only the seeming but the being—revealed itself the terrible tension that simmered beneath the surface: The tension of the predator poised to strike. The secret lay in his eyes, those cold blue eyes that took the measure of everyone and everything at once without ever seeming to. When Zorin spoke, his gaze always rested on his opponent, but there were those other moments, those fleeting moments of transient distraction—a smile, a frown, an occasional sip of whisky—and then his eyes would suddenly move through the room in one fell swoop—to survey, to assess, and to finally return to the starting point.

It happened again and again, then suddenly something changed—his gaze halted, the predator's eye finding prey in the crowd.

Sophie followed his gaze.

Silhouetted against the dim shafts of light, a man—squat and square-shouldered—was walking towards them. For a brief moment, he paused to greet Ivan, approaching him the way a supplicant would a king. The two men shook hands, spoke a few words, and then the newcomer took his leave with a cordial smile—requited by a less enthusiastic one on Ivan's side. Unfazed by his overlord's glacial send-off, the man turned and headed over to their table—one of Ivan's bodyguards in tow.

The bodyguard took up position in the shadows beside the table, while the squat, square-shouldered figure stepped closer.

"May I?" he asked, with a polite nod in Zorin's direction, as if his assent mattered more than Stiva's.

The moment the man spoke, Sophie recognised him: It was Ivan's Scottish informant. Andrew.

"Of course, Andrew. Sit down," Zorin replied.

With a stiff smile, the Scot sank down in a high-backed chair to Zorin's right.

"Ivan just told me the most fascinating story," Andrew said, taking a glass of whisky from the hand of a waitress. "Some obscure bit of Russian lore."

"Is that so?" Stiva asked, clearly bored.

Andrew picked up the glass and tilted it in the light, studying the colour of the liquor. "A few centuries ago," he began, his voice raised in that peculiar way in which people tended to tell anecdotes, "Some Muscovite nobleman tried to poison Ivan the Terrible. Only problem: the tsar was no fool. Word reached him that someone planned to slip something lethal into his nightly tipple. So, on one of those lovely Russian winter nights, Ivan invited the entire brood of suspects to a splendid banquet, including our would-be assassin. And of course, the sorry chap agreed. When wine was served, Ivan asked for a volunteer to serve as cupbearer and sample the wine, promising the emerald-encrusted chalice as a reward. Naturally, every guest leapt at the chance—everyone, that is, save for our would-be assassin. The tsar, now aware of who the traitor was, emptied the wine onto the floor, flipped the empty goblet upside down and put it back on the table. And that inverted goblet was the prearranged signal his guards had been waiting for." Andrew lifted his own glass a fraction. "The luckless would-be assassin was seized. The tsar, decidedly not the man for half-measures, had the sorry chap tied to a sled and dragged to the Moskva River, to be drowned in the icy water."

Stiva tapped ash from his cigarette, pretending disinterest. "I've heard many myths about the tsars. Most are nonsense."

"Probably so. Still, it illustrates a reliable truth: traitors always give themselves away in the end."

"How very insightful, Andrew," Zorin remarked. "Tell me, does the tale have practical value for us—or is it just a delightful anecdote?"

Andrew paused, lowering his glass. "Well, it just so happens that I'm looking into last night's incident and there are a few things I'm rather keen on discussing with the two of you."

Stiva arched an eyebrow. "I think you're playing out of your league, Andrew. That's business of the Twelve and those immediately advising the transaction."

"Well, I'm afraid it's my business too. You see, I'm running the investigation into it."

Stiva's eyebrow rose a little further—just a pinch. "On whose authority?"

"Ivan's," replied Andrew, evidently intoxicated with the power of his newfound station.

"You have risen in the world, Andrew. I'm impressed," Stiva said, his tone suggesting otherwise. "Well then, what did your... investigation yield?"

"A few rather surprising details."

"Is the current location of the launch codes among those... details?" Zorin asked languidly, so patently unmoved by Andrew's presumptuous announcement that he didn't even bother to shift his eyes away from the dancer.

"No, unfortunately not, but I have something almost as good."

Zorin's patrician head turned a little to the side, his eyes gracing the Scot with a disdainful look. "And what would that be, Andrew?"

Andrew leaned back in his chair with a deliberate lack of haste, his gaze shifting from Zorin to Stiva: "I have the traitor."

CHAPTER XX

Isola di San Clemente, Venice, Italy
Tuesday, 2nd July, 20:39

Sophie's apprehension gave way to outright terror. Andrew had beaten Zorin to the punch, and now the trap would snap shut right in front of her eyes.

Instinctively, her eyes shifted to Stiva. He was calm, utterly composed, but she could feel the tension beneath the surface. He was bracing himself.

"Is that so? Care to share the name?" Stiva asked, casually slipping an enamelled cigarette box from inside his jacket—the movement affording her a fleeting glimpse of the gun he carried underneath.

Andrew shook his head. "Well, I'm afraid I don't have a name. Not yet. But we'll get to that, after we've discussed the evidence I've found."

"Do tell, Andrew—what have you managed to dig up?" Stiva asked, slipping a cigarette between his lips, and offering one to Zorin, who declined with a barely perceptible shake of his head.

Andrew smirked and sat back. "I sent my boys down to the Faroe Islands this morning to get to the bottom of this mess, and what they found was really quite remarkable."

"Remarkable how?" Stiva inquired, blowing a puff of smoke in Andrew's direction.

"The man who killed Victor Orsin, and the man who stole the firing key are one and the same person. Same method of killing. Links him straight back to a Russian agent operating under the codename Mercury."

"I don't care about Russian agents, Andrew," Stiva interjected, both annoyed and bored. "He's just a pawn. A foot soldier. I care about the man who helped him. The man who fed

Mercury, and by extension the Russian state, with the kind of information that made all of this possible. I want the traitor."

"You should care about them both, Stiva, because it seems that our traitor and the Russian agent are one and the same man: Mercury doesn't have a collaborator in our ranks, he doesn't need one, because he's one of us."

There was a pause. Stunned silence. Then Stiva added. "Are you saying that a highly trained Russian deep-cover agent has been inserted in our inner ranks? A man we know absolutely nothing about apart from his bloody codename?"

"Oh, we know things about him, Stiva. A lot of things. First of all, he's clearly ex-navy."

Briefly, Zorin's words echoed in Sophie's mind, spoken so casually last night during their meeting with Ivan. *You're the naval man, Stiva.*

"But then, of course, there are other things. You see, Mercury didn't just appear magically in the Faroe Islands. He actually flew up there last night using a civilian aircraft. Mid-range jet. Quite pedestrian. You know where the flight originated?" Andrew paused, for effect. "Here in Venice."

Briefly, Sophie remembered the image of Stiva, dressed all in black, slipping into a speedboat. Undoubtedly to take the same journey that she had taken by helicopter, only in the opposite direction: From the island to Venice airport.

"At zero one hundred hours, a civilian jet departed Venice bound for Reykjavik. Two hours later, that very same jet reported a pressure drop over the Faroe Islands. The jet turned back towards the Norwegian coast, dropping to about four thousand feet. The height at which an experienced paratrooper can jump without having to rely on extra oxygen."

"Are you saying Mercury jumped from that flight?"

"Used the cargo hatch, most likely. Specialist chute. High-performance diving gear. That kind of thing. The weather was bad.

Heavy seas, strong rain, extreme wind, but he managed it anyway. Flawless quick-release a mere one hundred feet above the water. Then he dived two miles through the frigid, turbulent waters to the ship and climbed the anchor rod. But that's not even the best bit."

Andrew smiled.

"As you know, he made short shrift of the men who crossed his path, stole the launch codes. Now, the obvious way out would have been back into the sea. But he didn't choose that way. He opted for something more spectacular. He chose the fighter jet we were showing to our buyers." Andrew smiled a mirthless smile. "The J-20S prototype, a fifth generation Chinese two-seat stealth fighter with an almost unmatched ability to evade enemy detection and enter contested airspace. It's like riding an invisible magic carpet."

"He flew the damn thing off the carrier in heavy seas?" Stiva asked.

"No, he didn't. He isn't James Bond," Andrew replied. "He posed as the co-pilot. No one noticed. Not even the actual pilot. You know how it is: Heavy seas, bad weather, lots of rain. Pilots already wear their helmets when they walk out to the jet, no one sees their faces, no one questions them, communication happens only through the mics, voices are garbled, distorting them enough for it to be anyone's."

"What happened to the jet?" Stiva asked.

"Once up in the air, with the jet safely stabilised, Mercury killed the pilot. Snapped his neck from behind. And now, all by himself, he set course towards the Italian coast. Our last tracking of the plane was over Porto Levante where the co-pilot ejected. The jet, with the pilot's body, went on for another three hundred miles and then crashed into the sea, while Mercury, along with the stolen launch key, vanished in the waters a stone's throw from Venice, returning here just in time for breakfast."

Stiva smiled mirthlessly. "Spectacular, Andrew. Really. Is there any proof? DNA? Fingerprints? Anything?" Stiva smiled, because it was already evident that Andrew hadn't any of this. "Nothing then?"

"Oh, I do have something."

"And what would that be?" Zorin inquired with a hint of impatience.

"You see, someone who is this good acts cautiously. Rationally. He doesn't take reckless risks. And yet, our guy chose the most breakneck, devil-may-care escape route anyone could have come up with. Why? Makes no sense, does it? What does that tell you?"

"There was no other option," Zorin said, evidently bored by Andrew's lengthy explanations.

"Exactly. So why was there no other option?" Andrew paused, then answered his own question. "Because our guy was injured, and he was injured in a way that didn't allow him to swim a long distance in cold water but still allowed him to fly."

"You seem to confuse proof with speculation, Andrew," Zorin interjected, his voice cold. "Forensics swept that ship and not even Frost could find something. There is nothing there, not a speck of blood. Nothing to prove that your nameless, faceless suspect got so much as a scratch."

"Oh, unlike the charming Doctor Frost I didn't look on the ship, Alexei. I looked right here, on the Italian coast. And guess what I found."

Zorin smiled a mirthless smile that spoke of patience stretched to its limits and beyond. "Enlighten me, Andrew."

Andrew paused and sat back, his expression smug. "Our friend had to drag himself ashore, crawling through the thick, sticky mud between the rocks. There were footprints, evenly spaced, so he wasn't limping. And prints, left behind by a mud-smeared glove. The right hand only. Never the left."

"Upper body injury," Zorin concluded.

Sophie tensed. In that instant, as Zorin spoke the words, the loose pieces of the puzzle came together: the blood on Zorin's shirt, his oddly stiff movements, his absence the night before, his tired expression, his French skills, even his peculiar questions about the security arrangements for the ship during the meeting with Ivan.

Alexei Zorin was Mercury.

CHAPTER XXI

Isola di San Clemente, Venice, Italy
Tuesday, 2nd July, 20:52

What a fool she had been. The signs had been there, subtle yet unmistakable. But she had been too terrified, or perhaps too naïve, to see the truth: The man she had tried to escape from might also be her way out of here.

Sophie glanced at Zorin.

His face was a study in minimalism, stripped bare of all unnecessary expressions. His posture—one hand draped over the armrest, one leg stretched out, the other cocked—was almost deliberately dégagé. His eyes, though sweeping casually through the room, were those of a man completely at ease.

"So, tell me, Andrew," Zorin said, his tone deceptively mild, as if addressing some borderline incompetent underling, "should we all strip down for you so you can check for injuries? Just a final flourish before we dispense with these niceties?"

"No, not everyone." Andrew lifted his glass to his lips, downing the whisky in one pull and then setting the emptied glass—bottom up—onto the tabletop. "Just Stiva and you." Andrew gave him a conspiratorial wink. "With all the booze and whores around, I assumed you wouldn't mind a brief demonstration."

Stiva's eyes narrowed. He reached into his jacket, retrieving an enamelled cigarette box. "Really, Andrew? You expect us to comply with this farce?"

Andrew's smug smile faltered slightly, but he didn't back down. "It's not a request, Stiva. It's an order."

"I don't take orders from a servant," Stiva hissed, snapping his fingers at his companion to light his cigarette.

The raven-haired woman reached for the lighter and turned back to Stiva, gracing him with a smile. It was a smile stretched too thin, a brittle facade, fraying at the edges, betraying the fear that lurked underneath. Reaching out, the woman held the flame to the tip of Stiva's cigarette, but her hand trembled so violently that she failed to light it. For a moment, Sophie saw a hint of that terrible gathering wrath in Stiva's eyes that she had glimpsed before, and it seemed the woman saw it too because her lips parted, and the beginning of a whispered apology seemed to fall from her lips—but the anger in Stiva's eyes suddenly boiled over.

His hand cracked across her face, striking her so hard that her head snapped to the side and her diamond choker slipped up her neck. For a brief instant, Sophie saw the bruises that her jewellery had concealed—deep, mottled lines encircling her neck, as if she had been violently strangled almost to the brink of death.

Instinctively, Sophie reached out to steady her, but Zorin's hand stopped her with a fleeting touch when he felt her stir.

Sophie's eyes shifted to Zorin.

Zorin's eyes were fixed on the woman crouching at his feet—wiping the blood off her face as she picked up the lighter. At that moment—as his attention was entirely absorbed by the scene before him—Sophie saw something in Zorin's eyes: revulsion, bitterness, anger. The moment was so brief that it went almost unnoticed. But she had seen it. And then the mask slid back on, and there was nothing to be seen all.

Stiva was about to lash out again, but right in that moment Zorin reached for his whiskey—his outstretched arm now blocking the path between Stiva and the raven-haired woman.

The rage in Stiva's eyes flasher brighter, while Andrew looked on with something like a sickening delight. But before either of them could act, Zorin reached out, tipping the woman's chin up to look at her.

"I hear your pet was a Bolshoi dancer, Stiva," Zorin remarked, his eyes fixed on the woman's face. "Let her entertain us while we deal with less pleasant things. It will make this spectacle more bearable."

"Oh, Katya is glorious on stage," Stiva laughed softly, mirthlessly, then he flicked his fingers and said something in Russian.

In answer to his command, Katya gave a nod and went to take the dancer's place on the pole—and Sophie could almost feel the sigh of relief she breathed.

In fact, she did feel it, because the exhale was mirrored—though almost imperceptibly—by Zorin. And in that moment, Sophie understood what he had done: Under the guise of that cruel, sadistic demand, Zorin had given Katya a brief reprieve—removing her from Stiva's side, to shield her, for a few fleeting moments, from the physical danger of his wrath.

That small mercy was all Alexei Zorin was able to give—all he could do for her.

But he *had* done it.

And he had done it without anyone noticing. Not even Katya.

Sophie looked at Zorin, searching for answers.

Everything about this man was an illusion. His name, his life, everything about him was a lie. How much of what he had said and done to her had been a lie too?

In this world, Zorin held all the power, and she none. And yet, he hadn't made any attempt to consume their twisted relationship. There were no needle punches in her arms, no ligature marks on her neck, just the quiet terror of his words—of threatened punishment never seen through.

Who are you? Who are you really?

Andrew's words pulled Sophie from her thoughts. "Now, let's get this over with." Raising his hand, Andrew summoned two women to their table—their expressions empty, their eyelids heavy from drugs. "If you would be so kind, gentlemen, my friends here will help you."

In the shadows, Ivan's bodyguard, who had been lingering silently beside the table until now, seemed to catch the hint; he pushed himself upright, alert now.

One of the women walked up to Stiva and kissed him, the other slid onto Zorin's lap. With a vacant smile, she ran her lips down his neck and her hands up his chest—all the way up to the collar.

Sophie felt a thrill of fear. If she opened that shirt, Alexei Zorin was a dead man. And no matter if she was right or wrong about him, if Alexei Zorin died here, she would lose her only leverage, and thus her only hope of ever escaping this hell.

And so, in direct, terrible consequence, she would have to risk everything now, for a man she barely knew—balancing her life and freedom on the edge of a knife.

CHAPTER XXII

Isola di San Clemente, Venice, Italy
Tuesday, 2nd July, 21:01

Fear and apprehension made Sophie's focus narrow, and her vision taper to a single focal point: Alexei Zorin.

She acted on instinct. Moving with all the lasciviousness she could muster, Sophie shifted closer to Zorin, inserting herself between him and the other woman like some jealous concubine. Her body pressed against his, her hand coyly plucking at his shirt buttons. As Sophie moved towards him, their eyes met for just a fraction of a second—a silent understanding, a devil's pact—then she closed her eyes and kissed the side of his neck.

Zorin accepted this intervention fluidly.

"I want to sample my new toy," Zorin said, twisting his fingers in the brunette's hair and bending her head back. For a moment, he held her like this, then he let go. "Get lost."

Andrew didn't object. Apparently, he didn't care who stripped Zorin down, as long as it was done.

Sophie felt her heart race. It was one thing to plan, to strategise, to talk of danger in the abstract; it was quite another to stare it in the face. But there was no turning back now.

Sophie slid on Zorin's lap and let her lips trail along his. He tasted of whisky—smoky, heady, intoxicating. For a moment she let the kiss linger, steeling herself for the act, then she began to unbutton his shirt all the way down to his waistline. When her hands reached his waist, Sophie paused, then, slowly, she parted the fabric, easing it aside just enough to expose Zorin's toned torso while concealing the one place he could not afford to show.

It wasn't enough. Not for Andrew.

"Go on."

Sophie didn't hesitate, because hesitation meant suspicion, and suspicion was the one thing she could not afford to raise.

Her heart pounded so hard she was sure Andrew could hear it. Yet outwardly, she forced herself to remain calm.

Tremulously, Sophie let her hands slide inside Zorin's shirt—over his chest and all the way up to his shoulder. She felt his hot flesh under her fingertips, and then the smooth surface of a surgical plaster, applied over a spot just below his collarbone—the very same spot where she had seen that conspicuous speck of blood on his shirt. She placed her hand over the plaster, her fingertips cold like ice as they touched the heated flesh. And then, very gently, she pressed her palm flat over the plaster, covering it with her hand.

This was it. The moment of truth.

She met Zorin's eyes. For a beat they were both motionless, neither speaking nor moving as they held each other's gaze, then Zorin shifted a little towards her and let his jacket and shirt slip off his shoulders.

Under her fingertips, Sophie felt Zorin's heartbeat—a steady, measured thump that astonished her with its calm. Yet beneath the slow, almost lazy tempo, a rigid tension coiled in his muscles, poised to unleash lethal speed at the slightest provocation. An image flashed in her mind: the swift, effortless way he'd pinned her wrists in the car the moment she'd even grazed his gun. Zorin could kill in the space of a breath, and Sophie realised that now, with Andrew hovering over them, he was prepared to do so again. If anything went wrong, she'd see exactly how little effort it took for him to act.

The Scot leaned closer, his eyes glued on Zorin's chest. If Andrew ordered her to move, if he physically reached for Zorin to inspect further, it would be over. At this point their fate, Zorin and hers, had become inexorably tied—and if he died, so would she.

And it was only now that the possibility of death fully entered her mind and it made her heart race with a force she was sure Zorin could feel.

Andrew moved a little towards her, his eyes shifting to her hand and Sophie felt her blood run cold. She couldn't give Andrew time to focus on her hand and think about what lay beneath. She caught Zorin's eyes, and then she pressed her lips against his in a long, languid kiss. Zorin responded at once, leaning into the kiss with ease, as his palm slid up her spine in a show of lazy possession.

It was a deliberately indulgent display, an almost mocking demonstration of Zorin's innocence.

Even in the shifting half-light, Sophie noticed how Andrew's complexion turned pallid, almost translucent at the sight of Zorin's chest. He'd evidently expected open proof of Zorin's guilt. Instead, he found nothing.

At that moment, Sophie could sense how torn Andrew was: The logic that had brought him here screamed for him to check more closely, while sheer self-preservation warned him not to cross a line from which he might not return if Zorin proved himself innocent.

Out of the corner of her eye, Sophie noticed Stiva, watching with detached interest. She wondered if he was weighing whether to egg Andrew on or let him hang himself.

Slowly, Zorin broke the kiss, and for the fraction of a second, she felt the quiver in his breath, so subtle, so brief that she noticed it only because she *felt* it—the ghost of fear, or maybe relief.

So for all his lethal skill, Mercury too, could be rattled.

"Disappointed, Andrew?" Zorin asked, his lips still lingering on hers, watching her with a half-lidded gaze.

Beads of perspiration were forming on Andrew's brow and his eyes wandered briefly to Stiva—searching his chest and finding nothing there—then back to Zorin.

A muscle in Andrew's cheek twitched. And Sophie could almost see the exact moment, when Andrew lost the nerve to pursue his suspicion any further.

"I misjudged the situation, Alexei. I do apologise," Andrew whispered, shifting away from Zorin and her, as if to allow a safer distance between them.

Zorin gave a pensive nod as he slipped his shirt back on. "Oh, we all misjudge a situation sometimes, and then we end up thoroughly surprised."

Zorin's eyes shifted to her, and somehow, Sophie felt that his words had been meant for her rather than Andrew. For a moment, Zorin held her gaze and then motioned for her to button up his shirt.

Sophie reached out and as her hands moved down his chest, she felt the burden that they now shared with a grim acuteness: They were both playing a role and neither of them could walk off stage, not while the audience was watching. She would have to play her part until the bitter end, and so would the man she had just saved.

"The evidence seemed conclusive. Everything added up."

"Oh Andrew, I suggest next time you check your intel more thoroughly." Zorin paused, his lips curling into an evil little smile. "Because one might be tempted to think that your errors aren't quite the careless mistakes they appear to be. And we both know what happens to traitors, don't we?"

Sophie tensed. With Zorin's sudden exoneration, the power structure had sprung back into balance—casting Andrew once more in the role of the impertinent servant and Alexei Zorin in that of the displeased master. And Sophie had no doubt that Zorin would now wield that power to its fullest extent.

Shrugging on his jacket, Zorin motioned for her to get up and out of his way.

Sophie scrambled to her feet, as Zorin began to rise slowly from his armchair, like some great unfurling predator.

Andrew, sensing the danger, stammered some mumbled apology.

"Oh, Andrew, spare me your rambling explanations," Zorin said, his voice deceptively soft.

"Please."

"Only the guilty beg like that. Are you guilty, Andrew?"

"I'm not guilty of anything."

"Really? Then how come that got away in Paris with nothing but a scratch?" Zorin took a step towards Andrew. "Or did Mercury allow you to slip away?"

"I'm not a traitor."

"Really? I hear Moscow thinks differently. They think their man is a traitor and that suspicion is—in part—fuelled by the fact that he bungled the kind of shot that a fine marksman shouldn't bungle." Zorin smiled a mirthless smile. "Did he let you slip away, Andrew?"

Andrew blanched and shook his head, his eyes wide as he watched Zorin, whose eyes now went to Ivan's bodyguard.

"No, please, it wasn't me! Please," Andrew pleaded, turning to Ivan's bodyguard, who was stepping away from the table.

"It is said that the guilty proclaim their innocence often and loudly," Zorin remarked, his voice very soft now—terrifyingly calm. "Tell me, my friend, are you working both sides of the street, playing the Tsar's eager jester by day and his Majesty's loyal lapdog by night?"

Andrew blanched, fear flickering in his eyes. "I would never betray you, Alexei. I swear, it's the truth."

"The truth is rarely pure and never simple. Isn't that what your great British poets say?"

Andrew's eyes widened, staring at Zorin, then he glanced back at Ivan, who held court at the far side of the room.

Ivan's bodyguard had returned to his master's side, stooping over Ivan's shoulder and whispering into his ear. Ivan's shallow, slate-grey eyes shifted across the room to Zorin, whom he acknowledged with a vague but gracious nod of the head as if to acknowledge his exoneration, and then to Andrew. For a moment, Ivan simply watched his informant, then, with a calm expression, Ivan raised his glass, drained the last gulp, then, in a single economical gesture, turned it upside down on the table.

A small gesture but one of finality: the sound of a door slamming. A death sentence.

Zorin had seen it too. For a moment, he held Ivan's gaze, waiting for his nod. And as the silent permission was granted, Zorin moved his hand—a barely perceptible flick of the wrist. Instantly, two black-clad guards materialised from the edges of the room, closing ranks around the suddenly stricken Andrew.

"No, please," Andrew pleaded, his voice trembling as the guards grabbed his arms. "I had Ivan's permission to do this. Please, don't do this."

Zorin laughed softly. "We'll have enough time for that, Andrew. Save your breath for now." Briefly, Zorin held Andrew's gaze, as if to make sure the message had sunk in, then he dismissed the guards with a vague flick of his hand. "Take him away."

Flanked by two guards, Andrew was frogmarched out of the room. Caught in the inexorable current of Zorin's displeasure, he seemed to shrink with each step. Before Zorin's henchmen could muscle him out of the door, there was a brief exchange, Andrew's voice rising in a question or perhaps a plea, swiftly quashed by a sharp gesture from one of the henchmen. The words were lost to the distance, but the tone was unmistakable—a man bargaining in the face of dwindling options.

Zorin snapped his fingers, calling her to his side. And suddenly, the terror returned. Had she been mistaken about him? Would he silence her, now that she knew the truth?

As if he had sensed her fears, Zorin glanced at her. Their eyes met, and for a fraction of a second, he let her see through his mask. And that fleeting moment of truth was all she needed.

She wasn't alone.

She had never been.

Zorin held her gaze for another beat, then he reprised his grim role, turning his attention to Stiva.

"Forgive me for leaving early, Stiva," Zorin said. "But as you can see, there are matters that warrant my attention."

CHAPTER XXIII

Isola di San Clemente, Venice, Italy
Tuesday, 2nd July, 21:26

A butler escorted them back to Zorin's quarters. As they walked down the gallery, Sophie instinctively glanced at the windows, observing Zorin's reflection in the glass. He was undeniably handsome—regal and alluring—but the darkness beneath his perfect veneer was terrifying. It wasn't just Zorin's darkness she saw, but that of the man behind the mask—the man who had taken a dozen lives in a single night and who would take another soon, once he was done with her.

Without a word, they stepped into Zorin's suite. The butler left and closed the door as he went.

"Let's play," Zorin said, stepping closer, his eyes warning her to stick to her act.

Holding her gaze, he slowly ran his thumb along the line of her lip—and for a fraction of a second, his eyes shifted upwards, to the crown moulding, then back. Sophie followed his gaze. There, barely perceptible in the gloom, she saw the faint glint of a lens concealed in the pedicel of a marble acanthus leaf.

Cameras.

Sophie felt herself shiver.

Ivan's all-seeing eye was fixed on Zorin and this was why her captor's mask had never slipped, not even in private. And it would not slip now. Whatever would happen between them tonight, Alexei Zorin was bound to his act—and all it entailed. And so was she.

Their eyes met again.

For a moment, he held her gaze, then Zorin closed the distance between them, his lips brushing her temple, then her cheek, before finding her mouth in a gentle kiss—barely more than a brush of his lips against hers.

She felt the promise that lingered in his touch, that he would keep her safe—that the seeming and the being would be two different worlds.

For a brief moment, Sophie hesitated, then she leaned into the kiss, her arms wrapping around his neck as she sealed their silent pact. And then he moved one hand to her waist, guiding her backwards, his other hand finding the zip of her dress, slowly pulling it down. The silk slid off her shoulders and pooled at her feet.

And as the fabric fell, his hands moved to her wrists, lifting her arms above her head, walking her backwards another step, and then one more, until her back was pressed against the doorframe, her wrists pinned above her head.

Breaking their kiss, he caught her eye, his expression warning her to stick to her act. Then he released her hands and ran his lips down her neck, over her sternum, and—dropping to one knee—all the way down to her hip. His lips felt cool and firm on her skin, his touch sending a tingling sensation down the back of her legs. As he moved lower, running his right hand along the inside of her thigh, his other hand subtly brushed over some indistinct spot on the doorframe—as if searching for something that had been there but no longer was.

Briefly, his lips lingered motionless on her skin—as if he needed a moment to collect himself—then they moved back up, retracing their path along her body all the way up to her neck. And then, in one swift, effortless motion, he scooped her up.

Instinctively, Sophie wrapped her legs around his waist, feeling the solid strength of his body beneath her, kissing him as he carried her through the rooms. For a moment, she lost herself in the kiss, and when she opened her eyes again, they had somehow ended up in the bathroom.

He stepped into the shower, fully clothed, never breaking the kiss, then reached over and turned on the water with a swift, decisive motion. The warm spray cascaded over her skin, creating a steamy haze around them. His body pressed firmly against hers, pinning her to the wall. For a moment, Zorin simply held her like this, then his hand closed in her hair and bent her head back. He ran his lips down her neck—placing soft, lingering kisses along her skin.

"The water will render our words indecipherable even to the very best of microphones," he murmured, his breath warm against her skin. "We don't have much time, so listen very carefully and keep in mind that we're being watched—so if you falter for even a moment, if you fail to maintain this act, they will know."

Sophie nodded.

"Who are you?" she whispered, her voice low and hushed against the sound of the water.

His lips moved to her shoulder, kissing her gently before he replied. "I'm here to take Ivan down," he whispered, avoiding the direct answer she sought.

"On orders of the Kremlin? Or someone else's?"

He hesitated for a moment, understanding her unspoken question, weighing his own response. "For the sake of justice."

His reply was a confirmation and a denial in one. She looked up at him, searching his eyes for the truth. Part of her wanted to trust him, the other was terrified of who she was facing. But in the end, did it even matter? It wasn't like she had a choice.

"Why am I here? Why did all of this happen?"

"The stains on your fingertips, it was *metka*. Spy dust," he whispered.

Sophie shook her head, not understanding. "What?"

"A chemical substance used to covertly track someone's movements. It was planted on you back in London, and you unwittingly marked me with it. Then, after you had fulfilled your purpose, you became... a liability."

For a fraction of a second, the image of her scar-faced guest flashed in Sophie's mind. She had served him drinks, cleared his table, handled his cash. He had half a dozen opportunities to plant the substance on her if he wanted. Briefly, she felt impotent despair well up inside of her.

"I overheard Ivan say that Moscow sent someone after you, because they doubt your loyalty. A scalp hunter."

"I know."

"It was the man with the scar, wasn't it?"

As if sensing her distress, Zorin pressed his lips against her temple. "By all I know, he's Russian counterintelligence."

"He's the one who sent me to Harper, to be sold..."

"I know. I tried to find you, but I was too late. And when I finally got to you, my options were limited."

Briefly, her mind returned to the conversation she had overheard between Frost and Zorin: *Someone was going to extraordinary lengths to save her. Someone with a lot of clout.*

So it had been Zorin after all.

"Will you help me get out of here?"

"Sophie, you've saved my life and I'll do everything in my power to get you out. But I can only do that if you play by the rules."

"What rules?"

"What I told you when I brought you here wasn't a joke or some kind of depraved game—I need you to stick to the role I've laid out for you. I need you to be silent and terrified to maintain my cover. There can't be any games like the one this morning. I won't be able to save you again."

"You won't have to."

He gave her a small smile. "I have no doubt of that." He paused for a brief moment, then said: "We have to finish this, Sophie."

"I know."

"I won't force you, Sophie. If you say no, I'll find a way."

Sophie knew that he was offering to let her slip away, that he was willing to take this risk for her sake. Briefly, she was tempted to accept his offer, but she would be a fool to risk their lives for some ridiculous high-minded notion that she couldn't climb into bed with a man she had just met. And there was more. Part of her wanted to kiss him now, not Alexei Zorin, but the man behind the mask—the handsome stranger, together with whom she had just stared down death and won.

Closing her eyes, she kissed him again, running her lips over his. "I'm ready."

Sophie could feel the change in him, as the mask slipped back on, and he once again reprised his sinister role.

They were stepping on stage together now, and their every move had to serve the illusion they were playing out. It wouldn't be an illusion of love, it would be a display of dominance—of ownership.

CHAPTER XXIV

Isola di San Clemente, Venice, Italy
Tuesday, 2nd July, 21:49

Soaking wet, they stepped into the bedroom, the water pooling at their feet with neither of them caring. He claimed her lips and, without breaking their kiss, he guided her to the fireplace, trapping her between the flames and his body. Sophie felt the heat against her back, its sheer intensity drying the water on her skin within moments.

Zorin stood motionless, towering over her, his presence all-consuming. Then he released her and, by instinct, Sophie stepped back, increasing the distance between them—as much as the fire behind her allowed. And as she moved, a slow, languid smile spread across his lips, as if her fear amused him.

"Why so frightened, Sophie? We haven't even begun to play." With the magician's easy grace, he slipped the thin-bladed knife from his sleeve. Its edge caught the firelight, reflecting it. "But maybe it's time to start."

She watched the blade, transfixed, as he tilted it towards her. Her skin prickled with anticipation, the promise of danger intoxicating and terrifying at once. And then she felt the touch of the knife on her neck, cool against the heat of her skin.

She closed her eyes.

Slowly, the blade moved downwards, its touch light as a feather, its seductive terror all-consuming. When he reached the neckline of her lace bodice, he paused, then he cut through the silk with one swift motion, severing the lacing so that its ends slipped through the hooks.

The corset fell, and then her thong.

His hand brushed against her thigh, his touch infinitely gentle, wordlessly asking for her trust, holding her in place, reminding her not to move. Not even by a hair's breadth.

And then the knife moved again, lower this time, tracing a path along her skin, never cutting but always close enough that she felt the danger. The edge hovered just above the place where she ached for his touch, a reminder of how much power he held—and how much of it she had given him.

"Look at me," he said softly.

She did.

The reflections of the crackling fire ran in red flames over his hard-cut features. The illusion was diabolical. And calculated. Zorin's evil mask, honed to perfection, flaunted with deliberation for the benefit of their invisible watchers.

"Don't fear, Sophie, we will start gently"—the knife traced one final, agonisingly gentle line over her skin—"and save the pain for later."

He sheathed the knife and her knees nearly buckled with the sudden loss of it sharp, teasing presence. Warmth flooded back into her skin, but the memory of the blade lingered, sharp and unrelenting.

He kissed her, fiercer this time, as if claiming all of her. For a brief moment, Sophie melted into the kiss, her hands finding their way to his chest. And as she leaned into his kiss, he chuckled very softly.

"So you're eager for this after all," he whispered against her lips.

He broke the kiss and circled her slowly, his fingers trailing down her arm before closing gently around her wrist. For a moment, he paused, just standing behind her, then he kissed the soft curve of her neck, while his left hand closed around her other wrist, pulling both arms together behind her back.

"You enjoy this, Sophie, don't you? You enjoy having no choice," he whispered, his grip tightening around her wrists—trapping her.

In that moment, the game took on a life of its own. The pretence slipped, and genuine fear took over. And with the fear came the memory—of hands that had gripped her like that, that had taken without asking, without caring. For a split second, the terror welled up, raw and unfiltered, threatening to consume her.

But then Zorin's lips, still close to her collarbone, moved up her neck, over the throbbing vein, as if savouring her fear—but the kiss he placed there was infinitely gentle, a silent reassurance. A quiet message that only she could feel.

She could stop this. Even now. If she needed to, he would find a way.

She didn't move.

Neither did he. He remained still, his body pressed against hers, but there was no menace in it. No force. He wasn't pushing her. He wasn't asking for her to pretend. He was simply waiting, allowing her to decide if she could trust him in that moment.

And something in his patient silence told her that he wasn't merely asking her to take a leap of faith, but that he was promising to hold her if she did.

She closed her eyes, her breath steadying, and she leaned back against him, her body seeking his warmth, his presence. It wasn't submission. It was trust. A quiet, fragile thing between them.

His lips lingered on her shoulder for a moment longer, giving her time to fall back into her act. Then he added, "Answer me, Sophie."

"Yes, I enjoy it," she murmured, her voice trembling slightly, as she fully embraced the role that their unseen audience expected of her.

Zorin laughed very softly—that terrible, soft, melodic laugh, nearly inaudible, and almost pleasant.

But the façade didn't matter anymore. She could separate them now, the seeming and the being.

Keeping her eyes closed, she allowed him to guide her away from the warmth of the fireplace, across the room. And all she felt was his lips on hers, his hands around her wrists, and then his touch on her back, gently guiding her upper body downward, bending her at the waist until her heated skin met the cool stone covering the ornate Baroque centre table.

The marble beneath her was unyielding, its chill a sharp counterpoint to the heat building between them. It made her pause, not just physically but inwardly.

She felt him pause, standing behind her now, his fingers tracing along her spine, slow and deliberate, as if marking each vertebra, each inch of skin.

There was no rush—just the steady awareness of what was unfolding, as his hands moved down her sides, slow, controlled, testing her limits, his touch lingering just long enough to make her wonder if he was waiting for her to resist.

"Spread your legs."

She felt his hand tighten around her wrists, holding her in place, letting her feel the imbalance of power, allowing their audience to see it too. Then he ran his hand up her thigh. His touch was soft, infinitely gentle and for a moment, the world shrank to that singular point of contact, her skin alive with sensation.

It wasn't just pleasure—it was something darker, something more raw.

He bent over her, gracing her neck with a gentle kiss. For a moment it wasn't the sadist that kissed her, but the man behind the mask, gentler, kinder, yet—in his own way—just as dark as the guise he had chosen for himself.

"Open your eyes, Sophie, and watch yourself."

She did. Ahead of her was the wall of French windows, running the length of the room and all the way up to the ceiling. In the firelight, the glass had become a mirror, one in which she could watch herself—prone, helpless, her body spread for the pleasure of a stranger.

But there was strength in that vulnerability. She wasn't afraid, because she had chosen it.

Their eyes met and caught in the reflection. A mute understanding. A devil's pact. The power, the vulnerability—it was shared now, a delicate balance that neither of them wanted to break.

He ran his hand up the inside of her thigh, all the way up, and a little further.

She yielded to his touch, accepting it, seeking it—her eyes always on her reflection, watching herself, her body so terribly naked against his clothed form.

Each thrust, each stroke offering a momentary escape, filling her with a forbidden pleasure that was as intense as it was fleeting. And then his touch pushed her over the edge. But even now, he didn't take pity on her. He kept driving her further, even as she came down from her high. And as he continued, she crossed an invisible threshold; where sweetness began to cloy, where pleasure and pain became one, feeding off one another.

She didn't pull away. She couldn't. She didn't want to.

Closing her eyes, Sophie gave herself over to the sensation, unable to stop, driven by a need that went beyond hunger, beyond reason. They moved along the edge together, always along that narrow line between pain and pleasure, where she could neither escape nor fully embrace either. Release, when it came, was raw, intense, empowering.

When Zorin finally released her, her body trembling from the exertion, she collapsed at his feet. And then her lover stepped away, leaving her—the sadist's toy—kneeling on the floor.

Exhausted, she leaned her forehead against the soft fabric of the divan. She closed her eyes, listening to his steps, to the crackle of the fire and the waves that beat melancholically against the rocky shore.

He spoke her name, very softly.

"Sophie."

She looked up. Zorin sat in an armchair, watching her with mocking satisfaction through half-closed lids.

There was an undeniable allure about him, a dark magnetism that was dangerously enticing. And right now, she longed to lose herself in it—craving the sweet oblivion his touch could offer.

He held out his hand. "Come here."

She rose, and he beckoned her to him until she stood close enough to touch. Slowly, he ran his hands up between her thighs and spread her legs. For a moment he made her wait like this, then he slid his hands around her hips and guided her down onto his lap. Holding his eye, Sophie undid his zip. He drew her close, sinking himself into her all the way and wringing a shuddering sigh from her lips.

He drew her closer and then she felt his hand—the hand that had snapped a man's neck—close around her throat. And in that moment, she wanted it, she wanted the danger, the darkness of their union.

"Come for me, Sophie."

She shuddered, her hands clenching into fists, her fingernails clawing at the tender flesh of her palms. Then her body convulsed, every inch of her skin tingling as if her nerves had been stripped raw. And she felt Zorin move against her, his faint hiss barely audible as he followed her over the edge.

Sophie closed her eyes and sank against his chest, listening to the steady beating of his heart and the waves. Moments passed, stretching to a lifetime. Then, as her breathing began to slow, she felt his hand slip beneath her hair, fingers brushing lightly against the nape of her neck, the movement hidden from Ivan's all-seeing mechanical eyes by the mass of her chestnut locks.

At first, his touch was so light she might have imagined it, but it lingered, just long enough for her to recognise what it was—a crack in the mask, a silent unravelling of the man in the shadows, asking her to see beyond the role he played.

In the quiet of that touch, she sensed his own unspoken need, for solace, for connection—for hope.

And Sophie realised that in his stillness, he wasn't merely holding her up—he was asking her to hold him too.

And then, just as subtly as it had begun, the moment passed. But the memory of his fingers lingered, not as a mark of control, but as something infinitely more complex.

Then the ormolu clock on the mantelpiece struck the hour and finally, Zorin released her, both of them slipping back into their roles.

Like a puppet on a string—deprived of the puppeteer's guiding hand—she slid to the floor at his feet and remained there with all the due submissiveness of her assumed role.

For a long time, she didn't move, not even look up, simply listening to him as he showered and changed, going about his business as if she didn't even exist.

"Get up."

She looked up at him.

Zorin was dressed once again in an immaculate white shirt, dark trousers, polished leather brogues, and if not for the gun holster around his shoulders and the tattoos on his hands, she would never have guessed what lurked beneath the polished veneer of her lover.

On the table behind him stood the safe deposit box that had been delivered earlier that day. It was open now. And the item that had been removed dangled between Zorin's fingers: a glistening string of diamonds, held together by an intricate clasp of stylised acanthus leaves—their delicate curves and lines interweaving to form the shape of a heart.

For a heartbeat, her eyes lingered on the breathtaking piece of jewellery, then she stood very slowly, painfully aware of her nakedness and her audience which consisted of more than just the man in this room.

"Turn around."

Sophie complied, doing as he asked. Then she felt Zorin step closer, brush the hair from her shoulders and drop the string of diamonds around her neck. The necklace felt oddly warm against her skin, unnaturally so, and Sophie realised whatever he had just given her was more than a piece of jewellery.

"Let me warn you, Sophie, if you take this off without my permission, I'll replace it with something more permanent."

CHAPTER XXV

Isola di San Clemente, Venice, Italy
Wednesday, 3rd July, 09:43

Sophie woke slowly, her limbs tangled in the linen bedsheets, the morning sunlight sneaking in through the windows. For a moment she just lay there, her fingers trailing up her arm, over her shoulder, to her neck. The same path his hand had trailed up to her neck. And it was as if her body still held the memory of that touch, so dark and yet so gentle, as though coaxing her skin back to life, inch by careful inch.

She should have been afraid. A part of her had been, but his touch had been so careful and patient, as if he understood the precarious balance she was teetering on—gently coaxing her through the darkness, letting her find pleasure she had thought was lost to her. And he had made her feel something she hadn't thought she'd ever feel again: trust.

And in a strange way, she was grateful for that night, grateful for what he had given her under the guise of darkness.

Her eyes drifted towards the window, beyond which the water shimmered, and she wondered for a fleeting moment what it cost him to maintain the façade—hold it up, night after night?

The question crept in, sharp-edged and unwelcome, but she pushed it away, because she didn't want to confront the question.

Not yet.

Slowly, Sophie untangled herself from the delicate linen bedsheets. For moment she was tempted to cover herself in a sheet but didn't dare to do so lest it arouse the suspicion of her watchers. It didn't matter anyway, at this point there wasn't anything they hadn't already seen.

Forcing herself not to look up at the cameras, Sophie walked across the bedroom and boudoir to the bath. She showered quickly and pinned her wet hair into a bun, then returned to the spacious dressing room. Picking the least revealing item of clothing—a floor-length, linden green kimono with a red lining—she dressed. For a moment, she stood in front of the mirror, her eyes lingering on the necklace he had given her. Its weight suggested that the stones were real, but whatever held them together wasn't some precious metal—it was something else entirely.

Whatever he had given her, it wasn't just a necklace. Far from it. But she wouldn't solve its secret right now, and she didn't want to draw the attention of her unseen watchers to the necklace by studying it too closely.

No, for now, it's secret would have to wait.

She left the bedroom, walked along the spacious sunlit gallery to the reception room that formed the linchpin of Zorin's quarters. As she stepped into the sun-drenched space, the ormolu clock on the mantelpiece chimed the hour. It was already ten o'clock.

She folded herself into a low *chaise lounge* and picked up a neatly folded copy of the Financial Times from the table beside it.

The date below the title claimed that it was Wednesday, the 3rd of July. Under normal circumstances, she would have sat in her comparative politics seminar, discussing the merits of one or the other governance system and then, perhaps later in the day, she would have joked about some of that with Gabriel.

Gabriel's name surfaced uninvited, like a half-forgotten tune, but it no longer resonated the way it once had.

Sitting here, draped in clothes that weren't her own, with her every move observed by unseen eyes, she felt Gabriel's world slip further away. It was a world she would probably never return to. And then there was Alexei Zorin—a man who held power over her in ways Gabriel never could. The thought should have unsettled her, and yet it didn't. Not as much as it should have.

Forcing the troubling thought from her mind, she let her gaze trail the length of the room—along the walls lined by masterpieces that bore the hallmark brushstrokes of Renoir, Degas and Monet, over the marble pilasters, all the way to the windows, beyond which lay the emerald expanse of the Venetian lagoon. In the distance, she could see two helicopters heading out of the bay towards the open sea.

Indulging her idle curiosity, Sophie rose and went to the window. Squinting her eyes against the sun, she pressed her forehead to the cool glass and watched the helicopters fly in a close formation. For a moment, Sophie wondered what sinister business they pursued, then—knowing that she would never find out—she turned away and ambled along the window front, running her fingertips over the horizontal transom, and relishing its coolness against her skin. Then, stretching her taut limbs, she turned left and stepped through the open door into Zorin's private study.

The study, with its *Empire* writing desk, high bookshelves and carefully arranged flower bouquets looked unused. The only sign that Zorin had ever been here was the all too familiar blue-backed book that lay on a sideboard.

Hesitantly, Sophie let her hand run over the small volume, wondering again why Zorin kept the shabby edition of Pushkin's works. She was sure that it wasn't a keepsake, neither Zorin nor the man behind his evil mask would risk openly displaying this kind of emotional attachment.

Before her mind could dwell any longer on the issue, she heard voices in the forecourt. Harsh and clipped. Bellowing commands.

She stepped to the window. Ivan's black-clad bodyguards escorted a man towards the building, their pace brisk and unyielding, the steps synchronised as if marching to a silent tune. The man's hands were bound behind his back and a black hood had been drawn over his head, but there was something familiar about him. And as they muscled him up the sprawling exterior staircase just below her window, the sun flashed off the prisoner's cufflink, running over it in a playful cascade.

She stepped closer to the window, drawn to the scene and at that moment, a door was opened somewhere behind her in the suite, then brisk footsteps and voices echoed through the room.

No.

She recognised the voices—they were the same ones that had so casually discussed purchasing weapons of wholesale destruction on her first night here: Cavendish and Kirov along with their sinister overlord and the man who had become her unlikely ally.

"It seems Andrew has been feeding us lies—deliberately deflecting attention from the Kremlin's man by peddling us wild stories," Zorin said derisively, the disgust in his voice unmistakable.

"Good old Andy, I really didn't think he had it in him," Ivan replied. "But be that as it may, I've obtained new intel that might shed light on who we're dealing with. It's from a source inside Russian intelligence. Someone with... unprecedented access. My source tried to find out more about Mercury, but with limited results. The man is a ghost. There is no name, no face, no fingerprints. All that exists is... anecdotal evidence. But even that makes for a fascinating tale." Ivan paused, then continued.

"Mercury is what we may want to call the new model of the Russian spy, not some common leg man sent out to pull the trigger and eliminate whatever target the Kremlin dictates, but a man capable of holding himself on the world stage. There are rumours that he was educated at Oxford or Cambridge, PhD, subsequently worked as a staffer to the Russian president, either as a foreign affairs or defence specialist, then some time in the diplomatic service. After that, a two-year gap in which he is unaccounted for— possibly to undergo specialised military training, but we don't know. Then he begins popping up on the grid again: Paris, Berlin, Damascus, Washington, Istanbul, Tripoli, London and half a dozen countries in Sub-Saharan Africa. All the cosy spots. The traces he leaves are subtle, easily overlooked, but the results are... devastating. Unexpected electoral outcomes, destabilised governments, even the occasional coup d'état. It all happens very smoothly. No large-scale bloodshed. No war. Everything takes place in the backrooms of power."

"Is there any way to identify him?" Kirov asked.

"Maybe," Ivan replied. "You see, the Russian military attaché died in a car crash a couple of days ago. Apparently, his vehicle was forced off the road in the middle of Rome. Nasty accident. He's going to be buried in a closed coffin." Ivan laughed softly, mirthlessly. "But his... legacy will outshine him." There was a pause, the rustle of fabric, as if someone reached into his jacket to retrieve something. "You see, he was carrying this: Mercury's unredacted service file."

"You have a name?" Kirov asked.

"Not yet. The file needs to be decrypted first. And, as of now, I don't have the right resources to make that happen. But I'll find them."

Zorin, who had remained silent until now, finally spoke. His voice was calm, measured, betraying none of the tension he surely must have felt. "Ivan, if this is truly an inside job and not some wild story made up by Andrew, then we need to proceed carefully. A knee-jerk reaction could tip our hand."

"Are you offering to find the traitor, Alexei?" Ivan asked.

"I am."

"Very well, Alexei Alexandrovich," Ivan replied, his voice coming closer to the door—and the spot where Sophie was hiding. "You better not disappoint me then."

Holding her breath, Sophie carefully shifted closer to the wall. As she moved, the crisp silk of her dressing gown rustled, the sound was almost inaudible, but enough to catch the attention of men whose vocation had sharpened their senses to an almost superhuman level.

It was Ivan's voice that broke the silence. "I think we have a guest."

PART TWO
Alexei Alexandrovich Zorin

CHAPTER XXVI

Isola di San Clemente, Venice, Italy
Wednesday, 3rd July, 10:16

Alexei entered the sunlit study, his footsteps soft against the marble floor. The weight of his gun felt familiar, yet uncomfortable. He hated aiming a live weapon without lethal intent, but Ivan's presence demanded a show.

Alexei raised the weapon smoothly, finger firmly on the trigger guard, the barrel trained on Sophie, who stood by the bay window, bathed in morning light.

For a fleeting moment, she was merely a figure of light, an exquisite illusion far beyond his reach. But then the sharp metallic click of him chambering a round shattered the fantasy.

She turned sharply at the sound, her breath catching as she saw the gun pointed at her. A flicker of fear crossed her face—real, involuntary—before her dark eyes met his, steadying.

And there it was again. Trust. Fragile. A tether between them.

For a moment, they held each other's gaze, then Alexei lowered his gun and nodded to the door. "Get out, I'll deal with you later."

"Let her stay," Ivan's voice was velvet, deadly, slithering into the room before its owner.

In his mind, Alexei emitted a string of obscenities. But not even his crude and entirely silent outburst could change what was about to happen now. He would have to deal with this. They both would have to.

Stepping back, Alexei slid the Glock into his shoulder holster and turned around.

"I almost forgot about your little friend, Alexei," Ivan remarked, his grey eyes holding a kind of detached amusement, as though the world were an elaborate joke that only he understood.

"She's of no consequence," Alexei interjected smoothly. "A trivial distraction."

Ivan stepped towards Sophie, while Kirov and Cavendish filed into the room behind him, carefully staying in the background—quietly watching the drama unfolding before their eyes while making sure they did not get caught up in it.

"Quite a distraction indeed," Ivan remarked, running a finger along the line of Sophie's jaw—gently, though Alexei knew all too well that this gentle touch could turn into something else in a heartbeat—something that left bruises, something that could kill.

For a moment, Ivan looked her over with a critical eye, then his overlord's gaze fixed on the necklace, his eyes lingering just a fraction too long, as if he weren't simply admiring a piece of jewellery, but studying it intently—annotating, memorising and cataloguing its every detail for later use.

Alexei felt a trickle of unease run down his spine. If Ivan discovered its secret, it would be over.

"You have expensive taste," the Tsar remarked, his voice smooth and almost pleasant.

Sophie shifted slightly, lowering her eyes and then her head as though afraid, but there was steel in the set of her shoulders, in the way her gaze never faltered under Ivan's relentless stare. And then she turned her head a little to the side, letting her magnificent dark hair spill over her shoulder, the lush waves falling like a curtain of silk over the precious piece of jewellery around her neck.

It was a small gesture, unremarkable to anyone who wasn't paying attention. But Alexei was paying attention.

So his fair companion had sensed the truth, guessed that the seemingly innocuous piece of jewellery was more than it seemed to be, and now she was taking every possible step to prevent Ivan from discovering its secret.

"It really is quite remarkable," the Tsar remarked, tapping one elegant finger at the necklace, then looking at Sophie. "And you are quite exceptional too, I hear. Politics at SOAS and *Sciences Po*, Columbia before that and on a Marshall Scholarship no less. Awarded to intellectually distinguished students, isn't it? Your parents back in New York must be very proud. Tell me, do they approve of you moonlighting as a waitress?"

The words at once put Alexei on his guard; Ivan had looked much more closely into Sophie's background than he had anticipated—and something told him that his own ill-fated search for her wasn't the only cause for that inexplicable fit of curiosity. Ivan felt that something was off, and he was following his bloodhound instincts.

Sophie shook her head, her face deathly pale, but that determined line of her shoulders still intact. "No, they don't."

Ivan chuckled, a low, mirthless sound.

"Don't worry, my dear, parents are like that. We all want the best for our children." Ivan smiled vaguely. "But enough of the past. What about the present? Do you enjoy *Alexei Alexandrovich's* hospitality?"

Sophie closed her eyes, her dark lashes trembling faintly. At that moment, Alexei saw it, the tear that began to form, the kind of tear that would never fall, just linger there as a vague trace of her distress until it was wiped away. But she did not wipe it away, she let it linger for a moment, and then she closed her eyes—a slow, deliberate blink, that made the salty liquid trickle down her left cheek.

The most dangerous tear ever shed.

Somewhere between deliberate act and actual fear.

A marvellous deception.

In that moment, the agent runner in him felt fascination, delight even. She was a diamond in the rough, and with time and training, she would become exceptional at the smoke and mirrors game.

Ivan watched her silently, enthralled by Sophie's reaction—the sadist delighting in the distress of his victim, so caught up in his lustful delight of the game, so sure of his absolute power over his defenceless victim, that he failed to see that he was being played.

And then Ivan mastered himself, quelling those dark desires that had momentarily clouded his judgement and blinded him to the truth.

Reaching out, the Tsar ran one slender finger over the cook of her arm and Alexei knew exactly what he was looking for. Needle punches.

"You're going soft," Ivan remarked almost reproachfully, as if any act of leniency constituted an unforgivable weakness.

Alexei cursed himself. In an ill-judged moment of forbearance, he had spared Sophie the most harrowing aspects of their shared act. But now it was too late for regrets, he would have to roll with this.

"You know me, Ivan, I don't need drugs to make my women pliable, I prefer to break them the old-fashioned way."

Sophie flinched, but just like the tear, her reaction was only a half-truth, a reaction rooted somewhere between act and deception.

"And I see you're making progress." Ivan paused for a moment, measuring Sophie with a hint of cruel amusement, then he looked at Alexei. "Can she keep her mouth shut?"

"She knows the rules and the consequences of breaking them," Alexei replied.

"Well, it seems that your... benefactor has great confidence in you," Ivan said softly, stepping a little closer to Sophie. "I wouldn't disappoint him if I were you. It never ends well." Ivan smiled. "The charming Admiral Mercer would attest to that. Unfortunately, dear old Andrew can't do so anymore. You see, he's lying downstairs, cold as a fish." Ivan suppressed a thespian sigh, as if Andrew had somehow overstepped the bounds of good taste by dying in his house. "Oh, he took such a long time to die. And it wasn't a pretty sight—covered in his own blood, piss and vomit, begging for mercy as he bled out on the floor. But I'm sure Alexei will tell you all about it."

Sophie looked at him, and this time, the horror Alexei saw in her eyes was real.

A tear hung in her darkened eyelash, trembled there briefly, then coursed down her cheek in a slow black rivulet. And at that moment, as the tear fell, Alexei saw himself through her eyes—her false dawn, the monster in knight's disguise.

And then her eyes met his. This time, there was genuine fear in her gaze, but beneath it lay resolve—and a quiet, unwavering trust. She saw the danger but trusted him, somehow, anyway.

But he didn't want any more of that dark fear to spill into her eyes. It was time to end this.

Alexei holstered his weapon and stepped towards the Tsar. "You're spoiling my toy, Ivan. She'll have no tears to shed tonight if you continue like that."

Ivan smiled, took a step back and turned to Alexei. "Well then, make sure that she doesn't become a liability for us."

For a split second, Ivan held Alexei's gaze, the warning in his grey eyes clear, then he strode out of the room, gesturing to the men by the door to follow him.

Alexei didn't turn to look after them. He kept his eyes on Sophie. She was white, her lip trembling, her pulse beating frantically against the delicate curve of her neck. She had survived the trial by fire, but now she was coming apart right in front of his eyes—and those of their faceless watchers—and if he didn't intervene now, that brief moment of weakness would kill them both.

CHAPTER XXVII

Isola di San Clemente, Venice, Italy
Wednesday, 3rd July, 10:33

Alexei glanced up at the cameras. There was no way of getting her out of here, but he could at least try to offer some comfort.

He picked up the blue book with one hand and placed his other tentatively on Sophie's back. She tensed under his touch but didn't resist the gentle pressure of his hand steering her out of the room.

Without once glancing up at the battery of cameras that followed their every step, Alexei navigated their way through the suite. In passing, he picked up the newspaper that had been carelessly abandoned on the chaise lounge, then he steered his charge through an arched doorway into the sun-drenched breakfast room.

With its domed ceiling, arc of French windows and spectacular view of the lagoon, the room was indeed a magnificent sight, but Alexei didn't care for beauty right now and he assumed neither did his companion.

He motioned to one of the chairs. "Make yourself comfortable."

Sophie obeyed without a word, settling mechanically in the chair that he had picked. Alexei sat down opposite her—his back to the wall, his eyes on the door. Leaning back, he placed the book and the newspaper on the table beside him, then focused his attention on Sophie: She sat motionless, her eyes downcast, her delicate fingers playing idly with the gold-plated teaspoon.

For a fraction of a second, Alexei's eyes went up to the crown moulding and the fish-eye lens that glistened there. Ivan's eye was everywhere, his mechanical sentries turning his rooms into a stage upon which he had to perpetually perform. There was no escape, he was bound to his act and so was the comfort he could offer. But right now, even the coldest of comforts was better than none.

Alexei reached for the silver teapot and poured a small measure of its searing contents into Sophie's cup. Without a word, Sophie picked it up and took a sip. The moment she tasted the concoction, her lips curled into a grimace of disgust. Her eyes scanned the table, undoubtedly in search of sugar, but there was none. This was a Russian household and although some faceless household authority had evidently decided to forgo the unwieldy samovar in favour of a classic silver pot, other traditions were adamantly upheld.

With a small smile, he reached for the cherry preserves.

"In Russia, we sweeten our tea with *varenye*. Black cherries." He dipped the curved silver spoon into the dark preserves and added a small measure of it to her tea. The sugary mass swirled through the blend, slowly turning its rich tawny hue to a vivid dark red. "Try."

Sophie followed his request with the same silent obedience as if it had been a command. But as the cup touched her lips, Alexei saw some of the tension fall away from her, almost as if the searing concoction had achieved what his words had failed to accomplish.

For a long moment she simply sat like this—eyes downcast, almost closed, her mind focused on that most trivial and mundane of tasks—then she set down the cup and looked up, her eyes staring out at the sea.

"Where are you from?" she asked, without looking at him.

The question caught Alexei by surprise, but deep down he understood what had sparked it. Circumstance had cast her at the mercy of a man who—by any standard—barely deserved the term. She needed something, just one thing, to make the monster a little more humane.

"St. Petersburg."

It was a lie. It was Zorin's home, not his. But the legend would serve his purpose just as well as the truth.

She smiled bitterly. "I heard it's beautiful."

"It is, especially now, during the summer," Alexei replied, watching her with care. It wasn't enough. He had to give her more. "You'll see it one day," he added gently.

Finally, Sophie's eyes shifted away from that indistinct point on the horizon to look at him.

Despite all the bluster, she had heard his message. His promise, that she would make it out of here alive.

She gave him a ghost of a smile, vague and fleeting, with a tinge of bitterness, but a smile all the same. And that smile was all he needed. It was a promise, a pact, a silent pledge of trust.

They would do this together.

Sophie held his gaze for a brief moment, then she turned back to the window. The sunlight caught the diamonds and for an instant Alexei saw the face of another—one with the same dark eyes and chestnut hair.

Natalia

The memory of her came unbidden, as it often did, and he let it wash over him, just for a moment. He could see her as clearly as if she were standing beside him—and for a moment, he could almost hear her voice, feel her spirit, the powerful force she had been.

The memory twisted something inside him, something cold and hard, something that had kept him alive this long. Natalia was gone, and her death had left scars, deep ones. Yet they weren't the kind that time could heal. They were the kind that festered, that demanded retribution.

He closed his eyes briefly, allowing the last traces of Natalia to fade, as they always did—slowly, reluctantly, like a shadow resisting the first light of dawn.

Alexei collected himself for a moment, then he reached for the blue book.

It was time to attend to the matters that had brought him here.

CHAPTER XXVIII

Isola di San Clemente, Venice, Italy
Wednesday, 3rd July, 10:49

Briefly, Alexei double-checked the date on his watch, then he opened the blue book and turned to page 37—the numerical counterpart of today's date. Swiftly, his eyes ran down the page to find the rotating cipher key that changed with each calendar day.

It took him a second to locate it, but for the benefit of his unseen audience, Alexei pretended to read a few more pages, then creased his brow and shut the book, as if he couldn't find it in him to continue Pushkin's tedious tale of the hellbent Cossack and his failed quest to topple the monarchy.

With a glance at Sophie, whose gaze was lost somewhere far out at sea, Alexei put the book aside and reached for the newspaper. He flipped through the pages with an almost ceremonial casualness, while his mind briefly strayed back in time, to that moment about thirty-six hours ago, when he had tossed the used burner phone—meticulously dismantled into its constituent parts of battery, SIM card, and body—into the dark waters of the Thames.

By now, his message—carefully disguised inside the SIM card—should have been retrieved from the bottom of the river, deciphered, processed and answered.

He skipped to the commodities section and there—in the bottom right corner—was the article he had been looking for.

Special Report

Slick Moves: How Russia Eludes Global Oil Sanctions

by Maxim Mikoyan

Mikoyan—in truth a Russian cryptologist and signals officer codenamed the Poet—had been Moscow's man inside a vast array of different news outlets. He wasn't there for intelligence gathering or to do in the ever-growing armada of uncomfortable journalists who poked crater-sized holes into the never-ending stream of disinformation and propaganda that the Kremlin's troll farms churned out, but to make sure that agents in the field received orders even if communication lines were broken.

Mikoyan had been run by an entire string of Russian spymasters, and when Alexei went into the field, Mikoyan became his creature. A loyal soldier. A friend. One on whom he could depend. One who shared his goals. And now, with every communication line severed, the Poet had sprung into action, dutifully sending the signal into the void, hoping that Alexei would pick it up.

And he had picked it up.

Swiftly Alexei extracted the encoded message from the article—as always, the first letter of each sentence—then he closed his eyes and using the key from the book, began the mental acrobatics of deciphering the message, substituting letter by letter according to a predetermined pattern.

The result made his pulse quicken.

Зеленый.

Green.

It was the 'all-clear'. They were ready.

Alexei felt the cold rush of battle wash over him. His plan had always been a long game, a series of moves and countermoves. And now, finally, the time had come.

The game was his.

And his alone.

His eyes went back to Sophie. She was still staring out at the sea, her dark eyes lingering on some indistinct point on the horizon. Even though she didn't know it, her freedom had just moved within her reach. Soon it would be in his power to let her go.

For a moment, Alexei wondered if she had someone to go back to. The idea was surprisingly unwelcome. But the thought was mercifully cut short by a gentle tap at the door.

Alexei looked up.

He wasn't expecting company.

Slipping the Glock from his shoulder holster, Alexei stood and turned to the door. Sophie's eyes widened, and she rose with him.

"Stay here, Sophie," he commanded.

She obeyed without protest, backing up against the wall. He walked over to the door and opened it with his left hand, the index finger of his right on the trigger guard, ready for the kill.

But the man outside wasn't a threat. At least not to him. He was one of Ivan's guards. One of his *Oprichniki*, named so after the black-clad bodyguards of Ivan *Grozny*.

"We have a situation, sir," the man said, standing at attention as if he were reporting to a superior in the field. "An intruder was caught in the lockdown perimeter of a safe house in Rome where *Ivan Sergeevich* was storing sensitive data for transfer. A flash drive we'd taken off the Russian military attaché in Rome. We don't know who he is, but he was trying to gain access to the premises. Security rounded him up a couple of hours ago and flew him here straight away. He's downstairs."

Alexei felt a shiver of unease run down his spine.

"I'll deal with the matter," Alexei said, slipping the Glock back into his holster.

The guard nodded and then barked a sharp command into an unseen microphone inside his jacket collar. Alexei could hear the guard's earpiece crackle to life as one of his men confirmed the order.

Alexei cast a quick glance back at Sophie, silently reassuring her that she would be safe, then he slipped out of the room, closed the door behind him and locked it by pressing his thumb to the biometric scanner. There was the faint sound of metal grating over metal and then a dull thud as the twelve deadbolts lodged themselves into place. She was a prisoner now, but at the same time, she would be safe from everyone else in this house.

Anyone apart from Ivan.

"This way please, sir," the guard said, motioning ahead.

Pushing Sophie from his mind, Alexei followed the *Oprichnik* across the marble gallery, through a narrow service door and down three flights of stairs into the labyrinthic bowels of Ivan's estate—twenty feet under the sea level.

For almost a minute, the guard walked him through a maze of concrete hallways with unadorned walls, cold fluorescent lightening and steel doors on either side. Finally, the man turned right and stopped in front of an armoured door with a numeric keypad.

The guard punched in the nine-digit code and the gate—nine inches of bomb-proof steel—slid open without a sound.

Dismissing Ivan's henchman with a flick of his wrist, Alexei stepped into the brightly illuminated holding cell.

It was a cramped space, with a concrete floor and walls covered with high-performance polycarbonate plates that served not only as acoustic isolation but protected against electronic surveillance of any kind.

Exhaling a long breath, Alexei centred himself, ensuring that his mind was ready for the task, then he shifted his eyes to the man who knelt on the bare concrete floor.

The prisoner's hands were tied behind his back, and someone had placed a black hood over his head. Walking around him, Alexei switched on one of the man-high spotlights, training its garish lights right onto the man's face. Then he pulled off the hood.

The moment Alexei saw the man's face—dark-eyed and framed by equally dark hair—he felt his blood run cold.

So he had been right.

Kirill.

Alexei stared at his fellow agent.

CHAPTER XXIX

Isola di San Clemente, Venice, Italy
Wednesday, 3rd July, 11:29

Kirill.

Alexei stared at his fellow agent. The man he had last seen in London, in the middle of the night, in the lobby of the Valmont Palace Hotel.

For four long years, Alexei had managed to remain in the shadows. But then something had changed. Someone had slipped. Or perhaps someone had been turned. Wherever the error had happened, and however small it had been, its consequences had been catastrophic: And now, that accursed flash drive with his background file was in Ivan's hands.

He was with his back to the wall.

And so, in the moment of need, Kirill—who had orchestrated their operations from the wings with an unwavering hand—was forced to step into the limelight. In a last-ditch attempt to avert their collective undoing, Kirill had attempted to recover the drive and condemned himself in the process. And now, Alexei's unredacted background file lay somewhere in the depths of Ivan's safe, just waiting to be decrypted. And if the Tsar managed to do so, all would be lost.

"What do we have on him?" Alexei asked the guard that was obviously in charge of the room.

Kirill didn't look up, but Alexei knew he had recognised his voice.

"Travelled to Italy on a British passport. Passport is fake. So is his background. Our source in Moscow ran his prints, and got a hit," the *Oprichniki* replied, stepping out of the corner.

"And?" Alexei asked harshly.

"Colonel Kirill Fyodorovich Orlov. Russian Military Intelligence Services. Ural 16 covert action team."

Alexei didn't react because he had been trained not to.

Moscow's *special services* were so eroded that, until recently, all they were capable of producing was a litany of high-profile failures. But Ural 16 had been created outside the rotten establishment, operating far beyond the periphery of recognised structures. Their section wasn't just classified as top secret, it was *Osobaya Papka*—special folder. It was a state secret of the highest order. It didn't exist. Nor did its operatives.

And yet, somehow, Kirill's information had been leaked.

Deliberately.

The question was how. And more importantly, by whom.

Briefly, the memory of the scar-faced man in London flashed in his mind. He was Russian counterintelligence. There was no doubt of it. But he was just a leg-man. The buck stopped with Colonel Nikolai Morozov. Whoever he was. And wherever he was hiding. But this whole mess seemed to have a very distinct fingerprint about it.

He could almost feel Moscow's breath on his neck.

They suspected him. But they didn't have enough to go on.

Not yet.

Alexei forced the thought from his mind. He would have to look into this later on. But housekeeping would have to wait for now, he had to deal with Kirill first.

They had to work through this together now, and communication, however rudimentary, was of the essence. Taking a deep breath, Alexei stepped past the wall of light and moved into Kirill's line of vision.

"Welcome to Venice, Colonel Orlov," Alexei said softly, establishing eye contact with Kirill. "Tell me, what brings you here, apart from the mild weather and the sights?"

Kirill didn't respond. And Alexei hadn't expected him to. The training of a Ural 16 operative was rigorous—Kirill would maintain dead silence no matter what horrors Alexei inflicted upon him.

"Colonel, I'm not in the habit of repeating myself."

Kirill didn't respond.

He was completely detached from what was happening here. His mind focused inward.

And Alexei found himself needing to summon that same detachment, to endure the unfolding events not as a friend leading a friend to unspeakable horrors, but as a player in a game of chess, cold, calculating, always thinking three moves ahead.

He exhaled a slow breath, centring himself and then, without taking his eyes off Kirill, Alexei motioned to the guards. They stepped forward and hauled Kirill to his feet.

The goal of torture was always to break the mind before the body. Torturer and subject would inch along the precipice step by step, always one foot over the void, until the victim tipped over the edge. At that moment, when the mind shattered, the subject would do whatever was necessary to escape the terror—they would confess to any crime, betray any secret, and utter any lie just to appease the torturer. Andrew had done it. Countless others before him had done it too.

But this time, Alexei had to make sure that neither body nor mind was shattered beyond repair. And if possible, he had to limit the damage in a way that would allow Kirill not only to escape, but to assist him in his plans.

Slowly, Alexei stepped around his second in command, inspecting him like a piece of meat. A skilled torturer, just like a skilled physician, understood the intricacies of human anatomy. The rules were clear now. No joints could be broken. Spine, skull, legs, and fingers were off-limits. As were the eyes. He had to deliver maximum effect with minimum damage.

Alexei gave Kirill a moment to brace himself, then he moved, driving his fist into his abdomen.

The colour drained from Kirill's face, but he made no sound. And Alexei knew what he felt now: The pain spreading in his body, the bile being forced up his throat, the fear taking hold of his mind.

Under torture, every man had the same instinctive set of reactions, it was natural—but there was one key difference between those who broke under torture and those who didn't: Resilience—the ability to close the mind to pain and fear.

The guards held Kirill upright, then they let go. He collapsed to the floor, gasping for air, drawing his knees towards his stomach as the pain shot through his body. The moment of weakness lasted only a heartbeat, then Kirill tried to rise, but Alexei placed a foot on his subject's neck, holding him down.

"Let's try again, Colonel. Why are you here?"

Kirill didn't respond.

Alexei slipped the Glock from his shoulder holster, his eyes shifting to Kirill's arm—to the point just above the elbow. He pulled the trigger.

The bullet pierced Kirill's flesh just a hair's breadth above his elbow. There was blood. A lot of it. Enough to cover up the fact that the bullet had missed the joint and had gone cleanly through the flesh instead.

Removing his foot from Kirill's neck, Alexei stepped back, watching as Kirill slowly rolled onto his stomach, his body trembling slightly from the pain. Alexei motioned to the guards. They hauled Kirill up to his knees once again, yanking his head up so that he stared right into the bright light.

They had been trained for this. But training, no matter how harsh, always fell short of the real thing. And Alexei had to be careful that, in his zeal to uphold his cover, he didn't inadvertently cross some line that tipped Kirill over the edge.

Holstering his weapon, Alexei turned to the table where Kirill's effects had been placed: A Glock pistol with an attached suppressor can, a knife and a pair of elegant platinum cufflinks.

He picked up the links and turned them between his fingers. The light flashed off them, and briefly, he saw a dark dot at the centre of the cuffs. To the unsuspecting onlooker, it seemed like nothing but a fancy design feature, but the well-informed observer would—if he looked closely—spot the truth. It was a listening device. Standard issue GRU surveillance equipment.

Usually, he would discreetly get rid of them. But maybe, just maybe, he could make use of their presence here later.

Alexei placed them back on the table, then reached for the Glock and inspected it carefully. Finding that there was nothing unusual about the weapon, Alexei placed it back on the table and reached for the blade.

Slowly he turned it in his hand. It was standard military issue, used across all branches of the *Spetsnaz*. Discreetly he let his hand trail over the metal pommel atop the handle. It was warm. Too warm. And he knew instantly what it was.

The knife wasn't just a weapon, it was a concealment device.

Made from graphene and tantalum carbide, the heat-resistant, highly durable material was two hundred times harder than the hardest steel and could withstand temperatures of up to four thousand degrees Celsius. Its staggering price tag meant that it was reserved exclusively for the protection of highly critical equipment in the field.

He turned back to Kirill.

"Now, Colonel, since we're done with the foreplay, let's start with the fun," Alexei said softly, tipping the blade softly against Kirill's throat.

Their eyes met. Alexei hoped that Kirill had understood the unspoken question that he hinted at with his gesture.

For a moment, Kirill hesitated, as if he wanted to make sure that they both meant the same thing. Then Kirill lowered his eyes. The answer was clear, confirming what Alexei had suspected.

The knife contained *Sokrovishche*. Treasure.

CHAPTER XXX

Isola di San Clemente, Venice, Italy
Wednesday, 3rd July, 17:39

Alexei walked along the lofty gallery that connected the two main wings of Ivan's estate. Beyond the wall of French windows, the late afternoon sun bloomed in the sky, casting its golden rays over the rugged coastline and reflecting on the dark blue waters of the sea beyond. Across the lagoon, the massive hull of Ivan's three-hundred-foot superyacht glittered in the water, a dinghy rocking gently in the waves beside its stern.

Though not apparent at first glance, the postcard idyll was an illusion. Ivan's island palace was a fortress, guarded by leagues of mercenaries and state-of-the-art military technology. It would take an army to get in—or out.

Even if Kirill hadn't just endured six hours of ceaseless torture, he would never escape from this place. His only chance to make it out alive was Alexei's ability to bring this mission to an end. Fast.

And he was just about to do that.

With a touch of wry amusement, Alexei's fingers tapped against the pommel of Kirill's combat knife.

Smooth and cunning as always, Kirill had delivered the treasure right into Alexei's hands. At first glance, the silver flash drive—so elegantly concealed inside the weapon's hilt—was an exact copy of the flash drive that Ivan had taken off the Russian military attaché in Rome. But unlike the device in the Tsar's possession, this one didn't contain Alexei's official background file, but a set of carefully forged documents: Documents, that in their entirety, told the story of a shunned and humiliated son, who had sold his own father to the Russian government in revenge for a demotion that relegated him to second place behind the man he hated most: Alexei Alexandrovich Zorin.

Stiva, already insecure enough in his position to spy on his father—and do so with Russian made spy gear that he had eagerly bought from Alexei's strawman—had laid the foundation to his own undoing. All Ivan's son needed was a little edging on to incriminate himself further.

And if Alexei played this right, he wouldn't only clear his own name but also besmirch Stiva's beyond repair. The Tsar's son would take the fall for him, and Stiva's ruin would be Alexei Zorin's stepping stone to ultimate power.

It was neat, elegant—or it should have been. But Kirill's capture and the discovery that the Kremlin was harbouring its own suspicions against him had added a new and entirely unwelcome dimension to the game. He would have to act fast now, or all his plans would come to nought.

Entering the reception hall, Alexei slipped the knife into the concealed holster on his forearm. However inconspicuous the blade might be, he didn't want it caught on camera. It would be foolish to risk it.

There was music from the palm court. Guests came like moths to the flame, while flocks of servants scurried about the place to welcome the arrivals.

He would have to improvise now. And he couldn't do it alone.

Alexei's eyes swept across the room, searching for Ivan's head butler and finding purchase a moment later. With a contemptuous flick of the wrist, he called him to his side.

"I have an addition to the guest list."

"Of course, sir. Who may I add?" he asked in his usual courteous and slightly grovelling tone.

Alexei measured the man for a second.

Ivan's butler was utterly loyal to his master and Ivan rewarded him handsomely for it. And this was exactly why Alexei had picked him. No one would ever question his actions. Ever.

Some time ago, Alexei had been forced to form a sordid back-alley alliance with a fellow agent from a less-than-friendly state. In the process, they had agreed on a series of emergency procedures and chosen Ivan's butler as their unwitting go-between or floater. And now, the time had come to pull the rip cord.

"Tom Frost. And make sure the boy knows what to wear."

The butler graced him with a tense smile. "Of course, sir. I will add Doctor Frost to your personal guest list right away and will inform him regarding the dress code."

Alexei felt the prickle of impending battle. Half his army was ready, now he had to take care of the other half.

"Good. Is she ready?"

"We have informed the lady that her presence is required tonight, and I believe she is already expecting your return. Would you like me to check, sir?"

"No, I'll take care of it. You can go."

Dismissing the butler with a contemptuous flick of the wrist, Alexei went to the staircase and turned his mind to the woman who would be an indispensable ingredient for tonight's illusion.

She would be the star of his show.

His crown jewel.

CHAPTER XXXI

Isola di San Clemente, Venice, Italy
Wednesday, 3rd July, 17:53

His suite's lavish foyer bloomed with the red light of the setting sun. Sophie sat at the end of a chaise longue and rose the moment Alexei stepped through the door.

She had changed into an elaborate evening dress of translucent white chiffon, which fell in flowing waves over her slender hips and gave out a soft rustle as she walked towards him. At that moment, she looked so much like Natalia that he felt himself pause.

Alexei forced the thought from his mind and his attention back on his companion. She was all that mattered now.

"I see you've been admiring the sunset," he remarked casually, stepping to the sideboard and pouring a small measure of sinfully dark whisky into Baccarat tumblers.

"I did."

Alexei handed her a glass—cut-crystal, eighteenth-century, worth its weight in gold. "Well then, Sophie, let me indulge you a little."

He placed one hand on the small of her back and guided her over to the French doors.

Ivan's home wasn't just a fortress, it was a prison. Every door and every window was designed to keep unwelcome visitors out and cherished guests inside. And Alexei knew all too well how quickly a bidden guest could become an unwitting prisoner.

He pressed his thumb to the biometric scanner and, as always, experienced a vague sensation of relief when the French doors unlocked with a faint sound.

Side by side they stepped out onto the rosy-coloured terrace. The air was warm, a gentle breeze stirring the surface of the surrounding waters, carrying the scent of salt and ancient stones. Before them, the red-tinted waters of the sea stretched to the horizon and blended into the sky as if the two were a single, interminable space. In the radiant light of the setting sun, the glistening bodies of the landing helicopters seemed to hover in the sky like moths over a fire—entirely unaware that the flames were about to consume them all.

Sauntering leisurely to the balustrade, he held up the whisky glass and twirled it between his fingers. The sunlight refracted a thousand times on the intricate cut crystal patterns and made the pinhole camera in the corner flash up.

Well then, his hawk-eyed audience was in for a nasty surprise.

"Come here, Sophie."

Sophie stepped closer to him and placed one hand on his chest. Their eyes met. Alexei lifted his hand to remove a strand of hair from over her eyes, then leaned down and kissed her, very gently, on the corner of her mouth.

She kissed him back.

For a moment they stood like this, waiting, probing, both not quite sure of the other, and then, as one, they crossed that invisible line—leaving the hesitancy behind.

Without breaking their kiss, Alexei guided her slowly in a circle, like mute dancers in a tight-knit embrace. And as he slowly trapped her against the balustrade, his focus shifted from the woman in his arms to the world around him—to the crashing of the waves, the sound of the music, the rustle of the breeze. He closed his eyes, feeling the wind on his skin—determining its speed and direction with the unfailing precision of the battle-tried marksman. It was strong enough. But only just. Under these conditions, his words—and hers—would be carried away by the breeze before any microphone could capture them.

His hand moved around her hip and hers followed his—and there in secret, their fingers locked. A silent pact.

"Sophie, I need you by my side tonight. You just need to be present, play your role as my... reluctant companion as it lies. You despise me. You fear me. You prefer any man in the room to me. Nothing more. I will do everything else."

"You can rely on me."

"I know, Sophie. You've proven that already."

For a moment they stood motionless, her hand resting on his chest, her lips lingering against his, sharing that secret embrace that had been denied to them before—that moment of solace, bestowed and received, that had been impossible before.

"It's time to appease the watchers, isn't it?" she murmured against his lips.

"It is."

She slid her arms around his neck. Her lips touched his cheek just below his ear.

"Then make me forget that they're here," she whispered and kissed him once more.

In that moment, he felt a spark of something familiar, something he hadn't felt for a very long time—a deep, stirring emotion he dared not name. Briefly, he allowed himself to be lost in the sensation, returning her kiss and then he mastered himself.

Slowly, deliberately, he let his hand slip into her hair, twisting his fingers in her locks as began to walk her across the terrace, and back inside, towards the chaise longue.

"Lie down," he said, his voice soft, just loud enough for their audience to pick up. "And I'll show you just how much pleasure can be found in surrender, Sophie."

She obeyed, reclining onto the ivory-coloured silk, her hair fanning out on the pillows. Alexei took a moment to admire her, the way her body seemed to glow in the twilight, every curve and contour accentuated by the fading light.

Kneeling at the foot of the chaise, he placed his hands on her ankles, feeling the smooth silk slide beneath his fingers. Slowly, he moved his hands upwards, over her calves, past her knees, parting the fabric as he went. The soft whisper of silk against skin was the only sound in the room.

For a moment, he held her like this, spread for him, vulnerable—a motionless, soundless act of dominance, crafted with care to appease their faceless watchers. And then he bent and placed a gentle kiss on the inside of her thigh—the lover's gift, one that could only be felt, but never seen, even if it was given in plain sight.

With deliberate slowness, he kissed his way up her body—savouring every inch of her, as her body arched towards him, begging for more without words. But Alexei was in no hurry. He wanted to draw out this moment for her pleasure, and his own.

His hands held her hips, anchoring her as he worked his way up, her skin like fire under his lips. When his mouth finally found that most intimate place, Sophie let out a soft moan, her hips rising to meet him. He wrapped his arms around her thighs, holding her in place as he began to pleasure her—exploring her in delicate, teasing strokes.

Alexei felt her body respond, the way her muscles tightened, the way her breaths came in short, ragged bursts. He could sense her nearing the edge, and he pushed her further, wanting to see her unravel beneath him—wanting to sate that dark, secret part of him that revelled in the power he held over her.

And then she shattered, her body arching towards him, as a shuddering breath fell from her lips. He felt the rush of her release, the way her body convulsed under his touch, the way she melted into the mattress as the waves of pleasure ebbed away.

He gave her no time to recover, drawing her towards him, and guiding her down to the floor. They sank to the floor, the marble cold and hard beneath them, the room filled with the heady mix of their breaths. Her white evening gown spread out around them, like the petals of a pristine white flower in full bloom. He knelt over her, capturing her lips in a kiss, letting her taste herself on his tongue.

Her hands found the buckle of his belt, sure, steady. He felt a rush of desire, a need to possess her completely. He helped her, his hands guiding hers, until his belt was undone.

He entered her with a slow, deliberate thrust, savouring the way her body enveloped him. She gasped, her hands clutching at his shoulders, her legs wrapping around him, pulling him closer. He moved with a steady rhythm, and she matched his pace, their bodies moving in perfect, intoxicating harmony.

For a brief moment, Alexei lost himself in the timeless, boundless space of their union, and in that fleeting space of time, the world outside ceased to exist, leaving only the two of them, entwined on the floor, their bodies moving in perfect harmony.

When they finally came apart, it was with a shuddering sigh, a release that left them breathless and spent, tangled in each other's arms, the room around them silent once more.

For a long moment, they lay there, entwined on the cool marble floor, the only sound the crackling of the candles and their slowing heartbeats. He looked at her—her face flushed, her eyes closed, her hair splayed across the floor—and felt the pain he had kept buried so deep within his soul that it had almost ceased to exist.

He closed his eyes and placed his lips on her shoulder with a shuddering breath. *You won't share her fate, Sophie. You will live.*

CHAPTER XXXII

Isola di San Clemente, Venice, Italy
Wednesday, 3rd July, 19:32

Standing in front of a tall Venetian mirror, Alexei reached for the black bow tie and slung it around his neck, tying it into an expert knot that any public-school boy would have been proud of. Then he shrugged on his tailored dinner jacket and closed the topmost button. He assessed the overall result in the mirror, ensuring that he would pass exactly for what he wanted to pass tonight: The ruthless, amoral wheeler-dealer of the underworld, with an insatiable hunger for money and power.

And in case anyone doubted who the man under the polished veneer really was, a brief glimpse at his hands would always remind them.

Almost instinctively, his eyes shifted to the sinister inkings.

The tattoos that covered his body were part of his chosen cover—stories of a life he never lived, etched into his flesh.

And to those fluent in the secret code of Russia's criminal underworld, they told a compelling story: there was the skull and reapers scythe branding him a killer, the crown and eagle symbolising his authority, the eight-pointed stars on his knees stating that he would never kneel to anyone, and the dragon winding its way around his arm, marking him a "shark"—a thief of state property.

And Colonel Alexei Alexandrovich Zorin had stolen from the state. A lot. Weapons. Billions worth of military equipment that he had sold across the globe to willing buyers before he was caught by the FSB, tried before a military tribunal and sentenced to life at a maximum-security prison.

The cover was perfect. While Ural 16 destroyed twenty-three billion rubles' worth of equipment at a covert site—all stuff he had supposedly pinched and sold—Alexei was flown out to a penal colony in the farthest corner of Russia's Far East, just on the Chinese border.

There, at Khabarovsk penal colony No. 6—lovingly nicknamed *Snezhinka* or Snowflake in Russian—he had spent more than a year forming ties with ranking members of the Twelve—polished, white-collar criminals grateful for the protection of the hard-edged Russian soldier capable of killing with his bare hands. But of course, he had to offer his prospective employers more than simply the skills of a petty criminal.

And Colonel Zorin had a lot to offer.

The orphaned son of a Russian sailor and a factory worker of Ingush descent, Zorin had attended Moscow State University with a stipend, studying politics and graduating top of his class. After that a skyrocketing career in the Russian military, all the way up to the position of strategic advisor to the Chief of the General Staff.

But Zorin had one great flaw: He didn't belong. He wasn't one of the elite. Worse, the Cossack's blood was tainted. And that Ingush heritage, and all that it stood for, meant that the gifted Colonel's path to power was forever curtailed by his descent.

Hence, it wasn't drink or gamble or any other common vice that compelled Alexei Zorin to slip into the world of crime—it was the lust for power and the bitter realisation that only in the underworld he could attain what he desired.

The cover was perfect, lovingly crafted and eagerly lapped up by his fellow jailbirds.

When he was finally sure that he had gained their trust and admiration, Alexei had orchestrated his escape—first to China—just a puddle jump across the border—then to Istanbul, Beirut and finally to Moscow.

Back in the Russian capital, Alexei approached the Twelve not only with a recommendation from his fellow inmates but with a multi-billion arms deal that encompassed pretty much everything from top-of-the-range weapons systems, cluster bombs, fighter jets and guidance systems to mid-range missiles—enough toys to start a war... or end one.

The deal was closed swiftly. While the weapons were delivered to his buyer who was struggling with the repercussions of a dubious electoral outcome, six billion US dollars found their way to offshore accounts in Panama and Guernsey, and from there through a series of shell companies to a squeaky-clean Luxembourg SICAV-SIF.

The tyrant's money had been Alexei's entrance ticket into the ranks of the Twelve.

But while his buyer—due to ill-luck and a small intervention on Alexei's part—never had the chance to deploy his weapons, Ivan Sergeevich Volkov welcomed Alexei into his inner circle with open arms—paving Zorin's way into a world where ambition was constrained only by merit and one's own moral boundaries.

Thus, blinded by Alexei Zorin's talent and complete lack of conscience, Ivan—perceptive, distrustful Ivan—had nurtured the viper in his bosom.

And soon you will pay the price, Ivan Sergeevich, Alexei thought, his eyes flickering to the reflection of the woman behind him.

She sat on a curule chair in front of a vanity, pinning her hair elegantly to the side while the soft light cast an almost ethereal glow on her pale face. She looked alluring and expensive, exactly as he had intended.

Unaware of his prying eyes, Sophie bent forward to slip on her shoes. As she moved, the necklace sparkled brilliantly in the light, two hundred million dollars' worth of diamonds clinking together with a faint sound of crystal glasses being clanked together.

Tonight, these stones and the woman who wore them would herald the downfall of the Twelve.

Tearing his eyes away from the mirror, Alexei reached for his wristwatch and slipped it on. Then—acutely aware of his hawk-eyed audience—he picked up the card deck and affected to give it a playful shuffle, like a man growing bored of waiting for his fair companion. And as he did so, he glanced over his shoulder at Sophie, thus rotating his upper body out of the camera's angle, while his hand, with one swift flick, whisked the marked card from the deck and secreted it in his cuff.

"That's enough, Sophie, it's time to go," he remarked coldly, casually tossing the remainder of the card deck on the table.

It was time to play.

CHAPTER XXXIII

Isola di San Clemente, Venice, Italy
Wednesday, 3rd July, 19:52

The distant din of voices echoed through the foyer. At the foot of the staircase, guests mingled freely.

Stepping closer to the balustrade, Alexei surveyed the scene, quickly, methodically, with the spy's sweeping gaze, trained to take in everything at once. There were many familiar faces: Russian oligarchs, American politicians, European industrialists, an entire delegation of the world's rich and powerful, herded together under the crystal chandeliers of Ivan's palace to conduct business of the most sinister kind.

Alexei shifted his eyes to Sophie.

At first glance, she seemed calm, but the trained observer wouldn't miss the signs; The unnatural pallor, the fitful breathing, the rigid posture. She was frightened. And she had every right to be. They were up against a formidable enemy, one that could dispatch them to kingdom come in a trice. Still, it wasn't wise to step into the lion's den with rattling teeth.

"Don't worry, Sophie, I won't let anything happen to you."

She didn't look at him, but her fingertips brushed lightly against his, as if by accident.

"I know," she whispered.

In that moment, Alexei felt a sudden disgust at her touch. Not disgust of her, but disgust of himself. She didn't belong here. This wasn't her war. And yet, he had mercilessly dragged her into the trenches. *Just like Natalia.*

Unbidden, the harrowing image of Natalia's lifeless body flashed through his mind—her white gown stained with blood, her eyes wide, frightened, so terribly devoid of life.

Forcing the memory from his mind, Alexei directed his gaze back to the crowd. He couldn't afford to lose focus. Not now. Not tonight, when all the world hung in the balance.

"Come, they're waiting for us," Alexei said, closing his hand a little tighter around hers, to make sure that everyone could see just how attached he was to his *toy*.

As they descended the staircase, Alexei saw one or the other man glance at Sophie—undoubtedly wondering who she was. In this world of glittering frivolity, mistresses were unapologetically paraded in public, but women like her—women who served no other purpose than pleasure—were kept hidden away. By bringing her here, by flaunting her like some rare exhibit, he was provoking the envy or admiration of more than one man in this room, and if he played this right, Stiva—jealous, spiteful Stiva—would fall blindly for the oldest trick in the book.

"There he is. The man of the hour."

Alexei turned, his eyes shifting to Stiva who was strolling leisurely down the staircase behind them.

"Stiva," Alexei replied disdainfully, greeting the Tsar's son with a lazy nod.

Stiva eased a silver cigarette box from his jacket pocket, flicked it open, took one, and then held it out to Alexei.

Alexei shook his head. "No, thank you."

"Alexei Zorin... the man without passions," Stiva said contemptuously, snapping the cigarette case shut and slipping it back into his jacket pocket. "You don't drink, you don't smoke, and until a few days ago"—he slipped the cigarette between his lips and nodded at Sophie—"I thought you didn't even fuck."

Alexei smiled. *Time to set the stage.*

"You see, Stiva, my passions are few, and I indulge them only if I find a distraction that is"—Alexei paused and glanced down at Sophie—"worthy of my attention."

Alexei's words had the desired effect on both his companions: Sophie's lip—in accordance with her role as his reluctant companion—curled a little in contempt, the gesture leaving no doubt just how much she despised him, while Stiva's eyes shifted momentarily to Sophie, seeing her reaction and sensing his opportunity.

"Then let's hope the whore is worth it," Stiva retorted spitefully, lighting his cigarette and taking a deep puff.

Alexei felt the cold, satisfying rush of victory. In a beat, he had elevated the woman at his side from disposable plaything to serious contender for Alexei Zorin's more than dubious affection. Her newfound status would be enough to stir Stiva's interest and competitive spirit.

He had tickled Stiva's fancy, now it was time to get his hackles up.

"Let her be my concern, Stiva. I believe you have enough of your own to deal with."

Stiva's eyes narrowed. "What do you mean?"

"Mexico," Alexei replied. "It seems the subs are just the first verse of a never-ending litany of problems: Frozen assets, missing operatives, seized material. The list is as long as it is unpleasant."

Stiva's expression hardened. "My problems are none of your goddamn business, *Alyosha*," he spat, using Alexei's nickname, which so patently refused to cross his lips on any other day—but today, apparently, it served not as an endearing address but as an insult worse than any other he could come up with.

"I agree, Stiva, they are your problems. And if you don't deal with them, I will hold you accountable."

"I don't answer to you."

Alexei smiled faintly. "Ah, this is where you are mistaken: you see, quite soon you will answer to me. And if you fail me, Stiva, be it in matters large or small, I will call you to account."

Stiva blanched, finally understanding what Alexei was insinuating. This whole pompous event wasn't a conclave, it was a coronation mass. The Twelve had already cast their votes—and Stepan Ivanovich Volkov wasn't their choice.

Alexei let his lips curl into a triumphant smile, silently dispelling even the last wisp of doubt that could have lingered in Stiva's mind.

For a beat, Alexei held Stiva's gaze, letting him feel the imbalance of power that separated them now, then he turned away, his hand resting leisurely on Sophie's back. As they cut across the room, Alexei caught Stiva's reflection in the window front—he was watching them, his hate-filled gaze following their every step.

Yes, Stiva, hate me, show me that anger.

CHAPTER XXXIV

Isola di San Clemente, Venice, Italy
Wednesday, 3rd July, 21:48

Dinner was a splendid affair, accompanied by subdued music and hushed conversation. Liveried butlers served vintage bottles of Château Pétrus, while Ivan's esteemed guests sat over a carefully arranged forest of priceless crystal and porcelain, casually redrawing the world order on a napkin and enjoying an *amuse bouche* of Almas caviar.

Alexei sat to Ivan's right, sipping Pomerol, and listening to the soliloquy of a grizzled French nomothete while secretly studying the guests around the table. It was quite an illustrious assembly, one that, if judged by nothing but the rank and distinction of the attendees, wouldn't have looked out of place in the snow-dusted conference halls at Davos.

But this wasn't Davos. And what was discussed here wasn't the pristine side of the world economy, but those shoddy bits that stemmed from illicit trade and transnational crime. It was a multi-trillion industry built on human suffering. And the men around this table sat right at the top of the food chain.

Sitting back in his chair, Alexei let his eyes trace over the three dozen men in attendance, taking them all in one by one, then returning to those who interested him most.

There was Tarik Khan. A former advisor to a Middle Eastern despot, Khan was a staggeringly well-connected man—as well as a casual racist, misogynist and homophobe who raked in billons by aiding tin-pot tyrants in keeping their dissenting subjects under state control.

A little further down the table was Lord Arthur Cavendish. A former central banker and now a partner at the world's largest investment firm, Cavendish ruled over a financial empire that funnelled billions of illicit assets through the world's financial laundromats.

Then there was Leonid Kirov. Former Admiral of the Fleet, past pretender to the Russian presidency and uncontested claimant to the rank of Russia's wealthiest oligarch, Kirov was—bar of Ivan—perhaps the most dangerous man in the room. Cunning, capable and ruthless, he ruled over a global conglomerate that encompassed everything from dockyards and oil majors to private military contractors. A man capable of sipping champagne while entire strips of land were depopulated on his command, Kirov had an almost Stalinist approach to cruelty. Human life in the masses was nothing to him. A statistic at best. And yet when it came to those little dramas of life, he would always hold his protecting hand over the weak and broken.

They were the very worst that the world had to offer. But even in this congregation of the morally bankrupt, Ivan Volkov stood apart.

Alexei's eyes shifted to the Tsar.

Ivan was lounging like a king at the head end of the table. And like all great men, Ivan commanded the attention of his audience, not through the power of his station, but through his wit, his sharp intellect and his easy, disarming smile. There was an almost seductive pull about him, a sinister charm that compelled people to like him, without entirely understanding why. But underneath that polished surface, lurked a devil—a man who regarded war as business and human lives as a dispensable commodity.

And amidst this assembly of crooks and killers sat Sophie.

To Alexei's surprise, she held herself with ease—regaling her tablemates with her delightful conversation skills, engaging Kirov in an animated conversation over the dismal state of the world in general and Russia in particular and punishing her gloomy captor with a carefully calculated look of fear and contempt whenever there was no worthier admirer to command her attention. At one point, she caught Stiva studying her from across the table and—in perfect keeping with her role—caught his eye and held it, as if to challenge him, daring the Tsar's son to take what belonged to the man he hated most.

As he watched her, Alexei felt a touch of admiration for his beautiful protégé. She had a natural talent for the cloak-and-dagger game and briefly the agent-runner in him regretted that her gift for the black arts would never be fostered with the care it deserved.

But his moment of quiet admiration was cut short by the faint chime of the ormolu clock and the sound of Ivan's voice, inviting his guests into the reception room for some casual gambling and two-hundred-year-old cognac.

The guests rose and Alexei rose with them.

It was time.

With a matter-of-course casualness, Alexei reached out and slipped his hand around Sophie's waist, as if to prove his ownership of her. She didn't resist, but her face was set in the kind of rebelliously reluctant expression of obedience that, in the span of an hour, she had cultivated to perfection. For a moment, they stood motionless, two conspirators, immersed in their roles of captor and captive. Then he drew her closer, and—concealed from prying eyes by the folds of her gown—laced his fingers through hers with the lover's unconscious casualness.

"Come, Sophie, it's time to play," he whispered, knowing that his companion would understand his words for what they were: A secret prompt that the game was about to begin.

He tightened his grip on her hand, a silent reassurance that he wouldn't let her fall, and she reciprocated in kind. Then he let go. And with the calm assurance of actors taking to the stage, they followed Ivan and his courtiers into the opulent reception room.

The atmosphere inside the vast space was one of imperialist luxury—Renaissance paintings, Italian furniture and crystal chandeliers. In an alcove, a chamber orchestra was playing subdued music while butlers in dark tailcoats carried silver trays between the guests. The attendees were already forming small groups to converse, while a handful of men had assembled around the card tables to play Baccarat and *Vingt-et-Un*.

Alexei allowed his gaze to shift towards the centre of the room where Ivan, surrounded by his barons and retainers, was holding court under the watchful eye of a battery of highly trained and very discreet bodyguards who stood at precise intervals along the walls.

Keeping his visibly reluctant companion by his side, Alexei made his rounds, greeting his allies and ignoring his inferiors with the oligarch's habitual indifference. There was Cavendish and his latest conquest: a six-foot model clad in a ridiculously revealing gown. Then Kirov, in the company of his mistress to whom he was steadfastly loyal for twenty years. And of course, Tarik Khan, as always alone.

From across the room, Stiva was watching him with firm, steady-eyed impudence. It wouldn't take long before he would act.

Don't make me wait, my friend, Alexei thought slyly.

For a while, the game of wilful ignorance dragged on, then Stiva rose and strode through the sea of faces and voices and colour towards him. Briefly he shook hands with Khan—who had been late to dinner due to some commitment that couldn't be delayed—then he caught up with Alexei.

"Tell me, what does it take to get the man without passions to shed his iron principles for one evening?" Stiva asked, nodding at the card tables, where Cavendish was just about to gamble away half a million to Khan.

Well then, let's raise the stakes.

"One million," Alexei replied.

"Very well, Alexei, one million it is." Stiva motioned to the Baccarat table, his platinum cufflinks glistening in the light. "I trust you know how to play?"

Alexei laughed softly. "Don't worry, Stiva, I can hold my own."

"Good."

Alexei turned to Sophie. "Come, my dear, you will be my Lady Fortune tonight."

Sophie graced him with a cold smile—cold enough for their audience to not only see but feel its chill. "As you wish."

Slipping his hand around Sophie's, Alexei drew his visibly reluctant companion a little closer and led her over to the card table—well aware of just how perfectly this little display of forced proximity underscored the nature of their relationship. Releasing Sophie from his grip, Alexei sat down. Stiva took a seat opposite him.

Alexei took a moment to take stock of the table before him. The cards. The chips. The palette on which the croupier handed out the cards.

Neither the man he was nor the one he played had ever found pleasure in games of chance. But the boy in him had always loved cards—for their glossy texture, their dry riffle, but most of all, for their ability to astound in the right hands. And his hands were the right ones. His childhood passion for magic tricks had left him with the dexterity of a skilled pickpocket. As a boy he had delighted in the little illusions that a slight of the hand could create, as a man he cherished their deadly qualities of deception.

Stiva tossed a chip on the table. One million dollars' worth of black iron. Alexei followed suit. Then cards were drawn. Alexei traded a couple of cards, discreetly making sure that his hand would be the losing one. Stiva banked the win. The stakes were upped. The game repeated.

Sophie stood silently at his side, balancing a glass of cognac in one hand, while her other rested dutifully on his shoulder. Alexei felt her presence strongly. They were a silent team. A small army of two.

Stiva won again. Once more, the stakes were upped and the game repeated. Five minutes in, Alexei was already down sixteen million. And as expected, Stiva—a small stack of iron chips nestling at his elbow—revelled in the chance to pluck his opponent's feathers.

Time to make the rivers flow uphill.

"Let's play for something a bit more exciting, shall we?" Alexei asked.

Stiva laughed quietly. "What do you have in mind, my friend?"

"How about your Bermuda holdings? I hear they're worth two hundred million."

"Very well, Alexei. And what are you going to throw in?"

Alexei nodded at the diamond necklace. "383 carats, internally flawless. The current market value lies slightly north of two hundred million. And just for sport, I'm going to throw in its wearer as well."

CHAPTER XXXV

Isola di San Clemente, Venice, Italy
Wednesday, 3rd July, 23:28

Stiva laughed softly, a hint of cruel amusement dancing in his eyes. But for a moment, Alexei's attention wasn't fixed on his opponent, but on Sophie. Her hand cramped on his shoulder, and he was certain that it would feel cold to the touch.

His move had thrown her off balance.

Alexei turned to look at her, silently reassuring her that he controlled the game and all the players, then he said: "Now, my dear, since we're playing for you, I think you deserve the honour of dealing the cards." He dismissed the croupier with a dapper wave of the hand. "Scramble."

The man didn't even pretend to hesitate, vacating his position instantly.

Alexei motioned to the vacant place. "Please, my dear."

He could almost see how Sophie collected herself, regaining her footing and continuing her act with the same flawless elegance with which she had performed her part all evening. She smiled slowly, first at him, then the audience and finally she went to take the croupier's place.

And as his companion took centre stage, their audience seemed to grow, drawn to the table by the sheer audacity of the stakes and the vague promise of scandal: There was an Italian media mogul, a high-flying pretender to the French presidency, a titan of the German defence industry, two grizzled hedge fund technocrats and the assembled council of The Twelve, presided over by the Tsar himself.

Stiva—with the predator's lazy elegance—slowly picked up a sleek plaque and contemplated it for a moment. Then, with a cold smile of impending triumph, he tossed the chip on the table.

"Two hundred million."

Alexei followed suit, while Ivan—cigar in hand—stepped closer to the table.

"*Les jeux sont faits, rien ne va plus*," Sophie announced, indicating—just as her predecessor had before—that all the bets were made, and none would be accepted from now on.

Sophie dealt the cards, took a step back, and gave the audience a demure smile as she waited for Stiva to make his move. For a brief moment, Stiva sat motionless, then he reached out and turned his cards one after the other.

Queen of hearts and jack of spades.

Sitting back, Alexei once more took stock of the table. The card deck lay at the centre of the table, in full view of the audience. In the eyes of the spectators, the chance of tampering with the cards was non-existent. No one would manipulate the game, not while they were all watching.

How wrong they all were.

Alexei reached out, picked up the cards, gave them a practised slap to settle them comfortably in his hand, cut the deck, and placed it in front of him. Then Sophie, with one long, delicate finger, slipped out the first card for him and then the second, placing both face-down before him.

The stage was set. Now it was time to draw his audience into the illusion.

Alexei shifted his gaze to Sophie. "Tell me, my dear, who would you rather see win tonight?"

All eyes shifted to Sophie—the audience's collective attention focusing on the magician's object of choice. And his beautiful protégé, with her unfailing instinct for the dark arts, understood the cue. She removed a strand of hair from over her eyes and looked back at Stiva with a brilliant smile. And that small gesture, that quiet slap in Alexei Zorin's face, momentarily held not only Stiva's attention, but that of the entire room.

This was the moment.

That split second of transient distraction, when illusions were made—where real magic was born.

Keeping his eyes on Sophie, Alexei lifted up the two cards and as he did so, he discreetly tilted his wrist, allowing the ace to slither from his cuff into his waiting palm. Then he slid the bottom card ever so slightly sideways, keeping the top one inside his palm. And there, with the quick dainty movement of the practised magician, he swapped one card for the other, secreting one into his cuff and sliding the other back over the bottom card. And then he dropped them, face upwards, just before Stiva's inert hands, revealing the winning hand.

And it was Sophie's softly murmured 'no' that drew the attention of the audience back to the cards.

Alexei sat motionless, studying the cards for a brief moment, then he lifted his head and looked Stiva in the eye. "We should play again sometime, Stiva, I think I'm getting a taste for it."

Alexei could almost see how the thin veneer of Stiva's restraint finally cracked. "*Chernozhopy.*"

Chernozhopy. Black-arse. The racist slur used by Slavs for the indigenous people from the Caucasus region. The ultimate insult. And of course, Alexei Zorin, ever sensitive to the heritage of his Ingush mother that had barred his ascent in Russia's military, wouldn't brook an offence of such proportions.

Alexei raised his hand, moving it ever so slightly towards his jacket. And Stiva, with his unfailing predator's instinct, instantly saw the threat. He drew his gun. But Alexei, with all the superior calm of the true soldier, simply stepped back as if Stiva's threat had surprised him.

There was Ivan's voice, a sharp command, which made Stiva pause. And then the voice of Ivan's butler, softer, gentler, more subdued than his master: "Gentlemen, please be so kind and place your weapons on the tray."

With a curse, Stiva placed his SIG on it, then Alexei reached into his jacket and, with deliberate calm, placed his Glock on the tray.

Alexei felt a rush of triumph. It was done. He had what he had come for.

Stiva's gun.

CHAPTER XXXVI

Isola di San Clemente, Venice, Italy
Wednesday, 3rd July, 23:52

Slowly, Alexei shifted his gaze to Sophie. She stood motionless at a side of the card table, as if overcome by some unspeakable emotion, then she turned to him and caught his eye. For a fraction of a second, they shared their moment of triumph, then Alexei—keenly aware of their audience—held out his hand. "Come, my dear, let us drink to our victory."

Ignoring Stiva, as though his opponent were beneath disdain, Alexei took her hand and gently but firmly steered her away from the table.

With the game's dramatic finale, the audience had already begun to disperse, and the room was once more coming alive with the hum of voices and subdued laughter, which ran together in a gentle tune. Keeping Sophie firmly by his side, Alexei cut across the room. Taking a glass of whisky from the tray of a passing waiter, he let his gaze scale the crowd, searching for the tall figure of Tom Frost and finding purchase a moment later.

Keeping Sophie by his side, Alexei walked over to him.

"Ah, Tom, so you made it after all."

Frost, in perfect keeping with his role, gave a deferential nod. "I do appreciate the invitation."

"Well then, let's drink to the evening."

With an imperious snap of his fingers, Alexei summoned one of the waiters. The man, dressed in a crisp white jacket, almost rushed to his side, as if afraid of having incurred his displeasure.

"How can I be of service, sir?"

Alexei lifted his glass in a lazy fashion. "Doctor Frost will have the same," Alexei said, his eyes shifting from the waiter to Frost. "Exactly the same, down to a t."

For a fraction of a second, their eyes met and caught—the two spymasters holding each other's gaze, trying to read something in the other man's expression—then Frost gave the faintest of nods.

He had caught the message, however vague.

To his right, the waiter mumbled something and disappeared into the crowd. Alexei's didn't even glance at him, instead he kept his eyes firmly on Frost.

"Well then, Doctor, enjoy your drink. And don't miss the fireworks at midnight. The view on the gallery is marvellous I'm told."

"I wouldn't miss them for anything in the world. Well, apart from the sunrise over Venice, perhaps. It's absolutely spectacular. I'm religious about never missing it."

Alexei gave Frost a small, condescending smile. "Ah, the simple pleasures of the common man." He raised his glass in a mock toast. "Perhaps I might try them too one day."

"You should," Frost replied.

Alexei gave a condescending nod.

Like a man eager to leave a party that had lost its edge, Alexei glanced at his wristwatch and compared it with the hands of the ormolu clock on the mantelpiece.

Two minutes to go.

He shifted his attention back to Sophie. Closing his hand a little more firmly around hers, Alexei led her into the dimly lit arcade to his right.

Bounded by Corinthian columns on one side and a wall of French windows on the other, the arcade was the most private space inside the reception hall. The windows shone gold in the glow of the chandeliers, the refracted light bright on the marble floors and dull on the midnight blue velvet of the curtains.

"You're a gambler at heart, aren't you?" Alexei asked, leading her down the columned hallway, past orange trees in silver pots and Ming vases on marble pedestals.

For a fraction of a second, Sophie's gaze went up to up crown moulding and the lens that glistened there. "I don't like to push my luck."

Alexei smiled vaguely, as if something about her response had amused him. "Really? I'm surprised."

"Why's that?"

Ahead of them on a sideboard of carved oak sat a silver flambeau. Beside the flambeau was a silver plate with two guns on it. Stiva's and his. For a fraction of a second, Alexei fixed his eyes on the weapons, letting his gaze linger just long enough for Sophie to notice, then he replied: "I had the impression that you enjoy dicing with death."

Footsteps echoed at the end of the gallery, then the tall figure of Tom Frost walked around the bend. He gave a nod. Just the slightest dip of the head.

All clear.

The ormolu clock struck the hour. Beyond the windowfront, fireworks blossomed out of the night sky, their dull bangs echoing inside the reception room like a barrage of gunfire.

"So tell me, do you enjoy dicing with death?" Alexei asked, casually drawing her towards him, forcing her to face him.

For a moment, Alexei stood motionless, holding her in place, then he reached up, and—sliding his hand into Sophie's hair—guided her slowly in a circle, as if they were dancers. And in that brief instant, shielded from the cameras by his companion, Alexei reached out and picked up Stiva's gun.

The next fusillade of fireworks exploded outside.

Taking a deep breath, Alexei dropped his arm and pulled the trigger. The bullet buried itself in the soft earth of an orange tree, the sound of the suppressed round masked by the barrage of fireworks.

Half a second later, Frost walked past them, casually taking the gun from his hand. Briefly, Frost's eyes lingered on the silver pot, then he pressed on, casually replacing the gun to its original resting place before vanishing out of sight.

Alexei shifted his attention back to Sophie. "I'm still waiting for your answer, Sophie."

She held his gaze, the vein on her neck pulsing visibly. "I don't think it's wise to tempt fate twice in one night."

Alexei laughed softly. "Well then, enough gambling for today, let's enjoy the fireworks instead."

Taking her by the hand, Alexei headed down a columned hallway, then slid through the mahogany door out onto the terrace, joining the crowd that was watching the fireworks over the Venetian lagoon. The moment they stepped outside, Khan's voice rang out from behind him.

"How about another game of cards, Alexei? Trust me, I'd put your pet to good use if I beat you tonight."

Promising to himself that, if he ever got the chance, he would end Khan's life in a singularly unpleasant manner, Alexei turned around.

"I have no doubt of that, Tarik. Alas, I don't like to tempt fate twice in a single night," he replied, stepping closer to Sophie, as if to mark his turf.

But his intervention was barely necessary. Judging by the flash of indignation in Sophie's eyes, the only one who needed protecting right now was Khan.

"A shame. Well, I'd drown my sorrow in drink and gamble, but I fear business takes precedence."

Something about Khan's tone made Alexei pause. "Working on such a night? That's surprising, even for you, Tarik. What's going on?"

"A rather unfortunate incident. An hour ago, a commodities journalist was shot dead outside Perth, where he was supposed to conduct an interview with the head of a mining company. The Australians claim that it was a carjacking gone wrong." Khan smiled and shook his head in mock-disbelief. "Petty crime is really on the rise these days."

"Suppose someone with a keener eye than that of a provincial policeman would look at the incident, what would he find?"

Khan laughed softly. "You mean someone like you or me?"

"Indeed."

"I think he would find that the robbers weren't robbers, and the journalist wasn't really a journalist. In fact, he would find that the late Maxim Mikoyan—celebrated investigative journalist and commodity expert—was in reality a Russian intelligence officer who went by the codename Poet. A cryptology boffin attached to Ural 16."

Alexei felt his blood run cold but preserved his mask of outward calm. "And what do you want with a dead Russian cyphers' expert, Tarik?"

"Me? Nothing at all. Ivan? Apparently, a lot. So much, in fact, that he dropped ten million if I got him Mikoyan or rather the treasure he carried."

"What kind of treasure are we talking about?"

"Nothing too spectacular: A laptop, a cell phone and a single volume from a collector's edition of Pushkin's work."

Beside him, Sophie shifted a little, as if Kahn's words had struck a nerve. And perhaps they had.

"A poet indeed." Alexei remarked, while his mind reeled, doing the mental maths.

Perth to Venice. Eight thousand miles. A sixteen-hour flight. Seventeen if the weather was on his side. And then perhaps another seven to eight hours to get Mikoyan's decryption software working. That gave him until midnight tomorrow. This was the hard deadline to get the drive back and if he failed, there was absolutely nothing that would stop Ivan from decoding his background file. And if he did, then the monumental lie that held the persona of Alexei Zorin together would be exposed in all its megapixel glory.

Khan's voice cut through his thoughts.

"But enough of that, will you and your little friend join me for a drink inside before I check on my people Down Under?"

"No, Tarik, I think I'll retire and enjoy the fruits of my labour."

Khan laughed and gave him a pat on the shoulder. "Well, then, I shan't keep you." Khan gave Sophie a mocking little nod and disappeared from the balcony.

Alexei shifted his gaze back to Sophie. The light from the state rooms fell through the windows onto the sprawling loggia and showed him the silhouette of her body through the translucent fabric—its every perfect line laid bare to his eyes. And for a fleeting moment he felt guilt for having tainted her perfection with his touch.

"Come, Sophie, I think it's time that we retire for the night."

CHAPTER XXXVII

Isola di San Clemente, Venice, Italy
Thursday, 4th July, 00:48

As the door to the suite clicked shut behind them, Alexei took the measure of the room—a practised scan, quick and thorough. Briefly, his eyes lingered on the wall of French windows framing Venice like a painting, then his gaze moved on, scaling the length of the space—over those tiny tell-tale signs of intrusion and surveillance: all surfaces wiped down to perfection, his snares removed and replaced with precision, the glint of a lens in the stuccoed ceiling.

He had to act fast now.

He removed his dinner jacket and tossed it onto the chair beside the fireplace. He then reached up, untying the bowtie, pulling it loose and letting it dangle around his neck.

"Did you enjoy the evening?" he asked, his eyes shifting to Sophie, who was standing by the window, her silhouette still against the backdrop of the lagoon.

"I did," she replied, without turning around to him.

He unfastened his platinum cufflinks, the reflections of the red flames from the open fireplace glinting briefly on their polished surface. Unlike Kirill, he had made a point of avoiding any standard-issue gear. Everything he used was tailor-made. Unique. Not traceable back to its origins.

But even this had become too risky.

At this point, everything that wasn't strictly necessary had to go.

Tonight.

He pulled one link away, and as it came loose, he discreetly extracted the tiny listening device concealed within—no larger than a grain of rice. This minuscule masterpiece of German engineering was made of biodegradable material and once wet, the bug wouldn't simply stop working, it would disintegrate into a tiny puddle of mush.

With a subtle flick of his wrist, Alexei tossed the device into the nearby champagne bucket. The bug disappeared between the ice cubes—its electronic life extinguished by the water at the bottom. No sweeping device could find a signal that didn't exist.

One down.

Two more to go.

His eyes shifted to the table by the fireplace, the blue-backed copy of Pushkin's works balancing precariously on its edge. Now, with Mikoyan's copy on the way here, he couldn't risk keeping it. Even if it meant severing his final line of communication.

He shifted his attention back to Sophie. "Tell me, Sophie, do you wish the game had ended differently?"

She shook her head, ever so slightly. "No."

"You shouldn't lie to me," he said softly, closing the distance between them with a few measured steps. "I can always tell."

She didn't turn around, but she was watching him in the reflection of the window.

With a slow, deliberate movement, Alexei reached out, gently brushing her hair over her shoulder, the silken strands sliding between his fingers as he revealed the gentle curve of her shoulder. For a moment, he stood motionless behind her, his eyes finding hers in the reflection of the window, then he kissed the base of her neck.

"You know, that treacherous little vein, right here, on your neck… it flutters when you lie," he whispered against her skin.

Alexei felt her shiver under his lips and then she turned around to face him. And as she moved towards him, her eyes—for the briefest of moments—shifted across the room, to the table behind him, to the accursed blue-backed book beside the fireplace.

It was a question.

An offer.

One he was all too willing to accept.

For a moment, they stood, neither moving nor speaking as they held each other's gaze. Then he raised a hand and brushed the back of his fingers against her cheek.

"I didn't lie," she said, her voice soft, just loud enough for their audience to hear.

"Prove it."

For a moment, she stood motionless, then she ran her hand up his chest. Her touch was soft, her fingers trailing a slow path up his chest, her eyes holding a hint of playful invitation. As her hand reached the base of his neck, she stepped back slowly, leading him in a half circle, her gaze locked on his, her movements carrying the gentle cadence of invitation.

With fluid grace, Sophie let the straps of her dress slip from her shoulders, the fabric cascading down her body, revealing her naked flesh beneath.

And as she flawlessly morphed into the role of slave, she casually took the lead from him—becoming the guide, the protector, the true master of their game.

Alexei felt a fleeting sense of admiration for his protégé: Circumstances had cast her in the role of subject rather than ruler, but she clearly understood its possibilities.

As she moved, her back edged ever closer to the mahogany table beside the fireplace—and the book that rested precariously on its edge.

She was giving him the opportunity he needed.

And he wasn't about to waste it.

He slipped one arm around her waist, and with the other, he swiped everything off the table in a single, swift, forceful motion.

Glasses, decanters, and the small leather-bound codebook were swiped into the flames. And as he guided Sophie down on the table's cool surface, the searing flames consumed the book—burning its deadly secrets to cinders.

For a moment, she lay motionless, chest pressed against the cool surface of the table, her long hair spilling over the edge. Then, slowly, she parted her legs for him.

She was all too aware that they were being watched and that she would be the one to carry the moment, endure the humiliation to save them both. But they had made it their game before. Theirs alone. And they would do so again tonight.

He lowered his head, his lips barely touching hers, teasing her with the promise of a kiss. And then he ran his hand up her thigh, all the way up, and then just a little further. A shiver ran through her, her lips parting by a fraction of an inch as he slid his fingers in all the way to the hilt.

"Oh Sophie, tonight, I will make you scream," he whispered and part of him meant it, part of him wanted to take all of her, to own her.

It would be so easy to leave all behind, to become who he pretended to be. And right then and there, he was tempted to make it real, if only for a moment.

He pulled her to the edge of the table, his hand finding his belt. Hers finding it too. And then he took her, possessing her, all of her.

Her back arched, her thighs quivered. Alexei leaned down, their lips meeting in a fervent kiss. His hand found hers, their fingers intertwining naturally and then she came with a soft, shuddering breath. He followed her over the edge, and there was just the warmth of the moment, the heat of their breaths intertwining, and the sensation of being lost in time.

And then there was only quiet.

And their breath in the hush.

And the beating of their hearts.

He pulled her to the floor with him. They lay entwined in front of the fire like slumbering cats, her body glowing in the flickering light. Sophie leaned into him, her breath even, her eyes closed as she drifted into the sated half-sleep meant only for lovers.

And as Sophie drifted into sleep, Alexei lay awake, watching over her. He hesitated for a moment, then he leaned in for a kiss, a moment of genuine affection that doubled as a shield for his sleight of hand, he reached for the gun that lay on the ground between them, retrieved the small, steel pendant and—with the skill and dexterity of the magician—slipped it into the intricate clasp of Sophie's necklace.

If he failed, Sophie would carry the key to the world's most dangerous weapon over her heart. And her role as his *Cheget* bearer ensured that the Brits and the Americans would do anything in their power to get her out of here alive. In the case of his death, it was the best protection that he could offer.

A fifty-billion ticket out of hell.

CHAPTER XXXVIII

Isola di San Clemente, Venice, Italy
Thursday, 4th July, 04:59

Alexei awoke to the sound of Sophie's soft breathing. The dawn had scarcely touched the sky, its first light filtering through the French windows and casting an ever-so-faint glow on Sophie's sleeping form.

Her hair smelled of vanilla and a hint of jasmine. Gently, he brushed a stray lock of hair from her face and placed a soft kiss on her forehead. She stirred slightly in her sleep, but didn't wake, as deeply asleep as when he had carried her to bed last night.

The ormolu clock on the mantelpiece chimed the hour. It was five o'clock.

Alexei carefully disentangled himself from her and got out of bed, leaving Sophie sleeping in the tousled sheets, their shared warmth still lingering.

He quickly showered and dressed, then went to the window. He stood there for a moment, admiring the view of Venice, as the first light of dawn began to outline the city in a soft glow.

Soon.

He turned back to Sophie. She was still asleep, the linen sheets that tangled around her legs.

You will be free, he promised her in his mind, knowing with painful certainty that he would leave behind a part of himself when he left this room.

With a final, lingering look that sought to memorise her sleeping form, he turned towards the door and slipped away.

Without glancing up at the cameras, he made his way to the small drawing room, where a diligent member of Ivan's staff had already laid out the day's newspapers on the coffee table. Picking up an intricate cut-crystal glass, Alexei poured himself some cold water from a Lalique decanter while perusing the day's headlines. Then, like a man with nothing to hide and nowhere to be, he picked one of the papers at random and stepped out onto the balcony.

The world outside was still shrouded in the early haze of dawn, but the air was already warm, perfumed with a blend of sea salt and the faint, lingering scent of night-blooming jasmine. Below him, the lagoon was a mirror, reflecting the first timid hues of daylight visible in the cloudless sky.

It would be a brilliant sunrise.

With a brief glance at the ever-present camera, Alexei strolled across the terrace, first tossing the newspaper onto the wide-armed rattan chair, then sauntering over to the balustrade to watch the sunrise over the sea.

For a moment, he looked out at the lagoon, then his eyes shifted downward, observing the grounds below.

The silhouettes of black-clad soldiers wavered in the waning darkness of dawn, and—turning his head to watch them—Alexei saw that Ivan's henchmen were by no means alone. In the distance, almost completely obscured by the branches of a willow tree, a solitary figure was briefly visible. Although he moved with the fleet-footed grace of a much younger man, Alexei's instincts told him that it was the elusive Doctor Thomas Frost himself, come out to perform his own battleground reconnaissance.

Well then, it was time to get moving.

He took another sip of water, then placed the glass on the balustrade beside him. For a moment, the glass merely sat there, its intricate crystal pattern glistening vaguely in the light of dawn. Then the sun slipped over the horizon, and the glass caught its light, scattering it in myriad directions. The walls and floor were suddenly alive with dapples of rainbow light, quivering and dancing like ethereal fireflies.

With a casual flick, Alexei adjusted the glass, redirecting one of the refracted beams directly onto the camera's lens, rendering it blind.

Given the weather and sun's angle at this time of the year, the effect would last for no more than thirteen minutes.

Thirteen minutes he would put to good use.

Taking a step back, Alexei cast a last cursory glance around him, then—with his battleground reconnaissance complete—he scaled the railing, catching the balustrade and clinging to the balcony Romeo-style. For a moment, he focused on the grass below, then he jumped, landing in a crouched position, hidden from view.

He waited for a moment, ensuring no guard had heard the sound of his impact. But nothing happened.

He got up and, ducking into the shadows, headed towards the olive grove on the easternmost hill of the island.

Ivan's island palace was surrounded by a vast garden—a fantastic Mediterranean jungle where trees grew in a perfectly choreographed wilderness around grottos, artificial lakes, and monopteros housing the statues of ancient Roman kings, standing watch over the modern-day interlopers. Sitting on the edge of this fantastical garden was a sixth-century chapel, like a miniature basilica, its oblong nave adorned with scenes of martial glory and the visages of saints. It had once served as a place of spiritual solace to pilgrims and soldiers on the Greek island of Patmos, until—after a century of disuse and neglect—Ivan acquired, dismantled, and re-erected it nine hundred miles away on his private island as a place of spiritual solace.

Alexei had deliberately chosen the small chapel as their meeting location because there were only two places where he was sure that no cameras would be present: In the room where Ivan fucked, and in the one where he prayed.

As he stepped into the olive grove, it almost felt like he had crossed some invisible boundary—there were no cameras here, no prying eyes. This was Ivan's personal retreat, his spiritual refuge, away from all the bloodshed.

And today, it would be his too.

Alexei ambled through the olive grove, past a small hill overlooking the sea. On its crest stood a whitewashed pavilion, with French windows and billowing white curtains—an oasis of elegance overlooking the sea. It would certainly have made for a more fashionable meeting location than the one he had chosen, albeit a less dramatic one.

With swift strides, Alexei walked over to the church. With one last glance over his shoulder, he stepped through the door and closed it carefully behind him.

The church was narrow, with frescoed walls, an altar in the nave bay, pews on either side, and a passage between them. Save for a shaded light upon the altar and the blue glow of the sanctuary light, the room was in darkness.

Frost sat in a pew facing the screen of icons, which was of the particularly opulent kind—pure gold and precious stones. He sat very still, one arm draped leisurely over the ledge, one polished shoe tip resting on the kneeler. He looked almost relaxed, the way only a seasoned spymaster could look relaxed in the field.

And seasoned he was.

Frost had been recruited by MI6 straight out of Oxford at the height of the Cold War. Operating under the codename Absolem, he had served a series of prolonged stints behind enemy lines in Moscow and Berlin before he was outed by a double agent in his own ranks months before the fall of the Berlin Wall. And so, with his cover compromised, His Majesty's Foreign Intelligence Service had put its spymaster to pasture in the purgatory of desk-bound servitude, else known as the Joint Intelligence Committee. Relegated to the shadows of bureaucracy, Frost rose all the way to the top of his section's many incarnations until one of Ivan's underlings—in an unforgivable lapse of judgement—approached Frost with a lucrative if not entirely legal proposition.

Presented with a singular opportunity to gain leverage over the Twelve, Thomas Edmund Frost, the battle-tried, cold-war espiocrat, returned from his bureaucratic exile to active duty—this time not as a spymaster but as an agent in the field.

To ensure his success, British intelligence supplied Frost with a string of plush positions with, ostensibly, invaluable access to top-secret information. First as the head of the counter-narcotics and serious crime unit and then as the head of Interpol's European Response Team.

And so, for many years, Frost burrowed his way through Ivan's organisation, until betrayal within his own ranks once again threatened to unravel everything. But in one of life's little ironies, it was Alexei—as Ivan's chosen enforcer—who was first informed that Frost was an undercover operative of the British Crown. After a careful analysis of the risks, Alexei—on the condition of his anonymity being preserved—intervened on the agent's behalf. And so, in the course of a dreary November morning, Alexei rid British intelligence of a traitor and the world of two of Ivan's more disagreeable henchmen, while also securing himself a lifelong if, on occasion, reluctant ally.

Frost turned at the sound of Alexei's footsteps. "War party?"

"Afraid so," Alexei replied.

"And I assume you need this to play?" Frost asked, slipping a gun from his pocket. "Just as ordered, with some extras." He weighed the gun in his hand, with a look of pride on his face. "Its ballistic fingerprint is indistinguishable from Stiva's weapon. And the attached suppressor reduces the muzzle velocity to subsonic level, eighty decibels—about as loud as a popping champagne cork."

"Marvellous. Give my best regards to your quartermaster." Alexei held out his hand, but Frost didn't hand him the weapon.

"No, not yet," Frost said, pocketing the gun.

"Tom, I don't have time for this."

"Neither do I." Frost paused, measuring him. "You've saved my life, Alexei, and I won't forget that. But things have changed. This is no longer an uneasy whorehouse pact between non-allied states. We're back on Cold War turf. Russia is the enemy. And so are you."

"Then why are you here, Tom, fraternising with the enemy?"

"Because I'm no longer certain who you are and on whose side you really stand."

"Why is that?"

"The launch keys. Moscow doesn't have them. Neither does Ivan. And while both your masters find themselves short of valuable equipment, they are also both hunting for a traitor in their ranks. So I'm wondering whether you're playing both sides of the fence"—Frost hesitated—"or for someone else entirely." He paused, then continued, "Alexei, I need to be certain who you are before I commit treason to help you."

So Absolem had sensed something was wrong, and now the hookah-smoking caterpillar was asking him who he really was.

"In our world, certainty is a luxury afforded to the dead and the damned, Tom."

"We're talking about a nuclear weapon in space, Alexei. Certainty is no luxury in this case."

Alexei paused. He had intentioned to send this message directly, but if the route through British intelligence secured him Frost's allegiance, then so be it.

"Tell your American friends in Langley to pick up the phone and talk to Vandenberg. They should get ready to retrieve the warheads. Inactive. Secured. Fitted with a re-entry vehicle and configured for soft ballistic re-entry. The Americans are already tracking Pandora closely. They have the kit to pull this off and the clout to keep everyone else, especially the Chinese and the Russians, calm." He paused briefly. "I assume the boys in Langley would want to know who I am before they send in the fire brigade. I'll provide you with something that should light a fire right under their asses."

Frost paused for a moment, the reply frozen on his lips. "You can't be serious, Alexei. You're playing fucking Russian Roulette with the world if you do this."

"I don't think you'll like the alternative, Tom. Or would you prefer if Ivan or the Kremlin gained control of the weapon? Do you really want a buccaneering warlord or an unhinged dictator with imperialist ambitions to play Russian Roulette with the world, instead of me?"

"You can't guarantee a safe deorbiting of this weapon, Alexei."

"Dozens of good men have risked or lost their lives to deorbit this weapon safely. Engineers. Programmers. Soldiers. They did so because they understood the sheer insanity of placing a nuclear weapon in space, and they understood the risks of bringing it down. Everything is prepared, all that I need to do is initiate it."

"Why the hell can't this wait? Why the hell has this to happen now?"

"Because this is my last chance, Tom. It's do or die. By dawn tomorrow, I'll either be a dead man or sit in Victor Orsin's chair as one of the Twelve. And once I'm part of the Pantheon, I'll be one step closer to Ivan—one step from taking him down. But that means I might fail. If I do, the weapon will fall into the hands of either Ivan or the Kremlin. Neither of us wants that."

At this, Frost let out a low, humourless chuckle, the sound of it more a sigh than anything resembling amusement. He shook his head, a gesture that seemed to carry the weight of the world.

"You're a fool, Alexei. There is no question whether you *might* fail. You *will* fail." Frost pinched the bridge of his nose, as if trying to dispel a headache, then shook his head. "For fucks sake, man, you're trying to kill a hydra by chopping off one head.

Whoever you kill will be replaced. Even Ivan. You, on the other hand, *will* get caught, if not now then soon. And while you'll get a quaint burial with tearless guests, someone else will settle on Ivan's throne."

"That would be me."

"I'm sorry?"

"I will be the one to replace Ivan. And when I do, I will finally be able to tear down his rotten empire once and for all."

CHAPTER XXXIX

Isola di San Clemente, Venice, Italy
Thursday, 4th July, 14:22

With swift strides, Alexei made his way along the gallery that housed the temporary offices of the Twelve and those few select barons who were in attendance at Ivan's court.

Outside, the morning sun danced upon the sea, and although the windows were closed, the air was still filled with the scent of the ocean and the faint aroma of blooming flowers. It was a day that promised the kind of peace that had long evaded him, a peace he neither sought nor particularly desired.

At least not today.

He ran his hand over his jacket. Under the impeccably tailored garment, the SIG rested against his ribs. But before he could put it to use, there were less pugnacious duties that required his attention.

He stepped into his temporary office, with its hand-carved Italian writing desk, paintings by Rothko and Basquiat and a meeting table large enough to accommodate an entire armada of bankers, lawyers, and accountants.

Today, however, only three men were in attendance.

He didn't need more.

After all this was, ostensibly at least, only a formality.

The trio of impeccably dressed men, rose in unison as Alexei stepped into his office, their movements synchronised by practice. Their faces were masks of professional neutrality, but their eyes betrayed a hint of unease. They knew well the man they were dealing with—and they wished for this to be over as soon as possible.

"Good morning, gentlemen," Alexei greeted them, shaking their hands one after the other, before settling down at the head of the table.

One of the men—a wary-faced Swiss banker flown-in straight from Zurich—pushed a stack of documents towards him, with the polished, pleasantly neutral smile of the true predator, who didn't care if the contract was signed in blood and with the devil's name as long as it made him money.

Oh, my friend, you have no idea.

Under the practised guidance of his vultures-for-hire, Alexei worked his way through the papers. As expected, the entities and underlying assets of Stiva's holding company were clean—prime commercial and residential real estate in London, Paris and New York, a handful of stakes in the world's major ports, including Rotterdam, Antwerp and Ningbo, and investments in a handful of large-cap buyout funds which in turn held shares in the who's who of the world's privately-held companies. It was a portfolio fit for a pension fund, rather than a global crime baron. But Alexei had just changed that.

He reached for a copy of the closing accounts, flipping through the pages until he found the leger listing the year-to-date transactions.

And there it was.

Six hours ago, a well-known slush fund of the Russian government had wired a token of gratitude straight from Cyprus into Stiva's Bermuda accounts. The transaction was veiled, hushed up, but just sloppy enough for the keen watcher to undercover it. During the hasty wrap-up of the closing accounts, none of the accountants, lawyers and bankers—neither Stiva's nor his—had bothered to double-check the origin of the two hundred thousand euros. After all, as long as the cash on the balance sheet matched the amount in the bank account, no one really bothered. Why would they? It was the kind of thing that slipped through the cracks, and the cash would lay there, forgotten, until someone looked closer.

And someone would look closer.

He would make sure of it.

"It seems everything is in order," Alexei intoned and looked up. "Let's sign the share purchase agreement."

The Swiss banker gave a nod and handed him another stack of paper. Slimmer this time, a dozen pages perhaps, all in duplicate.

Alexei looked down at the papers, spread before him like an offering, then he went through the agreement clause by clause until he reached the final page, where Stiva had already signed his name. He reached for his fountain pen, unscrewed the top, then initialled each page and signed the one at the end with a flourish.

It was a death sentence, signed and sealed.

With a discreet signal from Alexei, the lawyers gathered their papers and departed, the door closing softly behind them.

Alexei pinched the bridge of his nose, trying to dispel the numbing haze from his mind. Soon, it would be time. He had to make provisions in case he failed. And that meant he had to ensure his allies in this game were reliable. Unequivocally so.

As if drawn there by the grim task that now lay ahead of him, Alexei's gaze shifted instinctively to the unmarked manila envelope that lay on the side of his desk.

Sophie's file. Collected on his command the day he had brought her here. All he had looked at then was the red flag summary. No known or suspected affiliations to any intelligence or law-enforcement agency, party, government body or criminal organisation.

Knowing that she wasn't a security risk was enough back then. He didn't need to know more. But things were different now. She was in over her head. And he could no longer afford to be ignorant of even the smallest detail about her.

He got up and strolled over to his desk and leaning against its edge, picked up the envelope. He opened it slowly, as if unwrapping a gift whose contents were both desired and feared.

It contained a dozen pages of cheap, off-white paper that was topped by the official seal of the Metropolitan Police and tailed by two red stamps that proclaimed the documents as 'copy' and warned that it was for 'internal use only'.

As he began to read, Alexei saw her life story unfold before his eyes. The unruly teenage years. The brilliant academic achievements. The soft-hearted causes. The violent lover and the ill-fated breakup that followed this whirlwind romance. The restraining order, twice overturned, to keep away the gilded scion of a Texan oil baron away who had refused to leave her alone.

Briefly the image of Sophie kneeling on his bedroom floor—bound and terrified—flashed in his mind. He had seen it then and glimpsed it again later, the fear that was more than just instinct, the kind of fear that was learned through pain.

Oh Sophie.

He felt a pang of guilt at what he had done to her, both at what he had unknowingly evoked and what he had knowingly done—and he feared that what lay ahead would hold greater horrors still.

CHAPTER XL

Isola di San Clemente, Venice, Italy
Thursday, 4th July, 19:22

Alexei pocketed the lighter, his eyes drifting to the mirror and catching his own reflection there.

For a moment, he wasn't sure if he was looking at himself or the mask he'd worn for so long. Perhaps, by now, the mask had become skin, or perhaps he simply couldn't tell anymore where one ended and the other began.

But he'd always known this was part of the deal. Going undercover meant surrendering a part of oneself, to live in a state of perpetual contradiction—bearing witness to the slow erosion of his own identity, while simultaneously filling the gaps with the role he'd been assigned. He was constantly wearing masks—many of them, all at once. He lived in layers, peeling one off to reveal another, all in service of some distant cause. And in the process, choices had become murky, grey, until eventually, the grey was all he could see.

In the end, there was nothing left but the lie. The lie he lived, and the lie he'd become.

In the quiet hours, he wondered if, when it all ended, there was still a self to return to. And whether he even wanted to. Or if he'd rather give in to the intoxicating thrill of power. It would be so easy, to lean into the lie and just fully become what he'd played at being for so long.

He glanced across the room at Sophie, who was standing by the window, her figure framed against the fading light.

She was standing by the window, her hands clasped tightly, her gaze distant, as if she was trying to steel herself for whatever was about to happen. Dressed in black, her slender frame was accentuated by the evening gown. Her beauty was undeniable—yet

Alexei couldn't help but notice the tension in her posture, the way her hands trembled ever so slightly.

He felt guilt for what he was doing to her. She didn't belong here, in the trenches. But soon, it would be in his power to let go—and when that moment came, he would make sure that not a shred of this world would ever touch her again.

He crossed the room towards her, his footsteps almost soundless on the marble floor. Sophie looked up at his approach, and he realised that he had pulled her from some unpleasant thought. Briefly, he wondered what it had been, but he let it go.

"Shall we?" he asked, offering his arm—the movement part command, part invitation.

Sophie took it, and together they stepped out of the room.

He led her through the suite and the gallery outside, but not to the foyer, instead he took her out to the gardens, and a moment later, they stepped into the humid evening air, the faint scent of salt and jasmine clinging to the breeze.

The sun was low on the horizon, casting a faint golden light over the water and the evening air felt cool against his skin. They walked in silence along the path by the sea, the gentle lapping of the waves providing a rhythm to their footsteps.

Finally, at a safe distance from the house and the guards that patrolled the gardens, he stopped walking, turning to face her.

Alexei paused, his gaze fixed on her. For a moment, he said nothing, letting the silence stretch between them. He moved towards her by just the fraction of an inch, just enough to pose the silent question, and then she placed her hand on his chest, running it up to his shoulder.

Then he reached for her, his hand resting gently on the back of her neck as he leaned in, pressing his lips to hers. The kiss was cold, controlled, meant for anyone who might be watching, but when he pulled back, his voice was meant only for her.

He pulled back, his lips lingering against hers.

"Sophie, I'm playing my end game tonight." He paused, knowing that what he was about to ask violated any protocol he had ever been trained to follow. A civilian's role was not on the battlefield, and even less so behind enemy lines. But it seemed that protocol was a luxury he could ill afford these days. "I can't do it alone, Sophie."

She nodded faintly, the colour draining from her face. "What should I do?"

"I need to take Stiva out of the picture, take him out to the balcony, for six minutes, that's all I need."

"He didn't raise to my bait last time, what makes you think he will this time?"

"Because he desires you and hates me. So you'll offer him the sweetest possible package: Your company and dirt on me in exchange for his protection. Make him believe you're ready to turn on me, that you have something important to tell him. Talk about me—give him a reason to trust you."

She nodded.

"Sophie, while you are out there, you need to stay close to the window, so that you're seen. At the same time, you need to make sure that Stiva stands somewhere where he isn't visible from the inside. Can you do that?"

"Yes."

As she spoke the words, he saw a spark of something quite unexpected in her eyes. Not fear, as he would have expected, but grim determination. And in that instant, he knew that she would pull through this. She was tougher than she looked. Capable of playing her role until the bitter end.

He looked down at her. "I promise you, Sophie, I will do everything in my power to get you out of here."

She gave him a faint smile. "I know."

"Are you ready to go in there?"

"Yes."

He placed a faint kiss on her forehead, his lips lingering for a moment on her skin before he let her go.

When he pulled away, his voice was steady. "Well then, Sophie, let's enjoy the night."

Walking ahead, Alexei kept his pace measured—one hand around hers, the other closing discreetly around the lighter in his pocket—that tiny little device, inconspicuous on the outside, and rigged with a small explosive charge on the inside.

A moment later, they reached the surveillance point—a pretty Venetian garden lamp. Elegant, unconscious, and with a hidden camera inside.

As they walked past it, Alexei discreetly removed the lighter from his pocket. And then, with the ease of the practised spy, he briefly brushed his hand against the cool metal of the lamp—in one fluid motion placing the lighter beneath the metal frame that housed the camera.

The lighter clicked into place—a silent promise of destruction to come.

And then they turned towards the illuminated foyer of Ivan's palace, walking towards the entrance shoulder to shoulder, both knowing that from this moment forward, every step, every glance, every word would be part of the performance.

The game had begun, the stakes had been set, and they were both playing for keeps.

CHAPTER XLI

Isola di San Clemente, Venice, Italy
Thursday, 4th July, 22:53

Dinner was a lavish affair, accompanied by subdued music and hushed conversation. While they ate, the lights of the crystal chandeliers seemed to grow brighter, the sky outside darker and when the guests finally spilt into the adjacent state rooms, the sky had turned black.

The reception hall was a bright semi-circular space, elegantly bound into the house by a wall of windows that offered a spectacular view of Venice. The windowpanes and marble floor gleamed gold in the refracted light a dozen crystal chandeliers—loot from the last tsar's place, lovingly preserved over the decades and finally purchased for a king's ransom by yet another emperor, albeit a modern-day one.

The air was alive with the hum of voices, laughter and the casual merriment of old friends meeting. Guests stood together in groups of two or three, brandishing champagne glasses and nipping on Almas caviar while flocks of servants scurried about the place to cater to every whim of Ivan's illustrious visitors.

Alexei looked at his companion. With her high cheekbones, gently curved brows and dark eyes she was indeed a woman of singular beauty. But what set her apart wasn't just beauty, but charisma—the same effortless grace and unbending spirit that he had so loved about Natalia. She was truly extraordinary.

I will get you out of here, Alexei assured her in his mind. *You won't share her fate.*

"Good evening, my friends."

The Tsar's voice interrupted his thoughts. Alexei looked up. Ivan stood at the centre of the room. Instantly, the muted conversations and hushed laughter dissolved into expectant silence.

For a brief moment, Ivan surveyed his audience, ensuring that he had their undivided attention, then he began to speak.

"According to lore, gods anoint kings, and people elect presidents. We all know it's a lie. It's money and power that dictate who rules and who is ruled. Victor understood this better than most, and he was unmatched in exploiting it. For those who could afford his benevolent intervention, he provided weapons, armies, or the means to whisper into voters' ears. His work helped build the foundation of what we are today: Kingmakers, the new gods of Rome. Yet, despite the depth of his loss, his place in the pantheon cannot go empty. And so, tonight, we have gathered here to bestow his mantle upon a worthy successor."

Ivan's eye shifted across the crowd.

"Over the past few days, the council of the Twelve has debated Victor's succession. And we have come to a conclusion."

Ivan's eyes shifted to Alexei.

"For four years, Alexei Alexandrovich has spearheaded our global arms brokering and military intelligence operations. His efforts have not only earned this organisation billions of dollars in profits but also reshaped the geopolitical landscape in favour of our esteemed clients." Ivan paused, raising his glass in Alexei's direction. "Tonight, my friend, you will reap the rewards for your outstanding work: A place among The Twelve."

There was a collective intake of breath, followed by a hushed silence as all eyes shifted to Alexei. And in that brief moment of unguarded surprise, Alexei could see what they all felt: Fear.

They feared him. They were all terrified of the man who had so swiftly and silently risen through their ranks, mercilessly clearing every obstacle until he had reached the very top.

Once again, Alexei could feel that cold rush of pleasure, a grim, sadistic delight at the thought of what was to come. Soon, they would be his, he would own them just as Ivan owned them now. *And then, my friends, you will learn the full meaning of fear.*

Ignoring their stunned surprise, Ivan raised his glass in a toasting. "To success."

Alexei raised his glass, so did everyone else in the room.

"To success," Alexei murmured, *but only mine, not yours.*

He took a sip, set down his glass and glanced discreetly at his watch. *Twenty-two minutes to go.*

Slipping his hand casually around Sophie's waist, Alexei allowed his gaze to scale the length of the room, all the way down to Tom Frost who stood a little to the side of the crowd, just beside Stiva.

As if he had felt Alexei's gaze resting on him, Frost looked up. For a heartbeat, their eyes met, and Alexei could almost hear Frost's voice in his mind, silently asking Alexei if he had the third man he had promised.

Like a man utterly taken with his companion, Alexei briefly glanced at Sophie, indicating to Frost that they had the third man required to see this through, then he shifted his gaze back to the Brit—waiting for his response.

Frost hesitated for a fraction of a second, then he lowered his eyes again.

Frost was ready.

Now everything depended on a clean execution.

CHAPTER XLII

Isola di San Clemente, Venice, Italy
Thursday, 4th July, 23:22

Keeping Sophie by his side, Alexei played the gracious guest of honour, politely accepting the attention lavished on him by his peers and grovelling underlings, while he discreetly scanned the room—conducting his reconnaissance with all the methodical rigour and due caution of a ground intelligence officer on the battlefield.

At first glance, there was little out of the ordinary: Those in attendance seemed to be at ease, standing together in small groups or dancing to the subdued music. But the levity was nothing more than a veneer.

Standing along the walls—motionless like tin soldiers— were three dozen stone-faced bodyguards, the bulk of their weapons visible under their dark jackets, their gazes sweeping the perimeter for threats, their earpieces and wires connecting them to the armed sentries and counter-snipers that guarded the site.

But however formidable this contingent of highly trained and impeccably equipped soldiers appeared, they weren't his primary concern tonight: Men, however skilled and vigilant, could be avoided, outwitted or killed, but technology was harder to outmanoeuvre.

Slowly, his eyes shifted upwards, to the sole camera in the room—discreetly hidden in the stuccoed crown moulding high above him.

He and Frost had done their best to account for each and every one of Ivan's miniature mechanical sentries. His performance was meticulously choreographed, and if it was flawlessly executed, he would move like a ghost through this house.

Alexei glanced at his watch. Seven minutes to go. It was time to brief his fair companion.

Tearing his gaze away from the camera, he directed his attention to Sophie. She stood close to him, half a step ahead. Under the dim glow of the overhead lights, she looked as delicate as a porcelain figure—her skin white against the black of her evening gown.

"Let's dance," he said softly.

She took his hand with a tight-lipped smile. Drawing her a little closer, he fell into step with the music, and she followed his lead with an easy grace—her hands resting on his shoulders, her lips a mere inch from his throat. Her breath was rapid, her hands like ice. She was frightened.

"I'm not sure if I can do this," she said, keeping her voice low.

"I know you're scared, and it is okay to be frightened," he whispered, sliding his hand over hers, lacing his fingers through hers. "But it's too late to turn back."

She closed her eyes and gave a faint nod. "I know."

"I will see you through this," he assured, giving her a small smile, hoping it would be enough to calm her fears.

He held her eyes for a brief moment, then he focused his attention back onto the crowd, searching for his quarry. Briefly, his eyes trailed through the room, searching for the Tsar's son, then finally, Alexei spotted him, lingering in a corner, deeply engrossed in conversation with an Italian defence tycoon.

At that moment, Stiva's gaze flickered to him. Their eyes met and Alexei responded with a lazy smile—cold, triumphant, condescending.

For a heartbeat, Alexei could almost feel the hatred in Stiva's eyes. Then the Tsar's son placed one hand on the Italian's shoulder—the soft glow of the chandeliers flashing of his platinum cuffs—and with the other he motioned to the balcony doors. A moment later, the two men vanished through them.

Alexei directed his attention back to Sophie.

"When I tell you to, you'll go out on the balcony and ask Stiva for a cigarette and a word in private. He'll readily oblige. Play a little with him, draw out your story, but make sure you keep him out there while I'm gone. Make sure you stay close to the window, while he doesn't." He paused for a moment, glancing at the glass doors through which Stiva had vanished only moments before. "But whatever you do, always keep in mind that—in this world—you're property and if you grant Stiva any liberties, I will have to punish you to keep my cover. Do you understand?"

Alexei felt her shiver under his touch, as the full meaning of his words sank in. Then she gave a slow nod. "I understand."

"I won't be long." He ran his hand over the watch on her wrist. "Six minutes, that's all I need. The count starts from the moment we separate."

She glanced down at her watch, her eyes fixed on its dial for a heartbeat. His eyes went to his own watch.

Three seconds to go.

"Are you ready?"

She gave a small nod. "Yes."

Their eyes met, and he paced her, silently counting down the seconds as he guided her to the edge of the dance floor.

Two. One.

Right at that moment, the small explosive charge beneath the surveillance camera outside would go off, turning off visual surveillance for part of the garden and the connected systems on the balcony. From the moment Sophie and Stiva stepped onto the balcony, there would be no proof of Stiva's whereabouts. For the duration of the heist, Stepan Ivanovich Volkov would be unaccounted for. Officially.

Alexei let go of her. As they parted, she graced him with a dazzling smile, running her fingertips down his arm from elbow to hand—like a lover parting from a loved one—then she turned away and began to walk evenly, purposefully towards the balcony doors.

He had six minutes now.

He turned and strode in the opposite direction, smoothing out his jacket as he walked. Concealed underneath the luxurious fabric, he carried not only his Glock, but also the copy of Stiva's left-handed SIG.

At the far end of the room, Alexei spotted Frost. Their eyes met. A silent confirmation.

Five minutes and fifty seconds.

Frost began to walk towards the dining room door. So did Alexei. He paced his strides, counting his steps, knowing that Frost did the same. They were a silent team now, moving in unison, with the unfailing precision of a fine-tuned clockwork.

They both walked into the crowd, elegantly evading the sentries' prying gaze in the congregating masses. Seven seconds later, their paths crossed, and for a brief moment, Alexei became invisible, hidden from the camera's all-seeing eye behind Frost's towering figure.

Alexei exhaled slowly. And as he pressed the air out of his lungs, he could feel his pulse slowing, his motions becoming more fluid, his vision gaining in clarity. Then he reached that elusive state of utmost mental concentration and physical mastery that a long-range sniper had to achieve before pulling the trigger. Only he, unlike a sniper, had to make this shot in full motion.

Five minutes and forty-three seconds.

Alexei crossed the threshold into the dimly lit dining room—deserted and unguarded but for the mechanical eye of a pinhole camera.

As he stepped through the door, into the shadows of the vaulted cloister that enclosed the room, Alexei slipped the SIG from the shoulder holster, took aim and pulled the trigger. There was a dry spitting sound, no louder than the pop of a champagne cork, then the pinhole camera at the other side of the room went blind, a mere fraction of a second before Alexei stepped into its range.

He was a ghost now. Able to move unseen through this room.

Slipping the SIG back into his shoulder holster, Alexei walked along the dining table, his eyes tracing over half-tidied silverware, crystal champagne flutes and pristine linen napkins folded back from dessert plates. Counting the chairs until he reached the one where Ivan had sat. In passing, Alexei picked up his glass and held it up into the light. There, right above the stem, was a thumbprint.

Without pausing his stride, Alexei slipped a small piece of translucent film from his jacket pocket and pressed it over the fingerprint with his right thumb. The heat of his flesh activated the highly sensitive gelatine mould, making it react with the lipid residue left behind by Ivan's touch and moulding its exact replica onto Alexei's fingertip.

It was wonderfully neat. Like an old-school copy of a key pressed into wax.

Without pausing in his stride, Alexei placed the glass on the corner of the dining table, then—continuing along the wall of French windows that lined to room on either side—he tapped the butt of his gun against the window catch, turning it just ever so slightly. Not enough to raise the alarm, but enough to suggest a hasty entry from the outside if anyone came looking.

CHAPTER XLIII

Isola di San Clemente, Venice, Italy
Thursday, 4th July, 23:43

Alexei drew his weapon and stepped out into the reception hall, his gaze sweeping across the room in tactical bounds. Keeping his finger on the trigger guard, he crossed the foyer and slipped through the double door on the other side. Swivelling the gun in a defensive arc, he cleared the dimly lit hallway by sight and moved forward.

He knew the layout of the building, the route and timing of every guard, the position and angle of every security camera. But there was always the unexpected—those tiny little changes which, if overlooked, had the potential to kill. And he had no intention of dying tonight.

Five minutes and thirty-three seconds.

Quickening his pace, Alexei rounded another bend and stepped into a gallery that housed Ivan's lavish office and private meeting rooms. And the setting left nothing to be desired: surveillance-proof communication lines and of course a biometrically protected wall safe large enough to store half a ton of gold. And there, he would find the treasures he was hunting for: The pendant and the drive.

Five minutes and twenty-four seconds.

Counting the steps, Alexei moved along the hallway, shifting course to avoid the cameras. Thirty feet in, there was a door to his right. He stopped in front of it. With a quick glance down the hallway, Alexei pressed his gel-covered thumb to the biometric scanner.

A tiny dot of red light flickered to life, flashing erratically while the system processed the fingerprint. Then, verifying it to be Ivan's, it turned green. There was a brief moment of silence, followed by a series of faint metallic clicks as twelve metal deadbolts slid out of place.

Five minutes and nineteen seconds.

He turned the handle and opened the door. There was a faint, almost inaudible click that made him stop dead in his tracks.

Oh Ivan, are you really that paranoid?

Reaching up, Alexei ran his fingers along the top of the doorframe and brushed off the dust. Then he took a step back, raised his hand and blew the particles gently off his fingertips. The dust motes swirled in the air like dancing snowflakes, exposing nine intersecting laser beams by scattering their invisible light. If anything bigger than a dust grain touched the optical barrier, the alarm would be activated and whoever was found here wouldn't live long enough to explain himself.

Lucky I passed on dessert, Alexei thought slyly, his eyes shifting to the narrow space between the floor and the bottommost light beam.

Taking a deep breath, Alexei let his body drop to the floor, rolled over his shoulder and came up behind the barrier, weapon in hand.

Everything was quiet.

Almost too easy.

Holstering his gun, Alexei crossed the room, strode to the wide desk and pressed the concealed button on its underside. Instantly, one of the wooden wall panels rolled back, revealing a massive four-foot-high safe. Alexei pressed his thumb to the fingerprint scanner and the door unlocked.

The sight that awaited him behind the six-inch steel door reminded Alexei momentarily of a brigand's lair, with piles of looted booty stacked up like trophies. On the bottom shelve lay wads of cash, at least a million US dollars and the equivalent sum in euros. The shelve above held neatly stacked files: Documents pertaining to offshore accounts and their corresponding shell companies, lists of middlemen and assets—ministers, generals and corporate big-wigs—and inventory records: B61 nuclear warheads, TERCOM guidance systems, sarin, napalm.

Not enough to wage a full-blown war, but certainly enough to start one.

Alexei spent five seconds reading through the documents, committing the information to memory, then he placed them back into the safe—careful to put them in the exact same spot as they had lain.

Then his gaze moved to the topmost shelve. In a leather-lined box lay half a dozen passports issued by a whole range of countries—the Russian Federation, Switzerland, France, Lebanon, Cyprus and, of course, the Caribbean Island nation of Dominica. And finally, he found what he was looking for. Hidden under the stack of passports lay the silvery flash drive containing his own complete service file and beside it, the launch key that—together with its counterpart—had the power to control Pandora.

Alexei reached for the steel pendant and carefully slipped it into the hidden compartment in his Glock. Then, coolly, he replaced the flash drive with the cloned version that Kirill had carried here.

And now, all my dirty secrets are yours, Stiva.

He shut the safe and locked it, then he strode to the door, rolled under the optical barrier and came up to his feet in the hallway.

Four minutes and twenty-six seconds.

Quickening his pace, Alexei moved silently along the corridor until he reached the corner. Pressing his back against the wall right beside the elevator, he drew his weapon and waited. One second later, the distant din of footsteps echoed through the hallway. A guard. And he was exactly on schedule.

Letting his finger drop past the trigger guard, Alexei counted the seconds. Two. One. The black-clad sentry rounded the bend, stepping into his line of vision.

It was time.

Alexei pulled the trigger. The bullet hit the man squarely between the eyes, killing him before he hit the floor. Bending down, Alexei slipped the security pass from the guard's limp hand. Just at that moment, his earpiece crackled to life. Dropping to one knee, Alexei took the man's earpiece and put it on.

"Alpha four, confirm status."

Smothering a curse, Alexei slid his burner phone from his pocket and dialled his own number. The moment his mobile connected to the cellular network, static began to crackle in his earpiece, its sensitive frequency momentarily disrupted by the phone's signal.

"Alpha four, confirm status," the voice asked again, now barely audible over the crackling static.

Alexei smiled. *Ah, the beauty of science.*

"All clear," Alexei confirmed, knowing that whoever was on the other side would no longer be able to tell the difference between his voice and that of the guard.

"Roger that, Alpha Four, confirm all clear."

Rising, Alexei turned to the narrow metal door beside the elevator and opened it with the key card. The cramped maintenance shaft beyond it was almost pitch black, the greenish hue of an emergency exit sign providing just enough light to illuminate the contours of a rickety metal ladder that ran six stories deep into the ground. There was a grate in the floor to prevent an accidental fall.

Alexei bent to remove the grate, grabbed the guard by the shoulders and flung the corpse down the chute. Then he slid through the narrow opening and, grasping the side rails, skidded down the rickety ladder. Five seconds later, he hit the concrete floor without a sound, stood and slipped back out into the hallway six stories lower.

Three minutes and forty-nine seconds.

Quickening his pace, Alexei moved through the corridor and turned right into yet another hallway. The moment he rounded the bend, the black-clad soldiers posted outside Kirill's cell raised their weapons. They were quick, but not quick enough. They both died where they stood, each with a bullet between his eyes.

Under usual circumstances, Alexei would police his brass, but today he operated under extraordinary conditions. He was here to leave a trail. And Stiva had just shot two of Ivan's men to rescue a Russian agent. And when Ivan's men came down here, the slugs from Stiva's left-handed SIG would lie all over the place to prove it.

Rushing to the door, Alexei punched in the nine-digit access code. There was a faint click, then the hydraulic-powered gate swung open.

Keeping his finger on the trigger guard, Alexei stepped over the bodies and entered the holding cell. Kirill lay stretched out on the floor.

"It's time to move," Alexei said, grasping Kirill's Glock from the table in passing and tossing it in his direction.

Kirill's eyes snapped open, his hand moving up to catch the weapon.

"Look who's here, and all dressed up for the kill," Kirill said, grasping Alexei's outstretched hand and hauling himself to his feet with a faint groan.

Alexei laughed softly. "If I die tonight, I sure as hell want to make a pretty corpse." He turned to the door. "Now let's get moving."

At that moment, he heard it: The faint click of a door, then the soft shuffling of rubber-soled combat boots on concrete floor.

Guards.

Alexei whipped around and flipped up the table with one hand to shield them from the spurt of bullets that would rain into the cramped space in less than a second. Diving down behind it, he raised his weapon and put a projectile into the lightbulb above him. Instantly the room went black. Half a second later, beams of light broke the darkness, then a hailstorm of bullets rained down on them, shredding the chair beside him and pinging off the table's steel surface.

Ducking down beside him, Kirill raised his hand, his fingers spread.

Five guards.

In near darkness, blinded by beams of light, the visual constraints were enormous. But they could deal with this. They had done so before.

Closing his eyes, Alexei exhaled slowly, forcing his pulse down. And then the barrage of bullets stopped.

And like they had done a thousand times in tactical drills, he and Kirill moved in unison. A bullet from Alexei's SIG took out the point man. He dropped to the floor, blood gushing from a wound in his forehead. Kirill shot the second man below the left eye.

The others regrouped now, keeping their formation tight. They were true professionals—experienced, coldblooded and deadly accurate.

Shots headed his way, tearing past his head and hitting the wall behind him. Alexei let himself drop to the floor, using the point man's body as a shield. Then he rolled over his shoulder, lifted his gun, and pulled the trigger three times in rapid succession. The third man fell with a kill shot to the head. The fourth collapsed a fraction of a second later. The fifth managed to fire a shot, but

Alexei's bullet had wedged itself in his brain before the projectile left his rifle. It hit the ceiling, ricocheted off it and buried itself in the lifeless body of the point man.

One minute and eleven seconds.

Pushing himself up from the floor, he motioned for Kirill to follow him. "Let's go."

Stepping over the body of the point man, Alexei moved forward, quickly crossing the room and slipping out through the door. The hallway on the other side was deserted.

Alexei moved forward, his finger on the trigger guard, ready to fire at any moving target within a fraction of a second. When they reached the end of the hallway, he handed Kirill the access card.

"Use the ventilation shaft to your left to get to the roof. Stay in place until you have a clear exit route."

"And you?"

"I'll finish the job. If I succeed, I'll clear the way for you. If I fail, Ivan and his detail will move out of the North-Western exit and head for the helipad. When he does, put a bullet in his head for me."

"I will."

"Good. You have exactly one minute until the alarm is raised." Alexei glanced at his watch. "The count starts now."

They parted.

Now came the hardest part: The act.

CHAPTER XLIV

Isola di San Clemente, Venice, Italy
Thursday, 4th July, 23:49

Alexei strode down the hallway, disassembling the SIG as he walked. Four seconds later, he slipped back into the maintenance shaft and closed the door behind him. Stepping over the guard's lifeless body, he bent, removed the drain hatch in the floor and tossed the weapon into it. There was a splash as the gun, clip and suppressor hit the water at the bottom of the disused drainage system. The rapid-flowing stream that fed the ancient channel would carry the components out into the sea—never to be seen again.

Now the only evidence that remained was the pile of bodies he had left behind: Ivan's guards, killed by bullets fired from a modified left-handed SIG. The very same that Stiva carried.

Making sure that he had left no traces, Alexei replaced the grate, climbed the ladder and stepped out into the hallway on the ground floor.

Nineteen seconds.

Straightening his cuff, he walked silently down the corridor, slipped out into the lobby, and headed for the dining room. Taking a deep breath, he entered and closed the door behind him.

Three seconds.

Alexei hurried to the end of the room, stepping into the shadows of the gallery and opening the door.

Two seconds.

One.

Schooling his face into an expressionless mask, he stepped out into the hall and closed the door behind him—knowing that at this exact moment, the unresponsive surveillance camera had activated the all-out security protocol.

From that moment on, he had three minutes to complete the handover.

Careful to stay in the shadow of the doorframe, Alexei scanned the darkened reception hall, searching for Frost, finding him a second later. Their eyes met. A silent confirmation. Then they both moved, crossing the room with military precision—Frost always in the camera's sightline, Alexei always behind—as invisible as a ghost. A moment later, Alexei vanished in a throng of dancers and emerged on the other side—reborn among the living, just as visible as anyone else in the room.

Two minutes and fifty-one seconds.

To his left stood Lady Anne, Lord Cavendish's wife. The moment she spotted him, Anne's stony features transformed into a radiant smile.

Once a great beauty, age and solitude had turned her into a pitiable creature, unloved by her husband who desired younger women and shunned by any potential suitors who feared Cavendish's wrath far more than they coveted Anne's attention.

No man in his right mind would dare to intrude on Cavendish's preserves. But Alexei was different, he stood at par with Arthur and could cross bounds that others couldn't. She was the perfect decoy.

Well then, Anne, let me warm that withering heart of yours.

Stepping to her side, Alexei greeted her with the most gallant hand kiss he could muster while his eyes swept through the room, scanning the crowd for Stiva and Sophie. Just at that moment, Ivan's son stepped back into the hall, chivalrously offering Sophie his left hand and holding the door for her with his right. She rewarded him with a dazzling smile.

Alexei smiled faintly: It seemed that in the span of a day, his frightened little protégé had cast her feathers and moulted herself into a cunning tactician.

Briefly, he felt the teacher's pride, which slumbers in every agent runner the world over felt at the sight of his creatures in the field.

Responding absentmindedly to Anne's question, Alexei shifted his sights to a liveried waiter who artfully balanced a tray with solid-silver cups on his hand. The server was walking in Alexei's direction, stopping every so often to cater to the whims of one or the other guest.

Tonight, the man would be his unwitting mule. And judging by his servile smile and grovelling attitude, he would do this job exceptionally well.

Satisfied, Alexei allowed his gaze to move back to the far end of the room, where Frost, standing a mere ten feet from Stiva and Sophie, was nursing a glass of single malt. Again, their eyes met; silently confirming that both were ready for the final handover.

Two minutes and eleven seconds.

With a gallant bow, Alexei took his leave from Lady Cavendish. Just then, the liveried waiter went by.

Discreetly slipping the silvery flash drive from his pocket with his right hand, Alexei stopped the waiter with a wave of his left. The man rushed to his side, eager to be of service. Alexei rewarded his zeal with the small, ever-ready smile that was always so beautifully effective when he had to manipulate someone into doing his bidding. Then, with all the skill and dexterity of an accomplished magician, he snapped up a solid-silver cup with his right, drained the Vodka in one go, let the flash drive fall into the empty beaker and set it down on the tray again.

"Make sure my friend over there"—Alexei pointed at Frost—"gets a shot."

"Of course, sir." The waiter nodded deferentially, turned away and hurried to fulfil Alexei's request.

Alexei watched him, a small smile lingering on his lips as the flash drive—like a cuckoo's egg in the sparrow's nest—made its way undetected across the room, hidden from prying eyes inside its solid-silver casing.

And from there, Frost could funnel it to his American counterparts, providing them with enough hard evidence to get them moving on Pandora.

Three seconds later, the server stood in front of Frost, holding out his tray and offering him a Vodka shot. Just at that moment, Lady Cavendish—having found auspicious prey in the form of the dashing Tarik Khan—rushed past the waiter, the hem of her gown brushing along his leg. Startled, Alexei's unwitting mule stepped aside just as Frost reached for the cup. The waiter's body twisted in a desperate attempt to regain his balance, then his left arm moved up, the tray on his hand pitching sidelong towards the ground.

Time ground to a halt.

Alexei froze. His entire focus shifting to the beaker that was now hurtling towards the floor, falling in slow motion—like a stone sinking slowly to the bottom of a sea. And then it hit the marble. Like a projectile, the drive was vaulted from its canister.

For a fraction of a second, Alexei's gaze followed the drive's trajectory, watching as it bounced off the floor twice, skittering across it towards Stiva, then his eyes moved to Sophie. She was chalk white, staring over Stiva's shoulder, her gaze fixed on the drive that slithered towards them. Before she could even react, Stiva began to turn around, his eyes shifting towards the source of the commotion.

Alexei felt his blood run cold. It was over: The moment Stiva caught sight of the drive, he would know, and in an instant Alexei's masterful plan—all those years of meticulous preparation and ruthless execution—would collapse like a card house.

Instinctively, Alexei's hand moved up to his weapon, his eyes scanning the room. His Glock 43 was a sub-compact weapon built for concealed carry. It had a single stack clip with a maximum capacity of six bullets.

Six men.

Six that he could take with him before he went down himself. At the back of the room was Kirov, Cavendish, Khan and a US senator who occupied the ranks of the twelve along with them. To his right was Stiva. And a little further away, protected by his loyal henchmen, was Ivan. Like a many-headed Hydra, the Twelve would survive their loss, but the injury would still be serious, perhaps severe enough to allow another to take down the monster in his stead.

Alexei's fingers curled around the Glock's grip, his eyes shifting to Stiva, focusing on the spot just below his temple. He exhaled, slowly forcing the breath out of his lungs, readying himself for the kill—and his own death.

For justice.

But before he could draw, Sophie shifted closer to Stiva and pressed her lips to his—throwing herself in the literal and proverbial line of fire to give him the distraction he so desperately needed.

She would have to pay for her bravery later on, and Alexei had no intention to let her sacrifice go to waste.

He moved with the speed of a viper, bearing his way across the room—for all the world nothing but a jilted and humiliated lover. Half a second later, he passed Frost, shoving him out of his way. Frost fell, all six foot something of him, tumbling to the ground with all the grace and elegance of a duck on dry land.

All eyes were on Alexei now, the promise of scandal far too tempting to pay any attention to Frost, who swiftly picked up the drive and slipped it into his pocket.

Stiva released Sophie and turned to him, a small triumphant smile spreading across his lips. "I must admit, Alexei, your new... toy is really quite exquisite. An untamed horse, wasn't that the analogy you used?"

Their act had to be flawless now.

"Untamed indeed, and easily led astray by the smallest of temptations," Alexei said softly, holding Stiva's gaze for a heartbeat, making sure that the slight had hit its mark, then he shifted his gaze to Sophie.

She flinched but didn't back away.

Good girl.

Slowly, Alexei stepped closer to her and moved his hand to her chin. Placing his forefinger just below the pretty little dimple there, Alexei raised her head to look into her eyes. Briefly, her eyes seemed to linger on Stiva, not on his face, but on his hand, then her eyes snapped up to his. The fear he saw in them was a little too real. Still, she was holding herself admirably. There was no doubt that she had every intention of sitting this one through.

Well then, let's not disappoint our audience.

"You see, Stiva, she's a fighter, fierce as an Amazon, always testing the limits, living on the edge," he said softly, holding her gaze while he spoke. "Women like her require a strong hand. Still, I prefer the exciting ones to your broken dolls. It makes things so much more... enjoyable when they dare to fight back." He paused, focusing his attention fully on Sophie now. "Wouldn't you agree, my dear?"

She didn't respond, and Alexei hadn't expected her to. Letting his lips curl into a small, malicious smile, he released her chin and turned back to Stiva.

"You're more than welcome to watch, so you can see what you've missed out on. Trust me, her screams are very pretty."

Before Stiva could respond, the dining room door swung open and six black-clad guards, led by Ivan's Circassian security chief, marched into the room.

Without pausing in their stride, the men cut through the throngs of dancers and chatting guests, purposefully carving their way towards Ivan. Three seconds later, the Circassian stood by the Tsar's side. They spoke in hushed whispers, their conversation taking less than two seconds. Then Ivan gave a nod. A mute command.

There was a brief moment of silence, the hush before a storm, then the room disintegrated into chaos.

CHAPTER XLV

Isola di San Clemente, Venice, Italy
Friday, 5th July, 00:01

Suddenly everything was in motion.

Two dozen black-clad guards detached themselves from their position along the walls, and, drawing their weapons, swarmed out with military precision. For a split second they moved in lockstep, their eyes searching for their allotted protectees. A moment later they regrouped into nimble two-man teams and cut into the crowd—ploughing through the throngs of dancers like icebreakers through the Baltic Sea.

Alexei let himself fall back, watching the drama that now unfolded: The guests retreating to the sides of the hall, the guards rushing to their charges, and Sophie—standing poised amidst the maelstrom of chaos.

For a second, Alexei held her gaze—assuring her that all would be well—then his own detail caught up with him.

"Code blue, sir. Kirill Orlov escaped with the Pandora launch key. Ten men down and counting. We need to clear the premises now," the point man said, pressing one hand against his earpiece as he simultaneously listened to whatever information operations was relaying.

Alexei almost had to smile. Just as planned, his little adventure had triggered a Blue Code—the security protocol for high-level threats that warranted the immediate evacuation of all high-value targets. As one of the Twelve, his safety took precedence over that of all others in this room. While the other guests remained behind, he and his peers would be spirited away to separate secure locations. And while they all waited, the guards would search the property—combing through the gardens, scouring through every room and shifting through all the surveillance footage and access rosters. Piece by piece they would find his trail—each shred of evidence another nail in Stiva's coffin.

Drawing his gun, Alexei glanced at Frost, making sure that the Brit would keep an eye on his protégé, then he nodded at the guards. "Let's go."

Obeying his command, the men formed a tight box around him—one to the front, a little to his left, the other behind. They would die to protect him.

"Cerberus in hands," the point man confirmed into his mic, moving forward through the crowd. Within seconds, they had cleared the reception hall, moving through a series of hallways and galleries up to the first floor, towards the one place Alexei hadn't expected to go.

Ivan's office.

Alexei felt his muscles tense, his body readying itself instinctively for combat. Boxed in by his own detail and faced by six armed sentries that manned the office door, he was both outgunned and outflanked. Retreat wasn't an option. Nor was an all-out assault. Whatever was about to happen, he would have to play the game. And he would have to play it to perfection.

The next moment the double door swung wide and Ivan's security chief walked out through them.

"Confirm Cerberus in hand," the Circassian barked into his radio, his eyes lingering on Alexei. Then he motioned ahead. "Step this way, sir."

Well then, the game's afoot.

Schooling his face into an expressionless mask, Alexei stepped over the threshold.

The room beyond was dimly lit, its polished marble floors aglow in the subdued light of outsized LED screens. Usually hidden behind the elegant timber veneer, the monitors were now in full view, displaying real-time security feeds, aerial footage and ground imagery. This wasn't just surveillance but battlefield reconnaissance.

Beneath the luminescent wall of flickering images stood six armed guards—motionless, arms ready, eyes scaling the bank of French windows from side to side. Beyond the armoured glass, Alexei spotted moving beams of flashlights, and a little further away, behind the line of trees, the pulsing glare of helicopter taillights.

The Hydra is ready for battle, Alexei thought, shifting his sights to the far end of the room.

There, flanked by four guards, stood Ivan. Calm, self-assured, as always in ascendency over the chaos. The stance of a general, feet planted firmly on the ground, a little apart, hands linked behind his back. His expression unreadable. His ever-wary eyes fixed on Alexei.

"Lock down the room," Ivan commanded.

Alexei felt a surge of adrenaline. None of his peers were here. And none of them would come. It was down to Ivan and him.

The ormolu clock on the mantelpiece chimed. The twelfth hour.

Ivan waited for silence to fall again, watching him carefully. Then he spoke. And in the stillness of the room, the Tsar's voice resonated from the walls.

"I have done this for a very long time, Alexei Alexandrovich, I know how much it takes to gain power and how little to lose it." Ivan paused. "The secret to staying on top is to never lose caution, to never trust anyone fully, even those closest to you."

Alexei remained silent, his every instinct cautioning him to maintain his act. *It's not over. Not yet.*

Ivan regarded him for a long time, searching his face for a tell-tale sign of his treason, then finally, he gave a slow nod.

"I kept my eye on you, Alexei, on you and all the others. I watched you, waiting for you to make a mistake, to expose yourself." Ivan shook his head, ever so slightly. "But you didn't. As always, you were perfect. Beyond reproach." Ivan paused, his grey eyes fixed on him. "You know, Alexei, you're the best I've ever seen. A prodigy. Larger-than-life. My showpiece general. And yet, you've failed to bring me the traitor. Why?"

CHAPTER XLVI

Isola di San Clemente, Venice, Italy
Friday, 5th July, 00:16

As though on cue, the jarring sound of cocking sub-guns echoed in the room. And then the weapons levelled on Alexei, their sight dots dancing over his heart like a swarm of fireflies.

Ivan didn't move as the weapons descended on his loyal lieutenant, but something changed in the Tsar's eyes, some quickening of malice, that—even more than the sight dots over his heart—gave Alexei absolute certainty of his situation: He was on trial, accused of either incompetence or treason, and unless he proved his innocence on both counts, he wouldn't leave this room alive.

For a second, Alexei's eyes shifted up to the screens, his gaze scaling over the alternating imagery of tactical teams rushing through hallways, black-clad snipers positioning themselves on the roofs and suited guards searching the scene with painstaking care.

The stage was set.

The trail—the bullets, the money, the flash drive—all had been laid-out with meticulous care. Ivan's men—the soldiers, the guards, the auxiliaries—were all in position. Each one trained to follow protocol in agonising detail. And now, like an army of string puppets, they would dance for their master. Piece by piece, they would uncover the evidence of Stiva's betrayal. And while the play unfolded in all its calamitous tragedy, Alexei would spin a marvellous tale of greed and hate and treason. Word by word, he would absolve himself from all guilt and brand the Tsar's son a traitor. And when he was done, not even a father's love would save Stiva from the headman's axe.

Time to lift the curtain.

He shifted his gaze back to Ivan. "Because I needed absolute certainty before I condemn one of ours to death."

Ivan smiled vaguely at the ceiling, like a judge tired of hearing the same lame excuse once again. "And are you certain now, Alexei?"

The flashing taillight of a helicopter illuminated the room like a thunderbolt.

"I am."

Ivan regarded him for a long moment, studying him pensively, then he raised his hand like a king giving his servant leave to speak. "Then convince me, Alexei. Give me a reason to spare your life."

Alexei gave a solemn nod.

"For almost two decades, the Twelve operated hand-in-hand with the Kremlin, fixing Moscow's dirty problems all over the globe while giving them plausible deniability. But there's nothing more dangerous than an ageing dictator, afraid that someone will snatch away his power and put him up against the wall. And it seems that our self-proclaimed Russian tsar was afraid that the Twelve were about to snatch his crown away, not by force, but by slowly undermining his empire. And so, the Kremlin decided to do away with us. Permanently."

Slipping his hand leisurely into his pocket, Alexei turned away from Ivan and—ignoring the sight dots on his chest with all the nonchalance of a vindicated man—began to stroll along the bank of French windows.

"But of course, it couldn't be done openly. The president still needed us, to launder his money, to build his weapons, and to prop up all those tinpot dictators around the world that gave the Kremlin a hold on a new sphere of interest, far beyond the sea. So instead of dragging you and yours to Siberia on trumped-up charges, Moscow devised another plan. A covert operation to undermine and finally topple the Twelve."

Once again, the flashing taillight of a helicopter illuminated the room like a thunderbolt.

"Given the scale and global reach of our operations, Moscow knew that a blunt force attack would hardly be sufficient to take us down. And so, in consultation with the GRU and SVR, they opted for a rather daring strategy: Infiltration." Strolling past the outsized fireplace, he continued in a steady voice. "With the help of an asset, the Kremlin inserted four deep-cover agents into our ranks. Slowly, step by step, they guided them up the ladder towards our inner circle. All they needed was one, just one, to make it to the top. And once he was there, he would be able to seize control and dismantle us from within."

"This is old news, Alexei," Ivan interjected. "Operation *Pugachev* was mothballed three years ago."

Ivan was right of course: None of this was news. Certainly not to the man who had executed his fellow agents on the shitty cellar floor of a Washington townhouse. But the best and most enduring of deceptions were always wrapped in the glorious shroud of verity. And so, like a cunning magician, Alexei would raise the past from its stinking grave and breathe new life into it.

Strolling past the door, he now turned back towards Ivan, establishing eye contact with the Tsar. "Operation *Pugachev* wasn't discontinued, Ivan, it was merely... adjusted."

Again, the taillight's pulsing glare illuminated the room, momentarily transforming the world around him into the garish interplay of shadow and light.

Raising his voice a little, like an actor on stage, Alexei continued his narration: "When the Kremlin realised that it would be impossible to insert an agent into our ranks, they opted for a different approach: Recruitment. And so they deployed Colonel Kirill Orlov, a senior intelligence officer attached to the First Directorate's Ural 16 black-ops team. His mission? Turn someone who already had a seat at the table." He paused for the briefest of moments, letting his words hang in the silence like a spell. "For more than two years, Orlov failed to deliver any results, but then his fortune changed: He turned one of ours."

"Who?" Ivan demanded, his voice cold.

Alexei waited a beat, well aware that the best and most enduring lies were delivered calmly, with an air of superiority and just a tiny pinch of well-calculated insolence.

"Your son."

Ivan didn't flinch, his expression betraying none of the emotions that he might feel right now. He was simply waiting for an explanation, and Alexei would deliver exactly that. For a heartbeat, Alexei's eyes went up to the screens, making sure that his puppets were still dancing according to plan, then he continued his narration.

"For six years, Stepan Ivanovich was the uncontested heir to the throne. Brilliant. Resourceful. Without fail. But then, all of a sudden, Stiva's rising star began to fade. Minsk. Washington. Manzanillo. Failure after failure. Mistakes that cost him money, power, and finally his position at your right." Alexei paused, letting his words sink in. "Stiva was frustrated. Humiliated. Angry. Prone to the Kremlin's offer to give him what he so desperately craved: Power and Revenge."

"Do you have proof for this claim?"

Alexei had anticipated this question. And he had provided for it.

"Orlov's confession, along with a payment made by a known Russian slush fund to Stiva's Bermuda holdings and a wiretap that I believe has been placed in your office by your son. I handed it to security for a follow-up."

"Who witnessed Orlov's testimony?"

"I witnessed it, so did the guards on duty."

Guards that were now dead, unable to verify or refute his claim.

The Tsar gave a slow nod, his eyes shifting to the monitors.

Alexei followed his gaze.

Ivan's security chief was now rushing back to the study, briskly brushing past the guards outside. Again, the helicopter's glaring lights flashed in the darkness. Then, the door swung wide to admit the Circassian.

"Orlov had help," the Circassian said, striding up to Ivan with the evidence bag in hand. "And whoever it was, he butchered at least eight of our men," He slipped the bullet from the bag and offered it to Ivan. "The scene is riddled with it."

Ivan took the slug, and holding it up between two fingers, took a step away to inspect the projectile. And as he studied the round, Alexei saw him shed his habitual air of controlled restraint and stiffen. For a fraction of a second, the Tsar seemed almost overcome with some unspeakable emotion, but then he recovered himself, turned and handed the shell to Alexei.

"Tell me what you see, Alexei, and be thorough."

Alexei turned the cartridge in his hand, studying it with due care. "That's a slug from a .357 SIG. Special ball, flat point bullet, modified to withstand higher bolt trust. I wouldn't say it's unique but certainly rare."

Ivan stood in silence for a moment, seemingly absorbing this information, then his eyes shifted to his security chief. "What did you find out about the wiretap that Alexei discovered?"

"This," the Circassian held up a platinum cufflink, one of Kirill's, its polished surface gleaming under the low light "belongs to Colonel Kirill Orlov."

The Circassian deftly twisted the cufflink, revealing a tiny compartment in the centre. From it, he extracted a minuscule device, no larger than a grain of rice. "It's standard GRU issue, fitted with this," he continued, holding the device between his thumb and forefinger. "A high-grade listening device. Quite sophisticated."

The Circassian placed the device carefully on Ivan's desk, then reached into his pocket, producing an identical one sealed in an evidence bag.

Alexei almost had to smile at the sight of the shattered bug, placed in Ivan's study by a desperate son trying to regain his father's love.

"This one," the Circassian said, his eyes narrowing, "belongs to Stepan Ivanovich. The working assumption is that your son received them from Orlov."

Ivan's jaw muscles tightened visibly. Alexei knew what went through the Tsar's mind right now: All the little inconsistencies and contradictions—Stiva's recent failures, his demotion, his hatred for the man who had taken his place. And now a Russian-made wiretap and the slugs of a rare, modified type of ammunition—both tracing back to Stiva. All of it was too much to be a coincidence. Too much to be ignored.

The game was under his control once more. Quietly. Without spectacle or force, Alexei had reclaimed the upper hand. And now, that he held all the strings again, he would steer his puppets into ruin.

"Continue your story," the Tsar commanded, in a tone laced with cold, controlled anger.

Pocketing the slug, Alexei gave a nod. "The Kremlin, knowing that they could only sway your son with the ultimate prize, went on to propose a diabolical alliance: They would ensure Stiva's ascent to the throne by removing you and yours from power. And in return for this lavish gift, the new Tsar would once again shore-up Russia's interests abroad."

Ivan pursed his lips. "I see, the Tsar in service to the Kremlin. A devil's bargain indeed."

Once again, the bickering taillight flared up like a bolt of lightning, momentarily transforming Ivan's even features into a sinister mask of shadow and light.

And as the garish light died away, the door opened to admit a dark-suited man. Without ceremony, he walked up to Ivan's security chief and handed him a single piece of paper. Briefly, the Circassian's eyes lingered on the page, then his gaze turned to his boss.

"Sir, we went through the security tapes of the past three hours. We initially lost control of the surveillance camera for the south-facing balcony and part of the garden. Subsequently, surveillance in the dining room went blind." He paused. "It looks like someone left the reception room over the balcony, re-entered the building through a window into the dining room and then went down to the holding cells from there."

"Who was on the balcony at that time?"

"Your son, sir. In the company of Miss Akehurst. During the six-minute window in question, we can consistently see Miss Akehurst in the surveillance footage from the interior of the reception room, however, your son is unaccounted for."

For a moment, Ivan stood motionless, his expression hard. Then he reached into his jacket pocket and handed the Circassian a key card. "Search Stiva's office and suite. And have someone check the financial records of his Bermuda holdings," Ivan commanded, then added. "What's the status of the flash drive with the service file of the Russian agent?"

"It's almost decrypted."

"Good. Bring it to me when it's done," Ivan replied, then turned to Alexei. "And while we wait for whatever my son might be hiding from me, there is one other theory that I would like to test."

"And which one would that be?" Alexei asked, suddenly wary of losing the upper hand.

"Your new plaything, Alexei. My son seemed unduly interested in her. I want to be sure that she isn't more than she seems."

Alexei showed no reaction, no blink of the eye, no twitch of the lips—keeping up the mask of cold indifference with all the skill of an accomplished deceiver.

Tonight's operation had been meticulously planned. Nothing had been left to chance. Every contingency had been provided for. But Alexei hadn't accounted for Sophie playing any part in this after the alarm was raised. This turn of events was certainly unpleasant, but he controlled the game now, and as long as he stayed on top of it, he would decide its outcome.

"Well then, let's bring her here."

CHAPTER XLVII

Isola di San Clemente, Venice, Italy
Friday, 5th July, 01:48

Seconds passed. Stretching to minutes. And then Sophie was brought into the room—frogmarched by two guards, two more walking on her heels. Each too close for comfort. Not a phalanx, but an execution squad.

As Alexei watched her, so vulnerable and frail, he felt a fleeting sense of guilt wash over him. All of this was his doing. He had brought her here, knowingly dragging her into his immoral power game. In consequence, her every moment of fear and pain and suffering would forever weigh on his conscience—yet another blemish on his unredeemable soul.

For a heartbeat, Alexei's eyes went up to the screens, watching as the Tsar's men rushed through the hallways, paving their way to Stiva's office—inching, step by step, towards the damming piece of evidence that he had planted there. Then his gaze shifted to Ivan, who stood by the window, his expression overcast, his face half-hidden in the shadows.

Silently, Alexei waited for Ivan to make a move, artfully maintaining the illusion of master and servant, while in truth, the balance of power had inexorably begun to tilt in the servant's favour.

Go on, old man, enjoy the crown while it still rests on your head.

For a second, Ivan stood in silence, simply observing Sophie, then, with half a smile, the Tsar stepped from the shadows, and—sauntering across the room with all the arrogance of a man who believed himself in absolute control—spread out his arms a little, as if greeting a long-awaited guest. "Welcome to the party, my dear."

She didn't reply.

Ivan pursed his lips as if he were disappointed by her lack of response. Stepping closer, the Tsar studied Sophie, then he moved his hand to her chin, tipping it up with his bony forefinger. She flinched away, a spark of disgust flashing in her eyes.

Ivan's lips curled into that cold, dreadful smile that Alexei knew all too well. "Oh, I can see why Alexei picked you. So very beautiful. So fiery." He chuckled. "Tell me, are you frightened of him?"

"No," she replied, looking straight into Ivan's eyes.

Ivan laughed softly, a hint of mirth dancing in his eyes. "You know, I'm an old man. I've seen many things in my life. But you..." Ivan shook his head, as though something about her was quite unbelievable. "You're young. Inexperienced. Unaware of the horrors that lurk in the real world. But I'm sure you agree that ignorance is never a good thing. So allow me to redress that by telling you a little story—one I think you'll find both entertaining and instructive."

Ivan released her chin and—clasping his hands behind his back—began to stroll around with slow, measured steps.

"About three years ago, there was a pretty little journalist that meddled in my business. She published a rather unkind article on my dear friend Victor Orsin in *The New York Times*. Of course, I had to put a stop to it, so I brought her here and entrusted her to Alexei's care. I'm not sure if you know that, but Alexei has a special talent: He understands how people work, what makes them tick." Ivan flicked his fingers. "Or snap. And so, as expected, it didn't take very long until your gentle lover had learned all her secrets. Personally, I would have done away with her after that tearful confession, but Alexei likes to play. So he kept her. You know, the kind of toy that you keep in a dark corner and only use when you need to... unwind. She fared quite well under his care, but then she crossed a line. Became a liability. And he put her down like a stray dog. Didn't even bat an eye." Ivan shifted his gaze to Alexei. "Tell me, my friend, how does your new plaything compare to the lovely Natalia?"

Alexei felt cold anger wash over him, a hatred so deep and pure that it almost made him lose his composure. Just then, at that moment of weakness, when hate and grief and pain threatened to undo all he had worked for, the taillight's pulsing glare illuminated the room, transforming Ivan's even features into a sinister mask of shadow and light.

And in the garish glow, Alexei saw Ivan as he had seen him the night of their first encounter, descending into a dusty trench on the Turco-Syrian border, tall and regal, clad all in black, walking between the bodies of the dead like the lord of the netherworld. And he had smiled as he looked down at the dead. Men. Women. Children. Their flesh eaten away by the toxic fumes of sarin gas. Killed at a tyrant's orders. Murdered by weapons sold at Ivan's behest.

This was the monster he fought—not just organised crime, not even war, but the inhuman, indiscriminate killing of the innocent. And whatever sacrifice this crusade would demand, he would make it. Calmly. In the steadfast certainty of his cause.

"One is like the other: Expendable."

"Indeed, they are," Ivan said with a nod. "Well then, let's find out what your pet knows, shall we?"

Alexei let his lips curl into a faint smile. "With pleasure."

Forcing the memory of Natalia from his mind, Alexei focused his attention on his protégée: She was deadly pale. Terror lingering in her eyes.

As he studied her, Alexei recalled their first encounter five days and an apparent lifetime ago: She had been so perfect then, a shining example of professional courtesy and reticence, the act wavering only when his cold reproach caught her off guard—faltering for a moment so brief that only one with his acumen and skillset would ever have noticed it.

What he had guessed then had been proven true many times over under the most difficult conditions: She had it in her, the ability to deceive, the sangfroid to play the smoke and mirror's game even with a gun held to her head. She was a diamond in the rough. Time and training would turn her into a master of this game. But here and now, they didn't have the luxury of either. And so, while an agent had years and guiding hands to learn his tradecraft, her rite of passage would take place under battlefield conditions.

Alexei lifted his hand. "Bring her forward."

As the guards forced her across the room, Alexei felt himself enter into that state of readiness and outmost concentration that he sought when pulling the trigger.

He had spent four years honing the character traits of the man he played, carefully cultivating a myriad palette of qualities and flaws that made up his persona. Each one of Zorin's many faces had proven useful over the years—the killer, the general, the dealmaker, the diplomat—but tonight, it was an unlikely one that would save them both: The sadist.

In this world, a man who derived pleasure from inflicting pain on others could engage in the most depraved acts without punishment or reproach. And this gave him leeway. It allowed him to intervene when the game was already over. When a prisoner had confessed all that there was to confide, when the only thing that remained was putting a bullet in the victim's head, Alexei Zorin could step in—keep his subject alive with nothing but the justification of deriving pleasure from the act of protracting their suffering. It had allowed him to save Natalia for a while. As well as many others. Assets. Men and women who were of vital interest to the Russian government. Alexei kept them alive, hidden away in some dark, forgotten hellhole, and after a while, they simply disappeared, funnelled into the caring hands of a GRU extraction team. And if anyone had the nerve to inquire after his toys, there was nothing surprising in the answer that they—quite unfortunately—hadn't survived the strain of his hospitality.

Tonight, the sadist's penchant for dirty foreplay would allow Alexei to prepare his pupil for what was to come—to teach, without words, the central lessons that would ensure their survival.

For a moment, Alexei's eyes went up to the screens, making sure that his puppets still danced for their master, then he shifted his gaze back to his apprentice.

Slowly, he stepped towards her, his eyes tracing down her body, taking in her expression, her posture, every little detail about her. An experienced interrogator knew the signs of deception, those little hints that the body gave: the unsteady eyes, the twitch of a muscle, that ever-so-faint flush of the skin and a thousand other clues. But there were ways to mitigate them.

On to the first lesson: Maintaining the illusion.

There was her hand, those fingers that were so inopportunely cramped around the folds of her gown. If she lied, they would twitch, just a little, but it would be enough to give her away. Then, there was her breathing, so shallow and quick, like a frightened deer. It too would change with every lie she told. It would slow, or quicken, perhaps pause for just a moment. And, of course, there was that treacherous little vein at the side of her neck, that pulsed visibly even in the dim light.

Slowly, deliberately, Alexei stepped around her—circling her like a predator its prey. And in passing, he let his hand glide over hers, as if by accident, casually untangling her fingers from the folds of her gown—letting his touch linger just long enough to let her know that this was important.

"Tell me, are you frightened?"

"No."

The word, when it came, was barely audible—a tremulous whisper accompanied by a single tear that ran slowly down her cheek, smudging her make-up and leaving a dark stain in its wake.

He let his lips curl into that cold, sadistic smile that was always so wonderfully effective in demonstrating to his victims how absolutely the balance of power had shifted.

"Liar," he sneered, halting behind her back.

Briefly, Alexei let his eyes linger on the smooth expanse of her back, then he moved a little closer, and bending down, pressed his lips to her cheek—just below her ear.

"Breathe with me," he murmured, his voice so low that it was inaudible to all but her. "Relax your body."

As he spoke, Alexei placed his hand gently on her back, feeling her breathing fall into sync with his. He waited for a moment, making sure they were attuned, then slowly, deliberately, he ran his lips up her cheek—licking off the tear.

"I can taste your fear," he said softly, raising his voice just enough for his audience to hear. "And it is oh so sweet."

She shivered under his touch. Alexei withdrew, took a step back and resumed his slow, predatory pacing, completing the circle around her. In passing, he let his hand run through her hair with the same absentminded gesture with which one might caress the head of a sleeping dog—casually brushing the mass of dark waves over her shoulder, concealing that perfidious, pulsing artery that would give her away in a heartbeat if she lied.

The basics were covered.

Well then, let's move on to the second lesson: Choosing the act.

Under torture, the subject's behaviour—reactions, words, recovery times and breaking points—told a story. It revealed a man for who and what he truly was. Agent. Liar. Traitor. Or simply an innocent bystander accidentally caught up in the game. Hence, the victim's mask had to be chosen with care. Under usual circumstances, this decision was left at an agent's discretion, but this was a trial by fire, and so, Alexei could give his student a nudge in the right direction—letting her know what kind of performance he expected from her.

Gracing her with a sickeningly indulgent smile, Alexei sauntered around her in a wide arc. "I'm sure you remember that spirited conversation we had on our journey here. In its course, I made you a promise." He paused, completing the circle around her, re-establishing eye contact before he delivered the decisive line. "I promised that you would lick the dirt off my shoes if you ever crossed me. Tonight, you did cross me. And it is your misfortune that I am a man of my word."

She closed her eyes, her lips trembling just a little, her reaction somewhere between genuine terror and wilful deception. Not perfect, but good enough for a first try. They could practise as they went along.

Time for the opening scene.

He stepped around her, very slowly, running his hand up her arm, over her shoulder, then up the back of her neck. And there, he stopped, waiting for just a moment, then he bent down over her shoulder, like a debonair rake whispering an indecent proposal into a lady's ear.

"Kneel."

CHAPTER XLVIII

Isola di San Clemente, Venice, Italy
Friday, 5th July, 02:01

"Kneel," Alexei commanded.

Sophie hesitated, reluctant to comply with his command. Gently, Alexei ran his fingertips down her spine, letting her know that his request wasn't a grandstand play, but a vital necessity—one that would give him the indispensable physical control needed to keep her safe.

"I won't ask again," he ordered, hooking his fingers in the sash that hung between her elbows. "Kneel down."

He watched her shoulders rise and fall with her breath, the final preparation as she readied herself for the curtain's rise. And then she sank to the ground—slowly, gracefully, the silk stole slithering through the crooks of her arms.

Alexei watched her for a moment, weighing the silken shawl in his hand, then he took a step back and, wrapping the scarf around his left, began to saunter around her in a wide arc.

Once again, Alexei took a mental reckoning of the score-line, his eyes going up to the screens—watching Ivan's black-clad sentries that stood guard in front of Stiva's office. For a split second, the scene behind the door flashed in his mind's eye with perfect clarity: The Circassian, standing beside Stiva's mahogany desk, as always in that conceited strongman's stance—hands linked behind his back, feet a little apart, eyes sweeping the room—calmly surveying his troops in action. And his bloodhounds—swift, precise and dreadfully thorough—searching every inch, turning every grain of dust until they uncovered the incriminating piece of evidence that Alexei had left behind for them to find. What came next would be a demonstration of the extraordinary power of the Twelve: Informants from dozens of intelligence agencies, military branches and government bodies would confirm the information on the drive, and their every word would be crosschecked against a myriad array of sources from mission reports and offshore bank accounts to diplomatic correspondence and satellite imagery. Until their work was done, another twenty minutes would pass. A lifetime. One they would have to devote to this performance now.

Alexei shifted his gaze back to his student. She was still breathing steadily, but her face was ashen, her eyes a little too wide, her position a little too rigid. She was frightened, not just of the act, but of him.

Alexei pressed his lips together.

It seemed that Ivan's tale had done its trick all too well. With just a few words, the Tsar had eroded that precious bond of trust between them. She doubted him, fearing that, if the choice came down to her or his duty, Alexei would sacrifice her to the cause without a moment's hesitation. Just as he had sacrificed Natalia. And that lack of trust would spell doom for his protégé, for no matter how well she maintained her act, the practised eye—Ivan's and his—would always see that shadow of fear. And while Alexei knew its origin, Ivan—oblivious to the secret that torturer and victim shared between them—would see it as evidence of her guilt.

If Alexei failed to heal that rift, she wouldn't survive this. In consequence, he would have to regain her trust while holding her at gunpoint.

He exhaled slowly, focusing his mind on the performance he would now have to deliver.

"Stiva is an interesting man," he remarked lazily, sauntering around her in a wide arc and making a show of tying the scarf into a loose snare. "Powerful. Affluent. Occasionally even charming. And just like me, an incorrigible romantic." He paused, giving his audience a moment to appreciate the show. "Tell me, what sweet nothings did he whisper into your ear to warrant such passion tonight?"

"We just talked, nothing important, about Venice... the sights. Please, I'm sorry. I didn't mean to anger you."

Her voice was barely audible, tearful, quivering with fear. Slowly, Alexei stepped around his student, pretending to ponder her response as he held her gaze, silently trying to soothe and assure her before he moved this forward. She held his gaze for a heartbeat, then lowered her eyes.

Come on, Sophie, have a little faith in me, he urged her in his mind.

She didn't look at him again.

So he would have to continue the game, leading his student along the edge of the precipice without letting her fall.

"Only fools risk their lives for no reason at all." He paused. "Now, I think we both agree that you're no fool. So in my book, this makes you a fibber, a fraud... a despicable little prevaricator of half-truths." Another pause. One filled only with the soft rustle of silk on skin as he slid the noose around her neck. Loosely. Nothing but a threat. A promise. "Tell me, Sophie Madeline Akehurst, are you a liar?"

He watched the small hairs on her arms rise, her breathing becoming more laboured, her nostrils flaring just a little.

"I'm not," she whispered, her voice wavering, betraying her fear as blatantly as the tear that ran down her cheek.

She wasn't ready. Not yet. The scars of the past and Ivan's tale were weighing too heavily on her. But Alexei had extended the grace period beyond any reasonable limit. The time for rehearsals was over. Whether his protégé was ready or not, they would have to cross the Rubicon now.

For the briefest of moments, Alexei felt a strange inertia descend over him—the silk scarf lying like lead in his hand, the need to delay the inevitable almost overwhelming.

She had undressed for him, come to his bed and knelt at his feet, each one an intimate act, but none of them close to what was about to happen between them now. All that had occurred was corporal, but this was different. Torture touched the mind. The soul. One misstep, a single careless action on his part, could do irreparable damage. If she broke under the strain, she would die, and so would he. And after them, countless more would follow—Ivan's future victims, who would die and continue to die years, and perhaps even decades from now, until someone else would have the chance to end the game.

Here and now, they were the last line of defence. They couldn't fail. That meant his performance had to be flawless now—an illusion worthy of the most skilful magician.

Forcing his mind to focus on the task, Alexei let himself drop to one knee behind her back, and as he moved downward, he slung the scarf around his right with a savage jolt—tightening it like a hangman's rope. And as the shawl began to constrict around her neck, he slid his left hand up her spine, all the way to the nape, and there—hidden under the guise of her sleek dark curls—he hooked his fingers into the silken band, stopping its deadly contraction—creating an invisible lifeline along which they would now move.

There was the brief moment of genuine terror, when her hands went up to her throat, trying to free herself, frantically fighting for her life. He pressed his lips to her shoulder.

"Trust me," he murmured, his voice inaudible to all but her. "Breathe with me."

Her breathing grew a little calmer. But still, she trembled under his touch—their physical proximity terrifying rather than reassuring.

This was all he could do for her now. More and his act would fall apart. Alexei closed his eyes, feeling her pulse, counting her breaths, making sure that the strain remained physically bearable. No matter how much his pupil struggled to maintain the act, the game was still his and so was the ability to shape it. He would drag her through this, help her act the part until she gained the confidence to spread her wings.

I'll get you through this, he assured Sophie in his mind, then he opened his eyes and reprised his role.

Slowly, with all the sickening depravity of a true sadist, Alexei let his teeth trail over the curve of her shoulder, up her neck, all the way to that pulsing vein just below her ear. There, he paused for a moment, placing a gentle kiss on that throbbing spot—as if relishing the physical manifestation of her fear on his lips—then he twisted his hand in her hair, compelling her to struggle harder.

"Yes, fight me," he urged with a soft laugh. "Fight for your life."

And she did, her body arching against his with the ferocity of a trapped animal. He held her like this for a moment. Thirty seconds. A minute. Letting her fight. Keeping her safe. Always between that narrow band of movement that would ensure that the hangman's rope remained nothing but pretence. Then he released her.

And then the ritual was repeated. A question asked. An answer given. A response deemed unsatisfactory. A punishment doled out.

Again and again, they went through the same set of motions. Ten. Fifteen. Twenty times. And as they performed the audience watched in rapt attention: The guards standing motionless along the walls, the occasional visitor slipping silently into the room to relay information, and Ivan, lounging in a high-backed chair—observing the scene with the vague smile of the connoisseur who knows the play by heart, but enjoys it nonetheless.

With every step they took, Alexei could feel his student's strength wane a little more, the act becoming harder to maintain. Once again, his eyes went to the screens, asserting that his puppets still laboured in his cause. Then he returned his attention to his apprentice.

He had tortured many. Men. Women. With a few exceptions, he had always tried to protect them. But more often than not, it had been in vain. When they broke, it didn't happen with a bang. There were no tears, no pleas, no physical breakdowns. It happened quietly, like death at dawn. It was in their eyes. He could always see it. The moment that the light died in them. And hers was dying.

The game was poised on knife's edge, and if she failed to entrust herself to him now, if she failed to immerse herself in the act without reserve, then the blade would fall and do so with devastating consequence.

Taking a deep breath, Alexei lowered himself to one knee in front of her. She averted her gaze. Unwilling to meet his eyes.

"Look at me," he commanded.

She looked up, a silent tear running down her cheek, along the line of her lips. And then it fell, dropping down on the tip of his shoe.

Very gently, he brushed her hair from her neck, exposing it to his view. He wanted to see that vein now. He needed to see it. Then, slowly, gently, he ran his thumb along her collarbone, silently assuring her that he wouldn't let her fall. As his fingertip ran over her skin, something changed in her eyes, as if—for the first time since the commencement of this twisted game—she was truly seeing him, not the illusion, but the man behind the mask. And in that moment, they crossed the line, becoming one in body and mind—two tightrope artists, balancing on the wire, moving across it in perfect harmony.

She was ready.

"It's time to redeem my promise, don't you think?"

She shut her eyes, and he watched her: His perfect pupil, Tchaikovsky's swan on stage, ready to deliver the performance of a lifetime. A second passed. Another. A lifetime. Finally, she opened her eyes, her gaze shifting down and then slowly, with all the weightless grace of a dancer, bent to fulfil his terrible request.

As she moved down, he rose, drawing his gun. Then, just as her lips touched the tip of his shoe, tremulously brushing off that offending testimony of her fear, he cocked his gun, aiming it at the back of her head.

"Shh, stay, just like this. This is your last chance to answer my question. Fail to convince me and you will die."

She looked up, meeting his eyes. Hers were puffed and wet with tears, and yet, the dying flame had rekindled, burning brighter than ever before.

"I've seen you and Stiva together. He hates you. He's jealous of you. He wants what you have—your position, your power, even me. So I went to him and offered him a deal: Information in return for his protection. I told him everything I knew—that you'd found the bug he'd placed in his father's study and that you suspected him of being a traitor. I hoped it would be enough to win his protection. But it wasn't. He turned me down." A makeup-stained tear trickled down her face, black against the whiteness of her skin. "I was so desperate. I was prepared to do absolutely anything to get away from you. And then I remembered what the auctioneer had said on the night you bought me—that you'd find a willing buyer in Stiva if I displeased you. So I did the only thing I could think of. I kissed him, hoping it would enrage you enough to discard me. All I wanted was to force your hand. Please, I'm so sorry…"

There was no hesitation, no trembling of the lip, no wavering of the voice.

She had done it. She had passed the acid test. As he watched her, Alexei felt a rush of fierce admiration for his pupil. The teacher's pride. She was truly one of a kind. Extraordinary in every aspect, not just a survivor, but a warrior.

He lowered the gun and turned to Ivan. "It's enough. She isn't lying. She might be a despicable little rat, but certainly no Russian asset."

As he spoke the words, Alexei could see the tension fall away from her. For a moment, she knelt rigidly at his feet, then she let herself sink to the ground. Exhausted. Every nerve stripped raw by the act he had forced her to perform. Here and now, under Ivan's watchful gaze, there was no comfort that he could offer his protégé. But soon it would be in his power to end this wicked game once and for all. And then she would be free. Of him. And this sinister world in which he dwelt.

Ivan gave a slow nod of agreement. And just at that moment, the door swung open to admit the Circassian, who rushed into the room, carrying a stack of papers under his arm, the Russian coat of arms—the Byzantine Eagle, bearing the imperial orb and the sceptre in its claws—emblazoned on its title page. And hidden within, in all its devious magnificence, the fabricated evidence of Stiva's treason.

Wordlessly, Ivan's chief henchman hurried over to his master and whispered a few words into his ear, then he produced the silvery flash drive from his pocket and handed both—the papers and the drive—to Ivan.

"Is this everything?" Ivan asked, holding up the stack of files.

"Yes, sir, these are the complete contents of the flash drive."

"Verified?"

"Yes, all of it."

With a nod, Ivan stepped over to the window to study the evidence in greater privacy. Alexei didn't move, unwilling to leave his pupil's side while she recovered. He glanced at Sophie, watching the outline of her tear-stained face in the dim light.

Not much longer, he assured her in his mind. *At dawn, I'll set you free.*

Pressing his lips together, Alexei shifted his gaze back to Ivan, who stood motionless by the window. The Tsar's habitual restraint had withered away. His face was hard with rage and a vein stood out on the forehead. And behind it all there lurked a diabolical fury.

"I think it is time to bring my son downstairs," Ivan said, his voice cold, devoid of emotion.

"What about his staff and security detail?" The Circassian inquired.

"Liquidate."

CHAPTER XLIX

Isola di San Clemente, Venice, Italy
Friday, 5th July, 03:48

Alexei didn't watch as Stiva's men died one by one, nor did he stay to bear witness as the Tsar's son was hauled down to Ivan's terrible dungeons to meet his fate. Instead, he carried his charge from the room, not back to his lavish first-floor suite where one wrong word or move could send them both to kingdom come, but outside, to the one place where he was certain they would remain alone.

Ivan's hilltop sanctuary, the small, secluded, hilltop pavilion beside the chapel—its surveillance cameras completely cut off after the explosion he had triggered in the gardens.

No one would watch them there.

Sophie was quiet as he carried her out into the night, accepting his touch with the resigned apathy of a convict awaiting execution—eyes closed, head bent, forehead resting on his shoulder as mute tears ran down her cheeks.

Don't give up on me, Alexei implored her in his mind, bedding her gently on a divan beneath a white fabric roof.

For a brief moment, Alexei's eyes went up to the billowing white fabric roof, instinctively checking for signs of surveillance: the glistening lens of a pinhole camera was visible between the fabric, but now, after his little act of sabotage, it would not transmit anything. Not anymore. For once, they were truly alone. Alexei could almost feel the tension fall away from his body as he knelt down beside her, finally able to shed Zorin's evil mask.

In the soft moonlight that sloped in through the bank of French windows, she looked so fragile and frightened.

He couldn't leave her like this. He had driven her to the breaking point, and now it was his duty to pull her back from the edge.

Rising, Alexei shrugged off his dinner jacket and placed it around her shoulders, then he sat down at her side and drew her gently to him, sliding his hands under the jacket and running his palms up her back. She yielded, resting her cheek against his chest, her dark hair spilling down over her back and his torso like a cloak of silk.

"Shh, it's over," he whispered to her, gently running his thumb over her nape. "No one can hurt you here."

She didn't respond, not even acknowledge that she had understood his words, but still, she accepted the consolation he was offering. So he remained silent, and it became a silence they shared.

Alexei studied the woman that had been thrust into his arms at the most inopportune moment and by no fault of hers: In the dim light, he saw the high cheekbone, the gentle curve of her jaw, those long dark lashes that rested on her pale skin. And the sight of one evoked the memory of another.

Natalia.

Like an evil spell, the name released a watershed of memories that he had always so carefully kept at bay and for a brief moment, Alexei abandoned himself to the visions of the past: Natalia, kissing him under the archway of Oxford's Great Tower, making love to him in the shadow of an ancient pine tree, Natalia—his beautiful *Natashka*—standing in the foyer of his London home, rain dripping from her coat as she pleaded with him not to return to Moscow, Natalia, shedding bitter tears on his shoulder as she realised that what separated the daughter of the exiled dissident and the son of Russia's great powerbroker was too much—a gap so great that not even their love could bridge it.

Thus, they parted ways, both following their chosen path in the opposite direction: He, ostensibly Moscow's loyal servant, labouring tirelessly in the backrooms of power, she, the Kremlin-critical journalist, filling the pages of the world's foremost publications with scathing articles about Alexei's chosen masters. And this should have been the end of their story: Two lovers, once united by a shared notion of the greater good, now fundamentally divided by their chosen path to serve it.

But it wasn't the end. Rather, it was the beginning of a far darker tale—a theatre of doom that turned the two lovers into mere walk-on characters in their own tragedy.

For many months, Alexei had been oblivious to the drama that had quietly unfolded under his very nose, his mind too focused on climbing the ranks of Ivan's empire to notice that Natalia was secretly undermining its foundations. But then—on that rainy March-day three years ago—the play came to a sudden climatic end, with Victor Orsin's face splashed across the front page of *The New York Times*, his story shaking the foundations of power from Washington to London and Moscow to Berlin.

Two days later, Natalia Vetrova, the woman who had unravelled Orsin's empire, had been brought to Ivan's estate, where—drugged, beaten and terrified—she was finally consigned to Alexei's custody.

In that moment, for the first time in his life, Alexei's strength of purpose failed him, his heart unable to make the terrible sacrifice that duty demanded of him now. And so, he had done the unthinkable: betraying himself, his oath and both his masters—feigned and real—to keep her alive.

When Natalia had finally confessed her secrets under tears at his feet, Alexei hadn't done what both Moscow and Ivan expected of him. Rather than ridding the Tsar of a useless source and the Kremlin of an inconvenient troublemaker, he kept her for himself. The sadist's toy, locked up at his seaside estate, to be used, tormented and killed at his leisure. It had been the perfect cover to keep her safe. And of course, Ivan, no better than the man Alexei pretended to be, had indulged him.

That night, when Alexei had taken Natalia to his home—bedding her broken body on his bed, cradling her to his chest and watching her in the soft glow of the moonlight—she had looked just like the woman that now lay in his arms: both shedding the same silent tears of sorrow and despair, both accepting their tormentor's mute offer of consolation. All night he had held Natalia in his arms, and at dawn, he had made love to her—softly, gently, the kind of love that only lovers shared. He could still taste the salt of her tears on his lips, the softness of her mouth as she kissed him. He had loved her then, in a way he had not thought possible, in a way that felt like drowning and being saved all at once.

Then, in the light of the rising sun, she had asked him about the sinister inkings that covered his body. He could still feel her lips on his hand, kissing every knuckle with such gentle care, asking him about the meaning of the letters there.

OMYT

"You can't escape from me," he had answered. And she hadn't. Neither of them had.

He hadn't realised at the time how prophetic those words would be, how irrevocable.

For months, they had maintained a blissful illusion of something like normalcy, in that house on the *Côte d'Azur*. They had strolled along the rocky shore, swam in the dark blue waters of the Mediterranean Sea, talked, and laughed and been silent together. And in those months, he had found something like hope. Hope for a future. Hope of saving her.

On that day, when Alexei had discovered that she had quietly resumed her investigation into the Twelve, it had already been too late: She had been so careful. But it hadn't been enough. A single, thoughtless, tiny mistake had sufficed to draw Ivan's attention to them both.

There had been no way out. No escape.

In that moment, Alexei had understood the terrible, immutable truth: that he couldn't save her, not even if he sacrificed his mission and his life for her, but that he wouldn't let her die alone. And Natalia had known it too, of course she had, she always knew—the woman that could look straight into his soul and see everything that he was. Every scar, every flaw, every secret, laid bare under her gaze.

Natalia so she had done the unthinkable.

She cornered him in his own game, beat him, and took the blame not just for her sins, but his. She gave Ivan the perfect suspect, the perfect sacrifice. And in doing so, she doomed her lover to go on alone—convinced that in this twisted game, his role afforded him latitude to succeed where she could not.

And it had fallen on Alexei to carry out the sentence she had written for herself, the final act.

It would be a kindness, he told himself. A mercy. But it didn't feel like that.

It felt like betrayal.

His hand had shaken violently, not with fear of the act itself but with the enormity of the moment, a grief so large it might tear him apart. How was it possible to hold all of it in? The weight of his love for her. The vastness of his terror. The certainty that he would have gladly ripped the world apart, given up his cover, his mission, his life, anything, just to save her. And yet now, here, in this awful, shrunken moment, he was powerless.

There was no grand act of defiance left to make. No heroic leap into the abyss. All that remained was this: a quiet, unbearable finality. To stay with her, to die beside her—that would be the easiest thing in the world, a coward's retreat into oblivion. But he couldn't fail her.

She had made her choice, and it wasn't for him to unmake it. She had chosen this so he could go on, so he could finish what they had started, their impossible dream, their rebellion against the cruel mechanics of fate. And if he failed her now, he would fail her forever.

He turned to her then, meeting her gaze, and it was all he could do to remain upright. Her eyes were steady, unflinching, filled with a strange, serene acceptance. No anger. No fear. Nothing but a calm so profound it almost frightened him. And in her eyes, he saw something else too—a strength that wasn't his but hers, held out to him like a gift. Her calm would have to carry him now, because his had long since vanished. Her eyes, luminous even in the shadow of death, were a command: *Live. Finish this. For both of us.*

Oh Natalia, what have I done to you?

Alexei shut his eyes, banishing the visions from his mind, but even as he focused his gaze back on the woman he held now, the memories of Natalia tarried—rich and deep yet bitter, like a fine wine gone bad.

Reaching out, Alexei brushed a stray lock of hair from Sophie's face, and as he touched it, the faint scent of jasmine seemed to drift around him—like a memory of another long-forgotten world.

I promise you, Sophie, you will survive, he assured her in his mind. *You won't share her fate. I won't allow it.*

An hour passed. And then another. And they spent it in silence. In the mute companionship that only those shared who have been through hell together. Then dawn began to creep up on the horizon, and with the light, he felt some of her strength return. Finally, for the first time since her confession, she found her voice again.

"How can you live this lie every day?" She whispered, her voice still hoarse from the tears she had shed.

Alexei regarded her for a long time, asking himself the same question, knowing the answer instantly, realising its prize a little later.

"Because I believe in the justice of my cause, I live and die for it."

"And you kill for it too. You killed Natalia for it."

Alexei heard the implicit question in her words, and let it lie, knowing that his silence was all the affirmation needed.

But she didn't let it go.

"When Ivan asked you about her, your lips twitched, just here." She raised her hand and gently laid her fingertip on the corner of his mouth. "Your face is always still. There is nothing there to see. No reaction. But the moment he mentioned her name, something changed. And it happened again, just now." She paused, studying him for a moment before she asked the question. "You loved her, didn't you?"

Alexei took a long time to respond, not because he didn't know the answer, but rather because it was too painful to voice it. But now, as he was about to place the same burden on Sophie's shoulders that had once weighed down Natalia, he owed her this answer.

"I loved Natalia more than my own life, but some things are great even than love—and she saw that, even if I did not."

CHAPTER L

Isola di San Clemente, Venice, Italy
Friday, 5th July, 06:11

Sophie regarded him silently, studying him with the pensive stillness of one who is able to see beyond what is presented. When she finally spoke, there was such sorrow in her eyes, and such unguarded emotion in her voice, that Alexei knew beyond any reasonable doubt that his mask had finally failed him: She had seen through it and looked right into his soul.

"When I look at you, I see a man tormented by an almost unbearable burden. I cannot lift this weight from your shoulders, nor is it my place to speak in the name of one you have loved, but I believe with all my heart that your sacrifice, in all its selflessness, redeems you—not just in my eyes, but in hers." She ran her fingertip very gently along his lips. "Maybe the time has come to forgive yourself."

Alexei closed his eyes, desperately fighting to regain control over a soul left adrift for far too long.

As Alexei sat motionless, absorbed by the pain of the past, he felt her lips on the corner of his, gently kissing that treacherous spot that had given him away. Her touch was hesitant, as if she were still trying to decide how much of her soul she could risk without losing herself. For a long moment he didn't move, neither withdraw nor lean in, trying to make the same decision. Then, at long last, he kissed her back, caressing her split lip, tasting its coppery tang, finally brushing the blood away as if—by removing that lurid vestige of his sins—he could undo what he had done to her.

He ran his lips down her neck and kissed the throbbing spot at its base. Sophie closed her eyes, sighing gently, her breath hot on the side of his face. Alexei paused, feeling the quickening of her pulse, then he ran his hands up her back and slid his jacket off her shoulders. It fell with a rustle, no louder than a sigh. In the dim light, she appeared spectral, otherworldly, yet to him, she was more real than ever before. He placed a gentle kiss on her shoulder, relishing the softness of her skin and then he slid the strap of her gown down. One. Then the other. And as the second one fell, she began her own exploration of his body.

Whilst they undressed each other, rain began to fall—droplets of water pelting against the windows, rolling down the glass like tears. And while the rain swept across the island like a cleansing force, they made love to each other—their union not that of heated bodies in need of release, nor that of kindred spirits in certainty of love, but that of broken souls in search of solace.

And solace they found, each in their own way, both together, their souls laid bare to each other's eyes. Thus, came daybreak. And as the first rays of the light swept across the countryside, the rain began to abate, leaving behind nothing but droplets of water that shone like diamonds in the morning sun.

He held her quietly, their naked bodies entwined in the lovers' gentle embrace, his eyes fixed on some point on the horizon, his mind all too aware that the moment of their parting was drawing close. Now all that remained was to bequeath his legacy on her—to make sure that she would carry on the torch if he failed.

Focusing his eyes on Sophie, Alexei reached out to brush a tousled chestnut lock over her shoulder. With her eyes closed and her long hair brushed down her back, she looked so delicate and young, so ill-equipped to survive in this merciless world. Yet, when—by no fault of her own—she had been cast into the deepest, darkest recess of hell, she hadn't yielded to its horrors, but faced them with a steely resolve that spoke of a warrior's heart and a mind to match it. He would choose well in her.

"Sophie, the game is drawing to a close. To get this far, I had to play my every trump card, and when I make my final bid for power, there won't be a rip cord left for me to use. It's all or nothing now. If I succeed, you'll be free to leave, but if I fail, you will be left to fend for yourself." He paused for a moment, weighing his next words with care before he spoke. "Should that happen, you have to make a choice: you can try to survive on your hands and knees, or you can stand up and fight this war in my stead."

She had listened to him with her eyes closed, but now she opened them slowly, lifting her head off his chest to look into his eyes.

"So you're offering me the choice between victim and warrior?" she asked, her voice soft, but firm.

He gave an affirmative nod. "I am."

For a moment she seemed to waver, but only briefly, and when he caught her gaze again, hers was resolute, and in it, Alexei saw all that he had hoped to see: In the hour of need, a warrior's heart unfailingly answered the call of duty, taking up arms without fear or hesitation. Her promise, as it was given, required no grandiose soliloquy or great gesture. It was the same quiet way he had entered into service, with a silent oath and absolute, unwavering faith in the justice of his cause.

"I will fight."

CHAPTER LI

Isola di San Clemente, Venice, Italy
Friday, 5th July, 07:43

They rose and dressed in silence, each helping the other. And as they prepared, Alexei felt the grim atmosphere of a looming battle descend upon them—that strange stillness in which men contemplate their own mortality. He had experienced it a thousand times, on the eve of a battle and later behind enemy lines. There was no uncertainty or fear, just that stalwart acceptance of death should it come.

And then they were done, and with the last button adjusted and the final wrinkle smoothed out, the time for silent contemplation came to an end.

Now all that remained for Alexei to do was to prepare his protégé for the case of his death.

He bent and picked up the necklace from where it had fallen in the throes of passion, then he stepped over to the table, cleared it with one sweeping motion of his arm and placed the glistening string of jewels on top of it: Stones down, setting up.

Glancing at his companion, Alexei beckoned her to his side. "Come, we don't have much time, and there are things you need to know."

While Sophie stepped to his side, Alexei directed his gaze back at the necklace.

"I assume you've realised by now that this necklace isn't quite what it appears to be." He gently dislodged the small, spherical container from its concealed compartment beneath the centre gem and held it up. "This is a concealment device fitted with state-of-the-art transmission technology. It is capable of transmitting the Pandora launch code to the one remaining ground station capable of controlling the weapon."

Alexei hesitated for a fraction of a second, then opened the container, and removed the firing key, its surface gleaming menacingly in the light. Then he reached for his gun and retrieved the second firing key from the protective casing hidden in his weapon's grip.

"Countless people have worked on this, all with the aim of destroying this weapon, and doing it safely. Most of them have died for their bravery. Now, all that is needed is for us to complete the last step and years of effort will be turned into motion."

He hesitated for a fraction of a moment, then, with a vague tremor, he joined the two pieces of the firing key and slid them into the purpose-built slot on the side of the necklace.

"Once it's activated, the transmitter will perform the last step in a series of security protocols that are needed to control the weapon. Maxim Mikoyan was the one who programmed the final uplink for the Pandora codes. And if his work holds true, then the nuclear warheads will disengage and decouple from the weapon today at 08:21 in the morning. About two hours later, Pandora will re-enter the atmosphere and burn up, while the decoupled warheads, which are capable of re-entering the atmosphere without being damaged, will be salvaged by the Americans."

He took a deep breath and activated the mechanism.

And right now, at that very moment, a secret, abandoned dead-hand station on an island in the Kara Sea would receive the codes to control the world's deadliest weapon.

And reliably, the *Perimetr*—designed to work even after the country has suffered a catastrophic nuclear strike—would do what it was programmed to do. Without human intervention. Without any means to stop it.

And he could only hope with all his heart, that Maxim Mikoyan, this brilliant mathematician and ciphers expert, had not erred when he had modified the command chain.

"So this is what you wanted all along, destroying the weapon, wasn't it?"

"It should never have been created. It's an insanity. One with the potential to kill millions."

Her eyes locked onto his. "What do you need me to do?"

"The weapon has a redundancy to stop unintended transmissions, which means as long as the weapon isn't destroyed, the re-entry process can be stopped. I need you to hold on to this for me. If there is a chance that the weapon will fall into Ivan's hands or the Kremlin's before re-entry, you need to destroy this."

A silence fell between them, heavy with unspoken fears and the weight of their shared history. Sophie nodded, her expression resolute. "I understand."

Alexei leaned in, his voice a whisper now. "Promise me, Sophie. Promise me you'll see this through."

Her eyes glistened with unshed tears, but her voice was firm. "I promise."

"There is something else I must ask of you."

For a moment, they stared at each other in silence, a mute understanding passing between them, then Alexei slipped a small blue USB stick from the grip of his gun. Turning it over in his hand, he placed it on the desk before him.

"This contains over twenty-six thousand records detailing the operations and organisation of the Twelve. The documents comprise evidence of illicit arms deals, large-scale money laundering, political assassinations, election rigging, the unlawful deployment of mercenary forces into conflict zones and the instigation of and intervention in two civil wars." Alexei paused, holding Sophie's gaze, making sure that she understood the full significance of what he had told her. Then he continued. "It's all the evidence Natalia collected. It will wipe out the Twelve, and half of Moscow's cronies."

"What will happen if you die?"

He fell silent, the words that he had meant to speak dying on his lips. During his time in service, he had turned and recruited dozens of assets, and he had sent them behind enemy lines without batting an eye. But now, for the first time in his life, something in him wished that he wouldn't have to give her these instructions.

Forcing himself to look into her eyes, Alexei pried the words from his mouth.

"If I die you will be passed on to someone else. A toy. An object to serve some other man's pleasure."

She smiled bitterly but didn't say anything, because there was nothing to say.

"Sophie, when that moment comes, do whatever is necessary to survive: Use your charm, your body, whatever assets you have at your disposal, and don't fight back, no matter what they will make you endure. This isn't about morals, or pride, or being able to look into the mirror the next morning—all that matters is staying alive."

She shut her eyes, visibly struggling to come to terms with his advice. But when she opened them again, the fear was gone, replaced by the steely resolve he had seen there before.

"I promise you, I will see this through, whatever happens."

He gave her a silent nod, a mute salute from one soldier to another—united by a common goal, each prepared to die for it. And then the ormolu clock on the mantelpiece chimed the hour, its toll like a death knell, reminding him that the moment of reckoning had finally come.

When this was over, he would either sit on Ivan's throne or kneel on a shitty cellar floor and wait for his execution.

"It's time. I must go." He paused and stepped around the table, closing the distance between them.

In the glow of the morning sun, she looked radiant, like a figure of light. Enraptured. Far beyond his reach. And he didn't dare to reach out and destroy the illusion with his touch.

"If we don't meet again, know this: It was an honour and a privilege to have you at my side."

She regarded him for a long moment, a strange sadness lingering in her eyes. "Do you have a name, a real one, that I can remember you by?"

He hesitated for a long moment, then he spoke the name that, for almost ten years, hadn't been his own. "Alexander Mikhailovich Sobolev."

She reached out and laced her fingers around his hand. "I won't forget you, Alexander."

CHAPTER LII

Isola di San Clemente, Venice, Italy
Friday, 5th July, 08:01

Alexei strode through the early morning haze towards Ivan's palace, the dew still clinging to the grass, leaving Sophie behind in the Pavilion. If he failed, she would be alone. For a heartbeat, his mind dwelled on the woman he had left behind, then he forced himself to focus on what lay ahead.

Well then, Ivan, it's time to pay for your sins.

Taking a deep breath, Alexei marched towards the main entrance. The dawn had not yet broken over Ivan's palace, casting long, eerie shadows on the ornate facade. The air was warm, laden with the scent of jasmine and the murmur of the sea. And then he stepped through the main entrance, past guards posted there for his protection, and staff who knew better than to approach him.

As he turned the corner, the distant din of running footsteps caught his attention. Stopping dead in his tracks, Alexei turned, his eyes falling on the dishevelled figure of Frost, rushing towards him.

"I need to speak to you, Alexei. In private."

For Frost to approach him like this, without regard for either Alexei's rank or their audience, was enough to alarm him. Whatever had happened, it was grave enough to warrant his immediate attention. Still, he couldn't let it go like this. Not in front of half a dozen spectators.

Concealing his alarm under an expression of unveiled disdain, Alexei regarded Frost silently, as if he had to contemplate whether his grovelling underling was even worth the effort of a sneering dismissal. When Alexei finally replied, he did so with the same indolent drawl that he always used to cow his subjects into terrified silence.

"I have people for that, Doctor. Speak to them."

Alexei's harsh reprimand had the same effect on Frost as a prompter's soft whisper on an actor: He collected himself and resumed his role with flawless grace—his head sinking forward into that gallant gentleman's bow that wasn't only an apology but an unveiled acknowledgement of his subordination.

"Forgive me, but I think it is a matter that warrants your personal attention: MI5 has opened an investigation into the death of Andrew Mercer, and I fear that we might have unwittingly drawn their attention to us."

Alexei arched an eyebrow.

"Good old Andy, an annoyance to the very end." Allowing his lips to curl into a faint sneer of disgust, Alexei motioned ahead. "Well then, let's talk."

Frost followed him wordlessly down the corridor, through the glass-paned orangery and out into the gardens. The moment they stepped into the open, Frost slipped a hand into his jacket pocket and took out a slender device. He switched it on with a flick of a finger. Instantly a tiny green light flared to life, while the device simultaneously began to emit a low, humming sound. Alexei arched an eyebrow. For Frost to risk using a radio frequency jammer to prevent anyone from listening in on their conversation, something very serious must have happened.

"What's going on, Tom?"

"You asked me to look into what happened back in London. With Harper, and whoever supplied him. So I did. Or at least I tried. But someone else was quicker. Both Harper and Liam Bryne—the guy that did some of Harper's dirty work—are dead. The kind of suicide where you know it wasn't one. So I followed the only lead that remained: Miss Akehurst. I went through all the footage at the hotel. Swiped the place for everything from electronic surveillance to chemical traces. Someone was following you, and they marked you with spy dust using Miss Akehurst as a go-between. And that very same person later killed off Harper and Liam to erase all traces."

"I'm aware of it. It was Russian counterintelligence. They guy with scar. You have him on tape."

"It wasn't just him."

"What do you mean?"

"Your scar-faced friend was just a legman. But the real deal was hiding in plain sight."

"What do you mean?"

"Nikolai Morozov. A Russian counterintelligence colonel. He busted your ass, Alexei. As an hour ago, you've officially been branded a traitor by the Kremlin."

"I've prepared for that eventuality, Tom."

"No, you haven't. Not that one. You see, your old masters in Moscow might be ready to strike a deal with Ivan. And they've sent their man to Venice. Morozov is here. And he's striking a bargain with Ivan for your head."

PART THREE

Sophie Akehurst & Alexei Zorin

CHAPTER LIII

Isola di San Clemente, Venice, Italy
Friday, 5th July, 09:14

They came for Sophie shortly after Zorin had left.

The moment the door was flung open, and Ivan's black-clad guards stepped into the pavilion, Sophie knew that all she had feared had just come to pass. For a heartbeat, her mind strayed to the man in whose arms she had spent the night, wondering if he was still alive and if so, what exactly he had to endure at this very moment, then she focused her attention on the task that lay ahead now: His instructions had been clear, and to her surprise, she felt no fear, not even a shred of doubt as to what she needed to do. No matter what happened, she would see this through.

"The boss wants to see you," the guard said, stepping to her side and thrusting his hand around her upper arm.

For a fraction of a second, Sophie was tempted to struggle, but she remembered Zorin's warning, and let it go. This was a fight she couldn't win.

Lowering her eyes, she obediently allowed the guard to lead her back to Ivan's menacing palace while his men followed on their heels—their weapons cocked and ready as if they expected to be ambushed any second. Surrounded by this frightening phalanx, Sophie was frogmarched to the door of the Tsar's office, where she was first searched and then thrust into the sunbathed room beyond.

As she stepped inside, Sophie's gaze shifted to Ivan, who stood by the window, hands linked behind his back, his eyes fixed on some point on the horizon. He was still wearing his dress jacket, and there was a little blood on the collar of his white shirt.

Ivan—tall, regal, oddly frightening in his stillness—was at first all Sophie could take in. His two companions, and the black-clad guards that manned the door and walls, were lost beside the Tsar's menacing figure.

It was only when the attention of Ivan's guests shifted to her that she noticed them: There was the familiar figure of Lord Cavendish, still dressed in his tailored dinner jacket, and beside him, the scar-faced man, and to their right, reclining leisurely in a high-backed chair in front of the massive fireplace, sat a tall, elegant man Sophie remembered all too well.

Gabriel.

"Forgive my manners, Miss Akehurst," Ivan said, turning towards her. "Of course, you know Lord Cavendish, but I believe you haven't been properly introduced to my other guest—so please, allow me to rectify that." He motioned graciously towards Gabriel. "Colonel Nikolai Nikolayevich Morozov, the commanding officer of the GRU's 12th counterintelligence and covert action team." Ivan paused, his eyes narrowing. "In other words, Nikolai is the man who keeps a watchful eye on the Kremlin's spies around the world. Now, usually, I'm not friends with Kremlin operatives, but as they say—the enemy of my enemy is my friend."

Gabriel rose and graced her with a derisive tight-lipped smile. "It is a pleasure, Sophie."

Sophie stood frozen, staring at Gabriel—the man who had been a friend, who might even have been more. His eyes, once warm and familiar, now held a cold, calculating malice. It was like looking at a stranger wearing Gabriel's face—gone was the easy smile. Gone was the teasing warmth. In its place, there was a hawk-eyed alertness, a poise that told her this man could snap bones in a heartbeat if he wanted to.

The sight made the words die on her lips.

As she started at him, Gabriel's eyes narrowed ever so slightly, as if he were watching her reaction closely. No, not watching, he was relishing it—his lips curling into a slow, cruel smile as he watched her flounder.

His expression, that cold detached delight in her horror, made Sophie's stomach tingle as if she were falling. Whatever he had pretended to be until now, it had simply been a mask, and the man who lurked behind it was one not simply to be feared, but one to be terrified of.

"I expected a warmer welcome from you, Sophie. After all, you really were quite infatuated with me, weren't you?" Gabriel graced her with a disdainful smile, as if her blindness truly amused him, then he continued. "But enough of that, I'm not here to discuss your adolescent fantasies. I'm here for business."

His eyes shifted to Ivan. "With your permission, Ivan Sergeevich, I'll run you through the unfortunate events that brought me here tonight."

Ivan nodded. "Go ahead, Colonel."

Gabriel turned to Cavendish, giving him a small nod, as if he were addressing a large audience. "As you know, the Kremlin's scalp hunters have been looking for a mole inside Russian intelligence. Someone exceptional, capable of undermining our operations on unprecedented scale. We've been watching, listening, waiting for him to make that oh-so-fatal mistake. But nothing. Whoever it was, he was too good to get caught. Too disciplined, too careful. But Pandora changed everything."

Gabriel smiled.

"The moment it became clear that Moscow had lost control of the weapon, the First Directorate went into full-blown crisis mode. Every branch of Moscow's special services was put on high alert. We were ready to move. And then, out of the blue, the Kremlin ordered us to stand down. Immediately. No one was to move, no one was to breathe. The path was to be left clear for Ural 16, because the Kremlin's golden boys already had someone on the inside. Someone capable of getting the weapon back. And that man was Alexei Zorin."

"So Zorin is a Russian spy," Cavendish said.

"Oh, not just any spy," Gabriel said. "He's the best Moscow has to offer. A prodigy. A man of unmatched skills. Someone capable of bringing Pandora back home." Gabriel pressed his lips together. "But unfortunately, he didn't bring it home. Quite the contrary. He let the firing key to Pandora slip through his fingers in Paris. But while he robbed Moscow of its most formidable weapon, he gave me something else in return. A suspect— someone who fitted the profile of the traitor we had been hunting for years. Alexei Zorin was skilled enough to pull off a deception of this scale and powerful, rich and well-connected enough to get away with it. So, the moment he let the pendant slip through his fingers in Paris, I knew I had my man."

"Then why didn't the Kremlin do him in right then and there?" Cavendish asked.

"Oh, Lord Cavendish, you have no idea who he is. To get a man like Alexei Zorin out of the picture, I would need the blessing from the very top. All the way up. Right to the president's desk. Before I could even think of making my case, I needed proof that Alexei Zorin was the traitor the Kremlin had been looking for all those years. But Zorin is a careful man. I could watch him, bug his rooms, breathe down his neck, without ever finding something to nail him down. So I opted for an old-school trick. Something that even Zorin wouldn't expect."

"And what would that be?" Cavendish asked.

Gabriel reached into his jacket pocket and pulled out a small phial. He tossed it to Cavendish, who caught it with a surprised fumble.

"*Metka.* Spy dust." Gabriel smiled. "An invisible marker, with a unique chemical signature."

Ivan smiled a mirthless smile. "You marked him with *metka*?"

"I didn't. Not directly. I used Zorin's pet as my go-between." Diverting from his path along the walls of the room,

Gabriel now strolled over to her and stopped. "Oh, and you were so good, Sophie. My perfect pawn."

Gabriel brushed a stray lock of hair from her face, and she flinched, but he caught her chin, stopping her from turning away.

"Would you like to know how it was done?" Sophie didn't reply, and Gabriel gave her a small, condescending smile. "Oh, I'm sure you do, Sophie."

Gabriel's fingers dug a little harder into her chin, as if to make sure she was listening.

"I knew how desperately you needed money to stay afloat—always taking the evening shift, always staying after hours. So I made sure that you'd be there when I needed you. You didn't even question my request." Gabriel smiled. "But since you served dozens of guests a night, I couldn't simply smear the *metka* onto those delicate hands of yours—at least not if I wanted to prevent the spy dust from spreading in an uncontrolled way and fuck up my operation by making everyone a suspect. So I opted for a biphasic product. The first component was on the newspaper that you so diligently cleared away from my agent's table." Gabriel's eyes went briefly to the scar-faced man who stood silent and motionless at the back of the room, then his eyes returned to her. "The second came directly from me." He brushed his fingers against hers, as if by accident, the way he had brushed his fingers against hers when he had instructed her how to deal with Zorin's security detail.

His touch made her shiver, and Gabriel felt that shiver—and it made him smile the kind of smile that made the hairs on the back of her neck stand on end.

"And like a good little mule, you went to work for your master—carrying the spy dust right where I wanted it to go. To Zorin. The plan was perfect. Or it would have been."

Gabriel shook his head. "But Zorin, being who he is, smelled the rat. He knew someone inside the Valmont had marked him. And, predictably, his first suspicion fell on you." Gabriel's lips pressed into a thin line, as if the thought displeased him. "Most agents would probably have let it go, getting themselves out. But Zorin is not like most. He took counter-measures. Instantly. He set up that little commotion in the lobby, making sure that, by making his men spread out around him, you would in some way be caught up in the mess. And of course, being the predictable annoyance you are, you got caught up in the mess. And of course, you had to ruin my operation."

Gabriel paused, watching her with disdain, disgust and something she couldn't name.

"And now Zorin had created a situation that forced me to intervene. I couldn't allow his bodyguard to touch you. Not while you had spy dust all over you. So I stopped him." Gabriel pressed his lips together. "Unfortunately, my little intervention on your behalf was enough to give me away. You see, my Russian background was part of my legend. My cover. It made me the Valmont's first choice when it came to dealing with our Russian clients, so it was perfect for getting close to Zorin or anyone else I needed to keep an eye on. But the moment I grabbed the bodyguard's arm, I changed from a Brit with Russian roots to a Russian-speaker with skills I shouldn't have. I had stepped right into Zorin's trap. And that meant I had to get rid of all the evidence." Gabriel smiled at her. "Including you."

Sophie looked away, but Gabriel's hand tightened on her chin, tipping her head up so that he could study her—his expression one of faint amusement.

"I really thought you were easier game, Sophie. I expected you to say yes when I asked you to come home with me." His voice took on an almost tender lilt, mocking, sickly sweet. "And I would have made it quick for you. A kiss, a twist of the neck. You wouldn't have felt a thing." He shook his head. "But you chose the hard path. Plan B."

He let go of her, as if she disgusted him.

"Usually, that kind of thing is a quick fix. A fall from a window. An accidental drowning. An unfortunate tumble down a staircase. You name it. But regrettably, there were already far too many bodies in the street for one week, and another one—especially that of someone who had contact with Alexei Zorin—might have drawn the attention of British intelligence. So I opted for something a bit more creative in your case. Something enjoyable." Gabriel smiled unpleasantly. "So, I called upon the services of Liam. I'm sure you remember him, he's the charming Irish gentleman who deals in women like you."

Gabriel watched her, his mouth curling into a lazy smile.

"It was such a perfect set-up. Now all I needed was a place I controlled to hand you over to Liam. And what better place than a nightclub operated by Russian intelligence in the middle of London."

Sophie felt a breath of air escape. "The Viper's Den..."

"Fitting name, isn't it?" He laughed softly. "All I had to do was make sure that your friends got free tables, and then get you there safely. And just like that, I had trapped you inside a place I controlled completely. Security. Surveillance. And the ability to jam communications if necessary." He chuckled softly, voice dripping with mock tenderness. "Like a bird in a cage." His smile sharpened, and he let the words hang in the air before he continued. "Now, all that remained was making sure you'd step out of the club at the right moment. And of course, you, being the eager little pet you are, would predictably return my call if I asked you to. And without any cell reception inside the building, you were sure to step outside." Gabriel laughed softly. "All it took was a simple trace on your phone, and I had you. Then I let Liam settle the rest."

Gabriel held her gaze for a moment, the faintest of smiles forming on his lips, as if he had just tasted something sweet and still relished its flavour.

"I instructed Liam to find a suitable arrangement," he said, voice smooth and condescending, as though explaining an obvious fact. "I didn't particularly care about the details, as long as it was... discreet. A place where you could remain suitably *forgotten*. You know, some quaint brothel in one of those miserable pockets up north, where you'd entertain the local dregs and town drunks for twenty quid an hour before a well-timed overdose would tie off any loose ends." Gabriel smiled vaguely, as if he found a quiet delight in the idea, and then he leaned in, his voice dropping lower, as if meant only for her.

"Who knows, I might even have paid you a little farewell visit—just to make sure you drifted off the way I intended you to."

He smiled, then straightened himself, his words once again addressed to the entirety of the room.

"It would have been neat. Tidy. Unlike a murdered American exchange student, a whore that pegs out after an overdose doesn't make headlines."

He took an indignant breath.

"But Liam, in his infinite greed and quite matchless stupidity, wanted to make a pretty buck off that lovely face of yours, and that's where things began to unravel."

There was a flash of anger in his expression now.

"Without consulting me, he traded you Harper. And Zorin, being who he is, tracked you down, spending eight million pounds to get you out of there." Gabriel shook his head as if he were truly impressed by that number. "You know, Sophie, you could buy a decent racehorse for that price. But having seen what I've seen, I'd say you were actually worth it." Gabriel ran the tip of his tongue suggestively along his teeth. "And don't tell me you didn't enjoy it."

"Fuck you, Gabriel."

Gabriel laughed. "Oh, Sophie, careful. I might just keep you instead of putting a bullet in your head. You'd like it, trust me. Alexei Alexandrovich and I have much in common when it comes to our... tastes."

Sophie kept silent. For a moment, Gabriel watched her, relishing the sight, then, very calmly, he stepped back and resumed his slow pacing—addressing his audience while strolling leisurely around her, like a predator circling its prey.

"Anyway, I had to do a little cleanup operation. Getting rid of Liam and Harper. And then, of course, you, Sophie." Gabriel gave her a condescending smile. "Like a bad penny, you resurfaced—this time in the company of a powerful benefactor. Zorin made full use of you. Not just as a distraction to get the edge off. No, he made you his mule, letting you carry all his secrets, including the key to Pandora."

Gabriel gave her a knowing little smile and gently tapped his fingertip against her necklace, then he turned to Ivan, addressing the Tsar directly now.

"After killing you, Alexei Zorin would have replaced you as Tsar, taking over The Twelve and all its formidable power. And no one here would have suspected a thing, not after the marvellous tale he had spun to pin all his crimes on Stiva and send your son to his doom."

Sophie's eyes went to Ivan, and for a fleeting moment, the man who had so callously ordered his son's execution showed a hint of emotion, closing his eyes, taking a deep breath, fighting to keep his composure. But she wasn't the only one who had noted the Tsar's momentary lapse. Gabriel had stopped his narration, his eyes fixed on Ivan.

"Continue," Ivan hissed, finally turning to face Gabriel, his face contorted into a mask of diabolical rage.

Gabriel gave a nod.

"And then, with the Twelve under his control, Alexei Zorin would rule over an organisation powerful enough to do what he had worked for all these years: Take on the Kremlin." Gabriel's mouth curled into a disdainful smile. "And I think he intends to start his war by staking his claim on Pandora."

"This is ludicrous," Ivan said.

"Oh, far from it. In fact, it's quite real. So real, that he has already begun the process of deorbiting the weapon in a controlled way."

"How the fuck did he do that?"

"Oh, Zorin, or rather one of his co-conspirators, found a rather ingenious way." Gabriel smiled. "As you know, Pandora, like any weapon of its kind, is operated from multiple ground stations, mobile bases and satellites. It's almost impossible to effectively take them all out. However, there's another way. You can make sure you have a back door to the weapon."

"Don't tell me Zorin's associate hacked the weapon."

"No, he built a back door into it."

"If he built it in, he can control it."

"He can't. Not anymore. You see, the man who built it is Maxim Mikoyan. A GRU signals officer and prolific mathematical genius going by the codename the Poet. He died in a roadside ditch near Perth less than twenty-four hours ago."

Ivan shut his eyes, and Sophie knew what he was thinking of now—of Tarik Kahn, and his command to kill Maxim Mikoyan.

"Mikoyan thought like Zorin. He believed that weapons like Pandora should never have been built, let alone been put into orbit. And he was all too eager to help Zorin get the weapon down. So he helped him." Gabriel pressed his lips together. "Given all I knew and suspected about Zorin, I was certain that he had some kind of associate to pull this off. He was good, but he didn't have the technical know-how to do it. There had to be someone else. And with some luck, the spy dust would have revealed who it was." Gabriel pressed his lips together. "Unfortunately, after the incident at the Valmont, Zorin shored up his operations. He played us. Faked an old-school brush pass in the hotel lobby, tricking us into trailing an innocent German engineer through London for three days, expecting him to contact Moscow. And while twenty men were trying to find a non-existent courier, Zorin kept up an avid and entirely undetected correspondence with the Poet."

"How?" Cavendish asked.

"Zorin passed on his messages concealed inside a burner phone that had to be recovered in a cloak and dagger operation from the bottom of the bloody Thames."

For half a second, Sophie's mind reeled back to her journey here, the image of Zorin tossing the phone out of the window flashing clearly in her mind's eye. But Gabriel's voice almost instantly pulled her back to the present.

"While the poet concealed his responses inside the newspaper articles he wrote." Gabriel shook his head in disbelief. "Zorin's final order to the Poet had been to reset Pandora's trajectory and put it in an armed waiting mode."

"What for?" Ivan asked.

"I was wondering that too. But now we know. An hour ago, our ground stations picked up a single signal. A Pandora code. It was transmitted through an abandoned transmission station in the Kara Sea. The command it transmitted to Pandora was meant to deactivate the nuclear warheads, dislodge them, and to steer the disarmed weapons system into the earth's atmosphere, where it will burn up. And I fear that celestial spectacle is preprogrammed for eleven hundred hours CET today."

Sophie's eyes went to her watch.

Less than two hours.

Gabriel paused, then continued.

"The command to disarm the weapon was sent from Venice. And just like that, I had the proof I needed, that the one man that was considered beyond reproach, entirely untouchable, was in fact, the traitor we had been looking for all along."

"So who are we actually dealing with?" Cavendish asked, his voice hard. "What kind of man are you trying to unseat that you need this kind of irrefutable evidence?"

"Colonel Alexander Mikhailovich Sobolev. The Kremlin's treasured protégé and commanding officer of the Ural 16 Black Ops Team. Officially he goes by the codename Mercury, but unofficially he is known as the puppet master."

"How very fitting," Cavendish said, his lips curling disdainfully as if he had just tasted something rotten.

"You have no idea how fitting it is, Lord Cavendish," Gabriel replied. "Alexander Sobolev is the son of General Mikhail Petrovich Sobolev, the grey eminence of Russian Intelligence, who spent four decades of his life pulling the strings on every Soviet and Russian covert mission and backroom deal. He spied on the Americans, the Brits, the Germans and anyone else. And while the mighty Mikhail spied on the world, his beautiful wife Maria spied on him to make sure that this notoriously difficult man remained loyal to the Kremlin."

"One hell of a family," Cavendish remarked.

Gabriel chuckled mirthlessly. "Indeed. And Alexander takes after his famous daddy: A soulless motherfucker. A one-man army."

"If he is as good as you say, he'll be gone by now."

"No, he won't. You see, like most great men, Alexei Zorin comes with that predictable soft underbelly. There's someone who mattered to him. Someone he let inside."

"Who?"

"Natalia Vetrova." Gabriel paused for a moment as if he were trying to recall that particular aspect of Zorin's past. "She was his lover while he studied at Oxford. But when the time came for Zorin to return to Moscow, he understood that not even his family's influence could pave the way for a relationship like theirs. The Kremlin's loyal servant and the enemy of the state. It was impossible. Unthinkable. So Zorin left her, but he never stopped loving her."

Ivan's lips curled into a cold, disdainful smile as if he relished the pain of the man who had incited him to kill his own son. "Oh, the pretty Natalia. So this was why he kept her."

"Indeed," Gabriel confirmed, shifting his gaze to Ivan. "And when you forced Zorin to pull the trigger on his lover, you made this personal for him. And now, with his cover about to be blown, his goals in ruins, robbed of his great love, all Zorin wants is to see you bleed. He has nothing to lose and everything to win. He'll come after you and me with everything he's got."

"Well then, let's make sure that we get to him first, shall we?" Ivan said coldly.

"I think it's already too late for that," Cavendish remarked, his eyes fixed on the monitors.

CHAPTER LIV

Isola di San Clemente, Venice, Italy
Friday, 5th July, 09:46

Alexei cocked his gun and stepped into the foyer.

He steered clear of the cameras. He didn't want to draw the attention of those who were watching on the other side. Not yet. For the next two seconds, his show was only for the three guards at the far end of the room.

Clad in full combat gear and armed with MP7s, the men had the bow-taut stance and concentrated attention of true professionals.

Alexei walked towards them, his steps echoing in the cavernous space.

Alerted by the sound of his footsteps, they turned, raising their weapons to take down the intruder. When they recognised Alexei, they paused, lowering the muzzles of their MP7s.

Their hesitation told Alexei all he needed to know: Ivan hadn't issued the kill order yet.

As always, the Tsar was waiting until he had everything under control before he struck. And while Ivan and his inner circle prepared for battle, his footmen and underlings were kept in the dark—utterly oblivious to the fact that Alexei Zorin, the mighty Tsar-in-waiting, was in truth the traitor they were all hunting for.

A fatal mistake.

Without pausing in his stride, Alexei aimed and pulled the trigger. Once. Twice. And then once more. His opponents died in less than a second, and they did so almost silently: No shouts. No burst of gunfire. Just the click of a trigger, the dull buzz of a subsonic bullet and the hard slap of a body hitting the ground.

Now it was time to reveal himself to his rapt audience who had just watched the three men die on screen.

Lowering his gun, Alexei slipped Frost's RF jammer from his jacket pocket and stepped over to the bodies into the sightline of the surveillance camera.

For a brief moment, Alexei saw the watchers clearly in his mind's eye: Ivan, standing in front of the outsized screens, his henchmen behind him, all watching his pixilated figure slither onto the stage. There would be half a second of mute deliberation, and then Ivan would issue the kill order, which the Circassian would relay to the troops on the ground. All in all, the order would take three seconds to trickle down the chain of command.

Too long.

Alexei dropped to one knee beside the heap of bodies, reached for the nearest man and ripped off his bloodstained earpiece. The distant murmur of voices issued from the device, that familiar, melodic flow of commands to which he too had once performed his deadly routine on the battlefield. He didn't pause to listen to it. Instead, Alexei wrapped the earpiece's sticky wire around the jammer and switched it on. Instantly, the faint murmur of voices was supplanted by static.

Alexei smiled grimly. As of this moment, every radio transmitter, mobile and satellite phone in the vicinity of half a mile had become useless. And while the ether went silent, the Tsar and his strongmen were reduced to the roles of silent spectators—unable to foment their footmen against the Russian agent in their midst.

His audience was firmly muzzled. Now it was time to tie them to the chairs.

He picked up a Heckler, rose and turned right. Slinging the sub-gun's leather strap over his shoulder, Alexei strode across the foyer towards a wood-panelled door that was half-concealed behind a marble pillar.

However plain and inconspicuous it appeared, this door guarded the linchpin of Ivan's kingdom: The switch room that controlled the security system.

Alexei pressed his thumb to the biometric scanner on the wall. The distant din of disengaging deadbolts echoed through the room, then the bomb-proof hydraulic door swung open. Raising his gun, Alexei put a bullet in the head of the guard behind the screens, then he began to walk backwards, counting his steps while his hand went into his jacket pocket to retrieve what he carried there: A fragmentation grenade.

He hadn't thrown one in many years. Brute force wasn't his style. But today he would make an exception.

Keeping his hand firmly on the safety spoon, he tore off the pin below the ignition cork, then he hurled the grenade through the open door.

Three. Two.

Counting down the seconds, Alexei crossed the room, took shelter behind a pillar and pressed his back against the cold stone.

One.

The grenade detonated. Instinctively, Alexei ducked and raised his arms to protect his face and neck. Debris and shrapnel scattered in all directions, shattering vases and chandeliers and shredding the paintings along the walls. Through the lethal hailstorm of fragments and dust Alexei saw bomb-proof shutters descend in front of doors and windows like falling guillotines. Half a second later, massive metal panels closed off the glass cupola above him, plunging him briefly into darkness before the blueish emergency lights sprang to life.

Brushing the dust off his suit, Alexei rose and let his eyes trace over the walls. Just as planned, the explosion had triggered the blast sensors inside the switch room and initiated a protective lockdown of the building. With this simple and rather crude legerdemain, he had transformed the Tsar's fortress into a prison—one with a fifty-million security system that was unassailable for both the troops outside and the prisoners within.

Just like that—with nothing but a bit of explosives and a technical trickery—he had trapped every single member of the Twelve who had knowledge of Alexei Zorin's true identity. And now he would erase that rather bothersome piece of information from the world's collective memory.

CHAPTER LV

Isola di San Clemente, Venice, Italy
Friday, 5th July, 09:59

Sophie watched in mute disbelief as a blinding flash erupted on the screen, its garish light accompanied by a ear-splitting explosion that shook the foundations of the building. Instantly, as if triggered by the blast, the dull sound of engaging deadbolts echoed through the room, followed by a series of droning thuds as metal slabs descended in front of every door and window, blotting out the sunlight and plunging Ivan's study into the blueish hue of computer screens and emergency lights.

"What is this?" Cavendish demanded, his gaze moving briefly along the wall of French windows before it settled challengingly on Ivan's security chief.

"Sir, the explosion has triggered a protective lockdown. As of now, this part of the building is inaccessible from the outside," the Circassian explained in a dispassionately methodical tone.

"Are you telling me that Zorin cut our communications and locked out the goddamn reinforcements?" Cavendish hissed, anger and a hint of concern edged into his hawkish features.

"He didn't lock them out," Ivan interjected, his eyes still on the screen, his expression somewhere between cold hatred and reluctant admiration. "He locked us in. Us and his secret. And he intends to bury it along with us."

"And what use would that be?" Cavendish asked, shaking his head. "The moment reinforcements breach the perimeter and find Zorin standing knee-deep in our blood, they will know who he is. And not even his silver tongue will get him out of it."

"He doesn't need his silver tongue," Ivan replied, nodding at a screen a little to the left, where a man in a blood-spattered black army camo just slipped through a door out onto the foyer's suspended gallery. "He has something better."

Cavendish turned to face the screens, his eyes focusing on the tall figure that marched along the balustraded walkway. "Orlov."

Ivan laughed softly. "His spear-carrier"

"No, not the spear-carrier," Gabriel said from across the room, pressing a rewind button at the bottom of one of the screens. Half a second later, the pixelated figures of Frost and Kirill appeared on the monitor: Frost stood with his hand on Kirill's arm, clearly trying to hold him back as he argued with the Russian agent. But Kirill ignored him, brushing his hand away and slipping through a hatch in the roof just moments before a metal plate sealed it off. "The pawn sacrifice."

Ivan laughed softly. "Sacrificing himself to place the crown on his master's head. All for the glory of God and Mother Russia. How very noble." For an instant, the Tsar's eyes were fixed on the screen, then his gaze shifted to his grey-haired security chief. "How many units do we have left inside the lockdown perimeter?"

"Only twenty-two, sir."

"Activate them all and bring me Zorin and his lapdog."

"I'll get him for you," Gabriel said, his voice as cold and controlled as ever, yet something in his eyes held a twisted spark of enjoyment.

"Give him a weapon," Ivan commanded.

The Circassian confirmed the Tsar's command with a nod and handed Gabriel a sub-gun. He checked it with practised ease, then turned and marched to the door, motioning for the scar-faced man and the guards to follow him. Sophie didn't watch them slip away, instead she shifted her gaze back to the screens.

There was Kirill, gun in hand, rushing around the balustraded walkway. And below him, Alexei Zorin, his tall figure oddly radiant under the glow of the emergency lights.

The two men moved towards each other, but before they caught up, the door at the far end of the hall swung open, disgorging a team of six black-clad soldiers from the darkened hallway beyond. An instant later, a second team joined them, then a third.

Eighteen men. Eighteen against two.

They won't make it.

Instinctively, Sophie's hand went to her throat, her fingertips touching the necklace. If her protector failed, she would have to destroy the key to *Pandora*. The thought sparked a prickle of fear that ran like ice water through her veins, making the skin on her back tingle and her stomach churn with an urgent simmer of tension. Briefly, the feeling of panic became so acute that her vision began to cloud with a red haze, and she closed her eyes, forcing it down.

Pull yourself together, she urged herself in her mind. *Focus.*

With pounding heart, Sophie carefully brushed her hair over her shoulder and let it spill down her chest, so that it covered the necklace. For a heartbeat, she was still, making sure that no one was watching, then she let her hand drop down to the centrepiece, unhitched the hidden compartment and slipped it into the pocket of her gown. When her fingertips dove into the silky folds of her dress, Sophie felt an exhilarating rush of adrenaline surge through her veins.

Just then, she heard Cavendish draw in a sharp breath. She looked up at the screens and froze.

The two agents stood shoulder to shoulder on the staircase, moving backwards up the steps. The high ground and the light behind their backs seemed to give them a terrible advantage over their opponents who fell like culms under the reaping hook.

Sophie felt a shiver run down her spine as she watched the man in whose arms she had spent the night slay his opponents without mercy. Zorin moved with an easy, unhurried grace, felling his enemies with terrible ease—as if the act of killing came as naturally to him as drawing a breath.

A second later, the pair reached the top of the staircase. They parted, each moving along the suspended catwalk in the opposite direction without halting the attack on their opponents. And then suddenly Zorin stopped shooting.

Beside her, Ivan laughed softly. "Ah, it seems our hero is out of bullets," he said almost gleefully, watching as Zorin dropped the useless machine gun at his feet.

The four survivors at the foot of the staircase took full advantage of the situation. Firing a barrage of bullets at the two agents, they charged up the staircase. Kirill took out three of them while they moved up the steps, but one of them—the scar-faced man—made it to the top. Keeping Kirill at bay with a rapid-fire attack, the scar-faced man encroached on Zorin.

Sophie felt a chill at the back of her neck, her muscles tensing as she watched the scar-faced man's relentless approach and Zorin's calm inch-by-inch retreat.

And at that moment, another figure stepped out onto the gallery—tall, lean, moving with the same feline grace as Zorin moved.

Gabriel.

A submachine gun hung in his grip, aimed unwaveringly at Zorin, his movements calculated and calm.

But Kirill didn't hesitate—he fired, his aim deadly, but Gabriel was quicker. He squeezed the trigger, a burst of gunfire cracking through the gallery. Kirill's arm jerked back as a bullet found its mark, pain slicing up his shoulder. His weapon slipped from his grasp, skittering across the stone floor as he lunged for cover behind a pillar.

He barely made it behind a marble pillar before Gabriel's next shots ricocheted off the stone, splintering it in an explosion of dust and fragments, forcing Kirill to stay hidden, trapped, as Gabriel advanced.

Gabriel now turned his focus on Zorin, now out of bullets and hemmed in on the opposite side of the gallery by the scar-faced man, who was standing in the direct line of fire between his commander and Zorin.

For the fraction of a second, Sophie hoped that it would buy Zorin the time he needed, but then Gabriel raised his gun, and without a hint of hesitation, he pulled the trigger, killing his subordinate to clear his line of fire.

The scar-faced man dropped instantly, leaving Gabriel with a clear shot.

Walking past where Kirill was hiding, Gabriel kicked Kirill's fallen weapon down the staircase, as he walked past the injured man towards Zorin.

But Gabriel didn't take a shot, instead he lowered his weapon a little and said something to Zorin.

The Circassian leaned forward, pressing a button to enable audio on the screen. A faint crackle echoed through Ivan's study as the sound came to life, just as Gabriel halted a few meters from Zorin, lowering his weapon slightly.

"Out of bullets, Colonel?" Gabriel's voice was low, almost conversational. "After all the talk of you being the best that Moscow had, here we are. Caught in the open. A poor final move, if you ask me."

Zorin's mouth twitched into a thin, humourless smile. "Perhaps you simply underestimate me, *Nikolai Nikolayevich*."

Gabriel chuckled, a dark sound that rippled through the speakers. "I doubt it. Unlike you, Colonel, I don't let myself get distracted by... sentiment." He gestured casually with his gun, his eyes never leaving Zorin's. "But you do. That's why you came back to save the girl. She looks like Natalia, doesn't she? Those lovely brown eyes. Like a deer. Tell me, whose face do you see when you screw Sophie? Natalia's, or hers?"

Zorin's face was like stone.

Gabriel's smile widened, barely a fraction. "Don't worry. I'll take care of your new pet when you're gone. I know what she likes." His voice dropped to a near-whisper. "And how she likes it. With a bit of a twist."

In that moment, Sophie saw it—the slight clench of Zorin's jaw, the flash of something raw, wounded, in his eyes. For a heartbeat, he seemed to falter, and Gabriel's smile widened, savouring his psychological victory.

"I've hit a nerve, haven't I? Does—"

Zorin moved before Gabriel could finish—a lethal, fluid shift of his weight. His hand snapped to Gabriel's wrist, twisting the gun sharply upward. Gabriel tensed, his grip tightening as he braced against the force. They locked together in a brutal, silent struggle, their muscles visibly straining as they fought for control.

For a fraction of a second, Zorin gained the upper hand, twisting the gun away, out of Gabriel's hand. It slithered across the floor, coming to a halt against the wall.

Zorin attempted to dive for the weapon, but Gabriel countered, delivering a savage back-handed blow to Zorin's gut, and then another, and another—each hit driving him back a step. Sophie could see the force of it in Zorin's gasps—and then Gabriel reached into his suit, drawing a glinting knife.

Without hesitation, Gabriel lashed out, the blade slicing through the air as he lunged forward. Zorin ducked, retreating fast, but his back hit the balustrade, stopping him cold. On the opposite end of the gallery, Sophie saw Kirill, bleeding and unsteady on his feet, raise his gun, training it on Gabriel— but didn't fire—the fight seemingly too vicious and unpredictable to allow for a clean shot.

Gabriel launched himself at Zorin who stood trapped with his back against the banister. But this time, Zorin didn't dodge the blow. He caught Gabriel's knife-hand, yanking it towards him. Gabriel stumbled, thrown off-balance by the unexpected resistance, his weight crashing into Zorin's chest. And then, in a move so fast Sophie barely saw it happen, Zorin's arm closed around Gabriel's neck, locking him into a chokehold. For one breathless instant, they were poised at the edge of the banister.

Then, with a fierce twist of his body, Zorin launched himself over the balustrade—dragging Gabriel with him like a ragdoll.

Clinging together, the pair plummeted into the abyss—Zorin with his back to the ground, Gabriel on top. And as they fell, Zorin twisted his body like a falling cat, nimbly reversing their positions. Gabriel's lips parted in a terrified scream, while Zorin hauled his knee up to his opponent's neck, positioning it right at his throat. Then they hit the staircase fifteen feet below—Gabriel's neck snapping visibly as Zorin's knee descended on it with the deadly force of a body in freefall.

"That fucking son of a bitch," Cavendish breathed beside her, an expression of utter disbelief edged into his face as he watched Zorin get up. "Is there a chance that he'll make it?" He finally asked, turning to Ivan.

"If he's only half as good as the GRU claims, then there's a good chance that he'll make it," Ivan replied, watching as Zorin picked up two more sub-guns before heading back up the stairs.

In that instant, for the first time, Sophie felt a glimmer of hope. Against all the odds, Zorin and his fellow agent had managed to take down eighteen men. Only four more. Maybe, just maybe, they would make it.

"Wouldn't put my money on your pretty boy," Ivan said, glancing first at Sophie, then nodding at the steel-enforced door. "Even if he takes down every man in the building, he won't make it through this gate." The Tsar's eyes shifted back to Sophie, measuring her disparagingly. "Nothing to shed tears over though, his lovers tend to be short-lived anyway."

Sophie didn't respond, her eyes returning to the screen. Just at that moment, Zorin moved a little to the side, giving up the close formation that Kirill and he had maintained so far. For a fraction of a second, their movements seemed out of tune, and then it happened. A bullet hit Kirill's shoulder. And as the bloodstain spread rapidly across Kirill's chest, four black-clad mercenaries, under the aegis of Ivan's security chief, emerged from a darkened hallway to their left.

Zorin showered them with a hailstorm of bullets and his opponents instantly returned the favour. The shootout lasted only a second. Then Zorin, seeing that he was finally outgunned and outflanked, slowly straightened himself, held out his arm and dropped his weapon.

There was no tension or agitation about him, just an astonishing calmness, as if everything were simple routine. Unhurriedly, Zorin dropped to his knees, his arms stretched out to either side of him in the universal gesture of surrender. A heartbeat later, Kirill followed his example.

Ivan laughed softly. "Ah, the White Knight is cornered at last."

CHAPTER LVI

Isola di San Clemente, Venice, Italy
Friday, 5th July, 10:11

Alexei felt the prickle of impending battle wash over him as he stepped through the door of Ivan's study. It had been the last obstacle. Unscalable without aid. But like the Trojan king—in steadfast conviction of his victory—Ivan had blindly opened the gates to his enemy and invited death into his kingdom.

And death he would deliver.

Stepping forward, Alexei shifted his eyes to the far end of the room, where Ivan—in perfect imitation of that mythical king—reclined in a wide-armed designer chair, one polished leather shoe perched disdainfully on the edge of the coffee table in front of him. He was reading Stiva's fake GRU file, his mouth set in a surly line as he studied the document. Cavendish stood behind him like a hawk, Nikolai Morozov's underling—judging by his uniform a GRU major—two steps away, head bowed like a repentant sinner.

To their left, a little apart, stood Sophie—her stance tense, her face white, her lips set in a firm line. Alexei saw the ghost of fear cross her fine features, but the grim determination in her eyes never wavered. He held her gaze for a heartbeat, a thousand unspoken words between them, then he shifted his attention back to Ivan.

"Ah, the fabled Colonel Sobolev in the flesh," Ivan intoned, making a show of closing the file while he shifted his sovereign's gaze to Alexei. "I hope it's all right if I call you Alexander, after all, we're almost friends." He tossed the file contemptuously onto the table. "Aren't we, Alexander Mikhailovich?"

Alexei almost had to smile at Ivan's caustic remark. What would follow now was a power game, a battle of wills and minds, rather than weapons and brute force. Ivan was a formidable opponent—perceptive, quick-witted and merciless—but his son's death had exposed the cracks in the veneer. And he would exploit them without mercy.

Briefly, Alexei's gaze shifted to the wall of French windows, surveying the men behind him in its reflection: There was the Circassian, standing by the door and watching him, a pair of black-clad wardens pointing their sub-guns at Alexei's head and their two colleagues steadying Kirill's limp figure between them.

For a fraction of a second, Alexei's eyes lingered on his fellow agent—his comrade, his friend for so many years. *Oh Kyria, you could have gone home to your beautiful wife and daughter.* But he hadn't. Instead, he had chosen to come back.

Forcing the bitterness from his mind, Alexei shifted his attention back to Ivan. Kirill's sacrifice—in whatever form it came—wouldn't be in vain. He would see to that.

He caught Ivan's gaze. *Time to play, old man.*

"Why so formal, Ivan Sergeevich?" Alexei asked, letting the Tsar's name and patronym roll off his tongue scornfully while he reached up to loosen his bowtie with an indolent flick of the wrist. "My friends call me Sasha."

The Tsar gave a mirthless little laugh and stood. "Oh, Alexander, even if you drop the act, you still are one arrogant, condescending bastard." Ivan stepped closer and stopped in front of Alexei, measuring him with cold contempt. "But don't worry, I'll teach you some humility. You'll kiss my feet before you die. And I'll make sure that you mean it."

Once again, Alexei's eyes briefly slipped away to windows, assessing the distances and angles at which the guards stood from his position. He moved a little to the left and shifted his focus back to Ivan.

He was ready to do battle. Now the time had come to force the Tsar's hand.

"Oh, come now, Ivan, be a sport—you know that I prefer to be on top when I play," Alexei replied, with mock offence, pursing his lips a little when he ended, as if he were truly appalled by Ivan's suggestion.

Ivan gave him an easy little smile. And struck.

The blow, when it hit Alexei's abdomen, was merciless—driving the air from his lungs and the bile up his throat. For a fraction of a second, red haze clouded his vision, then his legs gave way beneath him. The hard impact of his knees on the ground restored his senses, and his gaze went up, this time not to the window, but to the woman standing beside it, a mere three paces from the outsized fireplace.

Her face was luminous under the soft glow of the emergency lights—the pallor of her skin pronounced, the lines of her face regal, of an almost ethereal beauty. Their eyes met, and he saw in hers that quiet determination he had seen there before. And then her hand slipped into the folds of her gown and retrieved something from there. In the reflection of the window, Alexei saw what no one else in the room could spot: The double key to *Pandora* glistening between her fingers.

He felt the ghost of a smile on his lips: His Joan of Arc, ready to battle and burn to save the world.

I won't let you die, Alexei assured her in his mind, while he spread the palm of his hand slightly on his thigh—signalling her to stay and wait for his command.

And then she vanished from his line of vision, her small frame supplanted by Ivan's towering figure.

"The puppet master," Ivan mused, sauntering around Alexei with the menacing magnificence of a prowling lion. "I must say, I would have expected more of a man who bares such a lofty moniker."

Again, Alexei's attention shifted to the windows—confirming the distances and angles—then back to Ivan.

He had driven the king to the edge. Now it was time to tip him over.

"I was never keen on these... notions of grandeur. My pitch is not the field of honour, but that of deceit." Alexei laughed softly, condescendingly. "But you should know that, Ivan Sergeevich, after all, you sacrificed your son on it."

The transformation in Ivan was instantaneous: Cold, unrestrained fury finally won over as he lashed out, dealing Alexei a vicious backhand across the face.

The pain shot down Alexei's neck and spine, his muscles and tendons straining as his head was yanked to the side. He tasted the acrid tang of blood at the back of his throat. Then he felt the cold muzzle of Ivan's weapon against his forehead.

"I'm growing weary of the game, Alexander. Let's end it." Ivan cocked his gun. "Shall we?"

Alexei didn't look at Ivan, his eyes moving to the window again, watching the reflection of the men behind him, assessing the parameters with a quick glance: The distances, the angles, the speed that would be necessary. And as his eyes trailed along the reflections in the stained glass, he tapped his index finger lightly against his thigh, counting down the seconds for his protégé, just as he had done when they had danced.

Three.

He shifted his attention back to Ivan. "This is my game, Ivan."

Two.

"I make the rules."

One.

"You merely play by them."

Ivan smiled. "And yet, I win."

Time slowed to a trickle. And he saw all that happened at once.

The Tsar's finger slipping past the trigger guard. His protégé hurling the pendant into the flames. Cavendish shouting, his hoarse cry drawing the attention of the men around him. Ivan's momentary distraction, his brief glance in Cavendish's direction.

One fatal mistake.

Alexei moved, his eyes shifting to the reflections in the window, his hand grabbing Ivan's gun, tilting it up, forcing the trigger down. Once. Twice. Once more.

In the reflection of the windows, Alexei saw his wardens go down, the Circassian dropping to his knees behind them. And while they died, Kirill moved, wrestling a sub-gun from one of his guards and topping them both before he put a bullet in Cavendish's heart.

Then Alexei held Ivan's weapon. And there was only Ivan and him. Their eyes met and the Tsar's gaze stayed on Alexei. There was nothing left to say for either of them.

He pulled the trigger.

For justice.

CHAPTER LVII

Isola di San Clemente, Venice, Italy
Friday, 5th July, 10:39

Standing motionless in the gloom of Ivan's throne room Sophie watched as Zorin's finger dropped to the trigger and pulled back until it went no further.

The dull hiss of a bullet echoed in the room.

Time stopped.

A fleeting moment protracted to infinity.

And while the world ground to a halt, its facets seemed to become richer, as if time and visual acuity were an inverse function of each other—a trade-off between the senses where the awareness of one necessitated the ignorance of the other. And in that new state of mind, where time had no meaning, she saw the world around her unravel in spectacular detail:

Ivan's lifeless body falling backwards in slow motion.

Cavendish drawing a last shuddering breath at her feet.

A bodyguard lying beside him, still and limp, in a pool of blood.

And Alexei Zorin, standing motionless amidst the carnage, staring down at the dead and dying like the angel of doom.

For a moment, everything was silent, the world around her imbued with the hush of death. Then the metal shutters began to lift, and shafts of daylight poured through the wall of French windows—the sunrays casting dainty dapples of light onto the bloodstained floor and Zorin's face.

And it was that image—the dead on the ground, Zorin above them, all shrouded in the sun's ethereal glow—that burned itself into her mind. The sun-gilded snapshot of a nightmare. A glimpse of hell. Never-to-be-forgotten.

Then Zorin's eyes shifted to the screens, watching as a host of Ivan's mercenaries poured into the foyer and the gallery above. And then she heard his voice—distant—like a voice calling to her in a dream.

"They're coming."

As he spoke, the sound of his voice was joined by the echo of shouts and footsteps, and then all noises were drowned out by the deafening peal of an explosion.

Instinctively, Sophie retreated to the corner, her back hitting the wall as Kirill's knees hit the ground. And while she let herself fall, cowering down in a desperate bid for safety, Kirill raised his hands, arms wide, palms up, his eyes fixed on Zorin who calmly levelled his weapon at the kneeling agent.

And then the doors clattered open.

Guards—all black-clad, all armed, all shouting—poured into the room. Spreading out like a swarm of wasps, they secured the room—encircling Kirill, shielding Zorin and holding her back. And while the sinister legion of warriors held the Russian agent at gunpoint, Zorin—with the calm composure of someone in absolute control—holstered his weapon and shifted his attention to the men that had followed in the army's wake: Kirov and Khan, and two others she had seen but didn't know.

For a fraction of a second, Kirov stood motionless, his eyes fixed on Ivan's inert face, then his gaze shifted to Zorin. The tension was palpable, first in the silence, then in Kirov's voice as he broke it.

The words, uttered so softly in Russian, needed no translation—the cold tone of accusation and challenge in which they were spoken sufficient to transcend the boundaries of language. And Sophie realised that Kirov wasn't only here as prosecutor to establish Zorin's guilt or innocence, but as pretender to Ivan's throne: The next in line of succession should the chosen heir reveal himself as traitor.

The game was poised on knife's edge and Zorin's next move would see him either crowned or hanged.

Sophie shifted her gaze to Zorin, and as she watched her protector, she could almost feel how he steeled himself, preparing body and mind for the act. The change in him was subtle—the straightening of the shoulders, the hardening of the expression, the almost indiscernible lifting of the chin—but the effect was a grim and oddly frightening transformation: He seemed to loom over Kirov now, a malevolent overlord towering over his defiant vassal who had dared to not only accuse but challenge his master.

Briefly, Zorin's eyes lingered on Kirov, as if to relegate his rival to second place with nothing but a stern look, then he took a step back and directed his attention to his audience: The delegation of The Twelve, the kingmakers who would put the crown on his head.

"What happened here is the result of this organisation's collective failure—the dismal consequence of carelessness, arrogance and treason."

As he spoke Zorin began to move through the room with a slow, measured calm—less a defendant pleading his innocence than a king-to-be conducting his own coronation mass. In passing, he picked up Stiva's file from the coffee table. Briefly, he weighed it in his hand, then tossed it at Kirov, who caught it with surprising agility.

"What is this?" Kirov asked.

"A litany of failures, Leonid," Zorin replied, his voice resounding from the walls, like a voice in a cathedral. "A page-by-page account of a Russian operation, masterminded by the Kremlin's strategists, overseen by its puppet master and executed by a traitor in our own ranks. And had it succeeded, then all of you would now worship at the Kremlin's feet."

As he spoke, Zorin's voice seemed to echo in the room. It was a voice that made him shiver. The kind of voice that the ear followed as if it were a melody: every word a thrilling seduction of the mind—imbuing her thoughts with his sinister tale of greed and hate and treason.

Trying to banish Zorin's voice from her mind, Sophie shifted her gaze to his audience, watching them like figures in a dream: Khan standing over Ivan's body, Kirov leafing through Stiva's file, their companions stone-faced at their side, and Alexei Zorin—like a spider in its web—pulling the strings, spinning his tale, entrapping his victims in a deadly web of trickery and deceit.

Unbidden Ivan's words echoed in her mind: *He understands how people work, what makes them tick. Or snap.*

In that moment, for the first time perhaps, Sophie truly understood what the Tsar had meant with these words: Alexander Sobolev bent others to his will—not by force, but with a whisper.

He was an illusionist—a puppet master in the truest sense.

Wrapping her arms around herself, Sophie let her gaze trace over the faces of Kirov and his peers—each of them utterly absorbed by the tale—then back to Zorin, who strode around them with the sinister majesty of the magician, pulling his audience ever deeper into his illusion. And as he spoke, Zorin's eyes slipped briefly to the wall of French windows, watching the sea as if he were waiting for something to emerge from its golden waves. For a fraction of a moment, she glimpsed a hint of impatience in his eyes. He made another turn about the room, his eyes going once again out to the sea, and this time he seemed satisfied with whatever he had spotted.

Zorin ended his narration with a little flourish—a mockery at Kirill's expense—then turned to his audience, almost as if he expected them to applaud. His reward, however, came not in form of an ovation, but something far more valuable: The slightest inclination of a head. Kirov's first. Then Khan's. Then those of their peers. Each bow a silent oath of allegiance.

The genuflection to the new Tsar.

Sophie felt the exhilarating rush of victory. They had won. Zorin had claimed the throne. And now, as Tsar, he held the power to tear down this blood-sodden empire and bury its corrupt and decadent disciples under its burning wreckage.

And then the unthinkable happened. Kirov drew his gun, and for a single, terrible moment, Sophie expected him to aim the weapon at Zorin, but instead Kirov held it out to him. "The privilege is yours, Alexei Alexandrovich."

Zorin took the gun with a small nod and turned to Kirill.

Sophie felt her blood run cold, the feeling of horror, of utter helpless misery washing over her as she realised that the privilege Kirov spoke of was the Tsar's right to avenge his predecessor.

Cocking his gun, Zorin stepped around Kirill's kneeling form and levelled the gun with his head.

Something hot and warm ran down her cheek, and Sophie reached up to brush it away, realising only when she touched it that it was a tear. *Don't do this*, she pleaded in her mind, her eyes shifting from Kirill's kneeling figure to Zorin's face. *Please don't do this.*

But Zorin didn't look at her, his eyes fixed on the windows and on the sea beyond. For a moment he stood in rapt attention, his brow creased, like a man who is contemplating the world's mysteries in the surging waves, then anger—a terrible cold rage—transformed his even features.

With a curse, he grabbed Kirill's hair and yanked his head back to the point where the tendons and muscles of his neck strained visibly against the skin. "Invited a few friends to the party, haven't we?"

The eyes of every man in the room shifted to the windows, their collective gazes going out to the line of vessels that floated above the horizon: small, angular ships, painted in a distinct grey livery against which the *tricolore* on the stern stood out in vivid contrast.

The Italian coastguard.

Sophie shifted her gaze back to Zorin, who towered over his fellow agent, his eyes not on the ships, but on the men watching them. In that moment she realised that none of this was an accident: He had planned this. The magician's final hat trick to save his fellow soldier.

"Don't worry, Colonel, your death is only a pleasure deferred," Zorin hissed, dealing his fellow agent a savage blow with the butt of his weapon that sent him unconscious to the floor.

Stepping over Kirill's motionless figure, Zorin barked a harsh command in Russian and instantly the world around her sprang into motion.

Guards swarmed out, forming a phalanx around their masters, while Kirill, still unconscious, was hauled from the room. And then they came for her too. Hands going around her upper arms, men rushing her out of the room, guiding her through the hallways and galleries of Ivan's estate.

She saw her own reflection in the mirrored hallway, and Zorin in front of her, Kirov and Khan behind, all surrounded by a formation of black-clad bodyguards.

The hallways and corridors swarmed with soldiers, rushing from door to door, securing every corner, and giving the *all-clear* when they were done. Above her, on the gallery, some of Ivan's guests were rushed to safety. To her right, a door stood ajar. A second later, Sophie passed it, her eyes shifting to the man who knelt on the floor beside a woman, taking her pulse and shaking his head.

It was Stiva's lover.

She lay sprawled out on the ground, her brow resting on her forearm, her eyes closed as if in sleep.

For a heartbeat, Sophie tasted bile in her mouth.

And then she was out in the open, the garish sunlight blinding, the powerful throb of rotor blades audible above the sound of blustering waves. As her eyes adjusted, she saw five massive helicopters, dark and angular as if made for combat, sit on the lawn like predators.

She was rushed to the closest one. Zorin helped her up the steps, and as she slid past him, he paused briefly, his eyes going up to the sky.

She looked up too.

There was nothing to be seen, but she knew what he was looking for.

Pandora.

They didn't need to see the satellite's fiery tale to know that they had won. Pandora was gone.

He squeezed her hand.

A second later, she sat inside the chopper's plush cabin, Zorin beside her, Kirov and Khan across. The doors slammed shut, then they took to the sky with unexpected speed and silence.

A guard gave out headsets. And she took it and put it on, watching Kirov opposite her, who did the same. Voices crackled to life through the headsets, all Russian. Court exchanges. Commands given and received. Then Zorin's voice. Speaking just one word.

A command.

And as he spoke, Zorin's hand slid up her spine and neck, to the back of her head, his fingers spreading there as he pulled her close and down, his body coming down over hers, as the men around him ducked too. Then the helicopter was hit by a blast wave, while the estate below them exploded in a ball of fire.

Kirov's smug smile, as he straightened himself, left no doubt as to who was responsible for the detonation.

The Twelve didn't leave traces. Only scorched earth.

CHAPTER LVII

Istanbul, Turkey
Friday, 5th July, 14:59

Alexei felt a faint tremor of turbulence roll through the Bombardier's fuselage as the sleek jet began its descent over the Turkish capital. At a top speed of nearly Mach one, the plane had covered the eight-hundred-seventy flight from Venice to Istanbul in just over an hour.

Kirill would be in *Cap Ferrat* by now and Frost in the safe hands of a British extraction team. And while his colleagues were being hauled to safety, Alexei and his advisers had busied themselves with rolling up thirty-nine billion pounds of their Italian assets: Cash, stocks, real estate and of course inventory.

Stepping back to the mahogany conference table that stretched across half the cabin, Alexei let his eyes trail along its length, over the stony countenances of Kirov and Khan standing to his left, then around the table, over the tense faces of lawyers, bankers and advisors who assisted in the winddown of their operations.

During its long and turbulent history, the Twelve had been under siege more than once. But they were equal to the challenge. Prepared for every eventuality. And so, in the course of less than two hours, his team had shifted twenty-three billion of liquid positions out of the country, funnelling the proceeds through a series of offshore accounts and the Panamanian financial laundromat into a Luxembourg investment structure—gilt-edged, on-shore, whiter than the arctic snow.

The remainder of their assets—sixteen billion of real estate and an inventory of military-grade weapons—would have to be axed. It was a trifle. The kind of money they left on the table without batting an eye.

And while Italian law enforcement desperately tried to salvage a shred of evidence from the ruins of Ivan's estate and the coastguard scrambled to track the five missing stealth helicopters that had vanished under their very nose, the Twelve would already be gone—vanished like breath into the wind.

In the end, the Italians would have to make do with scraps: A couple of eyewitness reports stating that five black helicopters had touched down at Venice Marco Polo airport, a couple of fake passenger manifests and incomplete flight schedules pertaining to three Lagos-bound private jets that had mysteriously vanished from the radar and a handful of airport and law-enforcement employees who had seemingly just done a sloppy job.

There would be disciplinary measures. Official inquiries made and closed without further action. The reasons were always the same. Lack of evidence. Systemic failure. Gross negligence but no crime.

Of course, the Twelve's stooges would be generously rewarded. An inheritance here and there. Perhaps a particularly lucrative property sale. Sometimes some kind of other engagement. And while their helpers and underlings gradually vanished into their well-deserved early retirements, replacements would be procured to fill their positions.

Half a year from now, all cases would be closed and forgotten. And while the files started to gather dust in some official archive, the Twelve would funnel their money and assets back into Italy with the courteous assistance of international banks, bent politicians and paid-off officials. And then it would be business as usual.

Resting his palms on the polished tabletop, Alexei listened to Kirov's brief closing speech that detailed the measures he had taken to salvage or destroy the Italian weapons inventory. When Kirov had ended, a whey-faced lawyer with wire-rimmed spectacles handed Alexei the meeting protocol and execution documents. He signed and initialled both, the scratch of the pen on paper audible in the silence, then handed the stack to Kirov who signed it too.

With his signature, Alexei had completed all official duties. And now, as they descended on Istanbul, all that remained was for him to make good on the promise he had given to Sophie.

Taking his leave with a nod, Alexei slipped from the conference room through the tranquil living area to the back of the plane, with its bedroom and other private spaces.

He opened the door with care, stepped through, then closed and locked it behind him.

Sophie sat on the bed, eyes closed, back resting against the wall, knees drawn up to her chin. She had cried. But even with black makeup stains smeared down her cheeks and dark circles under her eyes, she was a woman of singular beauty. And with both the courage and the mind to match it.

"Sophie."

She opened her eyes and looked at him but remained silent—waiting for him to speak.

He motioned at the bed, wordlessly asking for permission to sit down beside her, which she gave with a nod. He sat down.

"I promised you freedom. Though I can't provide it in the form I wish, I'll make sure that you will be safe, and that none of this"—he motioned vaguely at their surroundings, as if it represented the entirety of the sinister world in which he dwelt—"will ever touch you again."

For a moment she looked at him, studying him, then she reached into the pocket of her gown and slipped out the encrypted USB flash drive. His treasure. His greatest prize. The whetstone to sharpen the sword of justice before he brought it down upon the guilty.

"And you have come for this, haven't you?" She asked, holding it up.

He gave a nod. "Yes."

She turned the USB stick in her hand, then placed it pensively on the bed between them.

"So you're really going to do this alone, aren't you? Just you. A hunted man."

Alexei smiled bitterly. How easily she had laid bare all his vulnerabilities: The Kremlin now knew the truth and that meant he was a marked man. From this day forth, he would be hunted by a truly formidable army. But there was no turning back. He had crossed the bridge and burned it. And he had chosen this path with his eyes wide open.

"Sophie, I have sworn to uphold justice and serve my country—even if its rulers don't. It is an oath that binds to the death. It's never abandoned."

"Then let me help you."

He closed his eyes.

As Tsar, he could force the Twelve to their knees, but to eradicate them, governments around the world would have to bring down the sword of justice without mercy or delay—governments who had looked on idly for twenty years as shoals of their exponents worshipped at the feet of The Twelve. There was only one way to end this game. And it would be a harrowing one. A public one.

"What must happen now, can only happen under the eyes of the world. Traitor or not, I'm a Russian agent, and if I try to drag this into the light, justice will be drowned in a cacophony of geo-political haggling and great power politics. All the world will see is the Kremlin's shadow looming over them and the guilty will slip away under the cover of ideology and politics." He paused. "Sophie, whoever I send out there to act as a witness in my stead will be hunted without mercy. It will never stop. Are you really prepared to pay this price?"

"You said it yourself, there are things that are greater than we are."

He held her gaze and in it he saw that she wasn't choosing this lightly. She was neither a fool nor an adventuress, but someone who was wronged and who had seen more wrong than was bearable. And her conscience and sense of justice wouldn't allow her to simply walk away—not if she could make a difference.

He hesitated for a brief moment, then reached for the USB stick. He held it up. "Together?"

It was the last chance for her to back out. To say no and leave all of this behind. And if she chose to walk, he would make sure that not even a wisp of this world ever touched her again.

She gave him a small smile and reached for it. "Together."

A disembodied voice from the overhead speakers announced that they were approaching Istanbul. He rose and helped her stand. And they settled in the seats by the window.

"What will happen now?" Sophie asked.

"I will send you back to England. The British government will watch over you. And I will make sure they do so properly. You will be able to prepare yourself in safety."

She nodded and fell silent, her eyes shifting to the window, lingering briefly on the airport's distinct dual runways that pointed like outstretched fingers towards the sea, before her gaze returned to him.

Sophie regarded him for a long moment, the hesitation in her eyes visible as she weighed the words that so obviously lingered on her mind.

"Will I see you again?"

He gave her a small smile and inclined his head in silent affirmation. Then the jet touched down on the runway, its engines howling as it reversed the thrust and finally skittled to a groaning halt. Across the tarmac, black limousines approached at breakneck speed while the crew lowered the stairs.

It was time.

"Are you ready?" he asked.

She nodded. "I am."

He rose and held out his hand to help her up. For a heartbeat they stood, facing each other—so much unspoken between them. One day perhaps, in a distant future where all that bound them now was done, these things could be said.

He brought her hand to his lips and placed a gentle kiss between her knuckles. And then he let go of her. It wasn't farewell. Not anymore.

Steeling himself, Alexei briefly closed his eyes, then he stepped out through the door. Without looking back, he strode past his subjects. They were all his now. Their loyalty to him as absolute as it had once been to Ivan. And he would drag them all into ruin.

Slipping on a suit jacket that a diligent member of the cabin crew produced for him, he stepped out onto the staircase and swiftly descended onto the tarmac. As his foot touched the pavement, he took a deep breath, inhaling the warm air.

Slipping on a pair of sunglasses, Alexei strode towards the car. As he walked, a grey-haired man carrying a stack of passports caught up with him—undoubtably Khan's factotum and master of identities who was tasked with smoothing their transfer through Istanbul. Alexei extended his hand without a word, and Khan's footman passed him the passports. All newly issued. All with an iron-clad fresh identity for each of The Twelve—or what remained of them.

Alexei didn't bother searching for his own. It didn't matter who he was on paper. The devil's name could've been printed on the first page of that passport, and he'd still breeze through every checkpoint at the airport. Money ruled the world—for better or worse, and no one played that game better than The Twelve.

He slipped the stack of diplomatic passports from the Caribbean Island nation of St Lucia—red instead of the usual navy blue—to the back, so that the blue British passport lay on top. It was fake like the others. But he didn't check it. It would hold. Alexei handed it to the guard on his left, then returned the others to Khan's officious underling.

"Fly her to London," he commanded.

"You're not keeping her?" Khan asked with a frown, catching up with him while he opened to collar of his shirt.

Alexei laughed softly, shaking his head. "Ah, you know how it is, Tarik. The novelty wears off fast."

"Where should we transfer her to, sir?" The guard with the passport asked, nodding at Sophie who, just at that moment, stepped down onto the tarmac.

"Send her to Frost's estate in Cornwall—a gift for his many years of loyal service," Alexei replied, slipping into the back of the car.

His bodyguard closed the door. Through the tinted windows, his eyes shifted to the woman on the tarmac: She would be his Joan of Arc, a shining beacon of hope in whose wake the just would rise to defend their cause.

EPILOGUE

The Hague, The Netherlands
Monday, 3rd February, 13:48

They had given her a bulletproof vest. It was very thin and light. Invisible under her buttoned-up shirt. An impenetrable shield. And yet the act of slipping it on had felt like the prelude of martyrdom.

The door opened and a woman in her mid-forties, gaunt and with faint wrinkles around the eyes, peered into the room, making sure that she was dressed. She gave Sophie a tight-lipped smile and vanished, leaving the door ajar. A moment later, a man stepped into the room.

He was tall and grey-haired, with keen blue eyes and a bespoke suit that spoke of money. His hair was combed back with a little elegant wave above the brow, his white shirt was monogrammed and his visitor's badge, which dangled around his neck from a light blue nylon band, announced him as Dr James Browning, Attorney at Law.

For the past six months, Browning had been something like a paternal presence at her side, guiding her through the legal process and keeping her out of the media's scrutinizing eye while reporters hunted feverishly for the anonymous crown witness whose revelations had rocked the spheres of power from Washington to Moscow.

But that anonymity would soon come to an end. Throughout the night and the early hours of the morning news of the forthcoming trial, relayed by reporters that had descended on The Hague like a bevy of vultures, had dominated global headlines. The moment she stepped into the court she would become a hunted woman. Forever.

Browning's voice pulled her from her thoughts.

"Miss Akehurst, it's time to go."

Sophie gave a nod. "Did you bring the newspaper I asked for, Dr Browning?"

"Yes, but maybe you should wait to read it until after the hearing. You need to focus on what is relevant."

"This is relevant. What I'm doing today is also for her."

"Very well," Browning said, handing her the printout of *The New York Times* article.

Briefly Sophie's eyes went over the title and the byline below.

VICTOR ORSIN'S LONG ARM

by Natalia Vetrova

For a moment, the name lingered on Sophie's lips, but she didn't speak it. Then she folded the page, slipped it into her handbag and turned to follow Browning out of the room. Surrounded by a close formation of police officers—British and Dutch—they descended to the underground garage where three black SUVs stood waiting—the beams of their headlights illuminating the whitewashed walls.

Sophie slipped into the car that was sandwiched in the middle. Half a second later, Browning slid in on the other side. The doors—six inches thick—were slammed shut and then the convoy began to move, ascending the curved ramp and pulling out into the street. The moment they emerged into the open, the motorcade was joined by a vanguard of police motorcycles that accompanied them with flashing lights.

As the SUV accelerated, Sophie turned and looked out the window.

Outside, a brilliant winter sun lit up streets blanketed by a recent snowfall and there was a certain hush to the city—an almost cathedral-like quiet that comes only with freshly fallen snow.

The route had been premeditated and secured to make sure that she survived the six-minute trip from the hotel to the International Criminal Court. Still, Sophie felt the tension in her shoulders, her eyes scanning the street, lingering briefly on a lone wayside observer—his stance oddly still, like a soldier. Or an assassin.

"Don't worry, Miss Akehurst, the security measures that have been taken to protect you are unprecedented and stringent," Browning said, his eyes following her gaze. "You're quite safe."

Sophie was certain that Browning wasn't referring to the state-sponsored army of bodyguards that accompanied her, but to another, equally potent protector who watched over her from the shadows.

Now, as the motorcade turned into a wide alley bracketed by birch trees, their slender trunks and bare branches frosted with snow. Sophie shifted her gaze to the colossal glass complex that rose before her: Six inter-connected buildings surmounted by a soaring glass tower.

As they approached the structure, the driver turned up the radio a little.

"... On trial for crimes against humanity according to Article 7 and war crimes according to Article 8 of the Rome Statute. Among the defendants are former Russian presidential candidate Leonid Kirov, as well as Tarik Khan, the majority-shareholder of Khan Industries and..."

As Sophie listened to the announcer's words, she could almost hear the man who spoke through him—the man who controlled and shaped the public narrative from the shadows, whispering into the world's ear and keeping its eye firmly on the stage upon which he intended to punish the guilty.

The motorcade came to a halt. In front and back, police officers in plain clothes slid out of the escort vehicles, forming a ring around her car. Then the door was opened.

Taking a deep breath, Sophie slipped out of the car. Instantly, a throng of journalists converged on her, the flashlights of their cameras blinding her momentarily. She felt Browning's hand on her back, leading her swiftly into the building.

The empty lobby echoed under their steps like a cathedral. They passed through it and entered a futuristic gallery with concrete and glass walls. An art installation projected the words Together for Justice onto a bare wall. They walked past it and entered the courtroom.

Judges in blue robes sat at wide cube-shaped desks, court clerks with stern faces and equally stern suits a row behind them. Browning conducted her to the table at the centre of the room, then stepped aside to an identical desk at its left.

For a moment, the judges regarded her, then one—a grey-haired man in his fifties—bent forward, adjusted his microphone, and said: "Miss Akehurst, as presiding judge I would like to welcome you to the courtroom on behalf of the chamber. Good morning."

For a moment, Sophie's voice failed her, and it took all her willpower to force the words from her lips. "Good morning, your Honour."

"Miss Akehurst, you have been called upon by this chamber of the International Criminal Court to give testimony. This is a solemn undertaking. You will now be sworn in. Please raise your right hand."

Standing behind the chair, Sophie held up her hand.

"Do you solemnly swear that you will speak the truth, the whole truth and nothing but the truth?"

"I do so swear."

"Thank you, Miss Akehurst. You have now been sworn in. Please be seated."

She slid mechanically into the chair.

"The prosecution has the floor," the judge said, his eyes shifting to the side of the room.

To her right she saw the prosecutor's head lift. "Robert Hawthorn for the Prosecution," he announced himself, greeting her with a polite nod that she reciprocated.

For a heartbeat, his eyes lingered probingly on her, as if he were trying to read her mind, then he leaned back and took off his glasses.

"Miss Akehurst, would you be so kind and identify the defendants?"

She turned, her eyes shifting through the room, tracing over the figure of Doctor Thomas Frost, sitting like a benevolent guardian in the first line of the audience, then her gaze moved on to the ranks of the defendants. Stopping there.

"Yes, I can. Tarik Kazim Khan and Leonid Petrovich Kirov."

Again, Hawthorn's voice echoed through the room. "Miss Akehurst, can you please state how you came to know the defendants?"

Sophie's hands stiffened and she instinctively placed them on her lap to hide them from view. "I came to know them in at the country estate of Ivan Sergeevich Volkov in Venice, Italy."

"And what was the nature of your stay at Mr Volkov's residence?"

"I was sold to one of Mr Volkov's guests by a ring of human traffickers and held at the estate against my will."

A whisper ran through the room, the murmurs almost instantly drowned out by Hawthorn's voice.

"Miss Akehurst, during your time at Mr Volkov's estate, did any of the defendants discuss matters of business in your presence?"

"Yes."

"Could you please, for the benefit of the here assembled judging body, state the nature of the business and the circumstances in which it was discussed?"

She began to speak, and as she spoke, the hushed murmurs in the room rose to a crescendo, almost drowning out her words.

Hawthorn asked a follow-up question. She answered it, just as she answered all those that came thereafter. Minutes stretched to hours. And then it was over, and she was back out in the street, conducted through the mass of journalists towards the waiting car.

Someone opened the door for her, and as she bent to climb in, Sophie's eyes went across the street, her gaze shifting to the motorcade that passed them. For a brief moment, she could see the man who sat in the back of one of the cars—the man who had become something more, something she hadn't expected.

For a heartbeat, they held each other's gaze, an unspoken exchange hanging between them, filled with everything they couldn't say.

Their love had been born in the dark. It couldn't survive in the daylight—not the way ordinary love did. But it lived in the stolen glances, the secret moments, and the knowledge that he would always be there, somewhere in the dark, waiting.

One day, perhaps, they would find their way to the light—and for now, that was enough.

THE RUSSIAN GAMBIT SERIES

The Russian Gambit series includes the following books, all of which can be read as standalone works.

The Spymaster – Russian Gambit Book #0.1 (June 2025)

Mercury – Russian Gambit Book #0.5 (October 2025)

Spy Dust – Russian Gambit Book #1 (January 2025)

Moscow Winter – Russian Gambit Book #2 (2026)

All release dates will be announced on my website www.themafiagal.com or on my Instagram and TikTok accounts @TheMafiaGal

COPYRIGHT & DISCLAIMER

Spy Dust by Laureline Ducros

Book One of the Russian Gambit Series

First published in 2020 under the title Russian Gambit

Copyright © 2020, 2025 by Laureline Marie Ducros.

The moral right of the author has been asserted.

ISBN: 9798863919560.

All rights reserved. No part of this publication may be reproduced, stored in a retrieval system, or transmitted in any form or by any means—electronic, mechanical, photocopying, recording, or otherwise—without the prior written permission of the copyright owner, except in the case of brief quotations in critical reviews or as otherwise permitted by law. Unauthorised reproduction, distribution, or use of this work, or any part of it, is strictly prohibited and may result in legal action. Any person or entity found to be in violation of copyright may be liable for civil damages, including statutory damages and legal costs.

This is a work of fiction. Names, characters, places, and events are either the product of the author's imagination or are used fictitiously, and any resemblance to actual persons, living or dead, business establishments, companies, events, or places is entirely coincidental.

Made in the USA
Coppell, TX
16 February 2025

45998658R00207